The com

Community Voice Musings
(2003 - 2008)

by

Peter Goulding

Published in 2008 by YouWriteOn.com
Copyright © Text Peter Goulding
First Edition
The author asserts the moral right under the Copyright, Designs and
Patents Act 1988 to be identified as the author of
this work.
All Rights reserved. No part of this publication may be reproduced, stored
in a retrieval system, or transmitted, in any
form or by any means without the prior written consent of the author,
nor be otherwise circulated in any form of
binding or cover other than that in which it is published and without a
similar condition being imposed on the
subsequent purchaser.
Published by YouWriteOn.com

Acknowledgements

In the autumn of 2003, I wrote to Fergus Lynch, the editor of the Community Voice, to sound him out about writing a regular lightly humorous column for the paper. The Community Voice is the paper of record for Dublin 15, covering the areas of Castleknock, Blanchardstown and all the new developments in the North West of Dublin, where we had moved to in September 2000. The paper has a print run of over 30,000 and is delivered free to homes in the area.
I attached an article for him to see and he agreed to go ahead with the idea.
The provisos were simple – nothing too controversial, roughly 1000+ words per article and if possible it should have some relevance to life in Dublin 15.
Thus began my "Musings" column. As well as the monthly musings, I have also been asked to include the occasional extra column for the Educational or Housing supplements, which are also included in this book.
In 2007, the paper went from monthly to fortnightly and I wondered if I would be able to keep pace. So far so good!
Each article is proof-read first by my wife Monica. This is not only to correct the many grammatical mistakes that occur in my writing but also to censor any bits that are "too personal" and "not for public consumption!"
These musings are also available online at www.communityvoicemusings.blogspot.com
My acknowledgements therefore are twofold.
To Fergus Lynch, my sincere gratitude for allowing me a showcase.
And to my wife Monica, for her diligent use of the black marker.

Front cover photo by the legendary Vincent Cahill

Index

The Stalker report - P9
A Christmas carol - P12
Someone tell me where I live! - P16
The garden birds of Dublin 15 - P19
A magical place - P22
Confessions of a bad driver - P25
Minding Emmet - P30
Should we be teaching our children this? - P32
Blue and Flagging - P35
Singing hosannas - P38
The new religion - P40
A day in the life of a Castaheany crow - P43
Give us a break - P46
My favourite restaurant - P49
New year, new change - P52
I name this ship... - P55
The snag list - P58
My career as a linesman - P60
St. Mochta - P64
Grass - P67
Tales from the North West frontier - P70
The weather - P73
Enjoying the neigh-buzz - P76
Harry Potter and the cobbler's mannequin - P79
The horror of purchasing a school uniform - P83
Dexterus immobilitis - P86
The curse of Hallowe'en - P89
The Clonsilla quaternion - P92
A Christmas quest - P95
Burgulars - P98
The art of selling your house - P101
Things to do in the garden in March - P104
Seagulls drink cider - P107
Solving the transport problem - P110

Index (contd.)

Supermarket checkouts - P113
McCrummo, ref! - P116
A load of walls - a conversation - P119
The night of the long hoe - P122
Wish I could be like David Watts - P126
The loneliness of the short distance runner - P128
Sunday dinners - P131
A winter's tale - P134
Beating the Westlink blues - P137
The Coolmine regatta for the appreciation of poetry - P140
Some tips for house buyers - P143
Worrying about wagtails - P146
A timely warning - P149
Advice for young people - P153
The magic composter - P156
The Castlehuddart principality - P159
The lawn forcement agency - P162
Shinners and grinners - P165
Making memories - P168
Sleeping on it - P171
Prime indicators - P174
Chickens and counting them - a ramble - P177
A watery end - P180
Chips, sausage and poached egg - P183
The seven wonders of Dublin 15 - P185
Love at the bookshop - P188
One hundred not out - P191
Giving blood - P194
The book of loud lamentations - P197
The stop and go man - P200
The curious case of the prison conversation - P204
A Christmas altercation - P207
Biscuitgate - P210
In love with the library - P213

Index (contd)

A warning to all house buyers - P216
The drive of death - P218
Alternatives to childminding - P221
A Pancake Tuesday wreath? - P225
Painting the town yellow - P228
Of blogs and blogging - P230
The lamentable letterboxes of Latchford - P234
Still fighting the bin war - P237
Just desserts - P240
Solving the school problem - P243
The Roquefort terrorist - P245
Dead tigers - P249
Oh, what a divine war - P251
A green fingered lament - P254
Rain magnets - P257
The legacy of Scaldwood - P260
The old school tie - P263
Sunrise, sunset - P266
Reclaiming the game - P268
Junk mail - P272
The joy of strimming - P274
A leafy suburb - P277

The Stalker report

The other week, leaving the Blanchardstown Shopping Centre, I fell victim to a stalker.
I had successfully negotiated the ramp outside the green door entrance, my uncooperative trolley barely missing an optimistically parked Starlet, and was proceeding along the roadway in search of my car.
Only on very rare occasions, do I make a conscious note of where I left the damned thing, although I usually have a vague notion of the general area.
This instance was no exception. I trundled merrily up a lane, turned the corner and trundled merrily back down the adjacent one. This can be quite a pleasant leisure activity, but only in fine weather, and not when your block of raspberry ripple is leaving a pink trail behind you.
It was only when I turned the second corner that I became aware of her. Middle-aged, plum-coloured hair, tinted glasses, behind the wheel of a silver Rover. As I began ascending the third lane, she purred contentedly along behind me.
Thinking that perhaps I was blocking her progress – although there was enough space to drive the proverbial bus up the lane – I moved over as far as my recalcitrant trolley would safely permit. But she did not pass. She kept coming effortlessly and slowly behind me, as though being towed by my trolley on a big invisible string.
Her actions puzzled me somewhat. Anyone who knows me understands that I don't come from the same gene pool as Brad Pitt or David Beckham, so it was quite unlikely that her interest in me was physical. Yet I had definitely acquired a shadow.
It was only when I stumbled across my giggling Almera at the top of the lane that the mystery was solved. As I fumbled desperately for my keys, in every pocket but the right one, my beetroot-topped admirer leaned out of her window and enquired hopefully if I was leaving.
It occurred to me then, with but a small pang of disappointment, that the object of her craving was not my imperfectly-formed and slightly overweight body, but my car parking space. Less desirable than sixty square feet of tarmacadam, I nodded and proceeded, in a fit of pique, to load my boot as slowly as I possibly dared, without arousing her

suspicions that I was tarrying deliberately. Then I made a big show of scanning the horizon for a trolley bank, in the manner of a matelot on the Santa Maria watching for the end of the world.

All in all, I must have procrastinated approximately five minutes, before she was able to zip into the newly vacated space. It must have been very important to her. As I watched in my rear-view mirror, I idly wondered if I ought to have haggled with her, perhaps recouping some of the money I had just handed over to the sullen girl at the checkout.

Driving home, I pondered the little scenario that had just taken place. The green carpark in Blanchardstown is always full by eleven o'clock on a Saturday morning. The only way to get a space in there after that time is to trawl up and down the aisles, hoping to hit upon a departing vehicle. This is a popular sport for many shoppers. Every lane normally has one car lying in wait, staking its claim, like a fox outside a rabbit hole. In the meantime, the rest circle and prowl menacingly, eyes darting hither and thither, ready to spring into action at the merest hint of a departure. The directional arrows, painted so beautifully on the tarmac, achieve perfect meaninglessness when confronted with the possibility of a parking space.

A spokesman for Sony, the Playstation people, has denied that Laura Croft's next mission is to park her Vectra in the green car park at two o'clock on the Saturday afternoon before Christmas. He claimed that the premise for such a game would be "too far-fetched."

The irony of the situation is that there are plenty of other carparking spaces in the centre. The blue carpark never gets full, the red carpark normally has spaces, except at Christmas, and the overflow, outlying carparks revel in a surfeit of vacant rectangles.

So why the urgency to get a space in the green car park? Why spend a quarter of an hour on high alert, circling frustratedly, when one can park with comfort and walk the extra distance in a quarter of the time? (Naturally, I am excusing those people for whom walking small distances is a hardship – the old, the infirm, mothers with defiant toddlers etc.)

The answer is depressingly obvious. This is the era of the dishwasher generation, for whom preparing fresh vegetables is a lost art and who haven't actually written a letter since the computer was installed. The generation who use their feet for clutch, accelerator and brake, and who cover their garden in bark to cut down on the weeding. The generation that saves time by having a shower rather than a bath and then uses the time saved watching "Pop Idols."

It isn't an age thing. Much as we may sneer at the younger generation for their laziness and lack of values, modern technology has made us soft too. Those of us who grew up carrying our shopping on and off buses are now unable to walk fifty yards from car to shopping centre. We regale our children with tales of our own hardships of yesteryear, but we rarely use shoe polish ourselves nowadays. These present day car-park circlers and stalkers are not fresh-faced youths who have only ever done long division on a calculator – they are the generation who suddenly got everything and have forgotten the meaning of quality, who never walk past the end of their driveway, who don't listen to birds singing or throw twigs in a stream or help their children with their geography. And yes, though I might be accused of adopting a holier-than-thou attitude, I often put cheese singles on my sandwiches rather than going to the bother of slicing block cheese and doing the washing up is but a distant memory for me. But I don't think I would ever become a car stalker.

Combatting the car stalkers is an art form in itself. The most common form involves nodding assent when asked if you are leaving, and then shouting out, "Sorry, I've changed my mind!" before running sniggering back inside. Pretending you have a bad back is also guaranteed to get beneath the skin of the finger-drumming stalker, particularly if you feel the need to straighten up agonisingly and ostentatiously after transferring each packet of crisps into the boot. "I'm just returning the trolley!" is another good one. Return the trolley and then crouch down behind the nearest car and time how long it takes before their impatience wears thin. Such is the demand for spaces that I often wonder if those of us who arrive and leave early should auction our car parking spaces on departure. It would certainly liven up Saturday mornings, and a small, sturdy gavel would quickly pay for itself.

(November 2003)

A Christmas carol

'Twas Christmas Eve in Dublin 15, and a light shower of snow was softly falling like, well, like snow. Bob de Builder, an engaging, garrulous and entirely fictional Dutch property developer, who bore absolutely no resemblance to any person past or present, was at home in the bosom of his family. His absent-minded wife, who, unfortunately for Bob, was also entirely fictional, was busy attaching the turkey to the top of the Christmas tree when the phone rang, as phones are wont to do.
"Hello? Hello?" barked Bob impatiently. "Tsk! There's nobody there!"
"You have to lift the receiver first, dear," chided his wife gently.
Bob did as he was advised. "Hello?" he barked a third time. "The Castaheany who? You want a what? Don't be so ridiculous! There are plenty of schools in the area. What? Prefabricated is good enough. Why, in my day, schools were made out of twigs and papier-mâché, children today…. What? Why in tarnation do children need to stay on in school after ten years of age? I'd made my second million by the time I was seven…No! Goodbye! No! And a merry Christmas to you too!" And he slammed down the phone so hard that the Christmas tree, with his wife clinging on for dear life, toppled elegantly into the fireplace.
"Who was that dear?" enquired his wife, crawling smoke-blackened out of the hearth.
"Castaheany Community Council," replied Bob. "The nerve of them looking for a school." He picked up a black and white sweet that had become dislodged from the Christmas tree. "Ahh, humbug," he said hungrily.
That night, Bob pulled the covers under his chin and settled down to go to sleep. The last thing he heard before dropping off into complete unconsciousness was the lash of whip on reindeer fur, and from somewhere downstairs, the sound of his wife and Christmas tree toppling over again.
But his usual dream of building rows and rows of houses was interrupted by a large, terrifying figure in a cowl. It was as if Jeremy Clarkson had joined the Capuchins. The figure held up a crooked finger

and beckoned Seamus to him.
"B-b-but I'm in my pyjamas!" protested the property developer lamely.
"You are a fictional character having a dream," intoned the figure solemnly. "Yes, I see your concern for your attire."
Faced with such heavy sarcasm, Bob sighed, flung back the covers, and fumbled with his feet for his slippers. However, when he rubbed his eyes, he was sitting in the passenger seat of a grey Morris Minor, travelling down a road that seemed somehow familiar.
"I am the Ghost of Christmas Past," announced the figure, cursing wildly at an unobservant squirrel that was crossing the road. "Does this place seem familiar to you?"
"There is something stirring in my memory," said Bob. "What are these snow-laden objects that line the road?"
"I believe they are called "trees"" replied the Ghost. "They were quite common upon this road once upon a time."
"I remember, I remember," said Bob excitedly. "Trees, and then there were little trees called hedges, and tiny flying things…"
"Birds," murmured the Ghost.
"…Yes! Birds! And the countryside was this funny colour called gr…gr.."
"Green."
".. Green, yeah. I know this place, Ghost. 'Tis on the other side of Blanchardstown. I believe it is called the Hansfield Road. It is beautiful. We used to come up here for walks, when I was small. Is it still here then?"
"I am the Ghost of Christmas Past," repeated the spectre. "With this question, I cannot help you. But I know someone who can."
There was a sudden flash of lightning and the Morris Minor disappeared. Bob was now standing on the same road in the dark of night. It took his eyes several seconds to adjust to the blackness, although other parts of his body took even longer. As his vision improved, he noticed an almost identical figure beside him, except he was a lot smaller and wore a Linkin Park t-shirt and jeans instead of a cowl.
"Ghost of Christmas Present?" he enquired, and the youth nodded glumly and said "Yup."

As they stood side by side, an old woman, heavily laden down with shopping bags hobbled up the road behind them. As she passed, Bob could hear her wheezing breathlessly, or maybe she was breathing wheezelessly. The point was, it was dark and he found it difficult to tell.

"Why is that old crone walking this dark deserted street at night, heavily laden down with shopping bags?" he asked the not-quite-so-terrifying being beside him.

But the answer was not immediately forthcoming. Two bright lights approached quickly through the gloom, and with a terrified yell, all three jumped wildly into the ditch to avoid the onrushing object.

"What.. What was that?" asked Bob, emerging from their prickly sanctuary.

"Just a car," replied the youth. "Unfortunately the property developer did not see fit to install street lights along this road."

A few yards away, the old woman was brushing the dust from her worn coat, and fumbling for her shopping.

"Is she mad?" asked Bob. "What is she doing here?"

"No, she is not mad," answered the Ghost. "She does not want to be here, but she has no alternative."

"What do you mean?" asked Bob, with a sharp intake of breath. "Does she not have bus fare?"

"Oh, she has the fare," replied the other. "Problem is, no bus comes up this way. Dublin Bus has said they won't provide a service until building is complete. And they just keep building and building."

"But all those houses?" protested Bob. "Surely she can shop somewhere nearer home?"

"Aha! There's the rub. All the brochures for these estates have promised schools and a church and shops and facilities and amenities, but none have been forthcoming."

By this time, Bob was starting to experience a rather uncomfortable feeling in the pit of his stomach, and another one in the crook of his left elbow. He put his hands on the shoulders of the Ghost and sought to reassure himself that all would be well. "It won't always be like this, will it?" he demanded. "When they've finished building the houses…"

But once again, there was another flash of lightning, which rather

puzzled him, as a mild, dry evening had been forecast. When his eyes focussed again, the Linkin Park youth had disappeared to be replaced by the most hideously deformed ogre imaginable. It had deep, sunken eyes and a deformed nose and a large jagged scar above its ear.
"Ghost of Christmas Future, I presume?" muttered Bob, with a sigh.
"Err, actually he's stuck in traffic on the M50 roundabout," replied the other, in a strong Drawda accent. "He asked me if I'd mind filling you in until he gets here. The name's Rasher, so it is. Mind yourself now, horse, here comes a car!"
Bob prepared to jump back into the briars, but the car slowed up in front of them, and, as it braked, four youths hopped out.
"Money. Phone." said the largest of them. It was, Bob guessed, a demand, rather than a Christmas wish list. He fumbled in his pocket and brought out a few notes. The hideously deformed creature at his side proffered his Nokia 9910. The lad, (he could have been no more than sixteen,) took them dispassionately and got back into the car. His guardian angels followed suit.
"Damn!" cursed Rasher, "I'm only after getting credit."
"We must contact the Gardai," said Bob, but his companion fixed him with a withering stare.
"They don't come down here," he said. "Discretion is the better part of valour. These are the badlands."
"But how on earth did it get like this?" demanded Seamus. "This was a good area. Fine houses. Built to last. Moulded architraves and everything."
"Oh, the houses are okay, granted. Nothing wrong with the houses." (Bob didn't like the way he emphasised the word "houses.") "Trouble is, that's all there is. Just miles and miles of houses. No shops, no churches, no facilities, no amenities, no transport infrastructure. Nothing for the kids to do. And you know what they say about idle hands and the Devil!"
Bob didn't, but he thought it safer not to ask. In the distance, he heard the sound of shots being fired into the air, and a long, drawn-out scream. He knew this place. It was Hell. Or Ronanstown. Trouble was, he could never tell the difference. He turned and started to run. Away. Must get away...

With a start, or maybe a finish, Bob awoke. For a minute, he stared at the familiar cube of raspberry jelly on his bedroom ceiling, and then he slowly slid out of bed, and pulled back the curtains. Outside his window, there was a blanket of snow, next to an eiderdown of fog, and further up the road he could see a luxury patchwork quilt of intermittent showers. Someone had built a snowman that resembled Kevin Kilbane on a bad hair day. With a jolt, it occurred to him that it was Christmas Day.

"I'm going to build them schools," he said to his wife, without turning around. "Primary schools, and secondary schools, as many as they want. And a community centre, complete with basketball court. And a sixty thousand all-seater stadium. And shops, and a dentist and a doctor's surgery, and maybe a chiropodists too. And a crèche. And a bus corridor. And a railway station. And possibly even a rail line as well. And maybe a deep sea port that can take ocean-going liners."

His wife turned over in the bed and propped herself up on her elbow. "You'd really do all that?" she asked, wonderingly.

"Absolutely!" Bob replied, enthusiastically. But then his face fell. Picking it up, he reattached it mournfully to the front of his head. "There's one slight snag though. Being an entirely fictional character who bears absolutely no resemblance to any person past or present, anything I build will, of necessity, be totally fictional too…"

(December 2003)

Someone tell me where I live!

"And whereabouts do you live?"

A straightforward question, and one that is asked, and answered, a thousand times a day in the Greater Dublin area. "Foxrock." "Darndale." "Fizzbra." "Mind your own business." Not rocket science, really, to identify oneself with a particular part of the city. Or so you might think.

When faced with this question, I need to pause and assess how familiar the enquirer is with the geography of Dublin 15. Probably anyone living south of the M50 will not have heard of Littlepace or Castaheany. I suspect that not many people outside of Huntstown parish have either. Sure, we're only a town of 10,000 people – why would anyone have heard of us?

In reply to the question, I usually mumble something about being between Blanchardstown and Clonee. A lot of people do the same. Best leave it vague. Too difficult to explain.

The slip road off the N3, up which the boy racers swerve every evening (boy, is there going to be a pile-up there one day!) has a sign denoting us as "Housing Estate," obviously quite easily recognisable to anybody not familiar with the area. As Nora Darcy of the local community council points out, how can we, as a community, expect to have a sense of identity, if we don't even have a readily identifiable name?

Brian Lenihan, one of our local TDs, recently expressed surprise that we did not regard ourselves as being part of Clonee. He was under the impression that most people here regard themselves as being from the quaint little co. Meath village.

Estate agents too have a predilection for describing our dwellings as being in the county Meath townland. One particular advert recently described a house in Linnetfields as being "in the heart of Clonee." I am sure that the residents of Clonee were surprised to learn that they had to walk over a mile down a very dark, pot-holed, unlit country road to get to the heart of their village.

Of course, for estate agents, Clonee is sexy. Clonee is rural, with a fire in the hearth and labradors bowling along the fields. And of course, many of us with exorbitantly high car insurance often wish that the Dublin-Meath border would lie a few miles south of its current position, and we could enjoy the lower rates enjoyed by our near neighbours.

Many of the original residents of the estate are under the impression that the estate is called Littlepace. Taxi drivers normally refer to the area as such, and the first estate to be built was, in fact, Littlepace. The bus timetable indicates the occasional bus goes "via Littlepace." The Littlepace shopping centre is regarded by many as being the hub of the community. The Littlepacers FC was set up, not merely for the children of the original estate, but for inhabitants of all fifteen current estates.

When we moved into our estate over three years ago, the deeds of the property stated that we were in the townland of Phibblestown. So we used that particular name for a year or two and then realised we were probably the only ones using it. With relief we ceased the practise, for we had always regarded it as a silly name anyway, particularly if, in the future, some poor unfortunate had to commentate on a match between ourselves and nearby Scribblestown.

Bord Gais, who one would expect to be on the ball, given the logistics involved in connecting up thousands of houses, always address our eagerly-awaited gas bills to the townland of Clonsilla! I have visions of the poor postman wandering around Clonsilla, scratching his head, unaware that over two miles away, householders are fretting over the non-arrival of their gas bills.

Religiously, of course, we are in the parish of Huntstown. But Huntstown is a much older, more established community, and its civil boundary is very definitely marked.

Fingal County Council, though, have made a definite statement on the issue. They have decreed that the estate shall be known as Castaheany, as that is the name of the townland. (Castaheany is also the name of one of the 15 estates, so I presume that people there have an address of "Castaheany, Castaheany") There is certainly some puzzlement as to who, in Fingal County Council, ordained that henceforth our estate should be known as that as, to my knowledge, none of the residents were consulted.

So there we have it. Castaheany, it officially is.

Or is it?

The local sorting office in Coolmine informs me that my correct postal address is "Clonee, Dublin 15." That is the address by which all correspondence should be labelled. They see no anomaly in the fact that Clonee is in county Meath. However, they point out that if letters are addressed to "Clonee, co. Meath" they will probably pay a visit to the sorting office in Navan before being delivered.

Incidentally, some of the houses towards the back of Beechfield seem to me to have strayed across the border into county Meath. As such, therefore, would their correct postal address be, "Clonee, Dublin 15, county Meath?" I suspect we are descending into the realms of the

ridiculous here.
After the reorganisation of county boundaries in Englan
good folk of Grimsby, proud Lincolnshire people, discove...
no longer in Lincolnshire, but in an entity called "South Humberside."
They responded by renaming their address as "Grimsby, South Bloody Humberside."
In a similar vein, I now suggest that until such time as we have signposts and maps giving us a readily identifiable name, we should inform our family, friends and businesses that our official townland name is "That Big Bloody Estate between Blanchardstown and Clonee." Who knows? It's better than Phibblestown, anyway.

(*January 2004*)

The garden birds of Dublin 15

Let me state clearly from the outset that I have had no formal training in the science of ornithology. Prior to moving out here from the city centre four years ago, I had always thought that birds were divided into two categories – pigeons and seagulls. Relocating in the comparative rurality of Dublin 15 has been something of an eye - [and lung-] opener for me.

It began with a couple of bird-feeders, purchased for peanuts and hung on hooks on the eaves of our shed. The seed and peanuts to fill them were ironically more expensive than the feeders but our newly-found love of nature deemed it worth it. We also invested in a cheap pair of binoculars and a pocket-sized bird identification book. Eagerly, we retired to the kitchen to watch the flocks of grateful, eager birds that would doubtless come swooping down from a five-mile radius to avail of our tempting offerings.

One thing you quickly learn from the art of birdwatching is patience. Just as it may take you a long time to find out that a particular shop in Blanchardstown stocks your favourite flavour of jelly, so the birds have no magical radar that hones in on particular tasty peanuts. They might be swanning around, showing off in front of land-restricted animals, when they suddenly spy the peanut feeder and come down to investigate. When one considers the number of gardens on a bird's daily flight path, though, it is a wonder that they discover the feeders at all.

The first to come are the sparrows. They are the most fearless and the most inquisitive. There are hedge sparrows and house sparrows and dunnocks, each with different pigmentation for male, female and juvenile. Basically, though, if it's small and brown with a non-sticky-up tail, it's a sparrow.

Hot on the sparrow's tail-feathers come the starlings. These are spotty yobs, who are just too big to perch on the seed feeder, but are well able for the peanuts. Like the sparrows, they tend to visit in packs, and frequently squabble with each other over feeding priority.

In our experience, the greenfinch was the next to arrive. When the peanut feeder is vacant, he will sit upon the washing line looking around nonchalantly, and then quickly make a dart for the feeder. He is often bullied off it by the starlings, though any sympathy one might have disappears at his absolute refusal to share with any other greenfinch.

We have a wren that visits occasionally, although it could be a brown tennis ball with a beak and a vertical tail. He doesn't hang around for long, obviously deeply distressed at being called a "wran" on St. Stephen's Day.

Probably the most colourful visitors to our garden [with the exception of my mad Uncle Toby] are the goldfinches. Decorated in vivid reds and yellows, we have a family that visits us several times a day. Actually, I am unsure of their relationship to each other. They could be five complete strangers for all I know and it is not the sort of information that they willingly volunteer. Timid little creatures, they are right at the bottom of the feeder pecking order [sorry] and even get muscled off by ladybirds.

The blue tit often visits in early morning, catching the peanuts rather than worms. A curious blend of blues, yellow and white, we have often confused him with a great tit, which annoys him immensely. The duller, coal tit is a less frequent visitor, due to his inferiority complex at only being in black and white.

The perennial Christmas favourite, Robin No-mates, can appear daily for weeks on end, and then disappear for months. The informed opinion is that this antisocial creature has some kind of drug-dependency problem, and makes frequent trips to rehab. Too fat to tackle either of the feeders, he will scavenge on the ground for the seeds that the sparrows drop in their feverish excitement.

The blackbird is often to be found in our shrubbery with his drab spouse. Contrary to Paul McCartney's assertion, I have never heard him sing in the dead of night, and I suspect he's tucked up in his nest at that hour, like most self-respecting flying things.

Another common visitor to our garden, though not the feeders, is a largish brown thing with a speckled breast. My wife and I are at loggerheads over whether it is a song thrush, a mistle thrush or a meadow pipit, though it rarely comes to blows. He bounds around the lawn searching for worms, while his mate keeps lookout on top of the wall. I have been tempted to tell him it is all perfectly legal but he seems to enjoy living on the edge.

Last year we had a family [yes, I'm guessing] of redpolls that took a shine to our lavender bush. For some strange reason, there is no sign of them this year, though I suspect the fact that the lavender bush withered and died may have something to do with it.

That would be the sum total of birds that venture into our garden. Not a great deal, but a darned sight more than visited when we were townies. And more than visited before we got the feeders. In addition to these, we also have fieldfares on the green opposite our house, and killer crows, rooks, ravens and jackdaws, that swoop and prowl menacingly, looking for small children to carry off to their lairs. And the massive blue and white magpie, who must be totally driven demented by that stupid children's rhyme. And every estate seems to own a pair of totally dense wagtails who stand in the middle of the road, watching as a car approaches, only to scuttle [not fly] out of the way at the last moment. And so my ornithological skills are progressing, and I am eagerly awaiting my first sighting of a hooped macaw and an albino penguin. It certainly livens up the winter months, watching the little creatures flitting about, although, as advised, we remove the feeders during the summer.

However, to my horror, I gazed out of the kitchen window the other morning, and there, sitting on the back wall, was a pigeon. Not a wood pigeon or a lesser spotted bearded Mongolian pigeon, but a common or garden Moore Street pigeon. He was the first I have seen out here. A sure sign that the metropolis is chasing after us.

(February 2004)

A magical place

The next time you are driving around the inside lane of the M50 roundabout, trying to leave as little space between yourself and the car in front to discourage that WW registered van from hopping in front of you, glance down at the centre of the whirling vortex below you. No, on second thoughts, don't. I'll tell you about it instead.
There, far below, above the M50 itself, and beside the railway track, there lies a most magical place, an oasis of tranquility in a maelstrom of vehicular activity.
The Royal Canal begins out in county Longford and wends it way eastwards across country before disgorging itself into Spencer Dock in Dublin. Footpathed throughout, its nature changes throughout its long journey, from the grey arctic tundra of Westmeath to the vast sprawling metropolis of Leixlip; from the hot, burning deserts around Mullingar to the blighted lunar landscape of Clonsilla. But nowhere is its magic more apparent than where it traverses the M50.
This world-renowned, yet paradoxically little-known, aqueduct is steeped in ancient lore and legend, half-lost through the mists of time, and shrouded in myths and fable. It is mentioned in the millennia-spanning "Annals of Castleknocke" where it is represented on an illuminated map as crossing "The Emme Fiftye," bearing the legend "Here be Dragons and Snarkletworps." Nobody is terribly sure what a Snarkletworp is but the general consensus of learned opinion is that they are unlikely to be cute and fluffy.
This is the place where Chu Chulainn is said to have fought the mighty Slug of Ashtown, a fearsome and vicious creature nearly four inches in

length. For three days the battle raged before Chu Chulainn squashed him underfoot. At the place where he died, a magical fire hydrant is said to have sprouted, the remains of which can still be seen today. This is not the only evidence of an ancient past groping through the centuries to greet us. Runic inscriptions abound on the imposing stone pillars surrounding the aqueduct and give us a glimpse of life two thousand years ago. There are references to a mysterious "Wacker," who apparently "was here," and further down there are bawdy references to the sexual activities of the goddess of fertility, "Shazza." There have been a few doubts raised in the academic world concerning the authenticity of these inscriptions, on the grounds that they are "done in marker" but most archaeologists are satisfied that they are genuine. That our forefathers were attracted to this place is beyond dispute. Charred circles are still visible where the four elements of earth, water, air and fire were summonsed in a magical incantation to pagan gods. Worshippers were encouraged to imbibe a strange, amber liquid called Dutch Gold, which they believed gave them terrifying powers. And in one of the great archaeological finds of the twentieth century, a bag of chips was unearthed, perfectly preserved and still as soggy as the day they were discarded.

After the demise of the Celts, the area remained hidden to the human eye until re-discovered by the legendary Scottish explorer, Doctor Livingstone, in 1829. Armed only with four thousand native troops, several camels and a teddy bear named Poops, Livingstone pushed through the dense undergrowth around the Little Chef and thus became the first modern man to view the "water-bridge" as he called it.

"In all my years," he later wrote, (in his seminal work "Travels to Darkest Mulhuddart,") "I never did see a more enchanted place. Except maybe the Angel Falls in Venezuela. And the Rift Valley in East Africa. And the Yangste Kiang. And possibly Bray Head. And several other places."

Tour companies were quick to cash in on Livingstone's discovery. A young Thomas Cook, advertising in "Ye Buy and Selle," promised prospective tourists "a trip to the bounds of your imagination, a cacophony of sounds to bleed your very ears." Very soon, the banks of the Canal were awash with hordes of exuberant Japanese tourists posing excitedly by the lock gates and doing quick watercolour sketches of each other.

The War of Independence put an end to large-scale tourism in the area. Perceived by the rebels as being a strategic crossing point of the M50, Rasher O'Shaughnessy and fourteen men bravely held out on the aqueduct for nearly a week, until the British discovered where they were, and told them to move on. And in 1922, dissidents attempted to blow up the canal, but were thwarted when it was found that their explosives "got wet."

Nowadays the canal over the M50 is a protected ecological area. Up until recently, it contained a strange green slime found nowhere else on earth. Slimus Humungus, to give its more technical name, was thought to exist almost entirely on empty crisp packets and coke cans, as evidenced by the large abundance of these that thoughtful passers-by deposited into the canal. Coincidentally, this slime reputedly formed the staple diet of the aforementioned Snarkletworp and Dragons.

Such was the rarity and importance of this slime that in 1980, the Rainbow Warrior made headline news throughout the world, as it successfully frustrated attempts by The Don't-Give-Two-Hoots-About-The-Environment Chemical Company to build a seventy six storey chemical plant in the middle of the canal.

The famous slime mysteriously disappeared a few years ago, when the newly-formed Canal Trust decided to "clean it up." Its absence means that you are unlikely to encounter a Snarkletworp, when traversing the M50.

Yes, this truly is a magical place. Here, with the traffic roaring above your head and the stationary traffic below honking their horns as they approach the toll-bridge, and with the overcrowded train from Maynooth steaming past with its cargo of miserably squashed commuters, here it is possible to lie back on the soft earth and imagine a simpler, yet richer world, a world where nubile young maidens would cavort naked in the canal's crystal waters and wash each other's backs, [mind you, I don't need to lie back near a canal to imagine that] ; a world devoid of bank charges and "Celebrity Wife Swap" and mobile phones; a world of perfect calm entirely surrounded by the maelstrom

that is modern life.
Such places are rare. We should cherish them.

(March 2004)

Confessions of a bad driver

My name is Peter. I am 43 years old and I am a bad driver. There. I've finally come out and said it. Those last five words are now etched in print forever, staring out at me from a white page, like my mother glaring at me from her bedroom the first time I came home drunk. I hope that admitting the truth will be the first step in my rehabilitation as a driver.
Oh, don't get me wrong. I have been driving for 26 years and the only accident I have had was when I spilt chocolate onto my white polo shirt [a harrowing incident for which AXA, amazingly, refused to pay up.] So how, I hear you say – which is quite worrying, as I thought I was alone in the house – how does that make you a bad driver? Surely with a record like that you could be considered the King of the Road, particularly as booze and pets aren't allowed and you ain't got no cigarettes? Let me explain.
Most people who step into a car, particularly males, think they are good drivers. Look, I can overtake you at 80mph with my elbow hanging out of the window. Travelling outbound along the Blanchardstown by-pass towards the Clonee turn-off is a real test of "good driving skill." Look at all those saps on the inside lane doing 59mph. Behold my superior handling control as I fly past you all, before cutting in with perfect dexterity just before the slip road.
Oh Lord, I hereby confess, to my eternal shame, that I was that man. And it took a scene reminiscent of Paul's vision on the road to Damascus to draw the veils from mine eyes.
We were returning home from a parents' evening in the school, where we had spent an hour being unilaterally pitied by all and sundry. Most cars as usual took the second Blanchardstown exit, and, as the Gardai are never seen further than that for fear of accidentally venturing into

"rural Ireland", I stepped on the gas, neatly overtook an elderly lady who could barely see over the steering wheel of her Austin A40, and roared off. 60mph, 65mph, 72mph – I overtook them all. As we rounded the final bend before the Clonee turn off, there was but a single truck on the road ahead, albeit a reasonable distance ahead.

My momentum, however, took me level with the truck, but time was running out. Should I accelerate and cut in, or slow down and fall in behind? I decided on the former, pushed my by now rattling Almera to the limit, and just managed to cut in and disappear up the slip road, as the lorry driver flashed his lights angrily at me.

At the top of the slip road, the lights were red. Naturally, I stopped and waited. [Oh, come on! I'm not that bad of a driver!] All of the cars and trucks that I overtook were obviously heading for exotic places such as Dunshaughlin or Navan, for no-one followed me up the slip road. Until – yes, you've guessed it – the distinctive shape of an Austin A40, with but a hint of blue rinse above the steering wheel – came purring slowly up the road and eased to a stop behind me.

My wife glanced at me. It was enough. It usually is.

That glance said, "You broke the rules of the road. You endangered my life and yours and for what? For the sake of overtaking a nonagenarian?"

"I had the car under control," I protested.

"And if the front axle had snapped? If a dog had come charging through the centre barrier? If a car had pulled out? If you'd dropped your Crunchie again?"

And thus I had my moment of blinding insight – not on the road to Damascus, but on the Clonee slip road. Not that I'm going to take the parallel any further, of course. I'm not going to be writing letters to the Huntstownians or the Corduffians, exhorting them to see the light. Nor am I going to walk the streets of Clonsilla and Mulhuddart proclaiming the Good News. I'm simply going to follow Michael Jackson's advice and start with the man in the mirror. [That's myself, by the way. Don't ask me how I ended up in Michael Jackson's mirror.]

The truth of the matter is that for years I've been lane-hopping along the Blanchardstown dual carriageway every morning, thinking that I'm being a great driver for skilfully overtaking a couple of cars on the way.

The reality of the situation is that not only have I been reckless in my driving [by not allowing for other people's mistakes] but I have also been annoying and frustrating those more patient than myself. And naturally, annoyance, frustration and driving are not the perfect combination required for attaining the M50 roundabout every morning. And just like a reformed smoker, I am totally dismissive of those who continue to put speed ahead of safety. These days, I drive down the old dual carriageway in the evenings at 59 mph, - yes, I still haven't got around to altering the mindset that I simply must do 1mph beneath the speed limit at all times - tutting pityingly at the boy racers who roar down the outside lane as if their houses were on fire.

That's not strictly true, of course. Inwardly, my competitive spirit is seething, not because I'm being made a fool of, but because I imagine that they believe they are making a fool of me. I pray to the Good Lord above to send a few adventurous Gardai with radar equipment to the dangerous city / country borderlands along the N3, and apprehend these vehicular transgressors.

Of course I shouldn't let it bother me. With my new safety-first mindset, I should be keeping a wary eye on these rubber burners but not allowing them to drive me to distraction. However, it does annoy me. I can feel the frustration welling up inside me like Coke in a bottle that's been given a good shake. Which is why, as I mentioned at the beginning, I am still a bad driver.

But I'm trying, Lord. I really am.

(April 2004)

Minding Emmet

Buying a Communion outfit is not a skill that I possess. Over the years, I have come to learn that the actual purchase of the dress is but a small part of this wearisome and time-consuming ritual. Veil and/or tiara, gloves, handbag, shoes, watch, prayer book, parasol – the seemingly endless list is an industry in itself, like Valentines Day or international football matches, and it is seemingly quite impossible for the females of our species to purchase the complete ensemble at one visit to the shops.

My niece, Kate, is making her First Communion in May. Her dress successfully purchased in town, a week or two ago, it was proposed that an expedition to the Blanchardstown Shopping Centre should be mounted, in order to buy the necessary accoutrements not obtained on the first visit. Furthermore, it was decided that the members of the foraging party would include Kate [naturally], her mother, [ultimate arbitrator], my wife, [special advisor to the ultimate arbitrator], Emmet, Kate's five year old brother [believing it would be fun] and myself [to mind Emmet.]

The only time that proved suitable for all the five protagonists happened to be Saturday afternoon, a prospect that did not exactly have me leaping around in excitement. If I were ever given the option of root canal work or traipsing around the Centre on a Saturday afternoon, you would find me skipping gaily off to the dentist. In this case, however, options were noticeable by their absence.

Now, Emmet is an extremely bright five year old, and it did not take him very long to discover that he had made a woeful error of judgement in believing that the adventure would be enjoyable. Surprisingly, he appeared remarkably uninterested in the differing merits of handbag clasps, preferring to concentrate on the far more important subject of ice-cream consumption. With supreme self-sacrifice, I volunteered to forego the fascinating Communion shopping experience for a while, to satiate my nephew's demands.

We descended the escalator very quickly; Emmet informing me that he knew exactly where the ice-cream shop was and why wasn't I running? I suggested somewhat maliciously that I didn't think there was an ice-cream shop in the Centre at all but my famished companion was having none of it, taking me by the hand and tugging me triumphantly over to the kiosk where the silver containers were amply bedecked with a myriad of ice-cream flavours. I made one rather half-hearted attempt to convince him that the brightly coloured scoops were in fact "medicine" and "tasted yucky", but he just stared at me incredulously, before patiently putting his obviously stupid uncle to rights.

Ice-cream duly purchased, we brought it over to the fountain area where it could be ravaged in comparative comfort. As Emmet decorated his face, I idly took out a two euro coin and with a skilful flick of the finger, sent it spinning elegantly on the black marble surround of the fountain. Emmet watched it revolving with awe-struck eyes, and only when it had finally spattered to rest did he utter "Wow!" Emboldened by this appreciativeness in my rapt audience, I proceeded to repeat the stunning feat. In a few years, he would cease to find such a simple trick entertaining, but five is a great age – old enough to be enthralled, but too young for world-weariness to have set in.

In terms of audience delight, my second coin flicking stunt eclipsed the first for, not judging the angle finely enough, the two euro shot across the marble and dived into the water. Emmet nearly choked on his cone with delight, as I made a frantic, futile attempt to catch it. Mournfully, I watched it sink to the bottom.

It is time, I think, to introduce another member of my family, my late father [he isn't dead – just late all the time.] Among the pearls of wisdom that he imparted to me as a child, two have stood the test of time and have survived into my middle age. "Find a penny, pick it up, the rest of the day you'll have a penny," was one. The other was "Look after the pennies and you'll have a lot of pennies." Suffice to say, I remain one of the dwindling band of mercenaries who will stoop down and pick a one cent coin off the pavement. I hate throwing money away, whether metaphorically, or, as in this case, literally.

Gazing down into the clear water, Emmet on his hunkers beside me, I could see the coin glaring up at me reproachfully. It wasn't easy to miss, nestling there, surrounded by self-pitying copper coins that mammies had cleared out of their bulging purses and handed to tiny kids who promptly flung them in the fountain, wishing for a Playstation or a Quad bike.

"Shall I get it?" asked Emmet, laying the remnants of his ice-cream down on the seat and starting to remove his shoes.

"No, its okay, son," I replied, rolling up my shirt sleeve. The water wasn't too deep and it seemed a simple operation. Just as I was about to plunge my arm in though, I noticed a very formidable looking lady on the far side of the fountain, eyeing me suspiciously.

Visions of newspaper headlines swam before my eyes. "Is this the meanest man in Ireland?" said one. "Uncle teaches boy [5] to steal from charities" said another. I hurriedly altered my actions, letting the cool water ripple through my fingers in a very contrived uncontrived fashion.

"Aren't you going to get the money?" asked Emmet. I told him that I'd get it in a minute, and didn't he think he ought to put his socks on? Disappointed, he returned to his ice-cream, now bathing in a pink puddle of its own.

After about five minutes of glancing sideways at the lady glancing sideways at me, she picked up her bags and disappeared in the direction of the red entrance. This was my chance. Nobody else was looking. A quick glance around. Was it my imagination or was that security guard squinting in my direction? Hard to see behind the sunglasses. [Why do they wear sunglasses in a shopping centre?]

I decided to hold off until he passed. There is something about a navy blazer and grey flannel trousers that makes me nervous, and not merely because it's such an affront to fashion. Dress them in camouflage gear and arm them to the teeth, and I probably wouldn't bat an eyelid. Yet another of my unexplainable idiosyncrasies.

Eventually I noticed that Emmet was trying to catch fish in his sock. A brief explanation of the natural habitats of aqueous animals ensued, while the security guard took up a position outside the flower shop, obviously having received a tip-off that an attempt was going to be made on the baby carnations. I glanced around. The fountainside was packed, but nobody seemed to be looking my way. I took a deep breath and then quickly plunged my arm into the water.

Another of my father's sayings concerns the importance of keeping one's fingernails short, though the reasoning is lost in the mists of time. That particular pearl of wisdom, however, proved to be my undoing. With the water up to my shoulder, I scrabbled frantically to prise the recalcitrant coin off the bottom of the pool, but my blunt, rounded fingers failed to get sufficient grip. Conscious that I would shortly be noticed, I leaned forward to get a better grip but, as I did so, around five euro worth of coin slipped gleefully out of my shirt pocket and into the water. With my free hand, I clutched vainly after the disappearing coins, just as Emmet jumped on my shoulder to get a better view of the charade.

It is many years now since I studied physics at school but, as my head dipped smoothly below the water level, I remembered that a force applied to one side of a fulcrum will change the equilibrium of the object. Or, put more simply, if you don't anchor yourself, you're going to fall in.

Certain fountains across the world, like the Trevi and Trafalgar Square, encourage spontaneous immersions. The fountain at the Blanchardstown Centre isn't one of them.

"You're soaking!" laughed Emmet, as my dripping head re-emerged. Shaking myself like a spaniel, I was supremely conscious that I had become the object of everybody's attention.

Naturally, I had neglected to bring along that most obvious shopping expedition accessory – a towel, so I was reduced to drying myself with my hands, which is not particularly effective, and was probably the cause of the considerable mirth of my new-found audience.

"Why don't you dry yourself in the toilets?" asked Emmet innocently. I looked at him, and then bent down and kissed him on the forehead, which he immediately rubbed off in disgust. Together, we hurried off to the toilets where the hot air dryer eventually restored me to something approaching normality.

"Now don't tell the girls," I warned him, as we returned to the fountain. "They won't find it a bit amusing."

To be fair to him, he managed to hold it in, at least until the others were in earshot. As the triumvirate emerged from Roches', successfully clutching a white handbag as though it was the FA Cup, Emmet dashed over to them and joyously spilled the beans on my watery mishap.

"Serves you right," opined my wife, when she got the whole story out of me in "twenty questions" fashion. "That'll teach you to begrudge a charity a few bob."

"We're going to look for a parasol," said Kate. "Now, Emmet, you will mind your Uncle Peter, this time, right?"

(May 2004)

Should we be teaching our children this?

I recently attended the final of the Aoife Begley Secondary Schools Debating Competition in NUI, Maynooth, not out of any great love for the art of oral duelling, but because my daughter, one of the participants, seconded me as transport provider. As a weary parent of two teenagers, who frequently argue with each other, the prospect of viewing an expanded version of this did not exactly set my pulse racing but, being the dutiful and obedient father that I am, I resignedly took my place in the auditorium of the brand new John Hume Building [named after the Northern politician, John Hume Building.]
The format was simple enough – four teams of two and four single speakers would debate the motion that membership of the EU should constitute membership of a European army. I kid you not. I was hoping for something along the lines of "Should Posh stand by her man?" or "Are any of the trolleys in Dunnes, Blanchardstown in working order?" Instead, the participants were expected to wax lyrical upon a subject that would rival "The Inside of a Ping-Pong Ball" in the Annual Most Uninteresting Topic of the Year Award.
Each speaker had to argue his or her case for seven minutes, for five of which the opposition were allowed to jump up and shout "Point of Order!" to try and put them off. This, I suppose, is the academic equivalent of trying to keep your balance on a log while people are throwing beanbags at you, so beloved by Stuart Hall on "It's a Knockout." I could only sit back and admire the cool way these irritating interruptions were dealt with. Me, I'd probably have lost it completely and thrown a wobbly, which apparently is not highly regarded in debating circles.
Teenagers, in general, get a very bad press. They are perceived as sullen, lazy, selfish and totally unintelligible, except when demanding money or lifts. Each generation apparently spells the death-knell for modern civilisation and always has done. I am sure that Charles Stewart Parnell was berated for "playing that Wagner rubbish too loud," with added admonishments that it was "tuneless" and "you can't hear the words."
Of course, one of the great ironies of life is that children grow into their

parents, no matter how unthinkable that seems in their formative years. It is another example of absolute power corrupting absolutely. Now that we, as parents, are in charge, we conveniently forget our own stomach-churning behaviour as teenagers, and try to mould our victims into mini-forty year olds, forgetting that being obnoxious and insufferable is a vital part of growing-up.

As the competition got under way, a myriad of differing emotions swirled around my head, obviously looking for a way out. My most overriding emotion was complete inadequacy. Here was I, extremely reticent about asking a fellow passenger on the 70 if the bus goes into Littlepace or not, listening to these calm, assured and very persuasive young people, who appeared to have no qualms at all about standing up before an audience of 200 complete strangers and espousing their views on world terrorism and defence budgets. Compared to them, I felt like an amoeba on the backside of a salmon.

On the other hand, I also felt strangely comforted. The future, as projected by these ambassadors of their generation, was in good hands. To counteract the joyriders and the cider-drinkers, here were Hugh McCafferty and Neil Reynolds of Castleknock College, intelligent and articulate spokespersons of today's youth. Wisdom and assuredness belying their years, their arguments made me want to rush from the auditorium and sign up for the New European Army immediately. They were ably backed up by Ciara MacNally from Pheasant's Run whose clear and determined support for future military involvement convinced me totally that my years as an armchair pacifist had been totally misguided.

Speakers came and speakers went, and the standard never faltered. One girl, Dasha Emelyanova from Blakestown Community School, had even reached the Final, despite the fact that English was not her native language. And yet, such was her passion and persuasiveness that the slight trace of an accent did not detract from a faultless performance. We were truly in the presence of greatness.

And then, another thought wormed naggingly into my brain, burrowing persistently through the soft, squishy layers of my cerebellum. What was happening here was totally unnatural and potentially very damaging to life on this planet as we know it. Something was definitely rotten in the state of Ireland.

For it is in the nature of the Circle of Life, that teenagers are teenagers and adults are adults, and never the twain shall meet. Teenagers demand to be allowed to go to the Plex wearing a few bits of cloth and elastic, and parents refuse. Parents win because we are both the judge and the jury. We adjudicate on moral issues, and teenagers slam doors and sulk in their bedrooms. These roles are written in the stars, they are predestined and inviolable.

However, when we train our subjugated offspring in the subtle art of debating, the train goes off the track. Instead of sullenly retreating to their Walkmans [Walkmen?] and mobile phones, they will be able to argue cogently and logically about the merits of going to a house party in Clonsilla until four o'clock in the morning. Parents, defeated, will retreat to their bedrooms and turn up their Jim Reeves and Frank Ifield albums to horrendous levels. May God have mercy on the souls of the parents of the sisters Aoife and Niamh Ni Mhaoileoin, who so eloquently represented Castleknock Community College in the Final. If these girls can successfully argue against the merits of forming a New European Army, what chance will their mother and father have when faced by a double-sided onslaught in favour of ordering Apache Pizza at two o'clock in the morning?

As a famous but fictional character once remarked, the country is in a state of chassis. When we tinker with the natural process of evolution, when we produce these genetically modified teenagers, when the Circle of Life is broken, strange things are liable to happen – mountains crumble, aeroplanes fall out of the sky, Iarnrod Eireann announce they are building a carpark at Clonsilla Railway Station. This is Armageddon time, with the Four Horsemen of the Apocalypse riding bareback down the Main Street of Blanchardstown.

Driving home after the competition, I mentioned this theory to my daughter, Louise. Naturally, she shot my argument to pieces, with a few well-thought out and logical ripostes, for which I could think of no intelligent answer.

You see what I mean?

(June 2004)

Blue and Flagging

The other week, I was sitting at home listening to the radio – which, I firmly believe is the best thing one can do to that particular contraption – when an article of news came up, regarding the awarding of the prestigious blue flags to the beaches of Ireland. Now, I had done some serious and detailed research on this subject as a project in National School and apparently, blue flags are extremely important to beaches. They tend to chatter about little else and get very defensive if they don't have one. The rumour-mill in the beach world asserts that Bettystown made its own blue flag out of a pole and appropriately coloured paper – a charge that the beach vehemently denies.
However, though I listened with bated earholes, once again Dublin 15 failed to capture a flag of any colour, never mind a blue one.
"Same as last year," remarked my wife dolefully.
"And the year before," I replied.
"And the year before."
It was a conversation that could have gone on for a very long time in a very repetitive manner, had our son, demanding money to go to the 'Plex, not interrupted us.
Over the next couple of days, the disappointment over the flaglessness of Dublin 15 turned first to anger, then to a small pain in my toenail and finally to a determination that something should be done about this lamentable state of affairs. I would contact our newly-elected councillors, distribute leaflets and, if all else failed, chain myself to Brian Lenihan. We could mobilise the troops to march on the County Council Offices or, if they were shut, we could march on Penney's. We'd have a sit-down protest with a difference – we'd all stand up. If it's good enough for Malahide and Killiney, it should be good enough for Blanch. Nothing, nothing would stand in our way of Blue Flag Status.
My first plan of action was to contact those individuals successful in the recent local elections, whose faces beamed down hopefully on us for weeks. I was actually amazed to discover that they have bodies like the rest of us, and not the bottom half of lampposts. Bizarre!
I have to say I was extremely disappointed by their response. The dogs

in the ever-increasing number of streets are all howling at the moon that housing is just shooting up everywhere, with little or no regard to infrastructure, amenities or facilities. Yet when I approached these civic guardians of our community, they displayed no enthusiasm at all for the campaign. One of them nodded sagely while I explained the situation, before promising that he'd get back to me. Several backed nervously away. One of them assured me that a letter would be winging its merry way to the Minister for Blue Flags in the morning. I knew he was lying by the way he opened his mouth.

Singularly unimpressed, I decided to tackle the County Manager on the subject. He was somewhat taken aback at being accosted in the yogurt aisle in Dunnes, and tried to flee towards the meat and deli, but I took a short cut down the frozen pizza lane and headed him off.

"Look!" he exclaimed tetchily, pinned between my trolley and the fresh fish display. "We're an inland postal district. We don't even have a coastline! How do you expect us to get a blue flag when we don't even have a beach?"

I looked him steadily in the eye. Then I looked him steadily in the nose. "Oh, you need a coastline to have a blue flag beach, do you?" I remarked, the sarcasm dripping copiously off my tongue.

"Err, well, yes, actually," he countered, though I could tell his answer lacked conviction.

Slowly I released him. There is no point arguing with that kind of defeatist attitude. The Ireland of Pearse and Connolly and Kevin Moran is dead and gone. Apparently it's with David O'Leary in a grave somewhere. No imagination, no dreams, just feeble excuses. No coastline! Pah!

What our civic planners obviously fail to appreciate is the tremendous tourist potential in attaining Blue Flag Beach status. Every sweltering Saturday and Sunday in the summertime, where do people head to? [Apart from the Phoenix Park Garden Centre, I mean.] To the beach! Ah, those halcyon days of our childhood! Kids happily throwing beach balls to each other on the back seats of stationery Cortinas, toddlers washing their dribbling faces with a combination of sand and ice-cream, mothers telling fathers that any fool could have known that all roads to Skerries would be choc-a-bloc and they'd have been better off staying at home in the garden.

Our councillors should be actively promoting Blanchardstown as a popular seaside resort. Instead they dismissively ignore the huge potential for the growth of the tourist industry. How much of Dublin 15 has been zoned as a beach? None of it. With all the talk of residential areas and green belts, what debate has there been on rezoning land as sandy belts? I can see it now. A long, wide front on the Snugborough Road extension with Victorian lampposts and oul' wans sitting on benches wolfing down 99s and admiring the bronzed surfboarders walking up from the old Research laboratories. B and Bs with names like Bella Vista and Sea Mist springing up in Corduff to cater for the massive influx from Leixlip and Celbridge. We could even have illuminations and trams and a pier.

With the next election a long way off, the chances of getting any action out of our public representatives are about as slim as getting out of first gear on the Clonsilla Road at 5.30 on a Friday evening. However, the campaign is gaining momentum. By now, you should all have received my leaflet, "The Corduff Riviera – Life's A Beach," in which I set out my ambitious plans for the area, and also give details how members of the public can rally to the cause by donating large amounts of money to my bank account. I have enrolled at the Ian Paisley School of Marching in order to learn to march both loudly and effectively. I have even made tentative representations to the European Court of Human Rights on the grounds that the awarding of blue flags actively discriminates against non-coastal sections of our community.

Some people look at the stars and think "Why?" I look at the stars and think "I dunno." In your dreams, nothing is impossible, as Benny from Abba once said.

Arise, Blanchardstown! It is time to shake off your inland shackles and your inland mentality and take your place amongst the Blue Flag beaches of the world!

(July 2004)

Singing hosannas

Earlier this year, I attended the highly entertaining football international between Ireland and a little-known South American side that plays in yellow. While marvelling at the silky skills of the flamboyant Kilbane and McAteer, I happened to remark upon the almost total lack of vocal encouragement emanating from the 44,000 people assembled in Lansdowne Road. The taunt, "You only sing when you're winning" could easily have been written for the Irish crowd, were it not fact that we don't. [Sing, that is. We do win occasionally!] We pride ourselves as a nation with a long list of positive attributes, but vocal dexterity is right down at the bottom of it, along with queuing patiently and using litter bins. As a race that was responsible for both Boyzone and Westlife, we rightly keep our heads low whenever the subject of singing in public is raised.

This fact was always brought home quite forcibly at Sunday Mass. With my wife, I usually attend the 10 o'clock service at the Church of the Sacred Heart of Jesus in Huntstown, which is our nearest place of worship, at least until the new church is erected in Littlepace.

As fellow members of the congregation will attest, Father Eugene is blessed with a deep, rich and mellifluous voice which reverberates around the pine panelling of the brand new church, a choral echo to the solemnity of the service, a rich evocation of the ancient spirituality of the Mass. If he chose to sing the entire Mass himself, it would be a beautiful performance, akin to attending a recital by Count John McCormack.

The problem though, as Father Eugene himself occasionally points out, is that the Mass is not supposed to be an entertainment. It is a participatory event, a coming together to worship. However, in Huntstown parish, and I suspect all around Ireland, the roof of the church is hardly in danger of being lifted off its joists by the vocal power of the congregation. A spider, idly spinning a web in the higher recesses of the roof, will not suddenly turn around startled by the sudden volume of joyful singing emanating from the pews below. Basically we mumble. We have no problem in joining in, but we deliberately pitch our voices at a level where people around us can't distinguish our own particular timbre. It seems as though the ultimate taboo is to have other members of the congregation glance sideways at you, as they distinguish your tones from the general muffled drone. We are extremely self-conscious when it comes to singing, and probably with good reason.

If a karaoke party we had in our house shortly after Christmas could be deemed representative of the Irish population as a whole, only one person in twelve is physically capable of holding a note, let alone carrying a tune. A video of this aforementioned entertainment causes us to cringe in embarrassment when it is replayed, despite the fact that we all thought ourselves pretty damn cool at the time.

Personally, my own voice is flatter than a hedgehog on the Blanchardstown by-pass during rush hour. I make Shane McGowan sound like Luciano Pavarotti. And I am very conscience of the fact. So, in common with a lot of the congregation, I suspect, I mouth the words of hymns with gusto, yet little sound escapes my pious lips.

However, I believe that, of late, our performance has been improving. The spider in the roof might not be leaping out of his skin in fright, but at least he is pausing for a second, while devouring an errant fly, to ascertain where the soaring voices are coming from.

The reason, I suspect, is the steady increase in numbers of non-nationals participating in Sunday worship. Their whole ethos seems to be quite different to ours. They are not afraid to sing out loud, they are not afraid to hit a wrong note in public, no doubt reasoning that if Jesus was crucified for our sakes, the least we can do in return is to sing His praises in a joyous and unrestrained manner.

I am reliably told by a Nigerian workmate that Mass in his homeland lasts for several hours. It is a happy, eagerly awaited occasion, and participation is total. Nobody holds back. Nobody mumbles the hymns. Nobody interprets the words "Sing Hosannah to the King of Kings," as "Whisper them as quietly as possible."

And when you think about it logically, they are perfectly right. A whole world has been created for our benefit, ranging from the physical beauty of a sunset to abstract concepts like love and hope. The wonder of childbirth, the friendship of equals, the great circle of life, the list goes on and on. So why shouldn't we let rip, let our voices, imperfect as they are, soar up to heaven in whole-hearted praise and thanks? Therefore, in today's global village, our immigrants are showing us how it is supposed to be done. Singing hosannas with gratitude and joy. I'm sure that Father Eugene is delighted with the increase in volume, relieved no doubt that he no longer has to drag us struggling and kicking through the verses and choruses of hymns ancient and modern. Of course, the change will not come overnight. It will take more than a few hymns on a Sunday to overcome years of tuneful self-consciousness but, under the guidance of the newer, more vocal members of the congregation, our own strength of lung is improving. We are still applying the same unwritten rule of pitching our voices so they can't be distinguished, but, as the general volume is now higher, so our own voices have grown marginally stronger. Granted, we still have a long way to go before we contort our mouths to the impossible shapes seen on "Songs of Praise," but at least we're heading in the right direction. And before too long, who knows? That spider might be scuttling off to look for a pair of earplugs.

(August 2004)

The new religion

It was actually in the doctor's waiting room that the idea came to me. Our teenage son had volunteered to help with the washing-up, so my wife and I brought him down to the surgery as a precautionary measure. Tired of idly guessing what terrible diseases the other occupants of the waiting room had, I started glancing through the countless women's magazines on display [Memo to doctors – men don't get sick, huh?] until I came across an article affirming that "Recycling is the New Religion."
The idea set me to thinking, a dangerous occupation that I normally try to avoid. If recycling was the new religion, I reasoned, then it followed logically that bottle banks were the new churches. My mind then strayed to a very pleasant day that my wife and I spent in Venice a couple of years ago. Armed with a guidebook and the obligatory

Cornetto, we had wandered the canals of that magnificent city, visiting a venerable host of magnificent, half-hidden churches, each with its own grandiose history and architecture, gilded with ornate flying buttresses and delicately carved stonework, before bolting hungrily into Alfonso's Pizzeria.

My mind then performed such an impertinent back-flip that the judges at the Athens Olympics would have been scrambling for their "10" cards. In the new religion, Dublin 15, with its wealth of bottle banks, could be the new Venice. Tourists with an artistic bent, or even an artistic straight, would come flocking here from across Europe, from across the world even, to admire our recycling facilities. Maybe if I got the franchise on postcards, I wouldn't have to work again....

Open-topped buses would ferry visitors around the highways and byways of the greater Blanchardstown area, stopping off at the more interesting environmentally friendly locations en route. A chirpy tour guide [myself, naturally] would rattle off the spiel with an assured air.

"And on your right, ladies and gentlemen, we are passing by the famous St. Kylie's Bottle Bank in Clonsilla. Designed by the famous German architect Schäfer, the bottle bank was constructed almost entirely of reinforced plastic. Note the intricate diamond design on the walls of the structures, said to symbolise the wealth – both social and physical – of the recycling movement. This particular style of architecture is art nouveau in feel, with all three types of glass seemingly being put in the same chamber, yet they are in fact compartmentalised. This three-in-one motif was common during the second great age of recycling history..."

"Ahead of you, there is the quaint bottle bank of Littlepace Shopping Centre. Dedicated to St. Britney, the patron saint of Recyclable Rubbish, this bottle bank is one of the earliest examples of its kind, having been designed at the very birth of the new religion. Note how the brown glass container is really a green wheelie bin, with a rough hole cut into it. The local congregation really venerate this bottle bank – so much so, that, as you can see, they present their offerings in plastic bags and leave them respectfully in front of the plastic edifices. If any of you feel like contributing to the Bottle Bank Restoration Fund, I am happy to accept all donations in any currency..."

"Just up ahead of you on your left, you will see what appears to be just a normal pavement. However, this "normal pavement" was in fact the site of the famous St. Ronan de Keating Bottle Bank in Porterstown, which mysteriously disappeared during the reign of Bertie the Bold in 2004. Legend has it that it comprised "three large cylindrical objects, each of whose girth outstretched that of the fattest man of the parish" according to the Annals of Castleknocke, "excepting maybe Jim McArdle." Local folklore states that a vigil is still kept upon the site on Candlemass Eve, in case the bottle bank should reappear…"

"Further on here, by Porterstown Church, we come across one of the most picturesque of all the bottle banks in the area. Overlooking the Liffey Valley, with the Dublin mountains looming in the distance, this is a place of quiet pilgrimage for many of today's recyclists, who feel the peaceful tranquility of the location is perfect for smashing bottles in. As you can see, many worshippers have been so entranced by this place, that they have scrawled their names and crude runic symbols over the bottle bank itself…"

"An unusual Bottle Bank here, as it is not for public worship, but is the private preserve of the Roselawn Inn. The three vertically grooved containers are chained together to discourage late night worshippers, who might try to remove them in a recycling frenzy. Note how the architect has installed lockable metallic coverings over the holes, lest the more fanatically orientated should try to make an offering of something other than glass…"

"Up in the corner, there is the newer five tier, bottle, can and clothing bank, named after St. Brian of Westlife. This stands on the site of an older recycling centre, which doubled as the largest breeding ground for wasps on these islands, before the elders of the tribe of Rehab came up with the notion of protective rubber flaps…"

"And now, ladies and gentlemen, the highlight of your afternoon, la piece de recyclance – the St. Martin de Cullen Recycling Centre in Coolmine. The Recycling equivalent of St. Peter's Basilica, this monument to environmental friendliness was opened in early 2004. You are free to wander around here at your leisure. Should you have any questions, the Guardians of the Sacred Temple – easily recognisable by their hi-vis vests – will be only too pleased to assist

you.
'I would like to direct you to a few special points of interest. The blue newspaper recycling container there is thought to be the largest in the civilised world, though rumours of an even larger one in deepest Finglas have yet to be substantiated. I would also draw your attention to the small red battery recycling container in the western nave, which is believed to be itself recycled from an old domestic kitchen pedal-bin.
'Although you are at leisure to visit all the great recycling domes in this magnificent citadel, I would ask you all to proceed in a respectful manner. The use of photography and other recording equipment is strictly forbidden. I do however have a large selection of souvenir postcards which are available for you to purchase. I do hope you have enjoyed your afternoon with us and will recommend us to all of your friends."
"What are you doing, snoring away like that, making a show of me?" hissed a familiar voice.
"Wha?" I asked, looking around wildly.
"Come on! The doctor says he's only looking for money to go to the 'Plex. Perfectly natural, at his age, apparently."
I meekly followed the pair of them out of the surgery. Somehow I felt a great opportunity had been lost. That's what thinking does for you, I suppose.

(September 2004)

A day in the life of a Castaheany crow

According to the adage, the early bird catches the worm. Not any old worm, mind you, but The Worm. The veritable King of the Underground Wriggly Things. The Worm to whom all other worms pay homage. He lives in a back garden in Deerhaven, apparently, but no matter what time you get up, you can't catch him, despite what the adage asserts.
Occasionally, though, I try my luck, and today was one of those days. The fledglings were awake half the night, so at crack of dawn, I gave

the missus a peck on the cheek to wake her up, and flew off to Deerhaven to chance my wing. I needn't have bothered. Place was swarming with sparrows, squawking and squabbling over the skinniest daddy-long-legs. Even the densest, stupidest worm wouldn't come to the surface with that racket going on, never mind el Honcho.

Flew lazily back to my tree in Littlepace. Kids awake again and screaming for their grub. Luckily it was Monday – never understood what Bob Geldof was rabbiting on about. Mondays are the best day of the week. Mondays are the new Saturday.

From my perch I could see many humans, attired in varying amounts of clothing, performing the weekly ritual of dragging their wheelie bins to the roadside. Yum! Yum!

Some of the ravens – particularly the younger ones – are wont to complain about humans. They claim they are selfish and pay scant regard to environmental concerns. In my experience, the reverse is true. When bin day comes around, the selflessness of some humans brings a little glow to my heart. Many of them deliberately fill their bins to overflowing, leaving the lids ajar. They obviously don't mind theirs and their neighbours' gardens ending up strewn with debris from our scavenging. Their viewpoint must be that it's a small price to pay to ensure that the local crow population is well-nourished.

Descended on a bin in Hazelbury and proceeded to go to town on it. Russell helped me out. He hasn't changed a bit since he made it big in Hollywood. Still the wild one, always boozing and looking for a scrap. Well, we found plenty of scraps in the bin today! Russell showed some great artistic flair by decorating the front lawn with used teabags, as a thank you to the owners for their largesse.

Brought plenty of titbits back to the avian rubbish compactors at home. Despite the fact they're constantly ravenous, they still complain about their meals, and absolutely refuse to eat carrots and peas. They have it too easy, if you ask me. There's poor jackdaws in the Sahara would be grateful for a nice pea.

Decided to spend the rest of the morning playing chicken with the traffic on the Blanchardstown by-pass. Sheryl joined me. She was worried that she was straying too far from her country and western roots, but I told her, hey, pop music brings home the bacon. Actually, she looked a bit overweight, probably from pigging out on all that bacon.

The game involves strutting along the inner lane of the dual carriageway in a totally unconcerned fashion. Then watching the look of growing horror on the faces of the speed junkies bearing down on you at 80mph, thinking they're about to turn you into strawberry jam. At the last moment, you casually sidle back onto the safety of the centre partition. It does be great fun, although Sheryl's currently working on a ballad about an old crow with failing judgement, who didn't correctly gauge the speed of an approaching Toyota Corolla. That whiled away a few enjoyable hours, and when we got tired, we flew over to the Littlepace Shopping Centre Car Park to do a spot of synchronised target practice. Of course, it kind of takes the sporting element out of it, when the cars are so tightly congregated, but at least it helps to get it out of your system. The ravens deliberately pick out the Mercs and Beamers, but hey, a car's a car. I always like to spread my talents as widely as possible. Naturally, I'm not quite as proficient as in the days when I got a bronze medal in the Olympics, but I can still hit the front windscreen of a Fiat Punto at an altitude of 200 feet.

My favourite time of the day is when these humans arrive home from work. I judge it to perfection. They go in through the hall door, and I give them enough time to kick off their shoes, go to the toilet, make themselves a cup of tea and sit down in a comfortable armchair in front of the early evening news. Then I start to caw irritatingly down the chimney at them. Sometimes, if I get no reaction, I drop small bits of grit and seeds down the flue where they land like bullet shots on the hearth. The language can be very colourful, ascending with venom up the chimney, though it always amazes me that they assume I can understand Anglo-Saxon English.

Met Glenn on the way back to the tree. Still a potent force with Bohemians, though he says he's not getting as much supply from the wing these days. He's excited at the prospect of playing against Effana Cuckoo.

With dusk rapidly approaching, it was time for our party piece. A load of us flocked together – as birds of a feather are wont to do - and sat in a long, silent line along the front gutter of someone's house. Then when they arrived home, we just stared at them silently. Fair freaked them out, especially as "The Birds" was on the telly recently.

There was just enough time then to get back to the tree before the little 'uns settled down for the night. I like to spend a bit of quality time with them, before they ascend the pecking order and fly the nest. Of course, the missus had been cooped up with them for most of the day, and she was like a raven lunatic. Accused me of feathering my own nest, which was a bit unfair, in my opinion. After all, many birds consider being able to provide for such a large family something to crow about.

(*October 2004*)

Give us a break

Not only do I have the privilege of writing for this esteemed newspaper but I also have the added benefit of being allowed to deliver it. One thousand one hundred and fifty two of them, to be precise, brought with decent haste, every month, to the good citizens of Littlepace, Hazelbury and Hunters Run.

It is an undertaking that I enjoy immensely. Not only does it pay for my trips to Tolka Park, but it gives me some much needed exercise that is scandalously lacking in my sedentary lifestyle. And I am also ensuring that my words of wisdom are delivered to over two thousand people, all of whom are naturally gagging to read my definitive opinion on whatever subject I have plucked out of the air that month.

Of course, I am but a small cog in the large distribution team that ensures the Community Voice is delivered to over 28,000 homes in the Dublin 15 area. And not the American delivery system, where papers are hurled from a bike in the vague direction of the porch. Try that here and the entire area would soon be smothered in a blanket of sodden newsprint.

Enjoyable as my monthly odyssey is, however, there are several ways that it could be turned into sheer distribution nirvana. I have taken the liberty of jotting down a few suggestions of ways that ordinary citizens can improve the lot of the door to door delivery people.

Walls. Littlepace is full of them. High ones, low ones, in-between ones. None of the other estates in the area have them at all, save for a few individual householders who have had them built at their own expense. An independent survey in Finland, found that in 100% of cases, it takes longer to deliver to houses with a dividing wall, than to houses without. To this surprising statistic, I can lend my wholehearted backing, based on my wealth of personal experience.

Of course, if I had the stature of an American basketball player, these walls would not present a problem. But I am what has kindly been described as "squat," not the most ideal physique in the world for wall-hurdling. I am obliged to grab my leg by the calf and forcibly swing it up and over the wall, hoping that there is no plant pot or cat litter concealed on the other side.

Now I understand fully how attached Littlepace residents are to their walls. They love them. They have wall parties and invite people from less fortunate estates. So I am not suggesting that they knock down their wall. Well, not all of it, anyway. Just the bit closest to the house, so we can walk right along in front of people's windows without straining our groins.

I used to deliver to Ongar too, but was forced to give it up out of fear that I might experience the joys of a cardiac arrest. You would not believe the number of steps in that place! You go up and down so often, your ears are constantly popping. The concept of having a post-box at the bottom of steps obviously hadn't occurred to the developers when the apartments were being built, for there's no escaping trudging up all these flights of stairs.

Again, the cost of converting one's steps to an escalator might prove to be prohibitive to many householders but most Sunday newspapers carry ads for these stairlifts for old people who can't be bothered climbing up and down and honestly, they're not that expensive and you can be sure your friendly Community Voice distributor would be very appreciative, not to mention your postman and pizza menu deliverers.

One of the brightest ideas I've come across is the letterbox three inches from the ground. This occurs in a dozen or so houses in the area, and I'm still trying to figure out the logic behind it. I only have to deliver there once a month, but I'm sure the regular postman loves it. Keeps your back muscles nice and supple, although the rush of blood to your head negates this somewhat.

Again, the solution is simple. Take your front door off its hinges, and turn it upside down. Okay, a bit of a stretch, but better to stretch upwards than downwards, at my age. And dead handy for any American basketball players seeking to get into the Dublin 15 distribution business.

I like dogs. Sautéed in a white wine sauce, the way they serve them in Vietnam. And I have no particular problem with those lovable canine friends of ours that grab the paper from the other side of the door and rip it into a mass of confetti. That's their prerogative. I fully understand that my writing isn't to everybody's taste and I respect their opinion. No, it's the lovable little rogues who lurk outside the front door and haven't been trained to recognise the difference between a burglar and a mild-mannered delivery person, that cause the problem, especially those who wag their tails delightedly at your approach and then start barking viciously the moment your hand reaches for the letter box. It's a great substitute for electric shock treatment, however, as it's cheap and there's no waiting list. But I feel at this time of my life, it is a bit of excitement I could easily do without.

This problem can be alleviated in a number of ways. Boiling, roasting, served up in a casserole, a nice stew. The possibilities are limitless for the adventurous gourmet.

Post-boxes make a creditable alternative to letterboxes. They are very prevalent in one particular estate, obviously a job lot from Poland or somewhere, as they all have a flower and "Posta" on them. They are an excellent idea, especially on houses that don't have a letter box, and save me the trouble of smashing one of the panes of glass in the hall door to deliver the paper. The problem is that the boxes are only big enough to hold a gas bill and a postcard from Puerto del Carmen. Each sheet of the Community Voice has to be folded individually sixteen times before it is small enough to force into the tiny aperture.

I think it was Albert Einstein who first promoted the concept that things could be increased in size simply by "making them bigger." Nowadays, even the densest astrophysicist understands this, and relatively experienced technical engineers should be able to construct a box with a larger slot. Their phone numbers are in the Golden Pages.

Believe it or not, but in Castaheany, sometimes it rains. Very rarely, I allow, but it does happen. It would help immensely if residents could whip out canvas awnings on these occasions, to help shelter us from the ravages of nature. This could be organised on a call-out level, much the way lifeboats are summonsed. At the first drop of rain, a siren sounds and householders spring into action, erecting a shelter in double quick time to protect the intrepid distributor from the deadly raindrops. I think this could work quite successfully.

I don't want anyone to get the impression that, despite what I said at the start of this piece, I'm dissatisfied with my monthly stroll around my local estates. I'm not. I really do enjoy it, particularly when I come across hydrangeas that aren't as well-developed as mine or when the smell of roast dachshund wafts through an open kitchen window. My blueprint for a better workplace need not be acted on immediately but can be implemented over time, so that we can ensure that the next generation of Community Voice distributors don't have to endure the minor inconveniences of their spiritual forefathers.

(November 2004)

My favourite restaurant

What constitutes a good restaurant? The ambience? Efficient service? Value for money? The quality of the food? Traditionally, a combination of some or all of these will have the gourmet dribbling with excitement. Low lighting, sympathetic wallpaper, waiters in white gloves – these have always been the prerequisites of a "good" restaurant. But in the twenty-first century, does the modern diner really need the elegant trappings that one normally associates with haute cuisine? In today's world of instant dinners and urgent appointments, more and more people are turning to unconventional establishments to satisfy their appetites.

The Grocery Department of Dunnes Stores in the Blanchardstown Centre might not have an abundance of stars after its name but I have always praised it for its ability to serve simple, honest food in an innovative way. There are times when it might get rather crowded, but reservations are seldom needed, which is a boon for both the serious and the casual gastronome, although it is true to say that the variety of the menu varies with the time of the week.

My partner and I – it is important for food critics to have a partner – decided to chance the Grocery Department one Saturday midday last month. As we entered, we were offered a complimentary glass of white wine by a charming hostess in a fetching white ensemble. The wine was rather a cheeky little Californian, which stuck its tongue out at us and pinched my partner's backside in a playful manner.

The theme of this restaurant is "supermarket shopping." Getting into the spirit of things, we liberated a recalcitrant trolley from its humiliating bondage and urged it gamely around the wide but crowded aisles, pausing occasionally to throw some strange and unfamiliar items into it.

Like the kids in the Bisto ad, it was the aroma of freshly made soup that drew us, as though hypnotised, to the Avonmore stand at the rear of the store. The disposable beakers were full to the brim with delicious Ptarmigan and Broccoli broth, served piping hot. My partner popped back to the bakery and returned with some still-warm wholemeal bread, lightly buttered and we stood and chatted with our amiable hostess about the benefits of playing a flat back four against teams who rely on a quick break as we feasted on our first course. By blocking access to the stand, we were able to polish off three beakers of soup, before our appetite was sated.

For our main course, my partner and I could not agree. I was inclined to dine on the grilled breast of chicken served effortlessly by a chef called Big Al – who, strangely, was quite petite and very definitely female – whereas my partner was leaning more towards the Chinese Sweet and Sour Chicken Balls that a Mrs. Knorr was tempting customers with in the condiments aisle.

In the end, we went our separate ways. I have to admit I was slightly disappointed by the size of the portions of chicken that Mrs Al was dishing out. However, by the simple method of shouting out, "Look! An eagle!" and pointing towards the yogurt section, I was able to obtain enough poultry to make Billy Bunter's stomach hold up its hand and say "No more!" Ignoring the admonitory suggestion that food should be consumed at the stand only, I retired to the cornflake display and devoured the succulent meat quickly, leaving behind the jealous glances of my fellow diners who had to make do with a single foil container each.

I was shortly joined by my partner, who had thoroughly enjoyed the seventeen chicken balls that she had managed to cajole out of the Knorr woman. After depositing the seventeen jars of sweet and sour sauce – that she had faithfully promised to buy - amongst the cornflakes, we decided to try each other's choice. I was very fortunate in that I arrived at the fully-laden Chicken Ball stand, just as the diligent merchandiser went off to replenish her stock. Broadening my back in a way that would have had referees blowing up for obstruction, I managed to polish off 90% of them before a small kid managed to wriggle between my legs and grab the last one. As I nipped around the corner, I heard him being berated mildly by the returning merchandiser.

We made our way down to the freezer section for dessert. Vienetta was on offer here and it was served up promptly and with good grace by a charming lady, who informed us pleasantly that it was "on special offer today" and thrusting a voucher at my partner, who thoroughly disarmed her by asking why we should pay for it, when it was being handed out for free. I was somewhat unsure if I enjoyed the flavour and had to try four helpings before deciding that yes, actually, it was quite scrummy.

At the cheese counter, I engaged mine hostess in a rapt and interested manner on the subject of the former French President, Georges Pompidou, while my partner polished off both the gorgonzola and the mature cheddar that had been laid out for her enjoyment. She later confided to me that she had found the latter somewhat bland and had half a mind to go back and complain but I laid a restraining hand on her mouth and ushered her quickly towards the exit.

Depositing our now overflowing trolley up against the precarious broccoli display, we left the restaurant, pausing only to sample again the cheeky little Californian that has teased us mercilessly as we entered. This time we were ready for it and as it blew a raspberry at me, my partner crept up behind it and clipped it sharply around the ear.

Comfort is not high on the list of priorities that this restaurant offers, but I defy any other establishment in the country to beat it in terms of value for money. In fact the bill was very reasonable, [actually, it was non-existent] and my partners knowledge of basic maths came in very handy in calculating that 10% of nothing was, erm, nothing, and so no tip was necessary. The merchandisers are always extremely friendly, and the food is cooked before your eyes, so its freshness can be guaranteed. All in all, I recommend it to any discerning diner with a strict budget and an eye for the unusual.

(*December 2004*)

New year, new change?

One year ago, on January 1st, my son limped downstairs in the early afternoon and stood in the middle of the sitting-room, his arms spread out wide. Slowly, very slowly, he turned around and around, performing perfectly-formed circles.
Eventually, my wife, who had been trying to watch Julie Andrews inveigle herself into the von Trapp household, could stand it no longer. "What," she asked, with the air of one who knows they are about to be hit with a stupid answer, "are you doing?"
"Isn't it obvious?" replied my son, who had doubtless been a tad concerned that nobody was going to ask him the obvious question, "I'm making my New Year's revolutions."
I've never been a great believer in New Year's resolutions, ever since the time, when but a pale and sallow youth, I decided that I would spend an hour jogging before breakfast every day. A glance out the window at the heaviest fall of snow in thirty years persuaded me that perhaps an extra hour in bed might be more beneficial to my general health and well-being and ever since then I have stoutly repelled all rashly-considered urges to turn over a new leaf on the first day of the year. Life-changing decisions, I feel, are somewhat trivialised by restricting them to January 1st.
As well as that, I feel that I am like the aforementioned Julie Andrews

in another of her evil manifestations (Mary Poppins), being "practically perfect in every way." My wife tells me this constantly. As such, of course, I have no need of self-improvement and trying to come up with meaningful resolutions – "must give up avocado pears, must learn how to fold a fitted sheet etc" – is quite a futile exercise.

I am however, despite my spotless character, very aware of the imperfections of others, and am willing to help those mere mortals around me to formulate New Years Resolutions for themselves. And of course, this being the season of goodwill, I am more than willing to dispense this advice completely free of charge, although any donations would be most gratefully received.

Exercise, for some totally unfathomable reason, is always near the top of most people's resolutions list, and so I would recommend for the entire body of Fingal County Council a nice gentle walk every morning at around 8am. Nothing too strenuous – just a stroll over the bridge at Clonsilla Railway Station and back a dozen times. After all, they appear to think it is perfectly safe for commuters to do this, day in day out.

More exercise is also recommended for the otherwise admirable glass-recyclers of Littlepace. Emptying a bag full of bottles into the recycling bins at the shopping centre is unlikely to cause repetitive strain injury and is actually quite helpful in the whole environmental scheme of things. Merely depositing the full bags in the vicinity of the bins does not, in itself, greatly benefit humanity.

To the strong, fit and athletic young men of Dublin 15 who journey into the centre of our great metropolis on packed buses every morning, I would suggest that standing up would be a great means of maintaining their robust physiques. True, it may mean that a frail octogenarian might take your seat but the benefit to the calf muscles is immense and will stand you in good stead when you are frail octogenarians yourselves.

Does anybody know if there are still clampers in the Blanchardstown Shopping Centre? The signs are up everywhere warning of the dire consequences of parking in an undesignated area - €80 fine or transportation to Botany Bay (whichever you prefer) - but it's been a long time since I saw an offending vehicle sporting the humiliating yellow contraption. My New Years Resolution, if I were a clamper, would be to requisition some new clamps. I'm sure they would find them a useful addition to their armoury, and a handy deterrent for those tempted to park in disabled spaces.

And on the subject of parking, it is incredible the number of people who find this exercise difficult. The spaces up in the centre are not unnaturally narrow or short, yet the number of drivers who fail to get their vehicle within the bounds of the rectangle is staggering. Either the car in the next bay is expecting Mr. Stick Man to pull up in his Stickmobile, or else the car in front is invading so far over the white line that only a Cinqecento parked on its end would be able to park. To these people, perfecting this really-not-too-difficult art would be a worthwhile resolution. Draw three lines on your drive and practise!

It has become quite a ritual around our area for people to push empty plastic sacks through our letterboxes. I think its something to do with charity organisations. They obviously appreciate that residents of new estates can't get enough sacks. Don't get me wrong – I'm not complaining. It's a wonderful gesture and the bags come in useful for a myriad of reasons. I was wondering though if these bountiful sack providers could resolve to make the bags a little bit stronger. Some of them are really quite flimsy and tend to rip when you're hawking things up to the attic.

New Years Resolutions often involve giving things up and I would maintain that it would be beneficial for all of us if the motorbike department of An Garda Siochana gave up its rather unhealthy interest in the Auburn Avenue roundabout. The mere sight of the white bike propped up on the kerbside makes every driver afraid to encroach into the beautifully drawn box-junctions that decorate that roundabout, with the result that total gridlock ensues. Left to our own devices, the traffic at least moves. Slowly, I'll allow, but any motion is better than none at all.

The list could go on and on. Interviewees on our national media could refrain from saying, "The reality of the situation is…" Shelf stackers in our supermarkets could give up lining the already packed aisles with trolleys, bins and empty packaging. Checkout girls could take aerobics classes to learn how to make the corners of their mouths turn upwards occasionally. Newspaper editors could surprise their faithful scribes with all-expenses paid trips to the Maldives. Gangs of youths could come to the realisation that hanging around street corners is perhaps not absolutely vital to a well-rounded education and that gardening is a much more pleasurable exercise. They could still enjoy the camaraderie of hanging around together, but instead use their time more profitably by descending on a local garden and giving the flower beds a thorough weeding.

Yes, the New Year can often be the optimum time to discard old habits and adopt a new approach to life, the universe and everything. A new start, a fresh beginning, the excitement of a challenge. Oh, how I envy people who are not as perfect as myself!

(January 2005)

I name this ship...

Last month's "Community Voice" contained a very interesting article about the re-naming or otherwise of the James Connolly Memorial Hospital. The subject itself was spawned by a discussion on Joe Duffy's radio programme in December about the Ballymun flats. Commemorating the seven signatories of the Proclamation, the names will not be transferred to the new developments when the tower blocks are finally pulled down.

It was mentioned on the radio show that James Connolly was not particularly associated with Blanchardstown and so the naming of a hospital after him in Dublin 15 was not very appropriate. A quick trawl through the archives in the National Library confirms that yes, James Connolly died for the cause of Irish freedom, "except in Blanchardstown." He apparently scrawled these words in red biro on Padraig Pearse's copy of the Proclamation. What he had against this part of Dublin is unclear, though one eyewitness claimed he once had trouble retrieving his money from a shopping trolley in the Centre and thus bore a grudge against the locality ever since.

The problem is, though, that if you were to restrict the naming of roads and hospitals after purely local celebrities, benefactors, philanthropists etc, your bag of names would start to dry up quicker than the Tolka in summertime. The Colin Farrell Memorial Hospital, anyone? Adjacent to the Councillor Rainey annexe? Perhaps not.

Personally, though, I feel there's not enough commemorating going on. I love a good commemoration and would probably pay handsomely to attend one. However, these days they are few and far between. In fact, I haven't been to a good commemoration for years and probably wouldn't recognise one if it turned around and nipped me on the backside.

So much so, that I have had to take matters into my own hands, and every time my wife buys a new plant for the garden, we have a commemoration ceremony. Currently the entire Shelbourne first team squad is represented out there, although I had to take a pair of shears to the Wesley Houlihan fuchsia recently. And Jason Byrne needs cutting down to size.

There are many things in Dublin 15 that are named in totally uninspiring ways. The methodology of naming the roads in new estates is to have some vaguely naturistic appelation (to commemorate the natural beauty that's been destroyed, perhaps?) like Applefields or Badgerhaven, and then add from a stock list of suffices — Walk, Road, Avenue, Chase, Green etc. The problem is that anyone enquiring for, say, Squirreldale Close will be met by a sea of blank faces, as nobody can differentiate Squirreldale Close from Squirreldale Park or Squirreldale Mews.

However, how much more enterprising it would be if the roads in new estates were themed? For example, you could call an estate Stuttgart 88, and name the roads Galvin's Cross, Sansom's Miskick, Aldridge's Leap etc. Somebody asks for Shilton's Despair, you direct them down to the end of Houghton's Header and take a left at Charlton's Delight. Or name a new development after pop songs - Thunder Road, Electric Avenue, Orange Street, Blackberry Way, Penny Lane, Don't-stand-so Close. All it requires is a bit of imagination.

Who decided on calling the car parks in the Blanchardstown Centre, Blue, Green, Red and Yellow? The Teletubbies? After four years, I still get them confused. Why? Because the names are totally bland and unmemorable. Why not call them John, Paul, George and Ringo, and stick posters of the respective Beatle up at the entrance to each. Problem solved. Maybe pipe some music from each of their solo careers post-1970 in order to reinforce the connection. Although, on second thoughts, perhaps that would tend to dissuade people from using the Ringo car park.

The outlying car parks don't even have names. Another great opportunity lost! Why not commemorate our Eurovision successes? It's hard to imagine anything setting your heart aglow more than driving into the All-Kinds-of-Everything Carpark. And what better opportunity to teach your children about the genius that was Johnny Logan by parking in What's-Another-Year? True, many people feel that it isn't exactly an honour we should be celebrating but how many of us sit down on Eurovision night hoping the English get nul points and berating the Greeks for voting for Cyprus?

Take a walk along the Royal Canal and you'll see that many of the bridges are named after people dating back over 200 years. Isn't that a brilliant epitath? Of course, nobody knows anything about them, but they were at least important enough to have bridges called after them. What about the bridges over the M50, or the Blanchardstown By-pass, or the River Tolka? Who do they commemorate? In 200 years, nobody will look at the bridge in Damastown and say, "I wonder who Ruth Coppinger was?" Unless of course she's still alive, which is not beyond the bounds of possibility.

Why stop at roads and car parks and bridges? Enterprising Norwegian explorers have whole degrees of latitude named after them in the Canadian Arctic. For a small fee, you can name craters on the moon or distant stars in faraway constellations. Of course, it's not easy going out and checking your property and you're probably at the mercy of some unscrupulous astronomer who just prints out a cert to say that Star XJ6T78 in the Constellation of Freddie the Fire Engine is named after you.

Be that as it may, though, would it be beyond the bounds of possibility for Fingal County Council to tender out the names of its roundabouts or traffic lights, thereby paying for their upkeep? The Goulding Family Roundabout has quite a ring to it, don't you think? And quite apt too,

for we're forever going round in circles. And it would tie future local historians up in knots trying to figure out why we were worth commemorating!
Bidding for sites could be done by public auction with proceeds going to the provision of local amenities. Get the local brass band out, invite Bertie down (he's bound to come) and solemnly hand over a scroll that states the traffic lights next to 'The Bell' will be henceforth and forever and a day be called "The Mrs. Daisy McGillicuddy Lights." Might not become imbued in the consciousness of the local population, but then again, neither was The James Connolly Memorial Hospital.

(*February 2005*)

The snag list

Many people regard buying a house as one of the most stressful experiences of their lives. There seems to be an interminable list of processes that need to be completed, and it can be a never-ending odyssey of frustration and despair. For many it is not so much the work that creates the problems, as getting the work done in the right order, for often you are at the mercy of tradesmen. Not a very good place to be.
I, on the other hand, did not feel in the slightest bit stressed during the whole house-buying process. I get stressed trying to reason with my teenage children, I get stressed watching Shelbourne trying to defend a one goal lead for eighty minutes, and I get stressed when the queue of traffic that I have chosen appears stationary compared to the queues on either side of me. But buying a house? It was actually rather relaxing. Of course, you are all eager to know how I managed to accomplish this tortuous and gargantuan task without feeling pressurised in the slightest. Well, its time for me to reveal the secret which, if followed, will benefit at least half the people reading this. I left it all to my wife. No point in the two of us becoming bogged down in a morass of bank correspondence and solicitor's appointments, I reasoned. The process is like quicksand, dragging you down into the murky depths, and it is just

as liable to overcome two people as one. So while my wife tried to follow the push-button instructions of the Bank's mortgage department and tried to get our old house sold before the new one was ready, I stayed supremely aloof in the background, occasionally murmuring encouraging words like "It'll all turn out okay in the end," and "When's dinner ready?"

Of course, I didn't manage to escape altogether. Towards the end of the process, when she was up to her oxters in removal men and packaging materials, she asked me to prepare a snag list for the new house.

Always eager to help, I set to work immediately and had reached number fourteen, (cocktail sausages with cream cheese) when, leaning over my shoulder, she pointed out that it wasn't a snack list but a snag list.

Naturally, I was entirely disbelieving when she explained to me that sometimes builders try to sell you a house without putting the finishing touches to their handiwork. Yes, I know, an absolutely preposterous notion and a complete slur on an honourable profession. But, in the interests of familial harmony, I grabbed a magnifying glass and a toothcomb and headed off for our intended abode.

We were buying a new house in a new development and I arrived there, pencil and paper poised, determined that no bad plasterwork should escape my beady eye. After all, we were paying hundreds of thousands for this house, so everything had to be perfect.

I started with the outside of the house and counted the roof. Yup, one. So far so good. I went around the back of the house, checking the shores, window frames, the fence, the patio area, the slates. To my untrained yet inquisitive eye, everything seemed in order, so I ventured inside.

To be honest, because a new house is empty, there's not much to check. Paintwork, holes in the floor, doors that won't shut. In our house, there were no such problems. I was a bit concerned that there didn't appear to be any bedrooms in the house, but I eventually located them up the stairs. I returned back to our old home quite confident that the house was practically ready to move into.

My wife took my list off me, when I arrived home and perused it swiftly. "So," she said, her lips pursed, and I knew immediately I was in trouble. "Apart from a cobweb on the kitchen window and a Mars Bar wrapper in the bathroom, everything's okay is it?" I nodded, cautiously, waiting for the catch.

By reply, she handed me a sheaf of papers. "This," she said, "is the architect's snag list. As you can see, he found 78 faults."

Now, architects, to me, are people who design luxury lakeside villas in the Bavarian Alps, for people with more money than sense. I was naturally horrified at the enormous expense we must have incurred from flying this gentleman back from Munich to inspect our U-bends. However, when my wife produced the invoice, I was mollified somewhat. Times must be tough for architects, for he was only charging a comparative pittance. And when she further enlightened me with the cost of getting a plumber, tiler or electrician out to rectify mistakes after we had moved in, I was positively beaming.

I flicked through the snag list. A lot of it was written in Building Language, with references to soffits and architraves that I didn't understand. I had to admit, I should have spotted that the kitchen ceiling wasn't painted, that the basin in the bathroom lacked a pedestal and that the banisters hadn't been varnished. The rest of it – the broken pane in the sitting room, the excess plaster all over the skirting boards, the damaged shelving in the hot-press etc, I felt he was nit-picking. Though I ruefully had to concede that it was better if the builder fixed them, rather than leaving it to me.

I tossed the snag-list back to wife.

"Didn't spot the Mars Bar wrapper, though, did he?" I proclaimed contemptuously.

(*Property Supplement February 2005*)

My career as a linesman

During the football season, you will normally find me on a Friday evening down in Tolka Park or whatever far-flung ground the mighty Shels are playing in that weekend. It is an activity that I rank slightly ahead of breathing in my list of The Most Important Things in Life, coming a very close second to Counting my Money and Bemoaning the Lack Thereof.

Part of the fun of following three-dimensional football, (rather than the over-hyped version of the sport served up on Sky,) is the great enjoyment to be got out of hurling abuse at the referee and the ludicrously-termed "referees assistants." A rose is a rose by any other name, and linesmen (and women) are still the lowest species of homo sapiens known to exist on the planet, despite attempts by the football authorities to re-market and re-model them.

Naturally, as a football supporter, I have the prerogative to vent my spleen on a trained individual who is in a much better position to make a split-second pressurised decision than I am. I can spot things from eighty yards away that he (or indeed, she) has failed to notice at a distance of three feet from the action. It is a football truism that the supporter is always right and the linesperson is always wrong. And long may it continue.

Recently, though, I got the opportunity to run the line at a local game, and thus was able to experience the trials and tribulations of the linesman from a different perspective. I went up to our local pitch to watch my son playing for Littlepacers against Malahide, a team they curiously seem to play every week. "Who are you playing this week, son?" "Malahide, Dad." Either I'm imagining it, or it's the joint smallest league in the world. The Scilly Isles, apparently, only have two teams. One of them wins the League, while the other prides themselves as being Cup specialists! But I digress.

Littlepacers very vocal and knowledgeable coach proffered me the flag as I arrived and I accepted with alacrity. My chance at last!

Now, those of you who have attended junior football matches know that a linesman's job – sorry, I'm going to continue to call him a linesman – in these circumstances, is to stand chatting to his mates and wave the flag airily and vaguely whenever the ball goes out of play. Sure, the ref can decide who it touched last. And as for keeping up with the last defender, well, that's far too much like hard work.

I, however, was going to break the mould. I was going to be strictly impartial and absolutely correct in everything I did. I was going to draw the ref's attention to off-the-ball incidents, I was going to prove it's possible to get offside decisions right and I was going to run that line without cause for reproach.

And, for the first ten minutes, I did pretty well, though looking back, that might have been because all the play was in the Littlepacers' half. But then the black and white stripes broke and in a swift flowing move, the ball was up my end. It was then I recognised the big hurdle that a linesman has to face. He must keep one eye on the last defender, one eye on the attacker and one eye on the kicker. Not an easy feat for mere bi-optic humans, but I made my decision in an instant. Up went the flag, straight, bold and decisive.

Unfortunately, the ref had his back to me and failed completely to notice my moment of glory. Now what do I do, I thought? Do I continue to stand here like a lemon until he eventually notices me fifteen minutes later and comes over to ask what on earth I'm flagging about? Or do I say, sod it, put my flag down and get on with it? In the end I chose the latter. Which was just as well for Littlepace, because Borner found Borky who crossed it for Deano to head home. Amid much backslapping and hair-tousling, the team made its way back to the centre-circle, as the Malahide manager went apoplectic on the far touchline, screaming something about the flag being up for offside. The ref glanced in my direction but I just shrugged – as linesmen in Tolka Park often do – though I was a little disconcerted that the Littlepace manager gave me the thumbs up as I trooped back to my position.

My feelings of guilt were assuaged somewhat by Malahide knocking in two goals before half time. They were a much larger and stronger team and the Littlepacers complained bitterly at half time that half of the opposition were "bangers." Why they should be likened to sausages was anyone's guess but our manager wasn't taking that as an excuse and lambasted the team for their generosity in defence.

My own view of our poor performance rested largely on the fact that there was no "Macker" in the Littlepace team. It is a well-known fact that every Irish team worth its salt needs to be able to count a "Macker" among its ranks. Our manager however seemed to be more interested in galvanising the lads into action than recruiting any prospective Mackers.

And to be fair to them, they came out for the second half and tore into their seaside opponents like whirling dervishes. I was getting good exercise trying to keep my sizeable girth up with the play and in fact was concentrating on my duties so hard that I never noticed the small child sitting by the touchline eating handfuls of soil. They don't tend to do that at Tolka, you see. Anyway, I went flying through the air like a human cannonball, while the child just looked up, unconcerned.
Darren had seen me though. "Hey, look at your Da, Neil!" he yelled, completely forgetting to get into the box for Eddie's cross. Several other Littlepacers turned around and burst out laughing.
"It was a dive, ref!" yelled Borky, who was actually a descendant of the famous Anglo-Hibernian family of Burke. "Hey Neil, your Da got tackled by a two year old!"
I picked myself up with all the dignity I could muster, which wasn't easy with a broad mud stripe running from forehead to kneecap, and glowered at him. "I'll have you for that!" I shouted at him, as the ball sailed harmlessly into an unpopulated Malahide penalty area. The ref turned around and arched a disbelieving eyebrow at me.
And sure enough, my opportunity came late on in the game. Borner – a member of the Clan Byrne – played a long ball out of defence and Borky, running through, beat the offside trap with a perfectly timed run. Or did he? The linesman's flag was up like a ramrod and it wasn't budging, equaliser or no equaliser. The referee's whistle blew loud and shrill and Borky, who had just coolly rounded the keeper, booted the ball into the empty net in disgust and was promptly yellow carded by the ref.
As he stomped back, he looked over at me and I gave him a big mud-splattered grin. There! Don't mess with me, sunshine! My great triumph at having bested a sixteen-year-old boy was short-lived however, when our assistant coach snatched the flag roughly from my grasp. Over his shoulder, the manager was looking daggers at me and I decided that perhaps it was an opportune time for me to withdraw. Making a big show of looking at my watch in open-mouthed astonishment, I turned on my heel and departed.
Unfortunately I haven't managed to make it back to cheer on the Littlepacers since that episode. Each week the Gods conspire against

my attendance, singling me out on Sunday mornings for such jobs as weeding the garden or trimming my nasal hairs. It's probably best I stay away for a bit anyway.

The experience though has given me much greater understanding of the difficulties a linesman faces. The job is a thankless one, performed under impossible circumstances in the knowledge that whatever decision you make is bound to be wrong. And when the Eircom League recommences this month, am I going to be so quick to hurl abuse at the poor unfortunate running the line?

Oh yes! Can't wait.

(March 2005)

St. Mochta

I am writing this on St. Patrick's Day, our national saint's day. Historians tell us there is not much we actually know about Patrick, except that he enjoyed the Guinness and a bit of craic. There is even speculation that he wasn't Irish at all but an American tourist from Cincinnati. And yet, on March 17th each year the whole country comes to a standstill as we celebrate the life of this remarkable man by downing copious amounts of alcohol in his honour.

Compared to St. Patrick, history has treated poor St. Mochta quite unfavourably. True, he was designated Patron Saint of Telephone Masts by Pope Pius VIth, which raised his profile slightly, but this Dublin 15 saint has largely been ignored by the population as a whole, and this part of the city in particular.

In order to rectify this, I have thrown together a brief biography of our local, almost-forgotten hero. Unfortunately, the Library is closed today, so I am unable to verify all the facts but I am confident that the accuracy of my research is practically faultless.

Mochta was born in either 444 or 454AD – whichever came first – the son of his father and mother. Legend has it that when the child was born, a raven swooped down from a nearby laurel bush and tried to peck off the boy's nose but was beaten off by the boy's father and his mates. Seeing this as a sign from heaven, they named him Mochta - which means "the boy who nearly had his nose pecked off by a raven swooping down from a nearby laurel bush."

Mochta grew up on the family farmstead in what is now Castleknock, but was then several miles from Castleknock. He could "run like a bantam cock, and fight like the very wind itself," according to one contemporary source, yet he spent most of his time tending the worms in the fields around his home.

One day, the youth was on the trail of some worm rustlers in Luttrellstown, when the Lord appeared to him in the form of a holly bush.

"Turn around, young Mochta," said the holly bush. "From now on, thou shalt be a minder of men not worms."

When Mochtas got home, he related what had happened to his parents, who smelt his breath suspiciously. His father though accepted his story and tearfully packed the lad's bags and escorted him off the property, even though Mochta hadn't mentioned anything about leaving home. At that time, Blanchardstown ended at the Garda Station and Corduff was still only a gleam in the property developer's eye, so young Mochta gloomily set off along the rough hewn track in the direction of the distant village of Cluain Saileach – literally "the group of houses just up from the Clonsilla Inn with the very dodgy railway bridge." However, before he reached his destination, he came upon a spot so tranquil and devout, that he decided to build a church and a three-bed semi in thanks to the Lord. Today, the Clonsilla Road still retains this peacefulness and restfulness, and is famous countrywide for being an oasis of calm in a maelstrom of traffic gridlock.

Here Mochta spent his time tending the sick and bringing spiritual enlightenment to the poor, although the place was practically uninhabited, which meant he was hardly burdened down by his ministry. Mostly he lay back on his bed in silent contemplation, or "sleep" as others called it.

One day, Mochta was sitting on the lych-gate cutting his toenails, when Diarmuid O'Diarmuid, High King of Ireland, came limping by. Mochta had seen him on the news, but pretended he hadn't.

"Hail, oh stranger, who I know not from Adam, your Highness,"

exclaimed Mochta. "Can I help you in any way?"
The King explained that his horse had bolted, and he had walked many miles and his shoes were wearing thin. Mochta invited him in to the church and brought him a bowl of broth and then presented him with a pair of knee length boots made of finest hamster hide.
"These truly are magnificent," said Diarmuid, trying them on. "What do you call them?"
"I suppose," said Mochta, cracking one of the first jokes in Irish recorded history, "you could call them High King Boots."
Diarmuid was so pleased with the joke that he made Mochta a saint on the spot and promised that he would force the whole country to convert to Christianity, "when I get around to it." St. Columbanus was rather miffed when he heard of Mochta's instant canonisation – he himself had spent seven years in Maynooth studying to be a saint and had indeed been forced to re-sit his finals exams when caught with a bible in his cassock – and started a rumour amongst his friends that Mochta was not a real saint at all because he "hadn't performed any miracles." When Mochta heard this, he strode up to Tyrrelstown and gazing down across the valley, he banged his crosier on the ground three times. At the time, Ireland was overrun by penguins, which enjoyed the temperate climate and the relatively low cost of living. Successive governments had tried to cull them, bribe them and generally dissuade them but they kept on arriving in ever increasing numbers. What the powers-to-be failed to understand was the only things that penguins fear is someone banging a crosier on the ground. Thus when Mochta made his famous Tyrrelstown Commandment, every penguin in the land rushed headlong over the Cliffs of Moher and didn't stop swimming until they reached Antarctica. Which is why today there are no penguins in Ireland.
Even Columbanus was impressed by this miracle and offered to share a chocolate bar with the new saint. Thereafter the two became great friends, although Mochta kept confusing him with St. Columba, who, admittedly, was the spitting image of Columbanus, except for the leather jacket and dreadlocks.
Mochta continued his ministry on the Clonsilla Road, founding a football club there, which still bears his name. Apart from this, though,

very little exists to remind us of the life and works of this great man, this saintly giant of Dublin 15. Recent excavations at the rear of No. 32 St. Mochtas Meadows – when creating a rather charming rose bed - unearthed several artefacts which are believed to date back to Mochtas' time. These include several milk bottle tops, half a breezeblock, assorted scraps of polystyrene and a ton and a half of builder's rubble. These are currently on exhibition at the National Museum at Collins Barracks.
Legend has it that Mochta met his end on the 19th August 534AD, hurrying to catch a train at the railway station in Clonsilla, when a druid on a horse knocked him down on the bridge. His last words, according to reliable witnesses were, "For God's sake, let them build a passenger bridge across this canal before somebody else is killed." Thirteen hundred years on his words, like the man himself, have been largely ignored.

(April 2005)

<u>Grass</u>

To some people it may seem strange, but I've always felt a close affinity to the Welsh balladeer, Tom Jones. Maybe it's because we're both fantastically wealthy and spend much of the year travelling the world. Or perhaps it's because we have both been blessed with a powerful singing voice that compels women to hurl their underwear at us in appreciation. More probably though, it has something to do with both of us longing to touch the green, green grass of home.
I'm not quite as fussy as Tom though. My grass need not be of the "green green" variety. Simple green would be good enough for me.
We enjoyed an enchanting family holiday in Lanzarote a few years ago. Away from the strip, we marvelled at the almost lunar wildness of the terrain and remarked on the comparative dryness of the climate. It was only after returning home, though, whilst taking a short trip through county Meath, that we realised how much we missed the splendid greenery of Ireland, the rolling fields, hedgerows and trees that give

this country the name of the Emerald Isle.

Grass is everywhere. The most common plant on the planet, it sprouts wherever there are reasonable amounts of precipitation and a thin scattering of soil. Take your car out beyond Clonee and it is everywhere, on roadsides, traffic islands, river banks. It is not a plant that really needs cultivating – it just appears by magic, as if to preserve earth's modesty, clothing the bare soil in a fantastic dressing gown of rich green.

So can somebody explain to me, why it refuses point blank to grow on my lawn?

Let me point out at this juncture that my fingers, unlike the aforementioned grass that I cannot grow, are very far from being green. I am not a natural gardener and the secrets of making compost and growing award-winning petunias have not been handed down through the generations of my family. Like many of the newer families in Dublin 15, I suspect, we moved out here from a much more centralised location, where housing was much more concentrated and consequently garden space was minimal or non-existent, as was horticultural expertise.

In our first house, the garden consisted of a window box on the kitchen windowsill, accessed via the back yard. As the children grew up, we realised it was not a particularly safe place for them to play, as they kept on falling out and landing in the shore beneath the window.

Our second home did, in fact, have a garden at the rear, approximately the same shape and dimensions as a postage stamp. I used to cut the lawn in five minutes with a pair of scissors. The children had to take it in turns to go out and play in it, as it wasn't quite big enough to accommodate both of them simultaneously.

Thus it was, on moving out here, to the wide-open prairie of Castaheany, that we looked forward immensely to a bit of lebensraum. We felt like settlers, hitching our horses to our wagons and setting out for the unknown, where land was cheap and plentiful and where a man could make a home for himself, yessirree!

Unfortunately, as I mentioned previously, it is one thing to have the luxury of space to make a garden. It is quite another to have the necessary skill to turn it into the idyllic rose-scented, colourful, balmy-

summer-evening haven that we imagined when first we moved here. I am no gardener. I empathise completely with William Wordsworth in his famous poem, "The Tulips," when he wrote:
"The tulips dance in sweet rapport,
Swaying lightly in the breeze,
A miracle of nature, for
I thought I'd sown a row of peas."
I have no idea if my soil is acidic or alkaline, nor how to find out. I read books on gardening but still have no idea what mulch is. I buy plants with colourful labels in garden centres and, when I plant them, they turn brown and collapse, clutching their throats in agony. But I can accept this. Gardening is a mysterious subject, built on years of experience and trial and error. That is why television personalities like Diarmuid Gavin are so revered. Their trade is a noble one and only slowly learned.

But grass? Come on! It shouldn't take centuries of primeval earth worship to be able to grow a bit of grass on your lawn. It grows everywhere, mostly in places that I don't want it. In my flowerbed, for example, it has no problems snuggling up to an ailing hydrangea or trying to strangle a pitiful dahlia. I spend hours each summer, digging it up from around the viburnum tinus and pointing it in the direction of the lawn, to no avail.

Of course, I don't want to give the impression that my lawn is a bare expanse of arid rock that would make Lawrence of Arabia feel at home. Au contraire, it has a rich greenness that contrasts very nicely with the brownness of the plants surrounding it. The problem is that the rich biodiversity that carpets the lawn so elegantly does not contain much grass.

We have clover in abundance, straggling gleefully across the lawn in a crazed dance. I am seriously thinking of going into the clover-harvesting business and applying for a grant from the EU. The large quantity of moss attests to the complete absence of rolling stones. I am thinking of digging up a few of the thistles and exhibiting them at next year's Ploughing Championships. Dandelions, daisies, and even mushrooms, after a particularly wet spell, all thrive. There are even weeds that, if I stuck them in a pot and called them by their Latin names, would not look out of place in the Botanical Gardens. David Bellamy would drool with ecstasy at the abundance and variety of flora that inhabits our lawn.

But grass?

I have a theory that the builders deliberately planted grass killer when they sold us our houses. They carefully prepared the ground with tons of rubble, cement, broken drainpipes, yellow plastic, milk cartons and carefully selected boulders – all conducive to great gardening – before covering it all with a quarter of an inch of topsoil. Then they liberally applied grass killer in the place where the estimated you would want your lawn. It's probably a builders' joke. At their conventions, I expect they swap stories about it, while we poor innocents scratch our heads and wonder seriously about the practicalities of concreting the whole lot over. Which is exactly what a lot of householders are doing. Benefitting from all these lawn conversions are of course the builders themselves, who, as part of the plan, have set up thriving cobble-lock businesses as a sideline, and giggle uncontrollably behind their cement mixers, when called into action. In years to come, there will probably be a tribunal about this, and I for one will have no problem spilling the beans. I'll grass them up, no problem.

(*May 2005*)

Tales from the North West frontier

The saloon was empty except for the bartender, three hundred customers and a grizzled old-timer propping up the counter. "Howdy," The Stranger said laconically and ordered a whiskey. The Old-Timer looked sideways at him, puzzling over the word 'laconically' as the interloper sat down beside him. "Care for one yourself, sir?" asked the Stranger and the wizened old gnome nodded with alacrity. The Stranger was not very good at estimating ages but he reckoned the Old-Timer must have been about 268, what with his battered old Stetson, long, white flowing tooth and yellow, decaying beard.

"You ain't from around these parts, are you, boy?" stated the Old-

Timer, cradling his newly-topped up drink with his gnarled hand.
"No sir," replied the Stranger, adjusting his sealskins and feeding his husky a piece of fish. "I'm a stranger round here. Listen, I don't mean to be impolite, but you must be one of the original settlers of this place."
"Sure am, mister," snapped the other proudly. "One of the first Littlepacers. Remember the day we first moved up here, ma maw and ma paw and myself. We came out here on the wagon, looking for freedom, to get away from the big city life. Last time I was on the wagon, sonny. This was prairie land, the buffalo ran free, and a man could set up a nice little home for himself, if he had the will. And a property in the city centre to sell, of course."
"Buffalo?" the other interjected.
"Well, buffalo, cows, whatever. All part of that great bovine family. We were pioneers, see. Things weren't easy. The stage coach didn't come to these parts at first..."
"Ah, come on..."
"No sir, too afraid. This was the Badlands, see? But we didn't mind, no sirree, 'cos we wuz all in the one boat. In fact, the thing we had to watch out for was the cowboys. They'd lay a cobble-lock drive for you in five hours flat, and the next time it rained, you'd find there was no drain."
Here he paused a while and spat in the vague direction of the spittoon, chuckling mildly as the bartender wiped the green globule from his sleeve.
"And boy, did it rain," he continued. "In them days, we had real rain. Not these 'light showers' so popular with youngsters today. I remember, it must have been back in October or November 03, it rained for forty days and forty nights. Never let up once. All the crops were destroyed - well the plants on the roundabout anyways - and all the houses were submerged. The mighty Tolka River burst its banks. We had to live underwater for a week, but it toughened you up. Not easy holding your breath for that length of time, but you had to sink or swim. Mostly we sank. Kids today wouldn't stand for it."
The Stranger arched a disbelieving eyebrow but the Old Timer carried on unperturbed.

"Then there was the tornado," he went on, a faraway gleam in his eye and a dewdrop clinging precariously to the end of his nose. "Never seen anything like it. Never hope to see it again. Slates went crashing through the air, whole vans were picked up and tossed like pancakes, trees were uprooted and re-planted a mile away in Clonsilla. People were crying, "Aunty Em! Aunty Em!" A family of Latvians was sent swirling, house and all, and set down on the strand in Rosslare. Took them ages to convince Sheriff McDowell they weren't refugees."
This time the Stranger arched a disbelieving earlobe, but the rambling monologue continued undeterred.
"Aye, we had it tough. But at least a man could ride free, providing he had a bus pass of course. No saloon at first, so many of the men made illicit runs across the border into county Meath, particularly when the womenfolk went to visit their mothers. And more and more people kept coming, 'cos the land was cheap, and eventually someone had the bright idea to open a saloon, and surprise, surprise, it did a roaring trade. Did you see the two clocks on the turret when you came in, sonny?"
The Stranger shook his head.
"Take a look when you go out. One's stuck on ten to three, the other on twenty past three. Bin like that for over sixty years. Rumour has it, just after it was built, a short-sighted crow, on his normal route home, flew slap bang into one clock, stopping it dead. Half an hour later, his twin brother did the same thing. That was just before the revolution…"
"Revolution? I never read anything about a revolution."
"Ah, history books don't tell you everything. Once upon a time, sonny, and you'll find this hard to believe, the town cleaners used to take your rubbish away for free. They figured it was better than letting you throw it in the street. Then they decided they were going to charge you for taking it away. There was pandemonium! People went on hunger strike, lay down in front of bin trucks and chained themselves to the courthouse, though many preferred to just click their tongues impatiently. It was the end of the world, the thin wedge. Of course, the government won the day, they rounded up the ringleaders and gave them a good talking to. Faced with that kind of institutionalised brutality, the revolution died away, but there's many still light a candle

on the anniversary of the first bin charge. The Charge of the Tight Brigade, they called it.

'The buzzword in them days was 'infrastructure' or rather, 'lack of infrastructure.' Trouble was, nobody in them days knew what infrastructure was, 'cepting those with dictionaries, because there wasn't any of it about. For years, I thought it was a variety of pack mule, except with longer ears. The politicians" – another large green missile shot from his mouth at the word, causing the bartender to take rapid evasive action – "the politicians would come into town and talk about it and say they'd get it for us, if we voted for them, but none of them ever did. Mind you, we never voted for them either.

'Speaking of voting, did you know that once upon a time, when you went to vote, you had to make a mark on a piece of paper with a small stick called a pencil. And then you'd put your bit of paper into a large box…You going so soon, sonny?"

"Sorry, Grandad," replied the Stranger, finishing his drink and standing up. "You had me going there for a while, but you overdid it a bit with that voting tale. Still, it's been a very entertaining conversation and I thank you most kindly."

He shook his head sadly at the Old-Timer and threw €100 onto the counter, telling the bartender to bring him another whiskey. Then he put on his wind goggles and sou'wester and strode out the door, glancing up at the broken saloon clock as he did so. "Ten to three," he murmured. "High time I was moseying out of this godforsaken place." And, humming an old tune his grandfather had taught him, he rode out towards the setting sun.

(June 2005)

The weather

"Everybody complains about the weather, but nobody does anything about it."

So said Mark Twain, or was it Ronan Keating? The two are so similar it's easy to get them confused.

Whichever of the two academic genii of the western world it was, they certainly had a point. I am rapidly becoming exasperated by our summer weather and, if I knew what a tether was, I'm sure I'd be at the end of it.

Don't get me wrong. My son informed me when doing his geography junior cert that Ireland enjoys (I use the word very loosely) a mild oceanic temperate climate. Basically, this means that winters are pretty dreary, but summers are quite pleasant, if not actually hot.

Therefore, I never complain about the weather in winter. It rains, but you expect it to. There are howling winds but you dress accordingly. Granted many of the younger generation venture out in bellytops in November and then complain of the cold, but to anyone with a modicum of sense, winter weather is pretty useless. You don't expect anything else.

However, summertime ought to be a time of lengthy spells of blue sky and a bit of heat from the sun, just as they were when we were young. And before you say, it's only an illusion, and summers were always very dodgy, err, no, they weren't. I remember spending much of my childhood's summer holidays on the beach. More than that, we'd go swimming in the sea, spending hours in there.

Have you tried swimming in Bettystown recently? Dip a toe in, and you have to be treated for frostbite. The coastal waters of Ireland are almost completely human-free, as compared to thirty or forty years ago. Kids play frisbees or football or build sandcastles, anything to avoid getting into the water. Global warming, me backside.

When was the last time we had a decent summer, a summer with weeks of hot, sunny weather? I'll tell you when – the summer of 1975, thirty years ago this year. Thirty years? That's far too long to be waiting for what should be normal, average weather for the time of the year.

People point to the summer of 1995 as being a great summer. Was it? We spent a fortnight in Spiddal in August and it rained virtually every other day. The indoor swimming pool and amusement arcades of Salthill got great mileage out of us that year. In August, please note. That was one of the last times that we spent our summer holidays in Ireland. Such was our frustration, that we've holidayed abroad ever since, save last year, when we ended up in a house full of steaming, drying clothes in Bantry.

I'm sure we're not alone. Can the Government not see that it's a false economy to have such useless summers? Foreign holidays are the norm now, and there's a crisis in Irish tourist circles. Imagine all those harp-stamped euro being handed over in Praia de Rocha and Puerto del Carmen, and think how much they would aid our flagging tourist economy.

Such is the scarcity of hot summer days in this country, that whenever we do get a couple of days of decent weather, we go completely overboard, strip off to our skin and end up like overripe raspberries. Everyone goes around saying what fantastic weather we're having. But it's not. It's only the normal average weather that we're supposed to get in the summertime. We should have weeks of this, not the odd day here and there when "it's not too bad out of the wind."

Rubbing salt into the wounds is the ever-cheerful Gerard Fleming and his grinning cohorts at Met. Eireann. Why does he wink at us, as though letting us into some great meteoroligical secret, and then inform us with a grin about the latest flash-flooding or severe weather warning? Joan Blackburn could at least attempt to show a bit of contrition for the abject weather she dishes up nightly.

Why is Joe Higgins not putting pressure on these weather gurus up in Glasnevin to serve up a nice long dry spell for July and August? I'm sure his crusade against the bin tax was very laudable, and his support for the Turkish workers likewise, but he seems to be overlooking the most fundamental issue of all – the weather. The weather is at the heart of everything. You don't mind sitting for hours on the M50 if you know that, come Saturday, you'll be throwing an extra burger on the barbie with the Beach Boys blaring out from the boombox. So your son is in a class of 70 in a ramshackle shed in the grounds of the local school? Who cares? We're bringing a picnic and going fishing down the Tolka at the weekend.

I read in the papers this week that parts of England are currently enforcing a hosepipe ban. The same England that lies just across the pond and enjoys the same oceanic, temperate climate as us? Yep, that's the one. Does something smell fishy to you? My nose hasn't stopped twitching since I read that.

Why have we agreed to take England's fair share of rain and added it to our own? What kind of hold does mad Tony have on Bertie that our esteemed Taoiseach has agreed to this? Doubtless it will all come out in the twenty-five year State Paper rule but most of us will have emigrated to Andalucia by then, if this present trend continues for much longer. I mean, it's not rocket science. All Winking Gerry has to do is to change a couple of those Ls to Hs, and push those isobars apart a bit. Maybe they're completely out of big smiley sun symbols or perhaps they've just rotted away through disuse.

It's not Gerry's fault. He's a rain man. He likes torrential downpours and winds rising to hurricane force 10, and that's his prerogative. But nobody is putting pressure on him to spread a little sunshine our way. Au contraire, he was probably picked for the job precisely because of his penchant for dismal weather. A subtle Governmental subterfuge designed as a sop to our English brethren across the water.

So, come on, Ruth Coppinger! Come on Leo Varadkar! We put you in, and we can put you out too. Once we get some long, hot sunny spells, all our other problems will decrease in size. Even if you have no influence over the druids of Dublin 9, then press for our own meteorological service in Dublin 15 and give the weather back to the people!

(*July 2005*)

Enjoying the neigh–buzz

As the relieved Antonio enthusiastically remarked in "The Merchant of Venice," as the last of his ships sailed blithely into port, "Neighbours, everybody loves good neighbours."

These words of wisdom were brought home very forcibly to me recently when a sign went up one evening in a neighbour's front garden announcing that their property was indeed up for sale. (My son maintained that it was merely the pole holding up the sign that was for sale but a quick crash-course in the business of selling property convinced him otherwise.)

Joe and Ann – I will call them Joe and Ann to protect their anonymity,

although that in fact is their real names – had moved into the newly-built estate at around the same time as ourselves five years previously. Like all of us along that strip of road, we experienced the same problems of moving into an unfinished estate, the dust, the access, the geography, the flat tyres caused by carelessly discarded nails, the building blocks buried one centimetre below the surface of the lawn, the excitement of discovering the best pubs in the locality. Thus it was that, sharing the same experiences, a sort of bond developed between us, an unwritten camaraderie that stated, "Look, we're all in this together. Let's all get on."
So when one neighbour suddenly decides to up and leave, it's not quite a bereavement or an amputation but there is a definite sense of regret. You realise, in the words of the heavy metal classic, that "good neighbours become good friends." You've got used to seeing them, having a chat, a wave, a nod. They are a part of your daily life and not unnaturally you're sorry to see them go. And obviously, you are somewhat apprehensive in case the Addams Family moves in two days later.
Those of us who are more paranoid than normal naturally fret a little, lest the reason for their leaving is something you have said or done. Did the wife see me sunning myself in my shorts? Do I sleepwalk? The worst scenario would be if three or four houses on either side all put up 'For Sale' signs. I've seen this occasionally in different estates, and idly wondered, probably unjustifiably, what was so terrible about the non-transient family in the middle.
My mother-in-law, a very perceptive lady, once remarked to me that you don't need to be in and out of other people's houses all the time borrowing sugar or lawnmowers to be classed as a good neighbour. Some of the best neighbours I've had have been the ones I only exchanged a few pleasantries with occasionally about the current meteorological situation. Some of them I didn't even know by their name, but referred to them merely as Number 26, though not of course to their face.
Of course, it's the classic syndrome of never missing your water till your well runs dry, or, as with Tyrellstown residents, until your reservoir becomes contaminated. It has often been said that you only

notice the performance of a referee if he is performing particularly appallingly (99% of the time). In a similar vein, Harold Wilson maintained you never noticed good government. And you will usually take good neighbours for granted too, provided of course they aren't inept politicians or hapless referees.

For, quite simply, it's not hard being a good neighbour. As with all aspects of life, if you treat other people with respect in the way that you would like to be treated yourself, then you can't really go far wrong. We are really fortunate that all our neighbours have the same broad outlook on life as ourselves and do not feel the need to play Black Sabbath (or Boyzone) at full volume at three o'clock in the morning. They keep an eye on our place when we go on holidays, and we keep an eye on their's.

"Location, location, location," runs the estate agents' mantra. It should read "neighbours, neighbours, neighbours." Sure, you could pick up a lovely little chalet on the shores of Lake St. Moritz with a Jacuzzi and a private indoor heated swimming pool nestling in the foothills of the Engadine, but if the Doberman pinscher next door spends every night barking at imaginary alpine intruders, then it would soon be time to pack up and move on.

Very few, if any, estate agents' literature, though, gives an indication of the neighbours you could potentially acquire. They don't tend to advertise a "Des. res. 4bd. Sfch. Number 35 is a bit of a nosey parker." A dream house can very quickly turn into a home from Hell if your new neighbour turns out to be a maniacal axe-murderer "trying to go straight," or a skunk-breeder.

Sadly though, many estate agents refuse to give details of the neighbours for fear of litigation, which is a shame. Imagine spending hundreds of thousands on a house only to discover that you are living next door to an Arsenal supporter! It doesn't bear thinking about. Even worse, at the other end of the spectrum would be a Ned Flanders Okeley-dokeley-neighbour type of individual who would cause you to spend whole evenings in the pub until you felt it safe to come home undetected.

Similarly, the charming "not overlooked" property you purchased would soon lose its appeal if the neighbour next door decided to build

Liberty Hall in their back garden and block out all your natural light. I once, as a small boy, lived next to a compulsive curtain twitcher. Every time I came home or went out, the curtains would be partially withdrawn. I had no idea what the woman looked like, but I imagined her to be a hideously deformed hag like the witch in the Hansel and Gretel story, just waiting for her opportunity to snatch me up and stuff me into a cauldron. Forty years later, I concede that probably she wasn't and my imagination did her a great disservice.

The other week, we arrived home one evening to find Joe and Ann's sign down. This was it, we thought. They'd been Sale Agreed for weeks and we'd been on a promise to have a night out in the local to see them on their way. Obviously time constraints had meant that we'd lost our opportunity to say goodbye to them in time-honoured fashion. Just as we were about to enter our house, we saw Joe on his drive. They'd changed their mind, he said. They weren't leaving after all. I bit my lip and commiserated with him that things hadn't worked out as hoped, whilst restraining an impulse to leap up and punch the air with delight. That evening I was in such good form that I didn't even complain when my daughter turned on "Big Brother."

(August 2005)

Harry Potter and the cobbler's mannequin

(Having purchased the contents of J.K.Rowling's wheelie bin on e-Bay, I was interested to come across the following sheets of paper, undeniably written on the author's own word processor. I firmly believe it will be an important source for literary critics in years to come, despite the fact that it had "No! No! No! This is rubbish!" scrawled across it in ballpoint pen.)

"Wow!" said Harry, straightening his glasses after the uncomfortable sensation of apparating. "What is this place?"

He looked around the huge tiled hall in wonder, vaguely aware of a tingling sensation in his legs. Looking down he found that he was standing up to his shins in cool water.

"This must be the Blanchardstown Shopping Centre, Harry," said a familiar voice beside him, "but what are you doing in the fountain?" Looking around, Harry saw that, as usual, Hermione had apparated perfectly and was sitting on the edge of the pool, watching him with a smile on her lips.

He gave her a withering stare as he squelched to the edge of the water and clambered out. "Aridamus!" he whispered, surreptitiously pointing his wand at the bottom of his trousers. "Any sign of Ron yet?"

"Sort of," answered Hermione, nodding towards the entrance to Mothercare. Looking over, Harry saw a red-haired boy hopping about on one leg. "He's been looking for his other leg for the last five minutes," she continued. "Reckons he must have left it behind."

"Well we can't wait for him all day," said Harry impatiently. "You're sure this is Voldemort's hiding place?"

"He Who Must Not Be Named, you mean?"

"For Chrissakes!" yelled Harry. "It's only a name. He's master of the underworld, the prince of the dark arts. You'd think he wouldn't be so touchy about having his name said!"

"This is the place, Harry," replied Hermione, ignoring the jibe. "I read it in "Secret Lairs of the Wizarding Community." And she reeled off the relevant section – "Beyond the Toll Bridge of Despair and the Roundabout of Confusion, along the Road of Desperation and up the Slip Road of Eternal Waiting, there shall ye find the Shopping Centre of Accursed Trolleys. Here lieth the hiding place of He Who Must Not Be Named. Brackets, Lord Voldemort, Close brackets."

Harry meanwhile was studying the hundreds of Muggles that were streaming past the fountain in every direction. To his eyes, they all wore an air of resigned desperation, as though they had just parted with large amounts of money against their will. Obviously, the evil lurking in this place had rubbed off on the shoppers.

"This place is so huge, Harry," wailed Hermione. "How are we ever going to find He Who – er, Voldemort, I mean?"

Suddenly, Harry felt a blinding flash of pain in the scar on his forehead, which he knew from old meant that his arch-enemy was close at hand. Whirling around desperately, he scanned the faces of the passing Muggles trying to see through any possible disguise. "He's here,

Hermione," he grunted, through the pain. "I can feel him."
Desperately the two schoolchildren, receiving odd stares for their wizarding robes, scanned the shops and passageways. Harry thought he saw him trying on a pair of wedges in a shoe-shop, but it turned out to be a shop-assistant from Penney's on her lunch-break.

"Look!" Hermione screamed suddenly. "Over there!"
Following the direction of her wand in her outstretched hand, Harry's blood ran cold. There, standing in the window of the Regency Cleaners, an evil smile playing about his lips, stood the Prince of Darkness himself, the evil Lord Voldemort. He had disguised himself cunningly as a mannequin, dressed in a navy baseball cap and a red Hawaii shirt, but there was no mistaking that heartless leer and steely gaze. As he watched, Harry could see Voldemort's wand tracing out patterns, putting the accursed Stupefacto spell on all the Muggles that passed by the window.

"How clever!" squealed Hermione. "The Muggles think he's holding a tool for cutting keys. No wonder they're all handing over their Sickels in large amounts, and leaving the Centre much poorer than when they came in. This must be how He…Voldemort is funding his Death Eaters!"

"And I've only just realised," exclaimed Harry, slapping his forehead in frustration. "The Blanchardstown Shopping Centre is an anagram of 'I am Lord Voldemort – Give me all your money."

"No it isn't," said Hermione, after a moment's reflection.

"Well, it would have been, if the letters were the same," replied Harry defensively. "Come on! We've got to stop him!"

With that, the two Hogwarts students sprang into action. Harry did a forward roll towards the flower shop, then suddenly stopped, turned and pointed his wand straight at the crazed mannequin.

"Expelliarmus!" he yelled at the top of his voice.

To his horror, the beam of light hit the window at just the wrong angle. Realising too late, that Voldemort must have reinforced the pane of glass with a cunningly contrived reflective spell, Harry watched his well-aimed shot rebound and strike Hermione full in the face. He could only stand helplessly and watch as she was pulled upwards, upwards, up the giant escalator, before disappearing with an audible Swoosh!

through the open entrance of Roche's Stores.

"Foolish boy!" cackled Voldemort, and did a little jig of delight on his podium. The sound of his voice seemed to echo round and round the cavernous walls of the Centre. Harry idly wondered why the crowd of Muggles passing by the window couldn't seem to hear the chilling words, but were instead staring at his own dishevelled appearance with amusement. "Just like that sad deluded father of yours..."

Harry felt the surge of anger well up in his bowels, and then rise quickly through his lower intestine, upper intestine and windpipe. Cutting through his trachea, it diverted through his lower jaw until it found full vent in his temples.

"NOOOOOO!!!!" he yelled at the top of his voice, and charged straight at the window, his wand sending a shower of fiery green sparks towards the grinning mannequin. Some Muggles screamed and ran for cover, while others took pictures on their mobile phones.

But just as Harry reached the door of the Regency Cleaners and saw the mask of fear on the faces of the two young shop assistants inside, Harry felt a firm hand clasp his shoulder tightly, and his wand was snatched roughly from his grasp. Whirling around in a panic, he found himself staring deep into the soulless face of a Dementor, one of those cold, evil creatures that suck all the happiness out of a body. A bit like Shamrock Rovers, Ron had once remarked.

The figure was wearing traditional Dementor garb – grey, flannel trousers, a navy blazer and a piece of plastic attached to a wire protruding from one ear. Its face was expressionless, as it bent Harry's arm up behind his back and frogmarched him off to the Security Office. Harry winced in pain, not merely from his arm, which he was sure was broken, but at the frustration of losing the chance of destroying Lord Voldemort for once and for all.

The Dementor brought Harry into a small room, furnished only with a small desk and two chairs. "We've got it all on CCTV, sonny," he snapped. "Attempted robbery with violence." He eyed the wand thoughtfully before bringing it down with a crash on the table. "Could do a fair amount of damage with that, I reckon," he said, not seeming to notice the sparks emanating from the end of the wand.

Just then, the door swung open and Ron hopped in, closely followed by

another Dementor. "Hi Alan," said the second figure. "This one got caught trying to remove a joint of meat from Dunnes. Mind him for me, will you. There's reports of a young wan battering a hole in the wall of Roche's. Kids today, eh?"
Harry put his head in his hands and groaned.

(September 2005)

The horror of purchasing a school uniform

On the second Wednesday of a fortnight's summer holiday, thoughts naturally turn to returning home and the resumption of the drab daily grind that is reality. Although one quarter of the holidays still remains, it is tinged, unquestionably tainted, by the realisation that the good times will shortly be coming to an end.
In much the same way, the realisation that the school summer holidays are about to draw to a close is marked by the annual trip to the local clothes shop to pick up the school uniform. I don't know which I hated more – the school uniform, going to collect it or the actual concept of having to wear a uniform in the first place. Probably all three combined to give me a loathing of the attire, from which I have never recovered. Towards the end of July, my mother would start to drop hints about going down to get the uniform "before the rush." Naturally, it is downright immoral to even think about school in July and so my mother's enthusiasm was greeted with copious amounts of cold water. From then on, it was imperative to have a full diary for the month of August. "Can't make it on Thursday, ma, I'm playing football." As August advanced, my mother became more and more persistent until the critical mass was achieved, and it was the lesser of two evils to get the school uniform out of the way.
Looking back, it was not the actual purchasing of the uniform that was the problem. It was being seen out in the shops with your ma that was the epitome of uncool. If my mother would have given me the money, and a list of things to buy, I'd have strolled down there with a spring in my step. Better still if, while there on my own, I encountered a

schoolmate or two with their mothers. That would have been absolute bliss.

However the notion of me being capable of purchasing a school uniform on my own was so alien to my mother that the thought probably never entered her head. (I actually still need my wife for moral support when purchasing a jumper, and much prefer to let other people buy clothes for me. This is because, as I am the first to admit, I have absolutely no fashion sense whatsoever.)

So we would go down to the local appointed shop, my mother leading the way and me slouching behind trying to pretend I was out on my own. I remember having to make sure none of my socks had holes in them, for fear of making a "holy show" of my mother.

Of course there were always two or three other boys there, (thankfully with their mothers,) though never any of your close friends. These were boys who might be in your year but moved in different circles. A brief nod of the head in acknowledgement was all that was required but my mother used to speak to the other boys, asking them what subjects they liked best at school. I would be mortified and petrified lest she committed some horrendous faux pas, like letting slip that I enjoyed geography, or that I kept on splitting the backside of my trousers.

The worst thing of all though was when she wiped a grubby mark on your cheek with her handkerchief. I was a boy. We're supposed to have grubby marks on our cheeks. What do you expect us to do? Give our faces a wash before we come out? So I'd recoil in horror on the production of the hankie in public, in front of kids in my year in school, for whom my over-fussy mother would bound to be the only topic of conversation when school restarted.

Trying the uniform on was another chore that I deemed totally unnecessary. The shirt was labelled "Age14" and I was, erm, let me see, 14. Where was the problem? If only they sized adult clothes by age, instead of this ridiculous insistence on waist sizes, I wouldn't be so daunted by buying clothes.

But no, everything had to be tried on, even the tie. I mean, how many different sizes can a tie be? One thing was for sure, my mother never sent the tie back, asking for "a longer one," but nevertheless I still had to put it on.

Then came the endless pulling and tugging and the imprecations to stand up straight. Again, why? For 95% of the time that I had the wretched uniform on, I was going to be slouching in it, so why not check it out for size whilst slouching, with hands in pockets?

My mother would invariably get down on hands and knees to check trouser length, which was a science in itself. Basically they had to be too long. When they were brought home, my mother would turn them up, and then, when they started getting too short, let them down again. In this way, we could eke out a pair of trousers to last for two years, even though the material on knees and backside was gossamer thin by this time.

My mother was a great believer in "buying big" so that I could grow into clothes. Looking back, my mother was way ahead of her time, because some of my school trousers had a crotch somewhere around my knees, which is a fashion very much in vogue today. Shirts could also be baggy – "you'll have your jumper on anyway" – and I could easily have worn them as a nightshirt.

Finally, my mother would pronounce herself satisfied and I'd be free to get back into my proper clothes. Everything would have to be refolded and placed in large paper bags and back we'd go up the street, this time with me leading the way, all eager to get home and play football.

But it was never as easy as that. I'd have to put on the trousers and stand on the kitchen stool, while my mother revolved around me with pins in her mouth, sticking them all around my ankles. By this time I was completely fed up and daylight was rapidly fading and we'd wasted a complete whole day in buying a stupid uniform that I hadn't wanted to buy in the first place.

Even today, my heart goes out when I see boys being dragged in to purchase school uniforms in mid-August. Girls, perversely, actually seem to enjoy the act, which proves what bizarre and unfathomable creatures they are. But for boys, surely there must be a better way.

(*Education Supplement September 2005*)

Dexterus immobilitis

Our daughter, bless her cotton socks, recently got her Leaving Certificate results. She was delighted with them, and so were we. For myself, her success is just another step nearer to the day that she will be able to keep us in the manner to which we would like to become accustomed. My sole reason for having her in the first place was so that I can retire early and sponge off her and so far the plan is coming together nicely.

However, this grand scheme was in danger of going badly off the rails last year, when we were obliged to take drastic action to ensure she got the exam results she needed. One Saturday morning, we had to sedate her heavily and carry her down to the James Connolly Memorial Hospital to have her mobile phone surgically removed from her hand. Not only is JCMH the country's leading hospital for treating gunshot wounds – as reported in last month's Community Voice – but it is also the country's premier centre for mobile phone removals.

"We currently treat around fifty young people a week," said Dr. Nokia O'Nokia, the leading consultant at JMCH. "and the numbers are rising constantly. Many of them are in a bad way when they come in. Because of the trauma involved, we insist on a full anaesthetic. The surgery itself is relatively straightforward, but the worry and sense of loss for the patient, means they often become aggressive during the operation, so it's best to knock them out completely."

The condition – known as dexterus immobilitis among the medical fraternity or Mobile Hand Syndrome – was first diagnosed in California in the mid nineties. Because the mobile phone never left the young person's hand for weeks and months, sometimes years, it was discovered that it gradually became grafted to the palm of the patient, until it was an actual physical appendage to the body.

Though widely reported in "Time" magazine at the time, this was largely dismissed as being a localised freak of nature. However, as Dr. Manic Texter of the University of Columbia explains, the condition has reached epidemic proportions.

"We have a database of reported cases from every country in the world," he says. "Except Nepal. And the Vatican. And Greenland, too, though many people still argue that it is an autonomous dependency of Denmark, rather than a bona fide country."

The symptoms of Mobile Hand Syndrome are very easy to spot, and parents should keep a close eye on their offspring to detect it at an early stage. Going to sleep with their hand plugged into the battery charger is normally a dead giveaway, as is enquiring about the cost of keyhole surgery whenever a SIM card needs changing.

Although JCMH operates a walk-in, walk-out system of performing the necessary surgery, they strongly advise that both the young person and their parent receive counselling both before and after treatment.

"It is best if the young person is persuaded that the operation is in their best interests," says Dr. Wotsme Pincode, eminent child psychologist and author of the seminal work, "Bloody kids! Who'd have 'em?"

"Here at JMCH, we try to stress all the negative aspects of having a mobile phone physically attached to one's hand – the inability to do homework, and to do washing-up or indeed any housework at all, the impossibility of holding normal conversations with their parents, the awkwardness of picking one's nose etc etc. If we can get them in the right frame of mind, if we can convince them that the operation will greatly improve their quality of life, then so much the better. If not, we just knock them out and go ahead anyway."

Post-operative counselling is also vital to integrating the victim back into society. In the early years, patients were thrown back onto the streets within hours of the operation and left to cope alone. They were often seen wandering around Roselawn, tapping the palm of their hand with their forefinger, whilst wearing a dazed expression. Some would hold their hands up to their faces and shout "Hello?Hello? You're breaking up!" much to the discomfort of passers-by.

Nowadays, it is accepted that the removal of a mobile phone is akin to having a limb amputated. Patients must be allowed time to grieve and mourn their loss. Mobile phone substitutes such as stress balls, alarm clocks and bananas are often prescribed by doctors to wean victims slowly off the horrors of the addiction.

Naturally it is difficult when society today is ridden with mobile phones. The pressure on young people is enormous when they look around and see their friends excitedly chattering away. Frequently, even with thorough and structured counselling, many patients suffer a relapse, and go out looking to score a Siemens or an Eriksson. They maintain it gives them a buzz, normally followed by a ringtone. One serial texter in Mulhuddart has had seven phones removed by surgery in the past year alone. "I can't help it," he says. "I just love playing Snake. The doctors say they're going to chop my hands off the next time I'm in. That should do the trick right enough."

Dr. Nokia O'Nokia stresses though that such drastic action is reserved for the most extreme cases only. "Normally we find people can lead normal lives again after the operation. They integrate back into society and can soon walk along the street without the need to hold one hand up to their ear."

Though there have been many calls for the Government to ban the use of mobile phones except under medically controlled conditions, in general the politicians have been slow to act. They have been accused of profiting from the mobile phone industry and some economists have gone so far as to suggest that without the blood money from the phone industry, the Celtic Tiger would be the Celtic Caterpillar, and Ireland would have trouble holding its own in the third world.

When I put this point to the Minister for Communications as he emerged from Tesco's recently, he said, "Can't talk now. I'll send you a text later."

There is a theory that Mobile Hand Syndrome may be the thin end of the wedge, a chilling warning of the future of mankind. Some anthropologists claim that we are mutating into technological entities and it is only a matter of time before the silicon chip replaces the human brain. Though considering some of the referees we get at Tolka Park, this may not actually be such a bad thing.

(*October 2005*)

The curse of Hallowe'en

I'll lay my cards very firmly on the table. I loathe Hallowe'en with the same sort of passion that Ebeneezer Scrooge reserved for Christmas.

The difference is that, in my case, it is unlikely that any ghouls, ghosts or things that go bump in the night will come along to point out the error of my ways.

It was not always so. As a child, I loved Hallowe'en. Of course, it wasn't as good as Christmas or your birthday but it nicely broke up the long stretch between summer holidays and the sheer ecstasy of the end-of-year festivities. Naturally, I refer to ecstasy in the old-fashioned meaning of the word.

Nowadays I dread it and I suspect I am not alone. Part of the reason for this lies in the fact that I hate to see children enjoying themselves. They should come in from a hard day at the pit, eat their bread and then slink off to bed, shattered. What the International Court of Human Rights doesn't know, they needn't worry about. Why should they have all the fun, while we adults have to re-mortgage the house to purchase all the synthetic, unhealthy tat that we're expected to donate to complete strangers on Hallowe'en?

Of course, my hatred for the feast day begins about a month prior to that in late September, when the first fireworks come sailing over the estate behind us and explode near my back door. What is the purpose of this? If a stack of fireworks has been purchased for Hallowe'en, why let them off three or four at a time in the month leading up to it? It's like finding your Christmas present in November, and then having nothing to look forward to on the big day.

However, that's nothing compared to the bright young sparks – I'm assuming they are young, but for all I know, they could be pensioners – who let their fireworks off in the middle of the day. Truly, the mind boggles! It really is quite unnerving that, as a nation, we can produce people who think it's a good idea to light fireworks on a sunny afternoon.

And then you have the interminable sight of processions of kids wandering around looking for wood for the bonfire. No problem there, of course, but it can be quite wearisome explaining that actually, I would like to retain my side gate, if at all possible, and that the young tree outside our house is not dead, but deciduous. Better by far, I always say, to go and rob the wood off the bonfire in the next estate. It promotes a healthy sense of inter-community rivalry and is always taken in good spirits.

But the night of Hallowe'en itself always fills me with despair. I pray desperately for rain but obviously, with the day that's in it, I'm praying to the wrong people, for it normally remains dry.

Where to begin? I suppose it mainly goes back to my own childhood. Hallowe'en wasn't such a big thing then and I can't really remember many of them well, except one, when I was about nine years old. I was invited around to a friend's house for a party. All afternoon, my mum and I toiled over my costume, a black bin bag, decorated with coloured bits of paper stuck on with sellotape. The hat was another masterwork of Blue Peter creativity, a piece of cardboard, folded into a cone and coloured black with silver stars. Lipstick and mascara suitably applied completed the job.

In the evening, we assembled at our friend's house, where his ma had a pumpkin and a knife for each of us. It took about an hour to hollow it out and make the eyes, nose and mouth, but nobody got fed up, or bored. Then we played ducking for apples, and another game where you had to try and eat an apple suspended from a piece of string, both of which I was rather good at, as even then I had a big mouth.

Finally, we donned our costumes – all of them home-made, placed lighted candles into our pumpkins, and ventured out into the night. We didn't knock on doors, looking for sweets, but still collected quite a large congregation of onlookers who came out of their houses to admire our costumes as we passed. It was a brilliant night, and one that I still remember vividly after all these years.

One wonders how many Hallowe'ens will be remembered by today's children in forty years time. I genuinely feel that the effort we put into it made the night all the more special. Today, the costumes come ready-to-wear from the Pound Shop, and the plastic Taiwanese pumpkins are no more frightening than a shopping bag. This is nobody's fault. The world has changed, people spent so much time commuting, that quality time as a family has shrunk alarmingly and thus the disposable society has emerged. Sadly, one of the costs of this is the diminution of the joy of creating. But I digress.

Another thing that irks me is the whole "Trick or Treat" scenario. What on earth does this piece of Americana mean? Kids knock at the door and ask you this question. By reply, you are supposed to fill their bags with sherbert and sticky fruity fizzy pops. Why? What would happen if you answered "Err, trick?" Probably the kids would mug you, and raid your house for chocolate.

Traditionally, I suppose, the children asked for fruit and nuts. Can you imagine the expression on the face of a child today if you dropped an orange and a handful of walnuts into their bag? Or better still, some broccoli. Actually that mightn't be such a bad idea and would certainly discourage them from knocking on your door next year. If all adults get together and decide to reward callers with sprigs of broccoli, we'd have this whole culture wiped out in next to no time.

Now, I'm not a great television lover, but I always manage to find some interesting programme on the telly on Hallowe'en. It's like wanting a pint on Good Friday – you'd not be interested any other time of the year but on that particular day, enforced absence makes the heart grow fonder. At Hallowe'en I'd just be settling down to watch some thrilling documentary on rock formations in Antarctica, when the doorbell would ring. And ring. And ring. Guaranteed I'd be up and down to the door fifty times until my programme was over, when the callers would mysteriously cease.

Combatting the hordes of children demanding that you give them the werewithal to rot the teeth out their heads is no easy feat. Not answering the door doesn't really work, unless you turn the lights off and crouch down behind the settee, which is not much better than answering the door to the little darlings. A lot more fun, though liable to get you into a spot of bother, is opening the door, saying "Oh thank you," taking the bag opened out expectantly in front of you, and closing the door again. Normally I just go down the pub for a few hours until the madness is all over, though I'm not convinced it works out less expensive than buying skip-loads of dolly mixtures. Whatever way you do it, you can't really win, though I'm sorely tempted to try the broccoli idea this year.

Bah, humbug!

(*November 2005*)

The Clonsilla quaternion

Once, as steely-grey October cast her pallor, cold and sober, o'er the rustic Dublin landscape in the year of forty three, staring out beneath the awning of his house that autumn morning, bold Sir William Rowan Hamilton called his wife while making tea.
"My dear," he said, in robust fettle, o'er the hissing of the kettle, "Let's not spend this morning doing chores we both find so banal. Shall we visit Myles the miller, up above, beyond Clonsilla? Let us stroll there, you and I, beside the sweet and still canal."
"I'll go and change this flour-stained blouson," (said his wife) "and put some shoes on. Cook can rustle up a luncheon to sustain us as we roam."
Thus, upon that day so pleasant, laden down with jams and pheasant, Sir William and his buoyant lady set forth from their urban home.
Sir William, on his own admission, was a brilliant mathematician, darling of the Royal Academy, Master at far-famed Dunsink. "People's problems," he reported, "should be broken down and sorted. Mathematics holds the key, if only folk would learn to think."
The only thing that ever troubled this great man, but lightly stubbled, was the oft repeated question, "Why the silly middle name?" Then he'd practise a deception, for he'd learned his own conception had occurred beneath this tree, as once he'd heard his father claim.
But this day, they left the hubbub of the northern city suburb, and marvelled as they smelt again the freshness of the country air. Through Cabra, heading west, they ambled, watching rabbits, as they gambolled through the fields that lined the borders of their leafy thoroughfare.
Neither spoke, but deeply pondered on life's beauty as they wandered, while the creamy sun ascended into the October sky. Overhead a chaffinch whistled. On the bank a cygnet bristled. Arm in arm, the couple sauntered, carrying their pheasant pie.
Down past Ashtown Bridge they headed, past the hawthorn deep embedded; on past scenic Castleknock, where otters swam and pigeons cooed; past great groves of beech and chestnut, all the time they put their best foot forward, as the arbour cov'ring cast a very sombre mood. By Coolmine they found a shady seat for William's weary lady, and

they picnicked, watching moorhens scuttle 'cross the leaf strewn beck.
Then, when they had both partaken of the pheasant, quail and bacon,
both stood up, refreshed, to carry on their long, but worthwhile trek.
"Westward Ho!" Sir William hollered, as a pigeon, lightly collared,
eyed him with a wary glance from high upon an oak-lined ridge.
Smiling now, they strode together, buoyant in the clement weather, till
they spied, beneath the trees, the grey stone of Clonsilla Bridge.
But, as they came upon it's buttress, brave Sir William drew his cutlass,
startled by unruly voices yelling hard from o'er their head. Up the
inclined path they stumbled, as the raucous curses tumbled o'er the
bridge's head, to grip them tightly on their wary tread.
But when they gained the road, which twisted o'er the water, it
consisted of a constant stream of traffic pouring o'er the parapet while,
on either side, a massive crowd, not patient nor impassive, cried in
anger at the drivers for their lack of etiquette.
Now and then, a blood-crazed urchin, through the constant traffic
lurchin', tried in utter desperation to dodge past the flowing tide. But
before too long, a flying wheel would strike him, leave him dying on
the dirty, dusty roadway 'ere he gained the other side.
Then Lady Hamilton posed the question. "Why is there such great
congestion? Can't the drivers pause a while to leave the peasants pass
on foot?"
"No," replied her husband slowly. "'Tis a rudeness most unholy!
Would a horse or two but leap ten feet below into the cut!
'This bridge will not allow these peasants share it's very narrow
presence with these rattling horse-drawn coaches streaming on to
Westmanstown. Thus the wealthy cross here simply, while the plebs,
all pale and pimply, wait their turn in deep despair, with futile yell and
murd'rous frown."
Then this famous mathematician viewed again the great attrition as an
algebraic equation to be worked out in his head. Width of bridge and
speed of traffic, size of crowd with language graphic – all were factored
in as either x or y or even zed.
However this numeric theorist couldn't seem to get the merest handle
on the formula required to solve this wretched sum.
Down the path he strode frustrated, information uncollated, while his

wife in torment followed, countenance morose and glum. Back along
the track he pounded in a temper quite confounded, back towards his
urban mansion down the earthen path he sped.

Gone were thoughts of Myles the miller and his home beyond Clonsilla
– all that filled his mighty brain were thoughts of x and y and zed.

Past Coolmine they blithely hurried, one possessed, the other worried,
past the spot where they had laughed and chattered but an hour before;
through the arching, cooling greenery they marched on, inured to
scenery, her with tender, aching feet and him with sturdy lantern jaw.
Castleknock was just a blur for him, and none the less for her, as
onward, onward, ever onward, down the ochre lane they strode. Down
past Ashtown Bridge they trotted, as Sir William planned and plotted,
working out that long equation 'pon the water-bordered road.

Then at Broombridge, by the creek, a cry went up from him, "Eureka!"
The formula had been discovered in a flash of blinding light. With
cook's knife, he carved out quickly, on the stony bridgework slickly,
the great quaternion inscription, lest its thought be put to flight.

One month on, he read a paper on the great Clonsilla caper, breaking
down the thorny problem of the bridge's right of way. Sadly, though he
had not planned it, nobody could understand it, and the bridge remains
quite untraversable by foot today.

Upon Broombridge, a plaque stands proudly to record the sojourn
loudly, when this algebraic discovery spawned so many learnéd books.
But further on, there's sadly still a whitened fury at Clonsilla. Those on
foot still run the gauntlet of the stream of cars and trucks.

The moral of this maudlin story may seem quite obtuse and hoary, but
is not confined to those with agile minds or privilege – despite the
finest reputations, complex algebraic equations never helped a single
body cross the cursed Clonsilla Bridge.

(December 2005)

A Christmas quest

The festive season had run its normal course.
Christmas Day had been too hectic to enjoy – well, for us parents anyway. Rising far too early at the insistence of our demanding offspring, we then spent the next eight hours performing unspeakable acts upon the turkey and trying to balance all the tasks required to produce the perfect Christmas meal, which was devoured in fifteen minutes and everybody ran off to watch Indiana Jones, leaving great piles of washing-up congealing on the table.
Two hours later and we were just about done in and it was time to go visiting. Great fun of course but not much relaxation and by the time we got home, we were determined that next year we would book the family into a hotel somewhere.
St. Stephens Day was the best day. Everybody lolled around in dressing gowns, yesterday's leftovers were reheated for a quick dinner in mid-afternoon and the sitting room got strewn with Quality Street wrappers. The next two days were very similar except the potatoes got boiled instead of roasted, and the frozen chips made their first appearance of the holiday. The turkey meat was finally removed from the carcass and to our great relief it didn't take the strength of four people to force the fridge door closed on it. The ham was practically finished, while the stuffing had long ago been devoured by ravenous teenagers who couldn't appear to pass by a fridge door without eating something from it.
And then came December 29th, with its hint of depression that the festivities were more or less over and that reality was flexing its muscles.
For me, this day always marks a watershed in the Christmas festivities. It is the day when you begin to tire of slouching around between the fridge and the couch and have a desire to go for "a nice brisk walk" as my Aunt Alice would put it. Not that you ever do, of course. There's always "The Sound of Music" on, or "Willy Wonka" and you feel compelled to pig out in the armchair with the last of the Roses, in case the film has altered since the last time you saw it.
This year December 29th dawned, as indeed it does everywhere after

the night of the 28th, and I woke with a feeling that perhaps I ought to be taking advantage of this brief sojourn from work by doing something a bit more constructive. A quick glance through the by-now well-thumbed RTE Guide however quickly disavowed me of that ludicrous notion and I propped myself on the couch to see if this time Steve McQueen would make it through the second set of barbed wire. When Donald Pleasance finally realised that he was going blind, I was so moved that I got up and went to see if there was anything tasty in the fridge. To my horror, it looked surprisingly bare. It seemed like only yesterday that we had a big turkey firmly wedged in its racking and cans of Guinness sitting in basins of cold water outside the back door, because the fridge had been stuffed to the seams with all things sweet and savoury. Now its appearance would have left Old Mother Hubbard feeling a tad disappointed. A bowl of dried turkey meat and five tubs of "Bless my Cotton Socks I Can't Believe its Not Butter" scarcely whet the appetite.

The realisation hit me like a sledgehammer. We'd have to go down to the Centre and do a shop.

Now don't get me wrong. I'm a big fan of the Blanchardstown Shopping Centre. When this impressive edifice is talked about in work, I bask in some kind of reflected pride as though in some way I am partly responsible for its success by virtue of living nearby. I proudly proclaim to all that will listen that I still haven't seen the Millennium Spire, because there's no need to go into town any more. And I also boast, quite untruthfully, that before Dundrum, it was the only shopping centre on earth that could be seen from outer space, though you'd need pretty good eyesight.

But by the time Christmas comes around I feel I never want to set foot inside its hallowed halls again. The queues of traffic up the slip road, the people milling for the last of the wrapping paper, running frenziedly around dozens of shops with your arms hanging off because "you've just got to get something for Aunt Ethel." Blanchardstown Shopping Centre in December is the definition of Purgatory.

My mother, God bless her, was an ardent anti-Communist. Her reasoning was that whenever you see footage of Russians, "they always look so miserable." If she were alive today and sitting by the fountain

people-watching, she'd think she was in downtown Stalingrad, surrounded by Vladimir Ilyich's finest. Nobody is having fun, nobody wants to be there and everybody can't wait to get home.
And so, standing there before my embarrassment of a fridge, my heart sank as I realised the trip to the Centre would have to be made. The signal that Christmas was truly over and another 51 weeks of reality was about to begin.
But then I remembered! In the last shopping expedition before The Big Day, in a fit of largesse, I had thrown some very small cheese portions into the shopping trolley, with the words "Sure, it's Christmas," as if that justified such extravagance. Normally we have St. Bernard's finest Cheddar throughout the year but for a treat I had plumped for some Brie, some Emmenthal and some Gruyère, albeit in the smallest quantities I could find. They would come in handy after Christmas, I had thought, when we were looking for a bit of a change from mince pies and mallows.
And wasn't this such an occasion? Blanchardstown could be deferred until tomorrow, if only… But where were these small cheeses? Now that I thought about it, I hadn't seen them since a bleary-eyed checkout girl had thrown them carelessly down from the register.
"Has anyone seen the cheese I bought coming up to Christmas?" I demanded, striding into the sitting room, but Richard Attenborough and "yer man from Upstairs Downstairs" were holding another briefing, and I got no response.
I checked the boot of the car to see if they had somehow fallen down into the spare wheel or in the empty ice-cream tub that we keep there "in case of emergencies." No joy. I checked the bag of shopping bags, in case some eejit had folded the bags away with the cheese still in it. I checked the fruit bowl to see if they were hidden under the rotting satsumas.
This was becoming a mission. Who cared about Charles Bronson's claustrophobia, when there were three small wedges of cheese out there somewhere, alone and unprotected? I'd scoured all the obvious places – now was time to rummage through the more unlikely spots. I checked inside Neil's working boots and through his underwear drawer. I manually spun the washing machine drum. I emptied out the contents

of the charity sack onto the road in front of our house and went through it with a toothcomb.
Then as James Garner was desperately plummeting out of the sky, I looked in the crib. There, nestling in the cotton wool that had apparently adorned your typical manger in biblical times, was a baby Brie, a baby Emmenthal and a baby Gruyere.
"Look!" I shouted to a completely disinterested family, pointing excitedly into the crib, "The Baby Cheeses!"

(January 2006)

Burgulars

In "The Annals of Polperro," the ancient Cornish saga which may or may not have been written by a practical joker in the 1950s, the inhabitants of the tiny coastal village of Burgle were often to be found leaving their neighbours' houses with armfuls of cauldrons, chickens and tawdry peasant garb. They were so proficient in this enterprise that the term 'burglar' became synonymous with house-breaking.
What history fails to record, probably because I've just made it up, is that justice was eventually served on this lawless society. Legend has it that they all went down to the coast one night to giggle at a particularly nasty shipwreck and when they returned home, the whole village had been stolen.
To counteract burglars, society has had to become more and more technologically minded down through the years. For decades, the simple operation of installing a front door confounded all but the cleverest thief and when the key and lock were invented –at around the same time as each other – it appeared that the burglary trade was on its knees.
The Great Burglary Symposium in Seattle in 1932 finally got the industry to shake off its lethargy with the publication of a number of startling findings. Windows, for examples, were found to break when struck by a hammer. It was reported that ladders could be used for gaining access to upper storey windows. And traditional burglar's

accoutrements of hooped sweater, mask and bag marked 'Swag' were not necessarily vital components of the house-breaker's armoury.

Today of course the burglar alarm industry is big business. Top of the range systems can not only notify weary Gardaí of an intruder but can also shout "Oi! Get your hands off that!" when said intruder goes to lift your stereo. Sensors can detect an earwig poking his head out from beneath a washing machine and many an unwary spider has spent time behind bars for thinking he had the run of the house.

Of course the big paradox is that very often today's burglar alarms alert the burglar to the fact that a house is unoccupied. This normally occurs on a Bank Holiday Monday morning, when the rest of the residents in the estate are sleepily looking forward to another three hours in bed. There is always one house, owners down the country or in Lanzarote, and they've left the key with her sister in Rathfarnham. A tiny sparrow will perch momentarily on the chimney guard or a snail will start to ascend the outside wall and all hell breaks loose. And it goes on and on and on and on, until you're forced to pack the kids into the car and go and visit dreaded Auntie Emily after all.

Naturally it does not take a person with the brain of an Einstein or a Keating to realise that, if a burglar alarm keeps on ringing, then the house is probably empty. When this happens, every burglar in the surrounding area is attracted to the noise and there's often a lot of jostling and pushing as competing robbers, all sporting gaily-coloured earmuffs, battle to gain entry.

Another problem with many "burgular alarms," as dreaded Auntie Emily calls them, is that they are just so expensive. In many cases, it actually works out cheaper to have your house robbed on a regular basis than to install one of these monthly-instalment "peace-of-mind" contraptions and many burglars are pointing this out in their sales literature.

Of course it is a typical Dublin trait to leave one's radio on at full volume when leaving the house unoccupied. This in fact is dealt with at Burglary School kindergarten. Pat Kenny gets massive listenership figures because every empty house in the country broadcasts his words of wisdom at full volume. Neighbourhood Watch groups have even gone so far as to warn people going out to pull up the blinds, leave a light on upstairs and "for God's sake, turn Pat Kenny off." Though of course this might be for humanistic, rather than crime-prevention reasons.

The aforementioned Neighbourhood Watch groups have a large part to play in deterring local crime, though there is a body of opinion that says they'd be better off watching for burglars, rather than neighbourhoods. Neighbourhoods, as a rule, don't tend to shin up your drainpipe and gain access through the bathroom window, according to Garda statistics.

Signage can also be instrumental in deterring house-breaking. Many burglars are aware that a savage dog's favourite meal is a lump of steak laced with sleeping draught, yet they will be in two minds about a "Beware of the Anaconda" sign. For years, we had a sign on the gate that read "Try no.32 – they just came into a bit of money," which was reasonably effective, until the man at no. 32 drove his cement lorry through our front room window.

A simple yet effective alternative to the burglar alarm is the cunningly-disguised "pit-in-the-hallway" ruse. Basically you dig a large pit in your hallway and lay some thick palm fronds over it when leaving your house unoccupied. When an unsuspecting burglar comes along, he (or indeed she) steps on the leaves and plummets into the inescapable hole below.

As an optional extra, many people these days are keeping a couple of ravenous crocodiles at the bottom of the pit. This is slightly more expensive, but it saves on the irritating business of phoning the police and filling out forms.

Some people have found that a taut length of wire between the bannisters and the sitting room door can also be very effective. Steve McQueen used this technique in "The Great Escape," though its popularity is on the wane, since Garda figures showed that the number of burglars who rob houses on motorbikes is declining.

For myself, the real trauma of burglary lies in those never-ending burglar alarm radio ads. You know the ones. A family comes home and the wife exclaims, "Oh, no! John, we've been burgled!" Does anyone discover a burglary and say "Oh, no!" Why are husbands in twenty-second radio ads always called John? Why do we need to know his name? It's a twenty-second, badly-acted radio ad, not Coronation Street. We're not going to develop a relationship with this lad, particularly as he's probably not even there and has gone to lug the suitcases out of the boot.

But really, how significant is the risk of burglary? The 2001 Census returns for Dublin 15 – the latest official records available – indicate that very few people list burglary as their primary occupation, though it is given frequently as a hobby. FÁS no longer offer apprenticeships in it, as many potential crooks find shoplifting easier, probably due to the absence of front doors and Pat Kenny. And you just try getting a hold of a burglar at weekends! Many are simply drifting away from the industry and becoming door-to-door broadband salesmen, or indeed burglar alarm salesmen, but it is hoped that the Government will soon provide some rehabilitation facility for these poor souls.

(February 2006)

The art of selling your house

Six years ago, when we were trying to sell our previous house, the phone rang one lazy Saturday morning in early April. I took the call, while my wife hovered inquisitively on the landing above.
"Who was that?" she asked, when I finally hung up.
"The estate agent," I replied. "He says he's very sorry about the short notice but is there any chance of bringing a couple along to see the house at 11 o'clock? I told him it was okay, but we'd prefer a bit more notice in future."
Now, our house was, and still is, normally in good shape, housework-wise. Regular dusting, tidying, hovering, mopping, washing and cleaning means that we normally do not have to resort to frantic blitzes. However, this particular Saturday followed about a week of distractions from the daily norm. We had been out looking at houses, attending PTA meetings, entertaining visiting relatives and bringing the children to football matches, hockey matches, feises etc. Housework had been put on the back burner, and consequently the house was the proverbial

porcine dwelling place.

The scream of horror that emanated from the landing indicated that my wife instantly understood the urgency of the situation. Bounding down the stairs three at a time, she intimated in not very pleasant language that perhaps I had been rash to agree to the estate agent's request. I was to get "the other two" out of bed "pronto" and then start on the living room. She herself would start in the kitchen.

Five minutes later, I ambled back downstairs and came into the kitchen. My wife was frantically hanging some unwashed jumpers onto the clothes horse, probably on the grounds that there was nowhere else to put them, while a mop and basin of water stood by the door.

"What date is it?" I asked casually, leaning against the door jamb and examining my finger-nails closely.

She leant over towards the calendar on the fridge. "I don't know. Does it matter? April 1st...." Her voice tailed off as comprehension dawned.

When I awoke in my hospital bed, I was forced to concur that selling a house can be a stressful occupation. If you believe everything you are told, people will not buy your house because the grass verge hasn't been cut. They will look elsewhere if your windows are dirty, and a living room that has been "lived in" is somehow not conducive to an early sale.

Our estate agent gave us a long list of items that needed attending to, to ensure we "maximised our profit potential," as he so eloquently put it. We had to cut our postage stamp-sized front lawn, sweep the drive, touch up the front door and window sills, empty the hall of shoes, reduce the volume in the utility room by three quarters, fix the leaky tap in the bathroom, tidy up the kids' bedrooms, fix that bit of the wall where the settee had been rubbing up against it, repaint the skirting boards, wash the windows, get the chimney swept, fill the house with pot pourri and fresh flowers and reposition the kitchen table over the tear in the lino. As my wife ruefully remarked, if we'd have done all that, there'd be no need for us to move.

Of course, he also came up with that well-worn cliché about baking bread in the oven on the morning of a viewing. The theory is that it gives the house a homely feel, as if potential buyers will be swayed into parting with their thousands by the smell of Hovis. Personally though, I would regard it with the same suspicion that my mother had for extra-strong mints. Is it masking another smell? Sewers, perhaps? Cigarettes? Dogs?

Besides, who wants a house that smells of bread? When we were looking at houses ourselves, we made a point of remarking to the estate agent, "Yes, it's lovely, but I don't think we could live with that smell." God help Messrs. Johnson, Mooney and O'Brien if they ever decided to sell up and move to a ménage-a-trois in the country.

The big drawback with selling your house is that the estate agent normally insists that you absent yourselves from the premises when he's showing people around. This is partly to stop you cluttering up the place and making the rooms look smaller, and partly so there will be no fits of giggling when he describes the house as a "highly desirable residence set in a prime location."

Admittedly, it is also embarrassing for prospective buyers to view a house if the occupants are following them around hanging on their every word. I remember on one occasion I was particularly forthright on the subject of a hideous pair of curtains and failed to spot the mistress of the house eyeing me murderously from an equally revolting armchair. As it happened, the house was not suitable for our needs, but I doubt that any bid we'd made would have been accepted.

Incidentally, when people are viewing houses, why do they always make a point of looking in the fridge? What on earth do they expect to find in there? "Fine big fridge, Mary. If we knocked down a shelf, we could maybe use it as a bedroom for Joshua."

Of course, in your absence, you have no idea what the estate agent is saying and this can prey upon your mind. Is he confiding that, "Look, the house is a kip, the owners are desperate and if you put in an offer anywhere near the asking price, they'll snap your arms off."?

The best way of warding off such suspicions is by donning a false nose, glasses and beard and disguising yourself as an enthusiastic purchaser. (Of course, if you habitually wear a false nose, glasses and beard, another disguise may have to be found.) I did this once, and to be fair to the estate agent, he did such a good job of selling me the house that I ended up putting in an offer for it, which was accepted. Not wishing to admit my subterfuge, I was obliged to follow through with the deal, and ended up purchasing the house from myself at a very generous price. Oh yes, selling your house is a stressful business.

(*Property Supplement February 2006*)

Things to do in the garden in March

The other day I was sitting on a stool in our kitchen, cleaning out the soles of my runners with a knife. Not the good, sharp knife that we use for cutting cheese, but an old one that we keep on the windowsill next to the cactus, the two useless salt and pepper sets (the holes are "too big" apparently) and the dish containing two screws, an elastic band and a small piece of metal that appeared one day on the kitchen floor. This knife is our non-food knife and is used, more or less exclusively for cleaning the soles of runners.

Now, cleaning the dirt out of runners, as many parents will attest, is a long, boring and ultimately futile operation. Suffice to say, that the inventor of the runner sole cleaner will earn a fortune, and if I had a spark of initiative, I'd have solved this problem long ago and retired to the Seychelles.

And so it was, I was idly scooping the dirt out of groove number seventy nine on the left foot, when my eye was caught by the headline on the newspaper spread out beneath me. "Things to Do in the Garden in March," it read.

I gave a wry smile. This was obviously some headline writer's attempt at sarcasm. Everybody knows that once the lawn-mower gets packed away for the final time in late September, still enveloped in wet grass (– sure, it will just fall off by itself when you take it out again in the Spring –) the garden ceases to exist for the next six months. What on earth would any sane person be doing out in the garden in March, when the winds are howling and the sun packs all the heat of a Wibbly Wobbly Wonder?

But as I read further, it was evident that the author of the article was quite serious about all the work the keen gardener should be doing in March. Keen? 'Barking' would have been a more appropriate adjective,

I'd have thought.

While I am at it, have you ever noticed that most 'keen' gardeners are old and bent with gnarled dry hands? Concrete proof, if any were needed, that excessive gardening is unhealthy.

Frankly, the only thing to do in the garden in March is to look out at it from the kitchen window and grimace. That empty plastic flowerpot that has been rattling around since the high winds in November is perfectly happy and is doing no harm to anyone. The slugs that sit contentedly inside it think it is a fairground ride.

That white plastic bag that somehow became impaled on your cotonaster on Christmas Eve is in fact adding a touch of colour to an otherwise drab vista. It is quite content to flap away merrily in the breeze until the slightly warmer month of April arrives and you can go out and retrieve it.

"March is the month when the experienced growers prune roses of the hybrid tea and floribunda types," warbles the article. There is no mention of spending the next six weeks in bed with pneumonia. March is actually the month when sensible rose growers make a mental note to prune the damned things in April or, better still, send somebody else out to do them.

"Prepare your lawn for the mowing season by brushing with a stiff broom," the enthusiastic author continues. Personally the reason for lawn psychology escapes me. Will your grass go into trauma if you suddenly appear the week after Easter, Black and Decker in hand? Why do you need to prepare it? It's grass, for God's sake. Honestly, this environmentally friendly lark can be taken a bit far.

Apparently there is "no earthly reason" why hardy annuals should not be planted out in the latter half of the month. A wind chill factor of minus twenty five is obviously not an earthly reason. Nor is the fact that there's a good Champions League match on the telly or the rugby is on. Or it's St. Patrick's Day, and St. Patrick hated gardens? How about sheer laziness? Hardy annuals can wait until April because frankly I'm still in winter mode and know that I'm going to spend many back-breaking hours in the months ahead prising up obstinate weeds and spraying gleeful greenfly and I'm going to put it all off as long as I possibly can. That's quite an earthly reason, I reckon.

Of course, to assuage the guilt, you can always hop in the car and spend an hour or two wandering around Atlantic Homecare, examining yet-to-flower pots of foliage and wondering if they will hold their own against your lavatera olbia. Of course, at this time of the year, every plant looks the same and you have little or no idea if the few straggling leaves in a pot really will grow up to be a cherry blossom tree or if some mischievous six year old has gone around mixing up all the little plastic signs. Maybe it's a nettle. You have no way of knowing. Better hold off until April when the first buds appear and the store's gardening buyer starts to worry if he's really going to shift a million hectares of primulas.

Of course, most of us in Dublin 15, particularly in the new estates, do not have gardens that warrant so much maintenance that we have to begin in March. Not for us the bed of snowdrops that sweeps down to the rock pool beside the greenhouse. We simply do not have the space for well-organised drills of vegetables that lead to a wicker gate opening out onto a woodland meadow with a bandstand in the middle. No, we have our little rectangles of lawn, around which we have stuck an odd plant here and there. Any potential growing area for weeds has already been smothered in four inches of bark, which is due to be replenished in 2012. If you went out there in March, you'd have nothing to do in April or May.

Besides, isn't wildlife gardening supposed to be the new thing? By moving away from the traditional well manicured lawn and pristine herbaceous border to a more unkempt woodland garden, we are in fact letting nature reclaim some of the land we have stolen from it for house-building. We are encouraging the restoration of a vanishing eco-system

That's my excuse, anyway, and I'm sticking to it.

(*March 2006*)

Seagulls drink cider

Last month's copy of *The Community Voice* carried a rather scathing, if entirely justified, review of the musical "Seagulls Dance" which premiered at Draíocht recently. While praising the lavish production and musical content, the reviewer felt the plot was about as credible as a plea from Westlife to be considered serious musical artists.

I ruminated on this. The production had all the ingredients to make it a smash hit on Broadway except a believable story line. I hurriedly fumbled in my pocket for a pen and an old Snickers wrapper, and in five minutes, had come up with a fully-fledged musical, tentatively titled "Seagulls Drink Cider."

Act One opens with a group of villagers converging merrily on Blakestown Roundabout. They sing a traditional Irish song ("All This, and Lidl Too") and dance gaily around the central island until a fleet of squad cars comes roaring up and moves them on.

On their way home, Kylie professes her deep undying love for Dwane in a heartfelt ballad ("Will You Ever Bring that Hape of Junk down to the Carwash?") Dwane is overcome with emotion and the two of them dance a pas-de-due, as an expression of their oneness.

They are then accosted by Mrs. Bulleted, a Nigerian woman, whose Puerto-Rican husband has been deported and now, unbeknownst to her, is having a whale of a time on a beach in Puget. She sings an aching and heartfelt lament for her homeland ("Jeez, It's Chilly Here, Inuit?") and all the villagers enter and sit at her feet, until a fleet of squad cars comes roaring up and moves them on.

Act Two sees Dwane and Kylie at home, while their two young children, Brad and Britney argue over the Playstation. Mrs. Bulalewe knocks at the door and starts to sing the haunting, aching and heartfelt ballad, "I Never Packed any Cardigans" but she is interrupted by Garda Jason Villens, who wants to query Dwane about his road tax. While the policeman is singing the amusing ditty "Is that Your Vehicle Outside Sir?" Dwane makes his escape through the kitchen window and promises a distraught Kylie that he'll write to her from Marbella. Garda Villens has a moustache and a little goatee beard to indicate that he is intrinsically evil. He is smitten by lust for Kylie and sets about wooing her, but her biting refrain "While There are Dogs in the Street?" sends him packing.

Act Three is a single scene set beside a pool in Marbella. It is 18 years later. This is conveyed to the audience by a woman walking out on stage carrying a sign that says "18 years later."

Dwane is lying on a sun-lounger, quaffing champagne and telling jokes to two beautiful young women cuddling up to him. He suddenly breaks into "Me Darling Little Blakestown Semi," an atmospheric, haunting, aching and heartfelt ballad of longing for his homeland. As he sings the line "And it was so convenient to the Blanchardstown Shopping Centre too," he breaks down and cries, and realises he must return home.

In Act Four, the now Detective Inspector Villens has not yet got the hint and is still pursuing the by-now-quite-frumpy Kylie. She fends him off with the feisty "Jesus, Get a Life, Will Ya?" He gets into his car and prepares to drive off, but is interrupted by Mrs. Bulalewe, who comes out of her house singing the unforgettable tune, "You Call This a Summer?" Distracted, D.I. Villens reverses over Kylie and kills her. As she dies, she sings the tearful, atmospheric, haunting, aching and heartfelt dirge, "I Don't Believe It! A Bloody Nissan Primera."

Outside the graveyard, the funeral cortege realises that nobody has picked up the key to the cemetery gates and, rather than waste a lovely day, they decide to bury Kylie in a nearby field. Brad, by now a strikingly handsome young man with a degree in Welsh Cookery, is determined to revenge himself on D.I Villens but Mrs. Bulalewe reminds him that the Coroner's verdict of 'Suicide By Running Herself Over' was the only logical conclusion. As the mourners file away from the graveside, Britney kneels by her mother's grave and sings the gut-wrenching, tearful, atmospheric, haunting, aching and heartfelt tribute "You Never Showed Me How To Work the Washing Machine (Mam)" D.I. Villens strides across the field towards Britney. He feels that, with the burial over, it would be a good time to approach her with a view to matrimony. She fends him off, despatching him cruelly with the acerbic "You Won't Get Your Size 12 Slippers Under My Table, Officer."

As she breaks down, Dwane comes over to see what is going on. He is back from Marbella. Britney runs into his arms and he comforts her. Curiously she does not ask where he has been for the past 18 years.

Brad appears from behind a sprig of spinach and the three embrace. Somebody breaks wind, and they all laugh. Suddenly a fleet of squad cars comes racing across the field and they run for it.

Finally, in Act Five, Dwane, Britney and Brad are stopped at a roadblock that has been set up on their driveway. Dwane has only just found out that there was nothing wrong with his road tax in the first place and blames D.I.Villens for his wife's death. D.I Villens leans into the car and informs Dwane that the readout says he was doing 80kph in a 30kph zone. This he imparts with the lilting air "On Our Way to Mondello, Are We, Sir?"

Britney opens the car door and tries to make a run for it but catches her leg in the seatbelt and falls under the wheels of an articulated truck. Her swansong "At Least Its Better Than A Primera" is guaranteed to haunt audiences for a very long time with its pathos.

Dwane tries to get out of the car, but his door is up against the pillar and he is trapped. Brad is in the back listening to his iPod, unaware that anything is afoot. D.I Villens produces a black spherical object from behind his back, lights the fuse and throws it into the car. It is not a bomb but a faulty ballcock and both Dwane and Brad drown, to the sound of the classic number "Glug, Glug, Glug."

D.I.Villens turns to the audience and regales them with a rousing rendition of "Frog Went-a-Courting" As the song reaches its crescendo, he is flattened by a meteorite.

Mrs. Bulalewe comes out of her house, sees the devastation and breaks into "These Home Heating Bills Are Costing Me A Fortune." Cue the curtain, and obligatory standing ovation.

Of course, penning such a strong script with such well-rounded characters is bound to pose its own problems. What do we move off the mantelpiece to make way for the Tony awards that will inevitably follow? Who do we want to direct the film version? Where should we host our Oscar-night party?

But, of course, artists are supposed to struggle. Just as the best footballers are produced from disadvantaged areas, so the best musical playwrights wrestle with their consciences and grapple with life's eternal conundrums. Ours is not an easy path and we go through torture for our art.

Unlike "Seagulls Dance" where it is the audiences that go through torture…

(April 2006)

Solving the transport problem

Let's face it. We've got ourselves into a bit of a jam with the traffic situation in Dublin 15 and tinkering with bus routes and putting more rolling stock onto the Maynooth line is not going to make any significant difference to the hard-pressed commuter.
The way things are going, it won't be long before starvation is listed as one of the major causes of road deaths in the capital, with drivers being advised to clunk-click-make-sure-you-have-your-emergency-rations every trip. Drastic problems call for drastic solutions, as a very wise man once said (I can't remember if it was Victor Hugo or Rick Astley) and, answering the call, I have pondered long and hard on the problem for the past fifteen minutes or so.
My proposals are radical, I freely admit, and possibly require a modicum of fine-tuning. They have also been registered at the patent office, just in case one of them sees the light of day.
What better way to travel in style to and from the City Centre than by hot air balloon? I propose building a heliport on top of Power City and a second one somewhere in town, say that funny little park in Jervis Street that no-one knows the name of.
Of course, they would not have tiny baskets and only carry four men in top hats at a time, but long, sausage-shaped baskets carrying up to sixty men in top hats. It probably would not be possible to run the service during thunderstorms or hurricanes but other than that, I see no obvious drawbacks to the scheme and the benefit to this country's ailing top hat industry would be enormous.
In Switzerland, they run cable cars thousands of metres up sheer mountain sides and never bat an eyelid. How much easier would it be for us in this country to run a cable car that travels seven miles horizontally? The cables would run thirty feet above the ground and run all the way from the Blanchardstown Centre into the heart of O'Connell

Street following the Navan Road most of the way.

The cables would be supported by giant wooden supports that rise vertically from the footpaths, which means you don't have to inconvenience road users for several years while you lay tracks. In fact, it could probably be done on a Sunday afternoon, before the Antique Roadshow comes on.

With a hundred cable cars running in a giant loop every thirty seconds apart, the amount of people it could transport would be phenomenal. It would be important, though, to build the cables high enough to clear double decker buses, or the consequences could be disastrous.

Speaking of footpaths, what is there to prevent them moving (apart from their natural inertia, that is)? They have non-rising escalators in Dublin airport, why not along all the arterial routes into the City Centre? One line moving quite quickly, and a slower line running alongside it, for when people want to alight. Stick a bit of an oul' bus shelter over the top, and Robert is your parent's brother. You could even have little foldaway seats, so people could travel in comfort.

With the recent construction of the financial centre in Spenser Dock, more and more people who work there are finding that their transport needs are not being met by traditional services. But there is a readymade road all the way from Clonee to the heart of this area. It is called the River Tolka.

Now, many of us have experienced the thrill of banana boats while on holiday in Puerto del Carmen. They don't seem very expensive, even allowing for inflation (sorry) and they would seem to me the ideal way of transporting financial whiz kids directly from Mulhuddart right into the heart of the city. Services might occasionally have to be cancelled due to drought or amorous swans, but there is surely a market there for the intrepid entrepreneur with a speedboat and a large quantity of rubber.

As we approach yet another energy crisis, with helpless motorists finding it cheaper to fill their tanks with Extra Virgin Olive Oil (extra virginity?) it is surely time to consider one of the cheapest, and greenest means of transportation known to man – gravity.

My proposal is very simple. We build an enormous spiral staircase in the Little Chef car park, say five times as high as the Quinn Direct building, and buy in a large quantity of straw mats. Commuters take a mat from the bottom and ascend to the top, thereby fulfilling their daily exercise needs. At the top there is a giant but extremely slippery slide that descends gradually all the way to the Garden of Remembrance. Naturally we would require a bored attendant in lycra shorts at the top of the slide to tell people when it was safe to go, though we probably wouldn't need to have reached the bottom before the next person is waved forward. And naturally again, you would need another spiral staircase in the Garden of Remembrance for the return journey. Fares would presumably operate on a sliding scale.

A couple of years ago, a research paper was published that has the potential to revolutionise transportation in all major cities. Written by an obscure British scientist, and going under the name "Harry Potter and the Chamber of Secrets," the paper claims that floo powder holds the key to easing gridlock in large conurbations. The commuter simply flings the powder into an empty fireplace, shouts out "The Pound Shop in Henry Street!" and hey, presto! He instantly finds himself being escorted out of the shop by a moustachioed goon with a piece of plastic in his ear.

Of course, this method of travel still requires detailed research, but with all the money that Dublin Bus are amassing, by handing out bits of paper instead of change, funding for the project should not be a problem.

(How can Dublin Bus get away with this? If I went into the butcher's in Ongar and bought a pound of sausages and three Euro worth of turkey mince, and offered him a twenty, would he hand me back a little piece of paper and tell me I can cash it in down in Moore Street?)

Of course, I am only scratching the surface with the ideas detailed above. My designs for giant catapults will have to stay locked away in the bank vault for now, and my research into human cannonballs is still at a very early stage. My proposal that we turn the City Centre into an exclusively residential zone and push all shops and industry out to the suburbs is currently before the Dáil, although the Minister is seeking to delay ratification until the run-up to the next election.

Remember, you heard it here first.

(May 2006)

Supermarket checkouts

They say – whoever "they" are – that the most stressful times of a person's life are moving house and getting married, two contracts that one enters into with a great deal of optimism, totally unprepared for the hardships that lie ahead.

For myself, I have moved house so many times in my life that I make the nomadic Tuareg of the sub-Sahara seem like positive stay-at-homes in comparison. As for marriage, I am fortunate to be enjoined to the most wonderful woman in the world, who just happens to be standing behind me with a baseball bat as I write this.

No, in my case, nothing in this life is designed to set the temples throbbing as much as supermarket checkouts.

Doing the actual shopping is bad enough. Trying to negotiate shelf-packers, totally unconcerned by the large-scale traffic jam their pallet of toilet rolls is causing, is bad enough. Fellow shoppers who leave their trolleys parked at right angles in the aisle while they sort through eighty packs of rashers are also inconsiderate. The hours spent fruitlessly searching the aisles when they decide to move the tins of prunes – well, that's just an occupational hazard. The screaming kids who seem to follow you everywhere you go…

But then you reach the checkouts.

Contrary to popular folklore, finding a counter empty with a checkout person waiting to serve you is Not a Good Thing. It may seem like a miracle, but it is something of a poisoned chalice, and should be avoided by anybody with more than the proverbial ten items in their trolley. For, while you are carefully loading up the conveyor belt, Ms. Flash Harry is sending them careering down the ramp at the other end and she will then stare at you impatiently when you set about trying to pack everything up.

For there is no pressure worse than not being able to keep up with the checkout girl.

The trick is to be the second in the queue, behind someone with two-thirds of a conveyor belt worth of purchases. Then you can start to load your goods on, while his are going through. By the time he has paid, packed and departed, you will be standing at the back of the checkout, first bag open and at the ready.

We are very careful how we arrange our goods on the belt. Frozen stuff, followed by fridge stuff, fruit and veg, tins and bottles, bread and packets and finally non-food items. If we can pack them up according to these categories, it saves time at home.

If however, you find yourself falling behind, a sense of panic starts to creep in and you make elementary mistakes like packing tins of beans on top of the Swiss roll, which is bound to cause Harsh Words further down the line.

The worst type of checkout assistant you can get is the speed freak, who seems to make it her business to try and hurl as many things at you as she can, while you desperately try to open the first of your bags. But of course you can't open the bags because she keeps throwing things down on top of you. Then when she is running short of space, instead of pausing a minute for you to catch up, she uses a highly adept forearm to shove everything down on top of you.

Of course the fruit and veg will slow her up. That's the only reason we buy it. Sure, nobody eats healthily in our house, but it's great for slowing madam down while you get the fridge stuff into the trolley. She realises this of course, and makes sure the subsequent bottles of minerals come hurtling down like skittles in a bowling alley to compensate.

A lot of people complain about the rudeness of checkout assistants these days. The ones who chew gum and hold loud conversations with Deirdre at the next checkout about whether Colm was going to ask her out or not may give off an air of inattention but while they are pausing to inspect their newly applied gel nails, at least you can triumphantly get the bottles packed and whisked away.

To the harassed shopper, bag packers may seem like a great help but in reality I groan whenever I see them. These are usually kids who have never seen the inside of a supermarket in their lives and, if they have, they were probably texting Jamie while the bags were being packed.

If they are not trying to squeeze seventeen tins into one flimsy plastic bag, they make sure that your coleslaw is firmly mashed into the bottom of the bag by the weight of the lemonade on top. The other week we retrieved a two dimensional lettuce from beneath the Sunday roast and no amount of plumping could revive it.

Of course the stress from supermarket bag packing is well documented. Basher Breslaw, the Clonsilla Composter who killed, dismembered and composted eight young telephone canvassers, recounts in his autobiography "Whoops!" how his homicidal tendencies first came to light.

"She kept pushing tins of tomatoes down on top of me. I couldn't get the bag open, possibly because it was upside down. The goods just kept on piling up and I was feeling more and more inadequate. Then she asked "Do you have a Clubcard?"

Research carried out at IT Blanchardstown between 2000 and 2004 reveals that bag packing stress lies third in the list of causes of marital breakdown behind walking in front of the telly when there's football on and the inability to read a map.

When a couple shops together, the male usually has the job of keeping up with the checkout assistant, while the woman performs the arduous tasks of ensuring nothing falls off the belt and making caustic comments about his packing abilities. This inevitably leads to bitter conflict and occasionally vegetable-flinging.

Of course the advent of internet shopping will in time serve to lessen the number of decree absolutes awarded by the courts but, seeing that many of us still haven't figured out how to get that annoying little smartass paper-clip man off our screens, the days of stressful supermarket packing look certain to continue for some time to come.

Hartstown Community School meanwhile has announced that they will be introducing a new course as part of their Evening Classes programme this Autumn - Supermarket Bag Packing for Beginners. Taken by legendary Laurel Lodge bag packer, Neetly Fillum - who achieved a bronze medal in the event at the Montreal Olympics - the twelve week programme will concentrate on technique, breathing exercises, yoga and being able to articulate the seldom-used phrase, "Could you slow down a bit, luv?"

With places bound to fill up very quickly, the course is bound to have a major positive influence on married life in Dublin 15.

(June 2006)

McCrummo, ref!!

Recently, I was browsing through the "On this Day…." section of one of the national newspapers when I came across the following mind-blowing piece of information: -
"On this day in 1890, William McCrum, a linen manufacturer from Armagh, invented the penalty-kick."
So amazed was I at this startling piece of information, I promptly spilled my bowl of Coco Pops into my lap. While mopping it up, I resolved to unearth the truth about this miraculous invention, to leave no stone unturned in my quest for the story behind the one-liner.
Minutes of detailed research later, I came across a story that will have movie producers knocking on my door.
William McCrum was born in Armagh in 1860, the son of his parents. According to local folklore, he was present at the birth, as was his mother, though he apparently remembered little of it.
From an early age, it was clear that the young William [or "Stupid" as his friends affectionately called him] was no ordinary youth. Instead of pulling the legs off daddy-long-legs, like normal boys, William would stick extra legs onto them and marvel at their increased velocity.
The McCrums moved south in 1870, when the Great Linen War between Ireland and Peru brought the industry, if not to its knees, at least to its ankles. Soup kitchens were set up at the corners of streets until people got fed up with soup and demanded quiche twice a week. Thousands of people took the boat to Liverpool but were forced to bring it back again by customs.
Jessie McCrum, his wife Kylie and their large-eared son William settled in what is now Diswellstown but was then a vast expanse of flax country. With his own hands, Jessie built a two roomed cottage by the road to Coolmine and then built a garage with someone else's hands. It was only after five years of hard toil and graft that the family realised that the bounteous fields around them were in fact full of weeds, not flax.
Such setbacks appeared not to have greatly troubled young William. After a hard day's gathering nettles, he would come in, eat a bowl of

warm water and then retire to the shed for a full evening experimenting. Of course it was his love of football, allied to his penchant for inventing, that brought about a revolution in the beautiful game. [In those days, of course, it was known as the "reasonably-good-looking" game.]

In 1884, the first breakthrough came when he invented the penalty spot, basically a lump of turf with a white circle painted on it. The prototype was a bit of a failure, as the circle measured approximately nine feet in diameter.

However, when Alexander Graham Bell, with whom he corresponded on a regular basis, introduced him to the concept of "scale", things really started moving. The penalty spot was unveiled to stunned crowds at the 1886 Scientific Exhibition in Paris, and McCrum's moon was on the rise.

Despite the success of the penalty spot in Paris, McCrum was stung by criticism in certain quarters that his invention had no practical application in the real world. Enraged, he shut himself in his newly-built laboratory and only emerged three years later, tousle-haired and rather hungry. A watching world held its breath as he explained the concept of the "penalty kick" and its place within the laws of association football. When he had finished, thousands of cheering fans carried him shoulder-high through the streets of Blanchardstown, before dumping him unceremoniously in the canal.

The first penalty kick ever awarded was in a game between Verona and Castleknock Celtic at Ye Olde Football Stadium (now Power City) in November 1890.

The history books tell us that the Celtic goalkeeper, Harry "Big Fat Hape" O'Hara actually saved the kick from Mr. Geoghegan (a gentleman.) However, a furious row broke out subsequently with Verona protesting vehemently at the positioning of the penalty spot two yards from the corner-flag.

An international tribunal was set up to examine the issue and, in their report delivered three months later, they recommended that the penalty spot should lie "twelve yards from the centre of, and perpendicular to, the goal line" where, of course, it has remained ever since, except during the war years, when it was brought inside for security reasons.

The tribunal also recommended that, whenever a penalty was awarded, the defending side should "protest vehemently at the decision" and that the referee should "listen intently to all cogent arguments put forward by the defending side and should be prepared to overturn his decision if so persuaded."

Nowadays, of course, the penalty kick is accepted by football teams all over the world, with the exception of Burkino Faso, where defenders still prefer to apologise and pay a small fine.

As for William McCrum, a great inventor he may have been, but unfortunately he possessed all the business acumen of a stoat with haemorrhoids. Had he patented or copyrighted the idea, he need never have manufactured linen again, and the "McCrum kick" or the "McCrummo" would have given sub-editors the world over much greater scope for headline writing. ("Few McCrums of comfort for Baggio", "Southgate McCrumbles" etc etc) Just imagine the amount of royalties that could have been earned at, say, sixpence a penalty, and you'll get some idea of the amount of money McCrum passed up.

Disenchanted, McCrum ran away to sea but got lost and ended up in Westmeath, where he carried on an affair with a pretty young badger-baiter until she found out. Returning home, he experimented for a while with the concept of centre circles, hoping to emulate his previous success but a raid by the Black and Tans and the ensuing destruction of his efforts, saw years of work go up in flames. (The centre circle was only introduced after McCrum's death by Dutch inventor Ruud van Driver)

As it was, he died penniless in Laurel Lodge when an affronted stoat attacked his nose. Thousands of people lined the streets of Blanchardstown for his funeral, which by some unfortunate route-planning fiasco, formed part of the St. Patrick's Day parade.

Fittingly he was buried beneath the penalty spot at Ye Olde Football Stadium, in a service that "touched even the hardest of hearts," according to the Irish Times, though Bishop O'Malley had to pause the ceremony several times to control his giggling. William McCrum now lies beneath the aisle between the dishwashers and the kettles.

A suitable resting place for a great man.

(July 2006)

A load of walls – a conversation

I suppose we looked an odd bunch as we marched around the borders of Littlepace / Castaheany – five forty-somethings carrying a boom box that blasted out "I Scream, You Scream, Everybody Loves Ice Cream." And to be honest, we all felt somewhat self-conscious as we completed one complete circumnavigation of the estate per day for six days, but sure, it had to be done.

It had all started a couple of weeks before with a casual conversation in the Paddocks on the subject of walls. Billy – or "Bully" as our newly-arrived Caledonian drinking acquaintance describes himself – remarked that, in all his travels, he had never come across a place with such a fondness for walls as Dublin 15. "They're everywhere, mon," he exclaimed with disgust. "Every new esteet that's built noo-adays has dutty great walls aroond it."

With the aid of Jimmy, whose occasional visits to Parkhead qualified him as translator for the group, we digested this profound remark and agreed that there was maybe something in it.

"Sure they tore down the Berlin Wall," remarked Notcher, twirling the remains of his pint, and glancing meaningfully at myself. "The international community decided they didn't much like it, so they got rid. And what about the uproar over that big wall in the West Bank, no planning permission or nothing. Everybody wants that taken down too."

"Seems to me that the rest of the world is busy tearing down walls and we're building them up," remarked Dave, draining his pint and leaving it down ostentatiously in front of me. "We're out of kilter with the rest of the world."

"Its Fingal County Council policy," chimed in Jimmy, who himself was "something in the Council." "Residents don't want their estates being used as rat-runs by young fellers on motorbikes and skateboards and the like, so it's now policy to have only one entrance in and out of every estate. Stop the joyriders."

"Yes, that's all well and good," said Dave with impatience, "but does it have to be a brick wall? It makes it look like a prison camp or North

Korea or somewhere. A good thick hawthorn hedge – now, that would solve the problem and it's more environmentally friendly. You ever tried riding a Honda 50 through a hawthorn hedge?"

"Trouble is, you canna plant a fully-grown hawthorn hedge," replied Bully. "By the time ets groon, the residents will have had their hooses pillaged and ransacked by hordes of unfidels from neebouring esteets. Sorry lads, ma throat's very dry and Ah've nae moor drunk left."

When I returned from the bar considerably lighter financially, the topic of conversation had turned from boundary walls to garden walls.

"There was a certain politician in the west of Ireland," Dave was explaining to Bully. "And he built a wall around his house two feet high, and charged it to the state, claiming it was a security wall!"

"They obviously have a denser class of criminal in Mayo," put in Jimmy. He put on what he fondly imagined was a burglar's accent. "Hey, Fingers! How we gonna scale dis damn wall? You brought a rope? No boss. I thought maybe we could step over it."

Garden walls was a particular bugbear of mine, delivering, as I do, *The Community Voice* on a monthly basis. I waxed lyrical on the trials and tribulations of the poor leaflet distributor, postman, Eircom Phonewatch salesman, whose lives had been made immeasurably harder by the erection of garden walls but I sensed little sympathy from the lads. "You want us to make things easier for these guys?" said Notcher incredulously. "Sure, a wall is an occupational hazard," he continued unfeelingly. "Get over it."

"That's just the problem," I retorted. "The older I get, the less I'm able to."

"I'm not a big lover of garden walls," said Jimmy. "Sure you never get your money back on them. A three bedroomed house in Littlepace costs the same as a three bedroomed house in Hunters Run, whether it has a wall or not."

"I dinna care for them masel'," opined Bully. "Up here the front gardens are too wee for walls. They make what luttle garden there is luik even smaller."

Thus a very pleasant hour was passed in the denunciation of walls, whether brick, block, stone or plaster of paris, though exceptions were made for dry stone walls, which, it was agreed, are very ornamental and stop fields from fraying around the edges, and the Great Wall of China, which the group generally decided was a great tourist attraction and dead handy for doing charity cycle rides along.

"Okay, so we dinna like walls," said Bully at last. "So what are we gonna do aboot them?"

"Dynamite?" suggested Notcher.

"You can't do that," put in Jimmy. "The Council wouldn't like it, and I'm sure there's a bye-law against it somewhere."

"Could we not export them to countries that don't have any walls?" asked Dave. "I'm sure there's some countries out there would give their eye-teeth for a few walls. We could set up a depot somewhere, and residents would bring in their walls, in exchange for the aforementioned hawthorn hedges, and then we'd send the walls on to Uzbekhistan or wherever there's a market for them."

I shook my head doubtfully, overwhelmed by the size of the logistical problem involved. "You'd pay a fortune in shipping charges," I said. "That is, if the ship ever made it out of harbour with all that weight. However, I do have another suggestion, but you may wait. There's a couple of details I want to check with the parish priest first. If all goes well, I'll meet you all here at 7.30 on Monday night."

Thus it was that the disparate bunch assembled outside the Paddocks the following Monday evening. I explained the plan to them, and they seemed somewhat perplexed, but agreed to give it a go.

"What's with the boom box blasting out Louis Armstrong?" asked Dave.

"Any of you play the trumpet?" I asked impatiently. "The recipe says you need trumpets. This is the nearest thing I could find."

It took us about one hour to circumnavigate the estate, not counting the bemused questioning from the two cycling Community Gardaí. So worn out were we by the exercise, that we were obliged to retire into the Paddocks for a rest and some refreshment.

We did the same on Tuesday and on Wednesday – in fact for six days we fulfilled our noisy procession. On the Sunday, however, we assembled early outside the Paddocks.

"I'm not walking around the estate seven times," asserted Jimmy. "Can we not go by car?"

From the general murmurings of sleepy-eyed assent, this resolution was adopted, and we all piled into Bully's Micra, with Notcher hanging the boombox out of the window. "If I never hear Satchmo again, it'll be too soon," he said. Off we set, little realising how far we would have to travel to completely circle the estate by car – we had to go along by Manorfields, Ravenswood, up the new Ongar Road, back by Hartstown and Blakestown, down to the N3 and up the Clonee slip road. By the time we completed the seventh circuit, Bully was wailing in true Caledonian fashion that the petrol gauge was hovering precariously above the red.

"Now," I said, as we pulled into the carpark, "Everybody out and roar at the tops of your voices!"

We all piled out and yelled, roared, shouted. Then we stopped, and listened. Nothing. We roared again, this time louder and with great passion. Again we stopped. No sound of crumbling mortar, no cascade of brick on brick. Just silence. Several neighbours peeped fearfully behind velour drapes to see what all the commotion was about.

"I can't understand it. It worked in Jericho," I said.

Just then, Bully espied the parish priest opening up the church gates in preparation for Sunday mass.

"Och, Father!" he yelled. "Are ye sure yon Joshua dinna use dunnymite?"

(August 2006)

The night of the long hoe

Bill Staines may well have affirmed that "all God's creatures got a place in the choir" yet it is tempting to think that there are a few of them whose sweet harmonies would not be missed in a laryngitis epidemic. Snakes and wasps and flies that buzz around your bedroom just after you've turned off the light – these are animals that would benefit humankind greatly by becoming extinct, according to this otherwise quite greenish observer.

However there is one other candidate for mass genocide that lends itself far more easily to extermination, as events in my back garden recently proved. Yes, it is the gardener's old friend, good old gastropoda pulmonata, or the slug to you and me.

It is difficult to see what is the point of a slug. It never tries to be constructive or provide some service. It doesn't make a good pet and will not fetch a stick when commanded. Rather, its sole purpose appears to be to sneak out at night and turn your marigolds into lace curtains. They have a voracious appetite and a single slug has been known to turn twelve acres of Amazon rain forest into a bowling green within twenty four hours.

However, they are idiosyncratic diners and will not touch the dandelions, clover and thistles that infest your lawn and cost nothing, but are attracted to the more expensive plants to be found in your local garden centre.

Yes, this particular gastropod – literally stomach-foot – is part of the subsection known as "pests." They might claim to have had a bad press, that they are merely cute little snails without the shell, but that is more to do with our bizarre tolerance of the snail, than prejudice against his homeless brother.

Stomach-foot – and I have been doing a bit of research on this blight on the suburban landscape – apparently enjoys cool, damp summers and mild, wet winters. With such criteria, Ireland is of course one of his favourite holiday destinations. They are hermaphrodites and a single slug can produce as many as 300 offspring in his / her lifetime, which equates to 90,000 grandchildren and 27 million great-grandchildren. This naturally can cause problems when they all come around to visit.

As many gardeners are aware, there are many different varieties of slugs. The smallest is the field slug – a thin and emaciated albino slug that appears to have an anorexia problem. Then there is the garden slug, who is small and black. The garden slug is not to be confused with the black slug, who is much larger and can be any colour from white, through red, orange and grey to black (a sublime example of sluggish nomenclature). Then there is the yellow slug, which, surprisingly, is luminous yellow, the netted slug, the great grey slug and the keel slug, which is my own personal favourite.

The keel slug is the fattish olive coloured one with the rather fetching orange trim. If you should touch him with an implement, he immediately tries to curl up in a ball like a hedgehog, not realising of course that he's just as squishable curled up as stretched out.

They say that animals adapt to their surroundings. This is not particularly true of birds who, if we are to believe everything we hear on "Mooney Goes Wild on One," face a constant struggle to gather enough food each day to feed themselves and their ravenous offspring. If however, they did not insist on skidaddling back off to the nest the moment that the sun approached the horizon, they would be in for a gastronomic treat.

For at dusk, the slugs emerge from under their rocks and bushes and claim the gardens for themselves. While the birds are snoring away up in their nests, dreaming of juicy worms, the slugs just below are swarming all over the place, making rude hand gestures up at them.

I passed by our kitchen window the other evening on my way to the wheelie bin to deposit an empty pizza box, that my son had managed to carry as far as the back door, when suddenly, I glanced over at the lawn. Or rather, the place where the lawn should have been. Even in the half-light, it had evidently become alive, a mass of slithering, rubbery shapes, not too dissimilar to the snake-pit that Harrison Ford got thrown into in "Raiders of the Lost Ark."

As it says in one of those Andrew Lloyd Webber musicals, this was my chance, this was my moment. A reluctant, as opposed to a keen, gardener, nevertheless, it made my blood boil to see good plants, expensively purchased, chewed to ribbons by the little blighters. I uttered a manic and half-crazed Dick Dastardly laugh and made my way to the shed.

Unlike moles, there are many ways to kill a slug. A gardener will always tell you there is only one way to kill a mole. The problem is that this method differs with every gardener that you speak to. With slugs, there is no such problem.

You can sprinkle salt on them, which apparently shrivels them up till they die of thirst. You can sprinkle the ground with slug pellets, or slug powder, or set little traps for them, or shoot them or electrocute them. Some swear by alcohol and pour good beer all over their plants to get the slugs so hammered that they start challenging starlings to fights the next morning. My grandfather, in the days before hygiene was invented, used to pick them up and nip them between forefinger and thumb. I daresay biting them in two would be equally as effective. For myself, I'm not quite such a subtle person. Normally, I like to raise the back end of a spade high above my head before bringing it smashing down upon the unsuspecting gastropod, despatching it in a nanosecond to that great cabbage-leaf in the sky. But with the great quantities of slugs revelling on my lawn, I felt that perhaps it was time to call in The Hoe.

Now I am one of the few people I know who actually owns a hoe. Well, I found one in a skip several years ago, so I reckon I can now claim ownership. Thing is, I've seen them hanging up in garden centres, but I've no idea what they are for. They're no good for digging with, that I can tell you. The only thing I've ever used it for, and which I reckon must be its sole use, is for killing slugs with.

There is a certain art in murdering slugs with a hoe. You hold the hoe poised above the victim like a guillotine, and then bring it down sharply. The perfect strike will bisect the slithery aristocrat cleanly, there will be a second of shock and then the blood starts pouring out of either end. Sometimes the blood is black, sometimes yellow, sometimes clear, any colour of the rainbow in fact and there seems to be no correlation between outer pigmentation and blood type.

And so I set to work. The hoe rose and fell and the silent screams went echoing up into the twilight. Ten, twenty, thirty, a hundred, all had come racing out from beneath fuchsia and hebe in expectation of a night on the town, and suddenly found that their worst nightmares had been realised. I was deux ex machina, the righteous man, armed with a second-hand hoe, slaying the weak and iniquitous, delivering vengeance in a series of short, sharp jabs. It was the Night of the Long Hoe, as it will doubtless be described in sluggish folklore history, and within ten minutes, two hundred corpses lay strewn in a putrefying mess all over the lawn.

And I looked down and saw that it was good.

(September 2006)

Wish I could be like David Watts

Anybody familiar with the Lancashire seaside resort of Blackpool will know that the town boasts three piers – the North, the Central and (wait for it) the South pier. All were constructed in the latter half of the nineteenth century and rapidly accumulated amusements to cater for the trainloads of mill workers that holidayed from the likes of Wigan and Salford.

Competition between the three piers was fierce. If one installed a helter-skelter, the others had to have the same. When the South Pier unveiled a Whack-a-Croc, the others quickly followed suit. Thus began what we know today as 'pier pressure.'

Schoolchildren, more than slave-traffickers and drugs barons, are the cruellest things on the planet. The marauding lion that hauls down the bucking wildebeest on the plains of Serengeti is a comparative pussycat in comparison. At psychological warfare, they leave Josef Goebbels in the tuppence ha'penny place.

Even in what us old fogeys like to term 'the good old days,' it was ever thus. There was a kid in our class with a glass eye who we named Isaiah, because "one Isaiah than the other." We poked fun at the kid with calipers, telling him to "hop to it," and woe betide the boy who cried in the schoolyard.

Looking back, of course, I feel ashamed of my part in these actions, although there was no real malice in them. It is one of the great mysteries of life that the children we look down on in school are often the ones we most admire when he have matured a bit, particularly if they cut up our Micras in their Merc.

One of our classmates didn't share our interest in pop music or football. He rarely came out to play as he had to spend a lot of his spare time helping his father with the pigs. Naturally, and with complete absence of logic, we decided he was smelly and had fleas and more or less shunned him. Now I look back, disgusted with myself for my shallowness and truly admiring the lad for his refusal to bow to peer pressure.

As a parent, I fought a long and losing battle with my children over the need to emulate Mama Cass and be in with the in crowd. I could never understand why a pair of runners with a tick costs €100 more than a pair of runners without the tick. My offers to paint a tick on their runners were met with derision and did I not realise that they would be the only child in school without this tick? Obviously, *I* was the t'ick.

I have often been accused of being tighter than a fish's rear quarters, but it seems to me that the peer pressure exerted in today's schoolyard is more to do with money than in our day. It was our attitudes that determined coolness. A kid in tatty plimsolls who could vault the horse (ask your parents) was pretty okay – the duffer in snazzy runners was derided. Basically, anyone had the capacity to be cool, whether prince or pauper.

Nowadays, it appears that only those with reasonably well-off parents, or possible those adept at shoplifting, can escape the ridicule of being uncool. Nerdy Kid suddenly transforms into SuperCool Kid by virtue of his gym top having a silly little green crocodile on it. If he splashes Joop onto himself after the shower, his legendary status is assured.

The big difference though is that in our day, we accepted our lot. There was always one kid in the class who got a Scaletrix for Christmas. For the younger generation, a Scaletrix was a racing track with remote control cars that shot onto the carpet at the first bend. Oh yes, we envied him and even pretended to be friends with him so he'd let you have a go but it was more than our lives were worth to go home whinging and whining to our parents that we wanted one too. We'd have got a good clip around the ear and a lecture on the value of money, and we knew it.

No, we just got on with tying our gaberdines around our necks and racing around the playground yelling the theme tune from Batman. We didn't feel excluded because we didn't have a Scaletrix. That's just the way things were.

Nowadays, in a much more affluent society, with parents who strive to compensate their children for their long periods of absence, children get most of what they demand, particularly if they keep harping on about it in a wheedling voice. Parental refusal is inevitably countered with comparisons with other more enlightened parents.

My wife and I were rounded on for being the only parents in the class who would not let their daughter get her belly-button pierced until she

was sixteen. Naturally I was unable to verify this assertion and would probably have been arrested if I had attempted to do so. The fact that I once told my mother just after "Pinball Wizard" came out that I was the only kid in the school wearing flat shoes is neither here nor there.
But it is a totally different world. The other day, I heard my eight year old nephew deriding another boy, not because he didn't have a mobile phone, but because he had the wrong make. I imagine the second boy running home and complaining bitterly to his astounded parents that he wants a new phone. At eight years of age.
Yes, occasionally I thank my lucky stars I'm not young anymore.

(*Education Supplement September 2005*)

The loneliness of the short distance runner

I still find it hard to believe.
One month ago, I was a normal, happy forty–something, drifting happily through life from work to home with the calm insouciance of the relatively content. Now – oh shame! I suppose the neighbours will have to find out eventually – I have taken up jogging.
Not since a lad named Saul was struck down just short of Damascus 2000 years ago, has there been such a reversal of mindset. For I have always been very anti-jogging and anti-fitness in general. Why didn't people just take the car or the bus, I used to ask, pityingly, as another potential cardiac victim hove into view.
Of course, for years, I was blessed with a digestive system that could cope with any amount of doughnuts, cream cakes and biscuits that I threw at it. This used to annoy my brother who couldn't pass by a Kylemore on the far side of the street without putting on a couple of pounds. For twenty five years, my weight remained constant at ten and a half stone (I have no idea what this is in kilogrammes and don't really care. Stones and pounds will be with me till I die)
Then, soldiering blithely into my forties, three things happened in a relatively short space of time that knocked my avoirdupois cockiness for six.

Firstly, I turned forty, as you tend to do at the end of your thirties. Fading family portraits of my father and grandfather both show a rapid expansion of waistline when they hit their middle years, so obviously this is in the genes, as well as being in the jeans.

Secondly, my lifestyle became more sedentary. For years I walked the two miles in and out of work every day. Then I moved jobs, I started driving to work, and found that more and more of my working day is spent behind a computer desk. Lack of exercise is obviously a large contributory factor.

Thirdly, I gave up the fags. Now, I don't want to give the impression that giving up cigarettes leads to bad health. Kicking the weed is not unhealthy in itself. It's just that I subconsciously replaced my evening cigarettes with something from the fridge. Chocolate bars, choc ices, cheese sandwiches, biscuits – they were all consumed in large quantities between dinner time and bedtime.

I crept past eleven stone, with a whimsical smile. At twelve stone, I told myself that I had always been on the thin side, and a little extra padding wouldn't go astray. At thirteen stone, I made a mental note that something must be done. When fourteen stone came and went, I decided that nighttime foraging must come to an end. It didn't.

On holidays during the summer, I was re-christened the evil Fatman, whose dastardly ambition in life was to creep up on children in the pool and throw them with a big splash into the deep end. "Watch out! Here comes the whale!" the cry would go up, from mock-terrified kids that I didn't even know. "Move away from the edge, Sumo, you're blocking the sun!" they would yell delightedly as I prepared to jump in, with a splash that left the pool a quarter full. Enjoying a Mexican meal one warm summer's evening, I could feel the rivulets of sweat trickling down the folds in my stomach.

Thus, returning home, I decided that Something Must Be Done. Now, I don't play sports. I've had two games of football and one game of Gaelic in the last 25 years, all of which rendered me quite unable to use my legs for a week. I am grossly unfit. I have no squash partner. I have a horror of bouncing up and down to music in a community centre somewhere with a load of other heavyish people. Personally I'd prefer to be hung from the ceiling by my nasal hairs.

No, it all came down to one thing – jogging.
It was strange, but once I had resolved that I needed to do some regular exercise, all my former prejudices against jogging disappeared in a flash. I would be like Harold Abrahams in "Chariots of Fire," face uplifted to the wind, borne along by the power of my own legs, intoxicated by the drug of speed (or should I say, velocity) breezing past my more pedestrian contemporaries with effortless ease, a smile playing on my boyish face.
It took approximately eighty yards of my first attempt at breaking into a run, to disavow me of my Olympian notions. I ended up leaning against a wall, doubled up in agony, trying to suck deep lungfuls of air into my sweat-ridden body. A small child wandered up and looked up at me concernedly. I hadn't the breath to speak to him, just spread a palm to indicate I'd be all right.
I hobbled on a bit further, and when my breathing had come down to something approaching normality, I tried again. Fifty yards, this time, and I got a stitch. This was unfair, I thought. Obviously the mind is willing but the body is weak.
That was three weeks ago. Yesterday, I managed to run as far as Latchford without stopping, a distance of about half a mile (no, I don't know what that is in kilometers, and I don't care) Granted, I have absolutely no speed at all, and a snail that was overtaking me on the outside of a bend was forced to cut in and nearly caused a horrific pile-up.
I meet other joggers as I am out. They sail past me effortlessly without a bead of sweat on their foreheads, while I lurch along like a drunken beetroot on legs, perspiring profusely and making strange rasping noises from my throat. I like to feel that a bond of companionship passes between us as we pass, though of course all superfluous movement, such as a nod of the head, is completely out of the question on my part. We are as one. We are the 1924 British Olympic team running along the beach, young, strong and carefree, with that annoying piano clunking away in the background.
The thing that surprises me though is the buzz I am getting out of it. The distances I have been able to keep going have been tangibly greater and this has given me great heart. If things continue at this rate, I will

have my sights firmly set on reaching the Ongar roundabout in one go, then the complete circuit, then next year's Dublin marathon, then perhaps my first triathlon, providing I learn how to swim.
The one downturn to all of this is that despite all the sweat I have pumped out, I have not lost a single ounce (I don't know how much that is in grammes and I don't care) of weight. The scales swing resolutely around to the fourteen and a half stone mark every Sunday, and I swear I can hear it giggling as it does so.
But I don't care. I know the fat will get burned off eventually, though my wife is forever cautioning me about overdoing it and reminding me how old I am. She obviously sees me as a potential cardiac case and says she would prefer a fat hape to a patient on an operating table.
But there's no fool like an old fool. I look forward to my runs every second day and am determined to get my body back in shape after twenty years of neglect. If the body is a temple, mine is in severe need of restoration.
But the scaffolding has been erected, the plans drawn up, and an architectural masterpiece is about to be created. Watch this space.

(October 2006)

Sunday dinners

Because we live in houses, away from the public glare, it is dangerous to assume that our own family idiosyncrasies are replicated in houses across the community. It was only when I got married, for instance, that I discovered that most families had their Shrove Tuesday pancakes after dinner, rather than instead of dinner, as practised by my "careful-with-money" parents.
So I am totally unsure about how common is the practice of enjoying a traditional Irish Sunday dinner – a roast with potatoes and vegetables, with family members sitting around the table, arguing about who is going to do the washing up afterwards.
Certainly I am aware of the current trend towards going out for a carvery lunch on a Sunday. We do it ourselves on occasion, and always

have cause to comment on the number of people eating out and wondering if anybody cooks on a Sunday any more. Of course, other families are probably glancing at us and thinking the same thing, so I have taken to wearing a sandwich board explaining that we normally dine at home on the Sabbath.

At this juncture, I would hasten to point out that I am in no way sitting in moral judgement on the pub diners. With the length of time it takes to prepare the vegetables, cook the roast, organise the dessert, eat the damned thing and tidy up afterwards, that's half of your Sunday gone, leaving precious little time for anything else. Not to mention of course, the stress of potatoes that break up into mush before you put them in the oven, gravy that steadfastly refuses to thicken, broccoli that kids turn their noses up at and wine that ends up on the tablecloth.

With all the above, it is natural that many people are prepared to spend a few pounds on a Sunday to avoid all the hassle of a time-consuming traditional dinner. And Dublin 15 has an abundance of hostelries catering for this demand. From Ashtown to Dunboyne, the area is well-served with excellent carveries that serve high-quality Sunday dinners without the seemingly obligatory family arguments.

For ourselves, though, we normally have the Sunday dinner at home. I prepare the vegetables and then my wife cooks the dinner, while I hover around, handing over ladles and wooden spoons with the same alacrity as an intern handing scalpels to a surgeon. Through years of practice, we have settled comfortably into our respective roles, though I often forget about drinks until everybody is sitting down.

What makes the task harder, though, is that whereas it is always easy enough to pick up a chicken of suitable size, the other meat options sometimes suffer from serious down-sizing. Supermarkets in particular seem to think that their meat-eating customers have tiny appetites. Lumps of pork are minuscule, cuts of lamb are puny and most corned beef cuts could fit into your pocket, if you had such a desire. Is there no demand out there for decent sized cuts of meat, except chez the Goulding household?

Of course, there is so much I do not know about cooking meat. If I buy two small chunks of corned beef and cook them together in a pot, should I do them for twice the normal cooking time? I have no idea.

Physics was never my strong point at school and I never could figure the one about the two trains travelling in the same direction with different speed capacities.

The different cuts of meat would baffle anyone except the experienced cattle slaughterer. What on earth is a Housekeeper's Cut and can you still buy it if you are not a housekeeper? Does a shoulder have a big bone in the middle of it? Why would anyone want to buy it if it has? Which cuts are susceptible to veins of greasy fat? This is the sort of thing they should be teaching in school, rather than how many elements you can balance on a periodic table.

Judging by the queues at the only butchers in the Blanchardstown Centre, I suspect that a lot of people are turning away from supermarkets in the quest for a nice joint. (Here I must explain to any teenager reading this that a joint is the word used to describe a cut of meat) But the very fact that butchers are so busy means that the nervous or unsure meat-purchaser feels very much intimidated by the superior knowledge of the aproned and blood-splattered master craftsman behind the counter.

I want a nice piece of lamb about 1500g in weight. Shoulder or rump, sir? I don't know, what's the difference? Different cuts, sir. Do they have bones? Sometimes sir, depends which piece you get. Which is the least expensive? Shall I get you a nice piece of rump sir? Very good. 1800 grammes, is that okay? Well, it's a bit big. I can cut a piece off sir. There. 1350 grammes. Is that okay? Well, it's a bit small...

When we lived in Stoneybatter, there was a butcher called Peadar who knew all his customers by name and knew exactly what they wanted. If he told you he had a nice piece of sirloin, you believed him, because you trusted him. It was meat shopping made easy. Sadly it's not so easy to find a friendly family butcher nowadays and the onus is now very much on the customer to know their own mind. Which I, for one, don't. Without a Peadar to nurture and guide his customers, traditional Sunday lunchers are reduced to sifting despairingly through ever-diminishing cuts of meat in the local supermarket or playing Russian roulette with the local victualler, hoping that their interpretation of "a nice bit of lamb" coincides with his. This is not progress. This is just another frustrating by-product of the modern age that we must struggle

to overcome. No wonder the local hostelries do a roaring trade on a Sunday.
Or maybe we should just simplify things and turn vegetarian?

(*November 2006*)

A winter's tale

It was Christmas Eve and the only sound that broke the evening silence was the faint sound of whips cutting into reindeer flesh. Large flakes of snow parachuted to the stony earth and then lay still, as if they'd broken both legs on landing. High, high above the clouds, a troupe of celestial angels quarrelled furiously over who should sing the soft parts of "Oh Come all ye Faithful."
Oliver O'Bituary took one final glance out of his bedroom window and drew the curtains. Then he rubbed them out and drew them again. Laying his sketchbook down, he gazed wistfully at the large empty stocking tacked to the fireplace. "If only Santa would come this year," he said to himself, which was a rather odd thing for a 43 year old tax consultant to wish for. Then he pulled the covers up under his nose, flatulated loudly and fell asleep.
Oliver lived in a large house in Clonsilla with his two airedale terriers, both also called Oliver. There was also a money spider who lived on the kitchen window and who was known as Ollie to distinguish him from the Airedales but, as he only enters fleetingly into this story, we won't dwell on him.
O'Bituary had spent a large amount of his spare time trying to get his two dogs to mate, showing them diagrams and playing cheesy Lionel Richie songs late at night, until he had been informed by the window cleaner that they were both, in fact, female. He had thought about renaming his dogs Olivia, but decided that this might induce a crisis of confidence in his canine house guests and decided to let sleeping bitches lie.
However, the window cleaner, a large uncouth man with sideburns and a hatred of lattice windows, had taken great amusement in relaying the

story around the neighbourhood, which resulted in the unfortunate dog-owner gaining the sobriquet "Two Bitch Ollie."

"Here comes Two Bitch Ollie," the local children would yell excitedly whenever Oliver's puffing figure approached with the two Airedales. "There goes Two Bitch Ollie," they would shout, whenever he was travelling away from them. Who says children have no imagination nowadays?

The first rays of the Christmas morning sun angled through the partially closed curtains in Ollie's bedroom and struck his sleeping face. "Ouch!" he yelled savagely and rubbed his cheek. Then, realising, the day that was in it, he dashed to the window and flung open the curtains.

Outside was a picture postcard winter wonderland. Young children were sleighing happily down Shelerin Road. Rosy cheeked carollers, bedecked in fur hats and scarves, were linking arms lovingly and wishing one and all a merry Christmas in perfect harmony. A fat little robin warbled cheerily on a yuletide log until it realised its feet were completely frozen to the wood. Lost penguins trailed around in single file asking people for directions.

Oliver flung open the window excitedly. "A merry Christmas to one and all!" he yelled at the top of his voice. Then, realising he was completely naked, he pulled the curtains hurriedly and went back inside to check his stocking.

There is something in it, he whispered to himself, as he approached. He knew Santa wouldn't forget. Already he could see a slip of paper and something green. This was just going to be the best Christmas ever. Actually, if the truth were known, Santa's presents turned out to be a trifle disappointing. They consisted of a single sprig of holly and a bill for a pair of bifocals that Ollie had purchased from the local opticians. Still, it was a start, and Ollie verily skipped downstairs, humming "The Holly and the Eye Fee."

He gave Oliver and Oliver their presents – a pair of musical slippers each, which they gnawed at contentedly - and then prepared to go out and join in the frolics. He put on a pair of moleskin trousers and then slipped on a pair of rubber boots, bruising his hip quite badly as he fell. Fully dressed, he pulled on his mittens and stepped outside his front door.

The first snowball playfully broke his nose while the second one caused a deep gash on the side of his head. "Kids!" he thought lightly, as he groggily peered through the film of red that coursed down his throbbing face. Bending down, he scooped up what he thought was a handful of snow, but was in fact a pool of battery acid. The acid seeped through his gloves and then started to burn the skin from his hand. In pain, he staggered backwards onto the upturned prongs of a rake which pierced both his feet and caused him to yell and career wildly into the path of a sixteen stone ice skater who was thundering up from the direction of the railway station at a hundred and forty miles per hour. It was perhaps somewhat unfortunate that the runaway steamroller, albeit bedecked in festive bunting, should have passed by at that very minute that Ollie bounced off the stocky ice skater. Certainly, Ollie felt that somehow the festive celebrations weren't quite turning out the way he'd anticipated them, as he crawled in excruciating pain through his open front door and kicked it shut behind him. The last thing he saw before he lost consciousness was a Christmas tree-shaped web adorning the kitchen window. "Gosh, that's clever!" he thought, as blackness descended.

"We must go and call on Oliver O'Bituary," said optician Dr. C. Cleerly to his wife a couple of days after Christmas. "We must go around and wish him the spirit of the season."

"He owes you money, I take it?" replied his wife, fetching her new boa from the wardrobe. She wrapped it tightly around her neck and admired herself in the mirror. "Should it really be squeezing me like this?" she asked, breathlessly.

At Oliver's gate, Dr. Cleerly left his wife still struggling with the snake and marched up the front path to the door. He rapped peremptorily, causing a large chunk of snow to shudder off the roof and fall on his head. The next time, he rang the doorbell, but the call went straight through to ansaphone. Peering in through the lattice window, he spied the comatose figure of Oliver lying in the hall. "Oh my God!" he yelled and, pausing only to comb his hair, eat a packet of crisps and rearrange the folds of his underpants, he put his shoulder to the door and barged in.

What struck him immediately was the smell of disease. Lying there for two days, Oliver had developed bronchitis, double pneumonia and treble Legionnaire's Disease. His head had turned gangrenous and he would undoubtedly lose it before he got better. The stench of illness, germs and rotting flesh pervaded the air, and Dr. Cleerly drew a handkerchief from his breast pocket and staggered backwards out onto the path.
"What is it dear?" asked his wife worriedly, as she stabbed an accurate stiletto through the boa's head. Her husband retched violently over a startled hedgehog, gasping for words to explain the situation.
"'Tis…'tis…'tis disease an' Two Bitch Ollie," he gasped finally, to which his wife responded, "Tra-la-la-la-la, la-la-la-la."

(December 2006)

Beating the Westlink blues

Let's face it, Dublin 15 has an awful lot to offer. We have the Tolka Valley, currently being maintained and developed by the wonderful people at TREA. The stretch of the Royal Canal between Castleknock and Clonsilla rates as one of the beautiful walkways in Ireland. We have a very modern and state-of-the-art hospital. We have a shopping centre that, if it entered "Strictly Come Shopping" – I thought of it first, RTE – would have Craig Revel Horwood bandying tens about like they were going out of fashion.
And we have the Westlink Toll Bridge.
There are a couple of things in this life that put the fear of God into me. Falling into a snakepit full of writhing cobras and black mambas is one. (I know, call me a big girl's blouse, but it wouldn't be what I consider an enjoyable experience) Getting stuck in a lift that plays Lionel Richie songs on a continuous loop is another. And being caught in one of those tailbacks on the M50, that Nicola Hudson so gleefully tells us about every evening, is the third.
I make it a rule to only travel on the M50 at off-peak times. The only trouble is that "off-peak" on Ireland's favourite motorway lies in a

thirty minute spot between 4:15am and 4:45am, not a time particularly conducive to travelling to work, relatives or football matches.

Even people like me, who don't use Ireland's great contribution to the pan-European transport system, can get caught up by events not of their making. Last month, a hubcap fell off a Fiat Panda on the Red Cow sliproad and the whole country was paralysed. The N3 was backed up as far as Letterkenny. The 39 from Ongar was so long getting the two miles to the Blanchardstown Centre that Oxfam were asked to bring soup and comfort to emaciated survivors. Travellers on the Orient Express clicked their tongues in frustration as the stationmaster in Budapest tried to work out an alternative route to Istanbul. A fit of giggling could be heard in the AA Roadwatch studios.

The National Toll Roads tell us that it's not the toll-booths that cause congestion on this great orbital feat of engineering, silly. It's those nasty exit roads. Now I am no infrastructure expert, but this reminds me somewhat of the boy with chocolate smeared all over his face denying that he stole the Mars Bar.

Senator Shane Ross has offered NTR to prove their theory by offering them €10,000 to raise the barriers for a day. To date, NTR have neglected to take up the chance to prove themselves right. Again this is like claiming you have an elephant in your bedroom but not letting anyone up to see it.

The Government's response to the whole fiasco is to build a third lane on the motorway. Now, sums were never my strong point at school but if, say, it takes 10,000 cars one hour to go through five toll booths on a two lane M50, then surely it will take 10,000 cars one hour to go through five toll booths on a three lane M50. Or am I missing some vital piece of information here?

If you insist on having these toll-booths, then surely the only way to get cars through them faster is to build more of them. Extend the toll-booths so that you have 100 of them all in a line. This will reduce every motorist's chances of getting stuck behind the Corsa driver who has to search his pockets, glove-box, ash-tray for the required toll, while drivers behind turn apoplectic with rage. Of course, the big drawback to this is when you have fifty cars all exiting the toll-booths at the same time and racing for the return to two-lane traffic. Naturally a white van will cut you up and leave you wedged in between the Roadstone truck and the mad taxi-driver, though even this is preferable to gazing at the bumper of the new Volkswagen for hours on end.

Alternatively, and this is my own idea which I am going to patent, build another M50 on top of the existing one, so its like a double-decker M50, travelling in exactly the same space-time continuum, only ten yards above it. Or below it, if you prefer. Or above and below it. Whatever, the point would be that there would be double, or treble, the amount of toll-booths, which would halve or reduce by two-thirds the queues that NTR say they are not causing and are only figments of our collective imaginations.

What we really need of course is a bunch of reckless truckers like in that song "Convoy" who insist they "ain't a-gonna pay no toll, rubber duckie" despite the presence of smokies and a bear in the air (kids, ask your parents) and are prepared to smash the gate doin' ninety-eight. But therein lies the flaw - the chances of approaching the toll-booths at anything approaching 98kph are relatively slim, even during the off-peak half-hour.

Of course, there is one surefire way to get the toll barriers permanently raised at all times, but I'm not allowed to tell you because that would be Incitement to Commit a Crime and of course I would not want to be breaking any laws, even though it might mean a break away from my children.

However, let me tell you a totally unconnected story about the dreaded island prison of Alcatraz in California. It was a fearsome place, ruled with a rod of iron. Breaking wind without permission meant a long spell in solitary for the abashed offender. Tapping one's foot to Lionel Richie music often incurred a severe beating by the guards (quite rightly too) Even impersonating garden vegetables was frowned upon and could cause loss of remission.

But the strictest rule in Alcatraz was the rule of silence. The authorities figured that if you could not communicate with your fellow-prisoner, then you could not conspire with him to escape. So, talking was out. The few Trappist monks in there simply shrugged and got on with it, but for the majority of the prisoners, having to forego conversation with their fellow prisoners for days, months, even years proved a severe ordeal. Some snapped and started gabbling unintelligibly and they were immediately hauled off to solitary, to emerge six months later, shattered and broken.

This state of affairs continued for years, decades even. The prisoners knew the penalty for speaking and silence reigned.

And then, one morning, everybody just started talking. Not one or two people, but the entire prison population started chatting away about the weather or the economic situation as if they'd been doing it for years. And there wasn't a damned thing the authorities could do about it. From that day on, the rule of silence was abandoned and conversation was allowed.

Now, some of you might be jumping ahead of me here, in relating the above wee tale to the situation relating to the toll-booths at Westlink. Some of you M50 crawlers, sick to blue death of being forced to sit for hours in a queue to pay money to NTR and the Government for the pleasure of travelling on a road that your taxes helped to build – some of you might infer that I am suggesting that we pluck a date at random in the near future – say January 29th – and everybody who gets to the toll-booth says they've left their money at home. You might assume from the Alcatraz story that if we all stick together and simply and inoffensively shrug and say sorry, no money, then they would have no option but to raise the barriers and let us through. And from that day forward, all our troubles would disappear and cars and trucks would henceforth chug along the toll-free motorway, waving genially to each other. And the good employees of AA Roadwatch would spend their days flying paper planes around the office and staring moodily out of the window.

That might well be the case but, of course, I couldn't possibly condone such criminality.

(*January 2007*)

The Coolmine regatta for the appreciation of poetry

Forgive me Father, for I have sinned. In the last week, I wrote a lengthy ballad composed of rhyming couplets, three haiku and a meandering free verse about the "dappled sky that o'er the slumbering earth now breaks."

Confession they say is good for the soul. And it is therefore with a certain lightening of mind and heart that I bare my soul to the readers of *Community Voice* and admit, "Yea verily, I too have been a poet."

It has always been thus. As a morose and frankly insufferable teenager, I was always prone to scribbling down maudlin and introspective verse into well-thumbed copybooks, perhaps with the hope that my genius would one day be discovered after my tragic death from consumption at an early age. Unsurprisingly, I survived and my teenage efforts are sadly lost to the literary world for ever (at least I hope they are!)

As I matured, so did my poetry, though, in truth, it couldn't really have got any worse. Instead of angst and tortured hearts, I wrote humorous light-hearted verse, often with a witty pun at the end, again with the hope that my genius would one day be discovered after my not-quite-so-tragic death from consumption in middle age.

Nowadays I write poetry about football and current affairs and, well, anything that comes to mind. I find it more satisfying than watching "Big Brother" or "Emmerdale" and whereas Seamus Heaney might not be shaking in his boots at the thought of competition, I have started to branch out and discover the real world of poetry in Ireland today.

As part of my self-education, I began to enter a few of the poetry competitions that appear on the Poetry Ireland website. After a while it became clear to me that every little town in Ireland, as a way of raising revenue in its local hostelries, seems to have organised some kind of literary festival associated with a famous writer from the area. Listowel has a week long programme of events which celebrates new writing and the legacy of John B. Keane. Kiltimagh in Mayo has a festival celebrating the blind Irish poet Raftery. Celbridge has grabbed Aidan Higgins, Donegal has gone for Allingham – the list is endless.

The basic premise of these weekends is that the local writers' group organises the festival. This consists of readings in local pubs – it is something different to loud wailing rock music for the pub clientele and it also gives poets the opportunity to read their work in public. The

White House pub in Limerick is a famous poetic pub where scribblers of all shapes and sizes grab the mike and strut their stuff. Poetry is the new rock'n'roll. Yeah! The landlords are happy as more people are attracted in, the poets are happy and the public enjoy the craic. Everybody is happy, except perhaps the tiny minority that recognise bloody awful poetry when they hear it.

Aligned to the festival, the smart towns organise a writing competition. Basically, like myself, there are thousands of hopeful scribblers out there who just know that they are the next Paul Durcan if only someone would discover them. So they set up a writing competition and a closing date and charge €5 a piece to enter. It can be free verse, rhyming couplets, limericks, tanka, descriptive prose – whatever you want. The World Haiku Championship in Donegal recently – I kid you not – was charging €10 per three line verse submitted. It can be themed or open. People like me, dreaming of our big break and perhaps a crack at the Booker Prize, then send in four of our poems for consideration ands a nice crisp €20 note.

The local writing group then nominates a well-known local poet to do the judging and, because all writing is subjective, nobody will argue with his final choice. In the meantime, those shortlisted travel to the town for the weekend of the festival and so help bolster the town's economy. The monies raised can help fund a Festival Anthology, perhaps, or the local writing group's new publication, or maybe it can simply be spent on more drink, as the organising committee think fit. Actually, I'm being a bit harsh here on these festivals. When you go along, they actually are a huge amount of fun, they can be very inspirational and they do introduce you to the best proponents of the poet's art. And of course you're away for the weekend!

Historically, my attempts to bolster Dublin 15 tourism in the August 2004 edition of *Community Voice* appear to have fallen on deaf ears. Seemingly the proposal to build a blue flag beach in Blanchardstown is impractical, although I do think it could have become a reality with a little lateral thinking.

However, I do believe this scheme could be a winner. An application could be made to the Arts Department of Fingal County Council, who I'm sure would be delighted to support such a worthy and cultural enterprise. There could be an 'open mike' poetry competition with the heats being held in local pubs and the final at Draíocht. Local poets could do readings and thus raise the profile of their own writing groups. We could give it a catchy title like the Coolmine Regatta for the Appreciation of Poetry, or maybe use an acronym if that title was deemed too long.

The only setback is that we don't really have a famous poet associated with the Dublin 15 area. (Forgive me if I have offended anybody living or dead – I am sure there must have been some poet out there who has achieved a degree of recognition who we might claim as "one of our own" but unfortunately, in my unread state, I am not aware of him or her) But all we have to do is invent one. We can call him Blind Michael O'Grady, the wandering poet from Tyrrelstown, who used to roam the highways and byways of the Greater Dublin 15 area, reciting his free-flowing verse and looking for his home. A well-known figure in the locality, he became a firm friend of Jonathan Swift who he bumped into at a cheese and wine party in Porterstown and the two spent a great evening swapping poetical anecdotes. Sadly, we can say, none of his verse has survived to this day but his legacy lives on through this festival etc.

I would suggest that we hold the Festival in the middle of summer and have a special showcase evening with invited poets from around the world waxing lyrical on magical sunsets and grizzled old men with careworn eyes. And hold it in the specially erected marquee on the blue flag beach.

(February 2007)

Some tips for house buyers

As Yossarian states in *Catch 22*, "all wars are fought over real estate." Property has always been the single most coveted commodity on earth and for most of us, buying a house is by far and away the most expensive investment we will ever make. The cost of a house these days is truly frightening, though not as scary as pulling back the bedclothes and finding a deadly black mamba coiled up ready to strike. Yet how many of us truly examine our prospective purchase with the proverbial fine toothcomb before putting pen to paper?

Here in Dublin 15, because of our expansionism and incessant search for lebensraum, we can lay claim to being the house-buying capital of the world. As such we would know more than most about what to look out for when purchasing that des res.

Most people in "Property World" – a mythical kingdom inhabited by people with clipboards and an ability with adjectives that defies logical comprehension – will tell you that the most important things when purchasing a house are "location, location, location." Quite how a single house can have three locations is difficult to fathom, but I suppose the general point is that you should try and choose a house that has a location. Whatever you do, never buy a house that doesn't have a location. It will only bring you heartbreak and you'll keep forgetting where you left it.

However, one man's meat is another man's cheese, particularly if the other man is pretty stupid. To some people living next door to a public house would be a living hell. To others it would be sheer heaven. Living facing a green is desirable to some people, but not to those who are allergic to green. Having a house near a bus stop is great but not if you have to keep picking used bus tickets and hastily stubbed-out cigarettes out of your garden.

What I'm trying to say is that buying a house is fraught with dangers and lack of thoroughness when inspecting the property can bring about untold misery further down the line.

For example, most of us bring out microscopes when examining paint on a light switch cover but how many of us would check for molten lava erupting through fissures in the garden? Geysers, too, and gaseous emissions are a surefire sign that the house is built on a volcanic fault and my advice in this case would be to choose a house a bit further down the road.

The house may look sturdy enough but have you ever tried to take a bite out of it? The practice is rare nowadays but in days of yore, builders often constructed property out of gingerbread to cut costs. Fanciful? Check out The State vs. Cheapskate Builders, Supreme Court

1698, and the real reason for the great caster sugar shortage in the Caribbean at the end of the seventeenth century.

In Iceland along the southern road between Reykjavik and Hafn there is a little shack built at the bottom of a cliff surrounded by massive boulders many time its size that have become dislodged from the heights above. It is colloquially called "The Optimist's House" and Paddy Powersson up there run a book on when the fateful boulder will fall. For those of you with a nervous disposition, it would probably be best to give this sort of house a miss.

The same applies to house-hunters attracted to a property which is perched on top of a cliff prone to severe wind and wave erosion. Thankfully there are not many such properties in the Dublin 15 area but if you should come across one, take a trip down to the Royal Canal first and borrow a bargepole. And then be careful not to touch the property with it.

That tiny ant languidly crossing the kitchen counter may seem innocuous enough, but the buyer beware! An acquaintance of mine once came home to find ten thousand termites curled up on his sofa making caustic comments at "Big Brother." When they refused to hand over the remote control, he was obliged to phone Panasonic to find out how to change channels manually.

Get your solicitor to check the deeds of the house very thoroughly, lest your prize possession should turn out to have been built on an ancient native American burial site. Again, the chances of this occurring in Clonsilla or Ladyswell are quite remote, but it is a small price to pay to avoid having vengeful war-painted braves rampaging through your sitting room walls at three o'clock in the morning.

Older residents may recall a similar occurrence at Cut Throat Cottage in Porterstown in the nineteen forties. The new owners tentatively pushed open the attic door and belatedly discovered that it had been cursed by the High Priest to Rameses II in 1275 B.C. The ensuing plagues of locusts and scarabs had an adverse effect on house prices in the area for the next twenty years.

Most of us employ the services of an architect to prepare a snag list when buying a house but how many of us think to get in touch with Astronomy Ireland? Its all very well to find out that your soffia board

needs a second coat of paint but it becomes pretty irrelevant if you find out that a meteorite is due to obliterate your house and all life forms within a fifteen mile radius in twenty years time. If you feel gung-ho, at least check out the small print on your insurance to see if you are covered for space debris.
Of course, not all potential hazards are preventable. Wherever you choose to purchase your house, you can never be sure that in twenty years time the runway of the second Dublin airport will not bisect your kitchen. This will cause mayhem at meal times and you may be obliged to eat out.
Or maybe some blindfolded planner in Fingal County Council will joyously stick a pin in your house to mark the site of the county's incinerator which will send twenty thousand tonnes of food packaging a year up into the ionosphere. Nothing you can do about it, I'm afraid, though you may get a reduction in your service charges to compensate. The point is that buying a house is always something of a lottery though you'd be wise to avoid plumping for kids' birthdays and anniversaries. A quickpick is usually best, though even here you could end up living next door to someone who likes to play "Lionel Richie's Greatest Hits" at all hours of the day and night.

(*Property Supplement February 2007*)

Worrying about wagtails

Out of all of the creatures that swoop down from the heavens to feed in our back garden, birds are the ones I like best.
As I have previously stated in this column, I get a tremendous amount of satisfaction from seeing the garden teeming with our feathered friends, squabbling loudly over the peanut feeders and fat balls. Some may find sparrows and starlings boring but I get a real kick watching their mannerisms and jealousies. A blue tit visits us early in the morning and late in the afternoon when he has the place to himself. A wren is sometimes to be seen skulking in the undergrowth (having no sense of date, he is probably afraid it might be St. Stephens Day).

Sometimes those big black bullies, the rooks and jackdaws, sweep down from their lofty perches, though they are always the first to scarper at a peremptory knock on the window.
And we have a wagtail.
He is a Pied Wagtail, a subspecies of the white wagtail, found commonly throughout Europe, according to my I-Spy Book of Garden Birds. Strictly speaking, he doesn't actually wag his tail, which causes one to doubt the compos mentis of the great ornithologist that named him thus. Instead he nods it up and down incessantly as though his backside is on fire and he's trying to cool it down.
Now, until recently, Mr. Wagtail (or motacilla alba yarrelli, as they probably refer to him in Rome) rarely ventured into our back garden. I would often see him in the mornings when I came out to get into the car hesitantly running backwards and forwards across the road, like a child taking swimming lessons. Whereas the other birds seem to prefer the foliage and food of the back garden, or the grass of the green opposite, the wagtail appears to regard tarmac and concrete as his favoured habitat, which has always struck me as somewhat odd.
But anyway, I would drive off in my car and watch him scurrying to the kerb as fast as his little legs would carry him. And here is another thing. If God had given me wings, I wouldn't waste all that energy running to avoid traffic. But I put that particular trait down to the fact that he likes to remain in shape and keep his figure, while robins and dunnets just let themselves go.
Last year, I had cause to visit another estate in the locality. Being an un-wagtail-like person, I hopped into my car, watched the little black and white shape hurry out of the way and drove around. As I parked on the roadside, I idly watched another wagtail ostensibly foraging at the base of the kerb where the dandelions grow. And the thought naturally occurred to me that maybe every estate has their own wagtail. Just as every gang has their own turf, maybe the wagtails divide suburban estates amongst themselves, each ruling the roost on their own patch and anyone who crosses the boundary is cruising for a bruising.
As time went by, I had cause to test this theory and it usually held up. Whenever I visited another estate, I would normally see the familiar black and white shape doing the widths of the road, apparently

unconcerned at the massive machines that approached him menacingly. He'd be pecking at something on the tarmac – surely not the greatest feeding ground he could choose in a location full of lawns and bushes and shrubs? – and then, judging it to perfection, he'd dash out of the way at the last moment.

So, I filed him away as a suburban estate bird, a little eccentric, considering his choice of habitat, but a familiar sight around the urban sprawl of Dublin 15.

And then I began to see him at work.

Now, I work out in Leixlip at a giant plant famous for producing pentium processors. It is right on the outskirts of Leixlip in a predominately rural area and as I pulled into the carpark one morning last November, I spied the familiar black and white figure scurrying out of my way. Ha, I thought. He's spread his wings a bit, venturing from his familiar suburban stronghold out to the countryside.

And then another thought occurred to me – what if it's the same bird? Now, I'm sorry to death such a disarming idea ever entered my tiny head, because it has lodged there and won't go away, pecking away at me whenever the nodding loner hoves into view.

What if the bird that I see when leaving for work in the morning is the same bird that is there ostensibly examining dandelions when I pull up in another estate? And is also there pretending to eat tarmac in my carpark at work? Spooky or what? Obviously he tails my car and swoops down unnoticed when I'm turning off the engine.

The more I think about it, the more the evidence seems to add up. This bird obviously has a personal interest in me and where I go. This explains why, unlike every other bird, he alone stays outside the front of the house. If he goes into the back garden, he might miss me leaving and won't be able to pick up the trail. It also explains why he pretends to be feeding on tarmac when there are gardens full of slugs and juicy worms all around. Because he's not really feeding – he's reconnoitring. And it explains why the little blighter runs everywhere – he's conserving his wing muscles in case he might have to make a sudden trip somewhere.

Farfetched? Well, would you be able to tell two wagtails apart? I, for one, am now pretty sure it is the same bird. Now, when I see him, I eye him closely and I am certain he is doing the same to me. We both watch each other out of the corner of our eyes and I fancy he is a bit disconcerted that I have blown his cover.

There are of course two possible reasons why this ornithological private eye is shadowing me. Instead of a guardian angel, he could be my guardian wagtail, watching o'er me to ensure I come to no harm, though quite what he intends to do in the case of an emergency is difficult to predict. Give me the peck of life?

Or his fixation with me could have more sinister undertones. Suppose Douglas Adams is right and white mice really do rule the planet? Could not this wagtail be part of their secret service, tailing me everywhere I go and noting down my movements? Maybe its tail hides a concealed radio transmitter that sends data back to the white mice's lair and that is why it is incessantly moving? Maybe every human being in Ireland has their own personal wagtail that follows them everywhere?

My wagtail has taken to coming into the back garden now. It doesn't squawk with the other birds on the pyrracantha or squabble on the peanut feeder. Instead, it runs around the concrete patio while we are eating Sunday dinner, occasionally glancing in through the glass door to make sure I am still there.

As the saying goes, just because you're paranoid, it doesn't mean they're not after you.

(March 2007)

A timely warning

Oh gather round and heed my tale,
Translate it into French and Braille,
And spread the word around the globe
About this chronomentrophobe.
To some I'm really just a melon,
Others see me as a felon,
A curse on our society
To show such impropriety.

But listen good and listen true
Lest my sad fate should come to you,
And learn from how I fell from grace
And ended in this wretched place.

One Sunday morn, as I recall,
When March's roar began to pall,
'Twas in the small hours of the night,
I saw a blue and flashing light.
And then began the klaxon's wail,
Like some demented nightingale.
Now when the moon and stars come creeping
I have little trouble sleeping,
Because my conscience is as clear
As unpolluted atmosphere,
But if a dog, a mile away,
Should break wind in a violent way,
I wake up in a merry sweat
And need to light a cigarette.
So, wide awake within a second,
Fun and games from outside beckoned.
Throwing back the crocheted spread
I clambered quickly from my bed,
And to the curtained window flew
To get a better, grandstand view,
For crime, thank God, is very rare
Along our quiet thoroughfare.
I watched the squad car turn the bend
And make its way toward our end.
I squinted round the curtain's drop
To see exactly where he'd stop.
Perhaps those lads at fifty four
Were on the wrong side of the law?
Or maybe him at sixty one
Was really someone on the run?
Had those Swedes down at the corner

Got permission for that sauna?
But holy moley, saints alive!
The squad car turned into my drive!

I put on socks and dressing gown
And very sharply hurried down
To answer their insistent knock
At very nearly two o'clock.
The neighbours would be wide awake,
Not knowing this was some mistake.
They must have seen the squad car come
And heard the pandemonium,
And now my name was likely mud
Throughout this genteel neighbourhood.

I pulled the bolt and turned the key
And opened up the door to see
Two burly cops, grim-faced and armed,
Which made me very much alarmed.
One yelled my name, and I said, "Yes?"
And in my state of half-undress,
They pushed me down upon the floor,
As shock ran through my every pore.
I felt as though I might be sick,
On hearing those strong handcuffs click.
There and then I made my mind up
One could see this was no wind-up
(Thoughts which, reader, you will see
Were laced with bitter irony)
They flicked the lights to lift the gloom
In kitchen and in sitting room
And then these swarthy time-police
Took photos of my mantelpiece.
They photographed my microwave
And clock above the architrave,
And laid my wristwatch in full view

And took some pictures of it too.
They read my rights, and when complete,
They hauled me brusquely to my feet
And bundled me into the car,
As neighbours gawped from near and far.

I sit here in my prison cell,
A malcontented ne'er-do-well,
And wonder what ungodly fate
Awaits this surly reprobate.
At first, I'd claimed my innocence,
But knew full well I'd no defence.
The clocks they brought into the court
Exposed my guilt in words and thought.
There really was no need to show
That they were all an hour slow.
And sweet Anne Doyle, from RTE,
Stood on the stand unflinchingly
And told the jury to peruse
The transcripts of the evening news,
In which she'd stated to her flock
That clocks went on at one o'clock

Yes, I'd been warned and paid no heed,
A criminal in thought and deed.
The clocks were changed at one o'clock,
And I admitted from the dock
That though the hour had come and gone,
Oh shame! I'd never wound them on.
So listen ye, who hitherto
Have left the clocks till morning's dew,
When told to add an hour more,
'Tis not "advice" – it is the law.
And woe betide the eager loon
Who winds his clocks an hour too soon,
For he may face a fate like me

Within the penitentiary.
I face a future breaking rocks
For daring to ignore those clocks.
Ironic though, that this foul crime
Will mean I end up doing time.

(March 2007)

Advice for young people

There is a famous list of eleven rules wrongly attributed to Microsoft magnate Bill Gates in which the author metes out advice to secondary school students who are about to enter the real world of life and work. From rule 1 – "Life is not fair-get used to it!" - to rule 11 – "Be nice to nerds. Chances are you'll end up working for one" – the list is a salutary wake-up call to young people who think that the world owes them a living.
I am well aware that ever since Moses told the children of Israel that life in the wilderness was a piece of cake compared to slavery in Egypt, every generation has moaned about the uselessness of their offspring. In fact, one of the reasons I looked forward so much to adulthood was the prospect of telling my own children in a sneering and condescending manner that they didn't know they were born and we had things much tougher in our day.
This is a theme I have developed to such an extent that I now view my childhood with grime-tinted glasses, regaling my uninterested children with lurid tales of being forced down the mine at five years of age and only owning my first pair of shoes when I got married. I have also developed my own set of rules that will guide my descendants through the pitfalls of leaving school and gaining employment:
Rule 1. Find out from your parents where they keep the bread, the butter and the cheese. Then ask them for a quick lesson on how to make a sandwich. Believe me, it only takes a few minutes and the money you will save in a year by not sending out for a jumbo breakfast roll in work will pay for that holiday in Santa Ponza that you seem unable to save

up for.

Rule 1a. Orange cordial plus water made up in a bottle at home can be just as nice but much less expensive than a can of coke.

Rule 2. Learn how to do some of those old-fashioned jobs like washing cars and sewing on buttons. One day you might be thankful that you did.

Rule 3. When you join the workforce, other people will not necessarily be impressed by designer clothes and branded runners. Working people are allowed to buy their clothes in Dunnes without fear of ridicule.

Rule 4. It is very possible in this enlightened age that you will still get that dream job if you turn up for the interview with bits of metal adorning various parts of your face. But don't be too surprised if you don't.

Rule 5. The cost of a hair-cutting kit works out at approximately the cost of three trips to the barbers. Think about it.

Rule 6. Despite what your friends say, a car is still a luxury for many people. I had to work for years before I could afford one. Believe me, you wouldn't be happy if we simply bought one for you. There is no greater satisfaction than working hard to achieve something.

Rule 7. Incredible as it seems, it is possible to be cool and not share your taste in music.

Rule 8. If you want to be treated as an adult, you are expected to share the "adults' jobs" around the house. Yes, really.

Rule 9. If you do not set your alarm clock, it is possible that you may not wake up in time for work. If you do not bring a key, it is possible that you will find yourself locked out when you return home. If you do not put your dirty clothes in the laundry basket, it is possible they will not get washed. None of these is your parents' fault.

Rule 10. You would be embarrassed if your mother and I started snogging passionately on the settee with you in the room. So please do not do the same with your boyfriend / girlfriend / whatever.

Rule 11. Your dinner may well be "gank" but at least your mother went to the trouble of making it for you. Honesty is not always the best policy.

Rule 12. Antiquated old wrecks we may be but we still remember the "staying out at a friend's" line. If we don't challenge you on it, it doesn't necessarily mean you have successfully pulled the wool over our eyes – we may be more enlightened than you suspect.

Rule 13. Please don't call me by my first name. This implies some sort of parity. Even when I am a weak and incontinent old wreck who giggles to himself for no reason, I will still be superior to you, sunshine.

Rule 14. Your contribution to the overall household budget comes nowhere near the amount it would cost you if you moved out. So if you really are "a bit short this week" try stopping smoking and drinking. As the sign says in shops, please don't ask for credit as a refusal often offends.

Rule 15. When you go around to other people's houses, they put on act for you, just as you put on an act for them. This is simple manners. In actual fact, every family is just as odd, weird and fractious as ours. You just don't get to see it.

Rule 16. As a parent, I have the right to bore the pants off you with long and uninteresting stories from my past.

Rule 17. Feel free to ask for advice. But as Brian Clough used to say, "If you have a problem, come to me, we'll discuss it and then decide that I am right." You will get to do the same yourself one day.

Rule 18. Shouting never wins an argument. I merely raise my voice to you whenever we have a disagreement. Learn to tell the difference.

Rule 19. There really isn't €60 worth of difference between one bottle of smelly water and the next. It is possible to get reasonably-priced toiletries that smell okay.

Rule 20. You don't have to take an interest in politics and I understand your point that it isn't cool. Just don't come complaining to me about income tax, the health service, public transport or employment legislation when you don't get a service you believe you're entitled to. And finally…

Rule 21. Whatever problem you might have, we always had it tougher in our day. This might or might not be true but you weren't around, so you'll just have to take my word for it.

The problem of course is that young people never listen to their parents anyway so the above rules are superfluous. It is the duty of the young to

rebel and make their own way in life. It is the duty of parents to worry. Even Bill Gates' parents must have had their doubts at times.
(April 2007)

The magic composter

Once upon a time in a land far, far away, close to the border with county Meath, there lived a man and a woman and their two teenage children in a nice semi-detached house in a nice estate. They were happy in their home because they used to live in the middle of the big, bustling city where there was a lot of noise. Here on the edge of suburbia, they had a bit of a garden and could enjoy the relative peace and quiet.

Now the woman of the house was a keen environmentalist. She was determined that she could help to make the world a better place for their children to live in and so she became a committed recycler. She would always sort her rubbish and would make sure that nothing went into the black bin that could be used again.

Her husband was not a committed recycler but he agreed with schemes that saved money. "Careful with money" was how generously minded folk described him and he willingly went along with his wife's recycling because it saved on the amount of times the black bin had to go out for collection.

The children, who don't really appear in this story very much, were not all that bothered about recycling but were more interested in somebody called Justin Timberlake. However they would share in the recycling for fear of being told off.

Now the recycling was going well. The woman would wash and squash plastic bottles and cut the little see-through windows off business envelopes in order to maximise the amount of waste that could be recycled. The man would gather up their unsolicited junk mail and return it to the sender in the freepost envelope provided. The woman would make the man wash the car with a thimbleful of water, in order to safeguard this valuable resource for future generations and woe betide anybody who left the cold tap running while cleaning their teeth. Then one day, the woman said to her husband, "Peter," – for that was his name, coincidentally the same as my own – "Peter, I think we should get a composter."

"What is a composter?" replied Peter, who was slightly dim, though in his defence had only ever lived in city houses with concrete paved back yards.

The woman tutted deprecatingly. "A composter is a big green plastic container. I have heard all about it. You put all your organic waste in at the top, and out of the bottom comes lovely rich dark compost which will make your roses grow tall and strong and will save you lots of money on fertiliser."

Of course it was the final phrase that caught the man's attention and he agreed to get a composter.

Now this land didn't have a King. Instead the King had been replaced by something called a Local Authority, though some people called him Fingal. The man went to Fingal and bought a composter and brought it home to his excited wife. The children just glanced up from their PSPs and said "Whatever."

The man and his wife read all the books about successful composting and even went to a workshop in a place called The Library to find out how it worked. Apparently you had to fill the composter three quarters full with a mixture of green waste and brown waste, although confusingly the green waste did not have to be green and the brown waste did not have to be brown. When the two were mixed together, they would produce lovely compost, they were told.

So the environmentally friendly pair set to filling up their composter. They threw in potato peelings, carrot tops and tails and broccoli stalks, although the man normally brought his Swiss Army knife into the supermarket to cut off the chunkier stalks, as broccoli is sold by weight. Then they got the brown leaves which were clogging up the shores along the side of the house and scrap bits of paper assiduously shredded by hand and added them to the mix. Then the man got an old broom handle and mixed up the concoction like the witches stirring the cauldron in Macbeth.

And then they waited.

And waited.

Every week, the man would throw in the week's supply of kitchen waste with a liberal sprinkling of shredded paper on top to keep off the flies. Every second week he would lift the flap at the bottom expecting to see shovelfuls of rich crumbly compost but all he saw was a mishmash of kitchen waste and bits of paper.

"I think the Local Authority have sold me a dud composter," he would say to his wife sadly on returning from another disappointing reconnaissance.

"Don't be silly," his wife would reply. "The Local Authority is wise and good. Shame on you for thinking otherwise. You must allow time for the breakdown process to begin."

So the couple gave the composter some more time. The man still threw in the waste every week but did not check the bottom flap for months and months. The months turned into years and every Spring, when the man had a momentary burst of gardening fervour, he would lift the flap and then lower it again with a sigh.

"I can't understand it," he said to his wife. "Every week we throw in a bucketful of waste, yet we never get any compost. But the funny thing is, the level in the composter keeps going down regardless." His wife was eventually forced to admit there was "something quare" going on. Where did all the peelings and apple cores disappear to if they weren't being turned into compost?

"Maybe the worms and slugs are eating it all?" she suggested lamely.

"Maybe our next door neighbour has dug a tunnel from the other side of the fence and is scooping out all the compost every week?" said the man.

"Maybe it is the horticultural equivalent of a space-time vacuum that sucks in all matter and turns it to anti-matter?" said the woman.

"Maybe there is a fissure in the rock just beneath the composter and the waste is falling into a giant molten cavern below?" said the man.

"Maybe a kitchen waste fetishist is creeping into our garden at night and regularly helping himself to a bucketful?" said the woman.

"Maybe it is a Magic Composter?" said the man. "I have heard of these things before. An old woman in a neighbouring estate had a Magic Porridge Pot that had the whole street knee deep in porridge."

Of course the man and the woman kept the secret of the Magic Composter to themselves. If everybody knew about it, the Local Authority would send out his servants to examine and dissect it in order

to find out how it worked. The woman was happy because it was eating up all her kitchen waste. The man was happy because he knew he had found somewhere to dispose of his wife's remains when she died and thus save on funeral bills. The children were happy because Justin Timberlake was playing at The Point. And the Magic Composter was happy because he was being well fed every week!
And so, as in the way of all such stories, they all lived happily ever after.

(April 2007)

The Castlehuddart principality

As some of you may already have surmised, this is an election year and the posturing and manoeuvrings have already begun. Already one senses a certain weariness, if not the sound of outright snoring, on the part of the electorate who see little to excite them in the impending bout of oral and verbal fisticuffs. The Government parties are promising to maintain the status quo, despite the fact that they haven't produced anything decent since "Down Down, Deeper and Down" in 1976 and the opposition parties are promising "radical change," in the very political and humorous sense of the word "radical."
In setting up the Castlehuddart Devolution Party – I am keen not to alienate the two major hubs of Dublin 15 – I believe that the only way to effect real and lasting change in the area is to vote CDP.
For too long, the good citizens of this green and pleasant suburb have been held to ransom by near-sighted planners, greedy developers and shopping trolleys with bockety wheels. We said we wanted extra places for our children in local schools and they gave us longer benches. We said we wanted a fast and reliable transport system and they pointed us towards the footwear in Lifestyle. We said we wanted proper health care for all and they gave us an Anadin. And the worst crime of all was doing away with Roches Stores (or so my wife maintains)
It is a general principal of life and business that the smaller an organisation or political entity, the more efficiently it runs. The kibbutz

in Israel generally operates well and is probably closest to the ideas that Karl Marx had before he chose to make the foray into Hollywood with Groucho and Harpo. The Soviet Union, on the other hand, was ultimately too unwieldy and declined and fell in much the same way that the Roman Empire did 1500 years previously.

The sad fact of the matter is that no matter what prospective candidates say about prioritising this area after the election, they will have to contend with every other area in the country looking for their own area to be prioritised. And despite our relatively small population, our politicians have yet to come up with a way of pleasing all the people all of the time, though resignations might bring a smile to most people's faces.

Here in the CDP (current membership of one, though I'm trying hard to get my wife and children to join through bribery) we (a royal "we" obviously) believe (and fully subscribe to the fact that) sentences (of all lengths) should contain as many brackets as is (humanly) possible. We also believe that only through total devolution from the island of Ireland (north and south) can the citizens of Blanchardstown, Castleknock, Mulhuddart and surrounding areas hope to achieve their full potential.

If we come to power – and in all honesty, a good old-fashioned coup d'etat seems more promising than an electoral victory – we would immediately close all borders with the rest of Ireland and insist that all non-residents must wear a funny hat if they wish to use our roads. This might not generate much income but if would lift the spirits of hard-pressed commuters travelling home from the foreign townships of Cabra and Glasnevin.

All citizens will of course require Castlehuddart passports and like Greenland we will secede from the EU, making our off-licences and pubs duty-free and thus generating a day-tripper tourist industry to avail of cheap drink. The first thing we will do when our status is ratified by the United Nations will be to apply to FIFA to host the World Cup in 2016, with matches to be played at Verona, Corduff, Parslickstown, Porterstown and possibly St. Brigid's, if we can negotiate a fee with them. Obviously this will also mean Champions League action for Whitestown United or Castleknock Celtic or whoever wins the domestic league.

We will stand firm on law and order, as we believe both are very good things to have, particularly order. This will be funded by the money collected in the fountain in the Blanchardstown Shopping Centre.

All building of houses and estates will cease forthwith and in fact we will pull a few of the newer ones down again and plant grass and thistles. We have also conducted extensive surveys and believe that the optimum solution to Clonsilla Bridge is to re-route the canal around the far side of the railway station and widen the road. All cars over 1.4 litres will be debarred from displaying witty signs in the back windows and we will of course push for Roches Stores to be reintroduced into the area. (Some people may regard this as a cynical ploy to go for the women's vote but frankly it is the men who are suffering through listening to their wives moaning about the store's demise.)

We will build another 37 bridges across the M50 to help alleviate traffic congestion on the N3 and we will also push strongly for the Phoenix Park to be cobble-locked to get rid of the jams on its frankly inadequate roads. This will also generate a considerable saving for the Parks Department of our neighbouring country which they can then use to promote environmental awareness.

The soon-to-be-renamed National James Connolly Memorial Hospital will receive its long-awaited scanner, purchased through Government funding in Dixon's with a free printer thrown in. The hospital waiting list will be dramatically reduced by the simple means of making more lists with fewer people on each.

Abbotstown will be rezoned as a luxury holiday resort, complete with blue flag beach, casino and lots of scantily-clad women strolling around eating choc-ices to entice in tourists from the mainland. It will also feature Joe Higgins World, a Disney-type theme park dedicated to the indefatigable campaigner. Excited children and adults will be strapped into black wheelie bins and hurtled around gigantic rollercoasters at absolutely no extra cost to the hard-pressed taxpayer.

As regards to the administration of the new principality, I have toyed with the idea of democracy but feel it probably wouldn't work. Just as you don't get schoolchildren to vote for their choice of principal, democracy entails people who know nothing about politics having a

say in who runs the country. It also entails the extra needless expense of ballot boxes, voting slips and pencils.
Instead, I would be broadly in favour of establishing a benign dictatorship with myself naturally on the throne. I realise fully that this onerous task will require a great deal of sacrifice on my part but in the interests of the community I am prepared to put the common good before my own personal well-being. Besides I thought of it first.

(April 2007)

The lawn forcement agency

It is one of the few consolations of our long, dreary winter months that the lawnmower can stay firmly nestled in the shed, untouched, unloved and forgotten. Few things in life give me such perverse joy as unplugging the infernal thing for the final time in late September and returning it to its natural home beneath the gardening gloves, one welly and a host of partly-deflated footballs.
Grass, the experts tell us – (they have experts in grass?) – will not grow below 5°C. This is not through any design of nature. It simply refuses to do so and who can blame it? If I had no financial concerns, I too would willingly hibernate for six months of the year.
Unfortunately these days there may or may not be an entity called Global Warming, depending on which paper you read and whichever day you read it. These winters, we rarely get enough snow to build a snowman's lower appendages and the mercury regularly creeps up above this magical 5°C mark between October and March.
One of my abiding principles in life, along with always changing your clothes after you have a bath, is to do nothing in the garden before April 1st, except maybe look at it from the kitchen window. The garden books all give us little jobs to do during the winter months like raking up leaves and preparing soil but I see no earthly point in any of it. Besides, it's always raining.
This year, however, such was the mildness of the winter, that I contemplated breaking the rule of a lunchtime and lugging my old

green pal out of the shed a whole month early. Actually, to my abject horror, one Saturday afternoon in January – yes January – I even heard the old familiar sound of a lawnmower engine in a nearby garden and I had to higher up Lionel Ritchie on the radio lest my wife heard it too and started getting ideas.

So, come mid-March, the grass was not yet out of hand but could certainly have done with a short back and sides. Two things stopped me. Every time I had a bit of spare time, it rained. (This happens a lot actually and I'm starting to get paranoid about it.) And we were going off on holiday on April 1st. If I could just reach that date, I could extend my non-grass-cutting hiatus by a further fortnight.

With a couple of days to go before we jetted off to what was a disappointingly chilly Orlando on our very early summer holidays, the heavens opened and I knew I was safe.

In line with our general holiday experiences, while we were donning sweatshirts and shivering in Downtown Disney (I have the photos to prove it), Ireland enjoyed one of those glorious fortnights that come only too rarely. The good citizens of this country should really have a whip round and send me away on holidays more often if they want to see some improvement in the meteorological situation. Evelyn Cusack would be able to explain to a gleeful public that "Peter Goulding is away on his holliers so a big H is coming in from the Atlantic and preparing to settle over Ireland."

The fine weather, of course, allied to the previous showery weather, meant there was no need to ask mad Mary Mary Quite Contrary how her garden grew. Like wildfire, I think the answer was (how do cockleshells make a garden grow?) When we pulled up outside the house on our return, the dense foliage all but obscured our abode and it was only through checking our neighbour's gardens, that we worked out through a process of elimination where our house should be.

We had actually left our two late teen offspring in the house in our absence but in the scramble to pack our t-shirts and shorts (ho! ho!), I had neglected to draw a map outlining the route from the kitchen door to the shed, so the grass had remained uncut. Only it wasn't just grass – nature had sought to reclaim what had once been hers and had really gone to town. There were shrubs and trees and dandelions as big as sunflowers and other exotic green things that looked decidedly tropical in nature.

I got away with it for about three days, claiming jet lag, which is really just a posh person's way of saying "I couldn't be arsed." There was also so much to be done inside the house, I claimed, that we needed to prioritise the work. We can't expect to get everything back in order immediately, I said, as my wife raised a disbelieving eyebrow.

For the next week or so, I would pull back the net curtains and peer despairingly at the vast expanse of blue sky. "Looks like rain," I would mutter. I even dug out an old *Community Voice* article about a workshop in the Library where Monica Shannon and the great people of the Dublin 15 Environmental Group were asking people to "garden for wildlife" and let portions of their garden run wild to encourage a greater biodiversity.

What made matters worse is that in our absence, all our neighbours had taken advantage of the fine spell to diligently mow and trim their lawns so that our patch stuck out like the proverbial aching digit. Like the new proposed Eye and Ear Hospital, it was a site for sore eyes. I knew I had to tackle it eventually but I was still in holiday mode, I said. Just a few days more.

The leaflets started coming in through the door. Do you need your lawn mowed? they asked, obviously rhetorically. I wonder do the people who deliver these leaflets only post them into houses with scruffy gardens? The reason I ask is that they never seem to come when my grass has just been cut. I know it is time to wash my windows when somebody pushes a leaflet through my letterbox offering me a window cleaning service. Come to think of it, there's no need for my wife to post a job list on the fridge – she can simply pile the flyers up on the hall table and I'll work through them one by one.

The final straw came when I came home from work one evening and my wife recounted that she had seen a troop of Masai warriors, carrying an okapi on a long pole, emerging out of our back garden in single file. I sensed she was exaggerating slightly but when she is in one of her sarcastic moods, its best not to challenge her.

Still, I managed to achieve a new personal best by not cutting the grass until the last week in April. This will be the new benchmark for future years and when I see grown men struggling to turn Black and Deckers around impossible corners in February, I will sit my enthralled grandchildren on my knees and recount to them proudly how in the Spring of 2007 I nearly made it to May without cutting the grass.

(May 2007)

Shinners and grinners

I don't know if anybody noticed but a general election campaign has been going on for the last month or so. Seemingly the more posters you can put up around the constituency, the more the electorate think that you're the man or woman for the job. Poster hanging is of course a vital part of running a Government and those who can shin up lampposts at local level are destined for great things.
Speaking of Shinners, the redoubtable Felix Gallagher was first out of the traps, getting his large Gerry's-buddy election posters up a full week before Bertie called into the Aras. Unfortunately, he chose to locate them on the rear of showhouse signs which were removed from roundabouts on the Sunday evening.
One thing about Felix, though – he sports a most engaging smile on his poster, as do most of his party colleagues around the country. His casual grin was seen in many places where other candidates feared to tread, on out-of-the-way lampposts, far from the mainstream spots favoured by the other parties.
One unusual feature of the SF posters was the addition, a few days before the election, of little Irish flags. Now I assume they weren't suggesting it is in some way patriotic to vote Sinn Fein, so I took it as a helpful little reminder that the election was being held in Ireland. In the last election, I spent hours wandering around Antwerp trying out my pidgin Flemish, before being told that I should go to the Mary Mother of Hope polling station in Castaheany, so Felix's little reminder ensured I did not repeat the mistake.
Brian Lenihan was another smiler, beaming down with all the confidence of a man who knows his seat is safe and that he doesn't

really need to put these posters up to get elected but he doesn't want to appear arrogant. He obviously favours the same passport photographer as his running mate Gerry Lynam, judging by the identical dark green curtain pulled behind them.

Gerry is not smiling in his poster. He obviously knows that he hasn't a snowball's chance in hell of getting elected and sees no point in flashing the teeth. What surprises me though is that nobody in the Soldiers of Destiny took Gerry aside and told him that moustaches hadn't had a place in Fianna Fail since the 1970s, with the exception of, erm, Willie O'Dea. As it stands, Gerry's photo reminds one vaguely of the bad man who used to tie the girl to the railway track in silent movies.

Another who was not best served by her party's electoral machine was the Labour candidate Joan Burton. I mean, let's face it, Joan is a damned sexy woman and you would have thought her posters would reflect that, in the same way that a football team always plays to its strengths. Now I'm not saying she should have gone as far as a bikini and a beach ball but at least she could have clamped a red rose seductively between her teeth and worn a long flowing scarlet dress with a slit up her thigh. But no, they missed the opportunity of a lifetime and showed this bombshell only from the shoulders up.

A week before the campaign ended, a second Joan poster went up. This was of a younger Joan, more sultry, yes, but still only from the neck up. Her bob haircut made her look like a member of a 1960s girl singing group – the Rabbettes? – and perhaps hinted at the raver we fancy she used to be.

One thing about the Burton posters though – because of the brevity of her name and the white background, her posters were easily legible when travelling up the new Ongar Rd at 80kms per hour (sorry that should read 49kms per hour, officer) It occurred to me that if Celtic striker Jan Vennegoor of Hesselink should ever go into politics, he would need extra wide posters to fit his name on.

Fine Gael candidate Leo Varadkar easily won the prize for putting up the most posters in the constituency. Barely had RTE breathlessly announced the date of the election, and Leo the Statesman posters were going up on every third lamppost. Obviously deciding that this was not enough, another set of posters went up a week later, and then, with even his finances surely running low, a third set of posters went up a further week after that.

The first poster was of a serious yet compassionate Leo, backed by a blue sky and white fluffy clouds. He also seemed to be standing in the middle of a field surrounded by hedges and trees, probably to give the impression of a down-to-earth man, a real salt of the earth type. The second poster was of a much younger, misty-eyed Leo, in the days before he could afford a jacket, that appeared to have been resurrected from a previous election campaign. And the third one, which he obviously thought would help to sway the floating voter, was a diamond-shaped effort urging people to vote him number one.

The Socialist Party was very quick off the mark, with their first posters going up by the time Bertie had got out onto Infirmary Road. Joe Higgins was the only one of the candidates to be photographed in black and white, which some might say mirrors his politics. Again, his posters appeared to have been recycled from a previous campaign and one would suspect his election budget was just a tiny percentage of Leo's. Less bin charges for Joe I presume.

The two late-comers to the poster frenzy were Roderic O'Gorman and Mags Murray. Roderic for the Greens somehow managed to end up with many prime location spots all to himself, though P.D.'s Mags, who concentrated mainly on junctions, often ended up sitting on top of Gerry Lynam or Felix Gallagher, or both.

Roderic had probably the most attractive poster with the green and white background, urging us all in the Littlepace Gaeltacht to make "an rogha cheart." Alone of the candidates, he favoured the slightly oblique stance, turning sideways to look at the camera, as practised at the beginning of 1970's American soap operas. True, Leo was at a slight angle in his field but that was probably because a bull was eying him menacingly and he was preparing for a quick getaway.

Mags went in for blue in a way favoured by Picasso in the early 1900s. Her blue mascara matched her blue eyes and her blue dress with Leo's blue sky in the background. Curiously she sported what appeared to be Queen Maedbh's torc in her election photo and looked a bit like a young Twink advertising her latest pantomime in the Gaiety. Still with

her long blonde hair wafting gently in the breeze, she posed coquettishly in a way that should be copied by Joan in the next election. But perhaps I am being too critical. I had occasion during the campaign to travel down to the Longford / Roscommon constituency and was deeply traumatised by the ugly-looking ibexes they have adorning the lampposts down there. Mothers, I am told, keep their children locked in during the day and even adults go about their business with their eyes fixed firmly on the paths. Compared to them, our bunch of candidates are positively good-looking and, if truth be known, would probably form one of the more attractive ballot papers in the country.
One thing is for sure, though. Like Christmas decorations, the place is going to look really bare when they come down.

(*May 2007*)

Making memories

While rummaging through the rubbish bins at the rear of the Tyrellstown Plaza Hotel, (as I am wont to do on fine summer evenings,) I came across a crumpled sheet of paper which I proceeded to unfold. It had evidently been an entry for the recent Fingal County Council "Memory Makers 2007" competition (essay section) but had not made the grade. This may have had something to do with the words "factually incorrect" being emblazoned across the text in red biro. However, after reading through the essay, I have decided to reproduce it here, as I feel it will be of interest to people of a certain age (over 115)
"I was born in a little cottage in Blanchardstown near the Tolka River. The cottage has since been pulled down to make way for a fire hydrant. That's progress, I suppose.
"My father was one of the first astronauts in the country but it was not an easy occupation in those days. He was often out of work for long periods of time, when he used to sit by the hearth and yearn for the birth of space travel. He had been arrested by the Black and Emeralds (a more fashion-conscious offshoot of the Black and Tans) during the

Civil War and only avoided summary execution by lying about his sex.
"My mother hailed from county Roscommon. She had walked to Dublin barefoot for the Eucharist Conference in 1932 and ended up squatting in a house in Brunswick Street with two Mesopatamian dope-fiends. My father had rescued her from this den of iniquity when his lunar module crashed through the roof in 1934.
"I had 32 brothers and sisters, most of whom had rickets. The others used to pretend they had rickets because they thought that was the norm. We all used to attend St. Whoopi's National School (now The Mace) in Blanchardstown. I remember one of my teachers was called Mr. Goering. He had a cane and used to administer six on the rump whenever anyone spoke in class, even when he asked them a direct question.
"Mother used to work at Comerford's Little Bits of Plastic that you find on the Back of Sticking Plasters Factory in Chapelizod (now the River Liffey) The company employed 20,000 people in its heyday until it inexplicably went bankrupt one week later. Mother used to work from 4am to 3am the next morning, seven days a week with Christmas morning off. Oftentimes she'd be held up on her way home by comely maidens dancing at the crossroads and have to turn around and go back into work before she arrived home. It was a hard life but I think she was happy
"Of course we had no television to entertain us in those days. Every evening the whole family would huddle together and stare at the corner of the room, waiting for it to be invented. I remember the first television set that appeared in the village. It was in the window of Lionel Richie's Hardware Emporium on Main Street (now a tree) and it attracted a huge crowd until Maxie "Mad Fecker" Murphy took an axe to it to see if there really was a little man inside of it or not.
"When I was sixteen, I was sweet on a boy called Notcher Farragher, son of the village's computer analyst. When he found out I was with child, he ran away to join the Navy until he discovered that it entailed a lot of travelling on water and joined the Army instead. I heard later that he had fallen in the Korean War but escaped with a badly stubbed toe.
"When I told my father that I was pregnant, he became acutely distressed, as he had always assumed I was a boy. "James," he said.

"The priest won't like this." Sure enough Father Away de Betta (a visiting Dutch cleric) came to the door with a roaring red face, threatening damnation and the workhouse. I hid in the scullery as Father confronted him on the doorstep. At first I thought it was going to come to blows but the whole incident was settled amicably by a game of kerb football. However, when the time came for the baby to be born, the midwife discovered that I, and I quote, was "just plain fat." Oh we were naïve in those days.

"Because times were hard, most of my brothers and sisters emigrated to England and America, where people with rickets were much in demand. My father contemplated emigrating to Cape Canaveral when the space programme started but a letter from John Glenn advised him that his wooden leg would likely put a hole in his spacesuit. This seemed to crush him completely and he spent the rest of his life sitting on a stool in the back garden staring up at the sky, while my mother entreated him to come in out of the rain.

"I got a job in Jacob's writing the word "NICE" in capital letters on the biscuits. Later I was promoted to drawing cows on the malted milks. "You draw great cows," my supervisor used to say. "You have a great future ahead of you." Sadly it was not to be and I was made redundant by the influx of a large group of Hungarian bovine-artists after the failed uprising of 1956.

"In the meantime, I had married a man named Denzel O'Loughlin who was apprenticed to a shepherd out in Luttrellstown. "Jobs may come and jobs may go," he used to say with great insight, "but there'll always be shepherds in Dublin 15." After a year, I had triplets (one of each) and the following spring I had twins. Three months later another set of triplets and by the end of the year another set of twins. It was a hard life but we managed. The older children, once they learned to walk, used to mind the younger children until my husband came home from a hard day shepherding.

"I remember the first car we bought. It was a little Morris Minor and the twelve of us used to go for trips to Skerries which to us seemed like the end of the world. Myself and Denzel used to paddle in the sea while the kids buried each other in the sand. One time the tide came in and they were all drowned. But we were happy."

I think I may appeal to the Memory Makers committee about the reasons for excluding this exceedingly moving piece on the grounds that its relationship with the truth might be somewhat strained. Just because it all may be a pack of lies does not mean that the facts may not exist in somebody's head.

(June 2007)

Sleeping on it

I used to think we lived in a quiet neighbourhood. Let me rephrase that. We do live in a quiet neighbourhood. It's just that I never realised until recently just how many different degrees of quiet there are.
My situation in work has changed recently, with the result that some months I work at nights. As such, I have joined that small band of people who have to sleep during the day. My wife and I discussed this – should I go to sleep immediately on coming home, or should I hold off until the middle of the day? It was decided to pursue the latter course as everybody else in the house would be getting up in the morning and I would keep getting disturbed by Krispies snapping, crackling and popping away in the bowls.
So at the ungodly hour of 11 o'clock when most decent people are safely ensconced in their offices, I got undressed and settled down to what I hoped was a good six hours sleep.
The first thing you notice is the light. It really is quiet unnatural to think about sleep with the sun streaming in through the curtains. I tried shutting my eyes, but obviously my eyelids are made of the same material as our curtains because the sun still got through. Only by turning away from the window and burying my face in the pillow did I manage to convince myself it was the middle of the night.
And then it started.
I was just nodding off when from an estate behind us, a house alarm went off. Obviously someone had put a pizza flyer through a door with too sensitive an alarm and all hell had broken loose. It's amazing how house alarms don't like pizza notices.

My double glazed window was shut but it was still like a workman operating a jackhammer in the bed beside me (don't worry – I checked and it wasn't.) From bitter experience, I knew that if it was not turned off immediately this would keep running for another fifteen minutes and then at fifteen minute intervals during the day. Reluctantly, I grabbed my alarm clock, shut the bedroom door behind me, moved to a bed in the front of the house, shut that door behind me and hopped into bed for a second time.

The sound of the infernal alarm was much muffled here and it was something I could live with. At any rate, it disproved my wife's theory that I would sleep through World War III. I settled down again and soon started to nod off for a second time.

Just prior to the point of no return, when you cross the Rubicon into sleep, the door bell rang. I ignored it, listening. It rang again. I waited. Why wasn't my wife answering it? For the third time, it rang. I swung out of bed, opened the bedroom door and was halfway down the stairs when my wife came out of the kitchen and beat me to the front door. It was the postman with a package for my daughter. I turned back on my heel and went back to bed.

By this time I was wide awake. On the rare occasions when this happens, I have a perfect plan for spiralling into the arms of Morpheus. I imagine a football match.

Don't laugh. I play out a fictitious football game from the kick off in my imagination. One player tips it to another, he plays it back to the midfielder, who sprays it out wide to the left full back who, under pressure, plays it down the line, for the defender to head it out. I guarantee you it works. Twenty passes into the game and I'm gone.

This time, however, my inside right (kids, ask your dad) had just made a cunning foray down the channel when he was brought up suddenly by a loud "Caw!" For a moment Graham Poll looked at his whistle with a puzzled expression, but when a second, slightly higher-pitched "Caw!" came, I realised with a groan that two killer crows (my wife's expression – they spook her) were having a conversation on the gutter above my bedroom window.

I don't speak crow (it wasn't on the syllabus in school) but I suspect they were discussing which over-full wheelie bin to ransack next.

Wearily, I got up on my knees and opened the window violently. A sudden flurry of wings told me that they had decided to carry on their conversation elsewhere.

I flopped down on the bed, feeling a bit apprehensive. I needed to sleep.

For the first time in my life, I could see what bad sleepers have to contend with every night. They are anxious that they can't sleep, so they don't sleep. It's a Catch 22, (rather than a Catch 40 winks) situation.

I went back to my football match but no sooner had an over-zealous midfielder gone clattering into his opposite number, than I heard the tell-tale sign of a lawnmower spluttering into life. Squinting out of the side of the curtain, I could see a man several doors down getting to work on his front lawn. I remember I had passed his garden a couple of days ago and thought absently that it needed a cut. I had a vague notion that the man also worked nights. Maybe he had given up trying to sleep and was mowing the grass instead, I thought ruefully.

I tried reading while the lawnmower clattered away out front and the house alarm scythed through the air out back. Reading normally puts me to sleep. However, this book, "Great Chartered Accountants of the Late Renaissance Period" (later made into a film starring Ernest Borgnine and a soundtrack by Lionel Ritchie) was fascinating and I read page after page before I realised that all was quiet in the neighbourhood.

With great reluctance, I lay the book down on the floor beside me and rolled over. Centre-forward to inside-left. Knocks it back to centre-half, diagonal ball down the wing…

Someone in the street walks past the house at the end of the road. This is fatal as the house has a big stupid dog in the side entrance who howls with fury every time somebody walks by. He's off again now, paying not the blindest bit of notice to the unfortunate passer by, head back, running up and down, howling like a banshee. This alerts another dog several doors down, who begins to bark in empathy. Somewhere far off, a terrier yaps away like a demented woodpecker. I wrap the pillow around my head and wait for the din to die down.

The ice-cream van comes around. The man on the little tractor starts to

mow the green opposite the house. The dogs start yowling again. The wheelie bin truck makes his round to thwart the killer crows. I pick up the Accountants book again and read to the end of the car chase on page 58. Silence reigns.
Centre-forward to inside-left. Tries to beat a man. Is fouled. Free kick. Opposition player protests. Ref changes his mind. No, he doesn't, that's silly. Three doors down, someone opens a car door without realising the alarm is on. I've done the same a hundred times. Alarm goes off. Fumble for the remote control. Alarm goes off again after five seconds. No harm done.
Except there's a man in a bedroom in a nearby house screaming at the top of his lungs as his wife rushes upstairs to see what's the matter.

(June 2007)

Prime indicators

The older I get, the more I realise just how many simple tasks I am unable to perform. I have never been able to blow bubbles with bubble-gum. I have never been able to whistle without pursing my lips into an O, I cannot do backward tumbles in the swimming pool and I cannot touch my toes without bending my legs. Nor can I change sparkplugs, do simple tiling, draw, sew on a button with any degree of rigidity or pretend to be angry without giggling.
There is however one small task which seemingly only I and a handful of others seem able to do with any regularity – indicating.
Now, to me, it doesn't seem a difficult thing to do. I want to let everybody know I am turning left. My left hand moves two inches off the steering wheel and flicks upwards. At most, the operation takes a quarter of a second. I do not feel physically drained after doing this, nor do I feel the need to pull over and massage my aching wrist. The manoeuvre has not taken very much out of me and I have fulfilled my objective in letting everybody know that I intend turning left.
I am immensely surprised however that more drivers don't seem to have the ability to do the same. Maybe, I tell myself charitably, that

they have cars in which the indicators are located behind the passenger seat and it is a considerable hardship to operate them. Maybe, I suggest to myself (though I suspect I am not listening), they have fragile left wrists and are suffering from repetitive strain injury through over-indicating. Or maybe, and here I find myself nodding sadly in agreement, maybe they just can't be bothered.

Sitting in my car at a busy roundabout, I find myself wishing disgusting toe infections on drivers who suddenly veer off to their left when I had been expecting them to go straight ahead. Sometimes, after it happens three or four times, I extend the curse to their kith and kin and to all their descendants in perpetuity. If, in 200 years time, half the country walks with an exaggerated limp, they need not pester the doctors for answers, as they will only have their ancestors to blame.

In these heated moments, I find myself marvelling at how ineffectual penalty points are. If we had cameras on every roundabout and fined everyone, say, €1,000 for every time they didn't indicate, think how much joy would be brought to people's lives. As well as the fine, drivers should be made to sit their test again or at least should be sent back to indicator school, where world-weary instructors can stress upon them the need for communication on today's roads.

Alternatively, the Japanese could be encouraged to develop cars that indicate automatically whenever they are turning at a junction. An irritating, disembodied voice, preferable in a Jade Goody accent, could demand of a driver which way they are turning at the oncoming roundabout and indicate accordingly. If the driver fails to respond, the question could be repeated ad nauseum in progressively severe tones of voice.

Almost as annoying as the drivers who can't be bothered indicating are the ones who indicate at the last moment, as a kind of afterthought. What good is that to anyone trying to anticipate a break in the traffic? Indicating once you have actually turned the corner serves no purpose whatsoever and you might as well not bother.

Dr. Wilhelm Grossenfahrter, from the European Institute of Road Etiquette in Leipzig, believes that a pathological failure to indicate is genetic rather than behavioural. "We have isolated the gene that is responsible for indicating and preliminary tests show that this gene is not present in almost 131% of non-indicators," he claims. "It is also true to say that people who have this gene twice are more likely to operate their hazard lights by accident."

The Crown Prince Franz Josef was a notorious non-indicator and it has been claimed that his blasé attitude to roundabouts was a major cause of Serb dissatisfaction with the Austrian Empire, particularly around the Sarajevo area. Field Marshall Goering, too, used to enrage Hitler by indicating wrongly when turning into Unter den Linden in Berlin. "Indicate right until the turn before the one you want and then indicate left!" Hitler would scream, sweeping the Corgi cars off the table in his bunker in a fit of pique. On these occasions, Martin Bormann would be prevailed upon to demonstrate and he would pretend to drive around the table making ticking noises until the Field Marshall said he understood, which often took several hours.

The great roundabout crisis of 1963 nearly led the world into nuclear war. Kruschev was adamant that there was no need to indicate when travelling straight ahead at a roundabout but Kennedy stood firm. "Ich bin ein Indicator," he told a million cheering Volkswagen enthusiasts at a rally in Memphis, though not many of them spoke German. Kruschev responded by threatening to pull the indicators out of every Lada in Eastern Europe but backed down when he realised the amount of time it would take him.

Of course the most famous non-indicator of the modern era was Nelson Mandela, who was sentenced to life imprisonment on Robben Island for the crime of "failing to indicate at a road junction," which was a comparatively lenient sentence for black offenders under the Apartheid regime of the time. Mandela's claim that he was "walking" at the time was laughed out of court, although his incarceration led to worldwide calls for reform of the rules of the road in South Africa.

"If everybody indicated correctly on roundabouts, the world would be a happier place," sang Bob Dylan at Woodstock and his melancholy lyrics ring as true today as they did then. In Australia, they have experimented with road signs saying "Have you indicated yet, you lousy wombat?" on the approaches to major junctions and in Italy, a major advertising campaign called "Si, si, indicatore, signore" featured a Genoese model who stripped down to her bikini bottoms to get the

message home. George Bush has recently said that he is in favour of bombing countries that don't share the American ideals of free speech, democracy and indicating, while Condoleezza Rice nodded sagely in the background muttering "God bless America."
I have a dream – yea verily I have a dream – that one day all the people of the world will unite in their approach to communication on the highways of this world and Bob Dylan's seemingly utopian view of life on earth will in fact become a reality.
In the meantime, I will continue to spit curses at offenders.

A very kind gentleman tactfully pointed out in the following edition of the paper, that if I move my hand upwards, I would in fact be indicating right not left. Mea culpa!

(June 2007)

Chickens and counting them – a ramble

We are often told not to count our chickens before they have hatched. The phrase is normally expressed as a command, rather than a piece of homespun advice, which brings up the whole area of civil liberties. If I insist on counting my pre-hatched chickens, I should be allowed to do so without censure. Tut-tutting might be permitted and disapproval for my actions in jumping the gun might well be expressed, but the choice ultimately is mine. My grandfather did not die on the battlefields of Monte Cassino so that I should only be allowed to count my chickens when the powers that be say so. (Actually, he didn't die on the battlefields on Monte Cassino at all, but hid in the wardrobe every time the military police called around to the house, but you get the point.) Personally, though, it is very rare that I have actually counted chickens before they have hatched. I have of course counted eggs and I suppose that there is little I can do if my mind translates the unbroken shells into a picture of fluffy yellow chickens running around a farmyard.
Counting eggs is of course perfectly okay according to the philosophers and indeed it is a necessity for those people who make a career out of

packing the eggs into egg boxes. Pack in too few and the customer will be most disgruntled when he/she gets them home. Pack in too many and the lid won't close, no matter how much you sit on it.

Not that I have had much opportunity for counting chickens since we moved to Dublin 15. We are hardly overrun with the little yellow flea-ridden feathery bundles. I have counted them occasionally in the supermarket when there have been very few and I intend registering a complaint to the meat manager. Of course these chickens are well-hatched, though judging by the state of them, they would have been better off remaining where they were.

Whereas the instruction not to count chickens while they are still in the shell might be sound advice to human beings, one would think that the Mother Chicken (or is it a Hen?) might be forgiven for doing a bit of forward planning. A mother who knows she is going to produce triplets might have to adjust some of her thinking on sleeping arrangements, equipment, bottles and asking the mother-in-law for help and I imagine that the Mother Hen (or is it a Chicken?) would be inclined to be the same. "I have six eggs," she would say to herself, "and, if they all hatch, I will have six chicks." (It is this sort of logic that makes you wonder why hens (or chickens) aren't higher up the evolutionary pecking order.) "Therefore" – she would continue – "I will need to plan for feeding, rearing and educating six chicks after hatching." It is only natural and one cannot really castigate a mother for dreaming.

The proverb is quite unclear as to whether it is acceptable to count chickens whilst hatching is actually in progress. In certain cases, this is instinctive. It is hard to say to yourself "Ah – a certain number are in the process of breaking out of their shells while a certain number have yet to do so." There is also the very salient point first broached by Wittgenstein in his groundbreaking book "The psychology of farmyard animals" that a chicken's egg that is actually hatching should not contain anything other than a chicken. "It is unlikely to contain a long-eared bat," he chortled with that wicked Teutonic humour of his.

Of course it is absolutely imperative that you start counting the chickens after they have hatched (If you are a member of the younger generation, you may bring a calculator as there could be anything up to ten of them) If you fail to count them, one might slip under the bit of wire at the bottom of the yard and you mightn't even notice. The poor little chick would then be at the mercy of any amount of predators that like to prey on uncounted chickens like hyenas, pterodactyls, certain species of whales etc

Again, if a chicken wanders off and you move house suddenly, the little beastie is unlikely to find its way to your new home. We have all heard heartwarming stories about families who throw a stick for the family dog to fetch and then move to Ulan Bator, only to find the poor wretch whimpering on the doorstep of their yurt six months later. Chicks do not have the same sort of homing instinct as dogs, although they would be unlikely to be fooled by the fetch-the-stick trick in the first place. Only by the scientific approach of "counting them" can you be assured that they are all packed safely in the suitcase for the long journey.

In days of yore, the ancient Celts used to employ chicken-counters who would be responsible for the inventory of chickens within the tribe. The chicken-counter was much exalted though not as much as the Druid, who seemed to get more perks. A little-known story from the Four Annals describes how Niall (of the Nine Sausages fame) once caught his chicken-counter hovering over a nest of eggs with a notebook and pencil in hand and had him hung, drawn and quartered until he said sorry.

During the Great Famine, the role of the chicken-counter all but disappeared in rural Ireland as most birds ended up on the dining room table an hour after emerging from the shell. Many turned their attention to root vegetables, though the job satisfaction was not as great. "Turnips," one demoralised counter recounted in his memoirs, "do not run around. They are too easy to count." With the advent of the steam engine, many farmers found they had time to learn the rudiments of counting themselves, which completely demystified the chicken counting art. Many counters were forced to emigrate or consider a career change, although some still eked out a living until the end of the nineteenth century.

I am approaching fifty years old and have never been involved in a traumatic incident to do with eggs or indeed chickens, though a fried egg once slipped out of a sandwich into my lap while I was waiting to be called for an interview. This blissful existence I attribute to having followed the above maxim assiduously for most of my life and I would urge all Dublin 15 residents to do the same. Counting chickens and eggs simply do not mix and those people seeking spiritual nirvana are advised to eschew all temptation to do so.

(July 2007)

A watery end

In a fit of environmental zeal last October, I splashed out on a water butt. I had been only too aware of the size of my environmental footprint (my wife had pointed it out etched on one of the tiles near the back door,) so I decided to reduce, reuse and regurgitate, or whatever the saying is. So, when I saw an advertisement for a water butt in my local free top quality newspaper, I felt the time had come to start protecting the planet for my children, neither of whom sees anything wrong in spending 30 minutes at a time in the shower.

To cut a long story short, Fingal County Council delivered the large green monstrosity promptly and it remained standing outside my back door for seven months while I contemplated assembling it.

Not that there should have been much to assemble – the blurb had said there was nothing to it but even so I knew things were never going to go smoothly. I'm not a DIY person. Flat packs can take me months to assemble. I hang wallpaper and come down the next morning to find it on the floor. Towel rails and toilet roll holders fall off the walls after three days.

Eventually, after much procrastination on my part and irritation on my wife's, I took a deep breath and ventured forth. "I may be gone for some time," I said as I closed the door like a latter day Captain Oates. Actually I wasn't gone very long at all. I came back in with the instructions. "Step one," I read aloud to my wife. "Get a hacksaw and remove eight inches of your drainpipe about four feet from the ground."

"That's an end of that then," said my wife, who is well aware of my deficiencies in anything practical. "You start cutting the drainpipe and

the whole gable end is liable to come tumbling down."
Call me stupid – and many people do – but I had never actually realised that you were supposed to connect the water butt up to your downpipe. I thought you just left it outside and you attached a tap and that was it. Notwithstanding my uselessness at sawing, we simply didn't have the room down our very narrow side path to fit a butt without blocking in the wheelie bins.
"Okay, Plan B," I said. "We just leave it outside the back door with the lid off and let it fill with rain water.
"If you think I'm going to spend my day staring at your butt outside the back door, you have another think coming," replied my wife. "If we have visitors, all they will see is your butt. Think about it for a second."
I thought about it for a second. "How about if I move my butt down by the shed?" I asked. "That way we can collect rainwater that rolls off the shed roof."
"Yes, get your butt down to the end of the garden," she replied and the finality in her voice left me in no doubt that there was no room for compromise.
The water butt had an inside part, like a huge plastic jelly mould, which I couldn't really figure out what it was for. It had another piece to replace the eight inches of drainpipe (ho, hum) and a hose to connect butt and pipe, now also obsolete. It also had a tap which I dexterously fitted in to the only place possible – about an inch from the ground.
I removed the jelly mould and other bits and hauled my butt down to the shed, placing it strategically beneath the sloping roof. Then with great manual dexterity, that surprised even myself, I affixed the tap. Brilliant, I thought, standing back and admiring my handiwork.
Of course I soon spotted the flaw. If the tap was an inch from the bottom of the butt, how could you get a bucket or watering can under it, when you needed to water the garden?
Like Winnie the Pooh and the Honey Pot, I wrestled with this problem, scratching my chin and biting my bottom lip to show how seriously I was taking this. Then, just to be different, I scratched my bottom lip and bit my chin. This seemed to work, for the light bulb appeared over my head almost immediately.
I disappeared into the shed and re-emerged with one of the patio chairs

bought in Tommy's last September when they were selling them off. I placed the chair against the shed and then sat my butt into it. It nestled there snugly and the tap was now a good eighteen inches off the ground. Pure genius, I thought to myself and dislocated my shoulder trying to pat myself on the back.

As you are only too well aware, this year's summer has been a trifle moist. Consequentially, my butt filled up very quickly, aided by the water collecting in the huge jelly mould which I also left by the shed and which I emptied regularly. Even my wife had to admit that for once I'd had a very good idea and that my contribution to the environment when/if the dry spell came would be immense.

Then, about a fortnight ago, in one of those rare relatively dry days that my wife and I managed to get out to survey the wreckage of our garden, I checked the butt to see how it was coming along. To my surprise, it was practically up to the top lip. "Just about full," I said and carefully poured the contents of the huge jelly mould in on top. Perfect! I placed the lid on top to stop any water evaporating and forming more rain clouds and walked back up the garden.

The next sequence of events happened in a split second but, replaying it in my mind, it all seemed to happen in slow-motion. I heard a loud crack and turned. My wife, duelling a rampant pyrracantha with a pair of shears, screamed. The patio chair buckled as the leg snapped off under the weight and the water butt went crashing to earth, spilling the entire 200 litres of rainwater over a startled viburnum.

"You idiot!" was all my wife could gasp noiselessly as two months of assiduous rainwater collecting went crashing to earth.(Actually there might have been a third word in there in between "you" and "idiot" but I an still too traumatised to recall.) I reached the water butt and pulled it upright but there was less than a teaspoonful left inside it. I picked up the plastic chair leg and idly wondered how I could have expected one plastic chair to bear the weight of 200 litres of water. With a sinking heart I noticed too that in the fall, a large split had appeared down three-quarters of the length of the giant container.

"That's it!" I said, turning away in disgust, already preparing myself for a lengthy stay in the kennel. "I've had enough of this environmental lark. You just end up breaking your butt for nothing."

(August 2007)
Chips, sausage and poached eggs

"We don't need no education," chanted Pink Floyd on their hit single "Brick in the Wall," and to be honest, as multi-millionaire rock stars, education is probably quite a long way down their list of requirements. The prospect of Roger Waters and Dave Gilmour sipping daiquiris on Martinique and discussing the latest list of evening classes at their local community centre requires too great a leap of imagination, even for Floyd heads.
However, for the rest of us, education has always been one way of maximising our options throughout the forty odd years of our working lives. The higher you ascend the educational ladder, the more jobs you are qualified to do. And the wider your choice of jobs, the more chance you have of actually enjoying your work.
Of course, the main charge levelled at education – usually by young people who aren't willing to put in the graft – is that it has no relevance to the world outside. And there is a large amount of truth in this. In the thirty years since I was last dismissed from class, I have had absolutely no call to write a letter to a penpal in Nantes, I have never even seen a slide-rule, let alone used one, I have never brought up the imagery in Milton's "Paradise Lost" in conversation and I have never had occasion to mix potassium permanganate with magnesium sulphide over a Bunsen burner.
Educationalists will naturally argue that it is not what you know that is important – it is the fact that you have been able to digest, understand and, in a pressure situation, regurgitate all the information force-fed you over a two year period that makes you a good prospective employee. If you have shown the moral character to be able to write an authoritative essay on anchovy fishing off Peru (from memory) then you surely have some of the qualities required for a management role in a multinational company, the argument goes.
Right at the heart of this non-relevant education argument is the subject of Irish. It's boring, say the kids. I never use it outside school. Sure, everybody speaks English anyway.

The obvious answer is that Irish isn't boring, just as Latin isn't boring. What may be boring is the way that it is taught and there seems to be a perception in schools that Irish is being taught in a boring way by boring teachers. However, teachers who attempt to liven things up a bit and who avoid the tedious repetition of declensions should hold the attention of class for longer. I would even go so far as to make the use of hand puppets in Irish mandatory for all teachers.

And if you ever go down to Spiddal and ask the postmistress in the Spar for a stamp for your postcard as gaelige, you will know the great feeling of satisfaction when she responds in kind with a smile.

However the one subject that young people are taught nowadays which was totally ignored in our day is CSPE. Both my children took CSPE in school, yet for the life of me I can never remember what the letters stand for – hence the chips, sausage and poached eggs.

To be honest, I would have loved to have had CSPE in school. I emerged from school totally ignorant of the ways of the world. I could spout Iago's "Reputation" speech to Othello but I had no idea about how a bank loan worked. I could calculate a hypotenuse with my eyes shut but I had no idea that councillors even existed, let alone what role they perform in society. And when I started work, I blindly accepted that my income tax was being deducted correctly because I knew no different.

While every member of our generation decries the appalling education standards of the current school population (just as the previous generation decried ours!) it is fair to say that the introduction of CSPE – along with Business Studies and Home Economics – is a major step forward in making schoolwork relevant. Children learn to explore – as opposed to being taught – topics like racism, immigration, trade unions, business trends, interview techniques and social welfare entitlements, which can only be a good thing. If your only exposure to immigration issues is clouded by a racist father or schoolfriends, chances are you will head in the same direction. If nothing else, at least the discussion of the issue shows that differing views exist.

What CSPE does, and what the education system in our day completely failed to do, is to prepare students to become active citizens who can participate in society in a meaningful way. Most of us are aware of our rights as citizens but not everybody is aware of the responsibilities that come with these rights. CSPE is instrumental in making children aware that life is not simply about being entitled to this and that.

In the reverse of the "Irish isn't boring, it's the teachers that are boring" argument, though, all the relevance in the world will not make children pay attention in class if CSPE is taught in a monotonal and unimaginative way. Droning on for an hour about Martin Luther King while Smudger and Notcher throw erasers at each other is not likely to be very productive. Though to be fair to schools, it is probably the one subject where teachers are encouraged to be unconventional, to use more teaching aids and to encourage class discussion and participation. Having said all that, the notion that schoolwork should only concentrate on subjects that have a relevance to the real world is equally ludicrous. As my father always used to say – well, occasionally used to say – the more you know, the more interesting a person you are. We are all familiar with the guy in the workplace who only talks about football. Now, I enjoy talking about football – particularly if Shelbourne have won at the weekend – but I am confident I could join in a conversation on other subjects if they arose. Football guy can't. Discuss share prices, the Holocaust, modern Irish poetry, golf, lunar eclipses or agriculture and he is struck dumb until the subject comes around to Robbie Fowler again. Ask him to balance his household budget and he'd probably reach for a pair of weighing scales. God help his poor wife.

(*Educational Supplement August 2007*)

The seven wonders of Dublin 15

There was a much-publicised survey recently to find the seven wonders of the modern world. Although many people treated it as an interesting piece of trivia, lobbying was feverish as governments eyed the billions of dollars in extra tourist revenue that could result from making the top seven.

In a similar way, the *Community Voice* also commissioned a survey to find the seven wonders of Dublin 15 in a bid to lure millions of foreign tourists to our neck of the woods and make us all rich. Sadly, the survey was not quite as extensive as had originally been envisaged, as both my wife and daughter merely raised their eyes to heaven and tutted when asked to contribute.

So, in no particular order, here is a list of my seven wonders of Dublin 15.

Possibly the most famous bridge in the whole world, the Clonsilla Bridge was constructed in 1500BC and was almost immediately declared too narrow to do the job. Nothing has altered much in the intervening 3,500 years. Today hordes of Japanese tourists pile out of coaches to take pictures of exasperated commuters taking their lives in their hands as they attempt to catch trains by squeezing in between the traffic and the bridge ramparts. This spectator sport has waned somewhat in recent months as extra trains have meant that the traffic is kept static for much of the time but the bridge is still deserving of being one of Dublin 15's premier tourist attraction.

It is said that the Quinn Direct building is the only insurance building in Dublin 15 that can be seen from the moon, though this has been very difficult to prove. By far and away the tallest building in the area, this colossal structure has been likened to the Empire State Building but only by very silly people. It has 97 storeys, though many of these are on the same level. But the main reason for its "wonder" status, is that when we are travelling along the bypass at night, I always say "Oh God, look at the queue!" and my wife is fooled every time.

Not too far from this magnificent structure is the "Games Workshop" unit by the yellow entrance in the Blanchardstown Shopping Centre. This choice might cause a few raised eyebrows and earlobes among adults as basically it is just an ordinary shop that happens to sell toy soldiers and warriors, just as Fields Jewellers sells diamonds and pearls and the Perfume Shop sells smelly water. However, this modest shop is perhaps unique in the western world in that not only are young people allowed inside without being spied on by suspicious security guards, but the assistants who work in the shop have a habit of treating them as adults and engaging in intelligent conversation with them!

My fourth choice as one of the wonders of Dublin 15 is the Urbus. Despite its name, this bus does not serve the ancient Mesopotamian city of Ur (much to the confusion of Blanchardstown's burgeoning Armenian population) but wends its merry way from Castleknock to Blanchardstown and onto the Airport and Swords. What makes it remarkable is that passengers travel in comfort and the buses are quite reliable. For those who have not enjoyed a journey on the Urbus, this may seem hard to believe in the context of the Greater Dublin Transportation System. In fact managers in Dublin Bus have been actively spreading rumours that the Urbus doesn't actually exist and is really only the commuter's version of Fiddlers Green or the Big Rock Candy Mountain.

No list of Dublin 15's wonders would be complete without the now legendary St. Mochta's telephone mast, a beautiful and aesthetic structure that is the pride and joy of the surrounding estate. It is said that St. Mochta struck the ground with his staff three times and the telephone mast rose out of the ground and convinced the dumbstruck villagers to become Christians. Sir Christopher Wren is thought to have modelled the nave of St. Paul's Cathedral on the mast and it has been reported that the dishes have picked up irregular radio signals from the vicinity of Betelgeuse that warrant further investigation by Jodrell Bank. However, rumour has it that mobile phone users nearby still have to go out into their back gardens to get a signal.

Another place that I would maintain merits a place on the must-see sights of the locality is the footbridge that crosses the M50 from Castleknock to the Royal Canal at the Twelfth Lock. Designed from an idea by Isambard Kingdom Brunel (namely, that a bridge should always span the distance between its two ends) this remarkable feat of engineering is one of the more unsung beauty spots of Dublin 15. There is nothing more relaxing than bringing one's deckchair onto the bridge on a Friday afternoon, sitting back and soaking in both the gentle hum of the traffic beneath and the fragrant fumes wafting slowly upwards. If there is any place closer to heaven on earth, it has yet to be discovered.

Finally and after much deliberation, I have plumped for the Snugborough Road intersection for my final selection. What a well-thought-out feat of civil engineering this is! There are five busy roads all converging on one spot which certainly gave a headache to traffic management. Would they use fly-overs, or filters? No, the ingenious solution was that each road should take it in turns to have a green light. Brilliance! Around Christmas, it has been known for the 39 bus to take an hour in crossing this intersection and the resulting log jam has certainly cut down on the risk of accidents.

Of course I realise that my choice is purely arbitrary and my mind cringes with embarrassment as I take stock of all the eclectic sights and structures that have failed to make it to the top seven. The Fingal County Offices in Blanchardstown with their shimmering translucence – a fine house of residence for those dedicated people who work tirelessly on our behalf; the Coolmine Recycling Centre, currently being restored, with its architecturally playful use of colour and shape; Rugged Lane which sweeps down from Porterstown to the Strawberry Beds and was obviously designed by the same pygmy roadsmiths that designed Clonsilla Bridge; the Georgian sweep of the Crescent Shopping Centre in Mulhuddart; the deceptively simplistic and artisanal prefabricated unit that houses Castaheany Educate Together National School. The list is endless and it certainly goes to show what a rich heritage we have in Dublin 15.

All that I can say is that if you have any further suggestions for sites deserving of inclusion, then by all means jot them down on a postcard and send them in. The list is due for revision in two thousand years time. (Please note – you may vote as many times as you like.)

(August 2007)

Love at the Bookshop

A few months ago, one of the very interesting morning programmes on RTE One radio had a competition to write a Mills and Boon story. The prize was the chance to meet a Mills and Boon editor who would more than likely tell you that your stuff was rubbish.

Notwithstanding this, I decided to turn my not very considerable talents to the art of writing romantic fiction and submitted the following piece, which I am sure will reduce most women to quivering wrecks. Get your hankies out, girls, you're going to need them.

There'd been a special offer on the spaghetti hoops in Tesco and as Brad exited the store he couldn't help thinking that the plastic bag he'd bought to carry the tin had wiped out the money he had saved in the first place. "Drat!" he said – or words to that effect – causing an elderly woman to go careering into the line of trolleys, which in turn rolled into the car park, making an oil tanker jack-knife and overturn.

Brad ignored the screams and the 200 foot plume of smoke that rose into the stratosphere like a giant mushroom cloud and marched off along the pedestrian pathway. "If Kylie had been here, she'd have warned me of that," he thought, swinging the bag idly and accidentally shattering the plate glass of Boots window. "She always knew about bargains."

He passed Fothergill's. "Purveyors of fine food," he read absent-mindedly, as he headed on towards Ladbroke's (Purveyors of Fine Betting Slips) and Roselawn Hardware (Purveyors of Fine Bathroom Tap Washers.)

As he passed the Roselawn Bookshop, he glanced inside and stopped. Sure it looked like the same bookstore but it was under new management "for the summer months only." Same as Kylie, he thought. Under new management.

Soon the brightly coloured shelves festooned with a vast array of novellas, poetry anthologies and paperbacks would be a gloomy shell. Dust would cover the fixtures and the floor and grinning spiders would abseil delightedly from the light bulb.

This was where he had first set eyes on Kylie, he remembered. They had both reached for the same Dr. Seuss Cat in the Hat book and their eyes had met. After a short tussle, she had wrestled the book from his grasp and ran to the counter to pay. He had executed a full-length rugby tackle on her and the book flew out of her grasp. Turning round she clicked a flick-knife and held the blade at his throat and he knew in that instant that he loved her.

Her eyes were like lucent rockpools, even as far as the tiny shrimps darting here and there among the seaweed. Her cheeks were ruby red like the Manchester United home jersey from the late nineties and her full pouting lips seemed to quiver like a blancmange on a rollercoaster. As they locked in a passionate embrace, he reached down and grabbed

the book and placed it on the counter with a €5 note.
All had gone well at first. He had moved into her tiny basement flat on the Clonsilla Road and had shared her bed for three months until she found out. He used to wave her goodbye as she went out to work in the evenings, selling all-night home insurance along the Quays. Idly he used to wonder why she would return home in the early hours with her hair dishevelled and her clothing in disarray. "All part of the home insurance business, sweetie," she would say, placing her fat finger on his lips and standing on his foot.
They used to go for walks in the park and he cut their initials in the bark of a tree until the knife slipped and he lacerated her cheek. Hand in hand, they would skip through the long grass and deer excrement while up above the birds twittered in the trees annoyingly. Nothing it seemed could ever go wrong with their love. It was a match made in heaven.
It was when he came home one afternoon and found her naked beneath the local rugby team that he began to suspect something was wrong. He had believed her explanation that they were simply "looking for a shinpad" but he noticed how she crossed her fingers as she said it. Occasionally he would wake up in the night and think there was a third person in the bed until a big gruff voice assured him he was only dreaming.
Matters came to a head when he started receiving letters addressed to "Mr and Mrs Cohen." She denied it at first, vehemently and passionately, but after five seconds, she admitted that yes, she was indeed Mr. and Mrs. Cohen.
It was like a bomb had hit him and in fact a piece of shrapnel did penetrate his right buttock. It was not the fact that she was an elderly Jewish couple – it was the fact that she had lied to him. This was what hurt him the most, apart from the shrapnel. He had always been open and honest with her about everything, except maybe the incident with the liquorice allsorts.
That was three months ago and he still found her smiling face haunting his every waking moment. Even now, as he gazed into the plate glass window of the bookshop, he fancied he saw her beautiful reflection, all gappy and gummy with a Woodbine hanging out of the corner of her

mouth. In a sudden fit of rage, he drew back his fist and slammed it through the glass. "Get away from me!" he yelled as the blood spurted triumphantly from his main artery.
"Why?" said a voice behind him and he swung around to find himself staring into that familiar face with its four inch scar down the side of her nose.
For a minute, neither of them spoke, though Brad involuntarily broke into a few bars of "Dancing on the Ceiling" by Lionel Richie. Then they rushed into each others arms in a hot passionate embrace that had all the tramps in the neighbourhood coming around to warm their hands.
"Oh Brad," she whispered, as she came up for air. "Let us never part again. Let us be always as one, entwined together in the great embrace of love."
"Oh, Mr. and Mrs. Cohen," he managed to reply weakly. As the last pint of his blood splashed gaily onto the window of the boutique next door, he vaguely wondered if a second can of spaghetti hoops would have made the trip to Tesco's worthwhile.
Well I guarantee there isn't a dry eye, or indeed a dry pair of trousers in the house after that. The only problem is that the competition finished three months ago and I still haven't heard anything from the judging panel. Still there's plenty of time yet. I expect the contract's in the post.

(*August 2007*)

One hundred not out

The other day, an A4 sheet of paper bearing what can only be described as a royal crest was hurriedly slid beneath the door of the *Community Voice* offices. As the sound of yelping corgis retreated down the street, my editor picked up the paper and read it out loud.
"My husband and I," he read, "are delighted to offer congratulations on the occasion of one's hundredth birthday / issue / international cap (please delete as necessary) Signed E.R."
Of course it is unlikely that we will ever discover the identity of the

semi-anonymous well-wisher but her sentiments are typical of the thousands of letters and cards that have been pouring in from around the world on the occasion of the 100th issue of *Community Voice*. There is something magical about the number 100 that sparks the imagination. It is like a long thin rasher with two fried eggs by the side of it. It is often referred to as a round number, though not as round as 800, which is a veritable feast of circular shapes.

For many, the newspaper is like a favourite jacket, though without the rolled up tissue and sticky sweet in the inside pocket. Together with Phoenix FM, it provides the only real source of information about what is happening in the local community and, in an age when a sense of community often comes a long way down the list of people's priorities, this service cannot be underestimated.

Of course, it has other uses too. It is great for spreading out on the kitchen floor when the wife cuts your hair because, unlike the Northside People, it doesn't have any staples in it. It is also great for swatting flies and wasps and even otters when they become too inquisitive and one enterprising sculptress in Porterstown takes multiple issues from her supermarket every fortnight because "they make great papier mâché" as she later told the jury.

But it is for its well-written local news coverage that the paper is held in high esteem throughout the western world, as just a sample of the well-wishing letters show.

"I always read the *Community Voice* from cover to cover, and sometimes the inside bits too," writes a world-famous trapeze artist from Vaduz.

"It is full of good reading, especially the articles," says a V. Putin from Moscow.

"It has everything a good newspaper should have – pages and writing and pictures and things," applauds R. Murdoch from Australia.

"It is great for spreading on the kitchen floor when my wife is cutting my hair," writes a ghost-writer for a D. Beckham from Los Angeles.

Believe it or not, the *Community Voice* is not the first newspaper to reach one hundred issues but it is the first one to do so without straying outside of its Dublin 15 catchment area. The Times of London may be in its 3,000th year but events in Ongar and Littlepace often do not make it into the news section, let alone the front page. Pravda, too, occasionally eschews bringing its readers up to date information on Draíocht in favour of armed conflicts, nuclear disarmament and global warming, much to the dismay of the cultural Muscovite population. Of course we have all passed a lot of water under Clonsilla Bridge since "*The Voice*," (as it is affectionately known to those who know it and view it with affection) first hit the streets many many years ago. In those days, Blanchardstown consisted of a couple of farm dwellings and several outhouses, overwritten with "Here be dragons" on the Ordnance Survey maps of the time. Horse-drawn barges traversed the territory by way of the Royal Canal on their way to exotic and far-fabled destinations like Mullingar and Longford. The Blanchardstown Centre, yet to be built, was a thick impenetrable forest inhabited by wild boar and wolves and houses made out of gingerbread.

Into this wilderness strode a man with a typewriter in one hand and a copy of Roget's Thesaurus in the other. Fergus Lynch was that man's name, though many people simply called him Fergus, especially members of his own family. He was determined to put Dublin 15 on the map and he did so in a size 11 Tahoma font.

He had all the attributes of a great editor – he championed the poor and downtrodden; he fought corruption wherever it reared its evil head; he refused to reproduce press releases verbatim to the public; and most importantly, boy, could he spell! Even words like "minuscule," "marmalade" and "Tyrrelstown" wouldn't faze him. "Show me a word I can't spell," he used to bark at the copy boy, "and I bet you it's Polish. Or maybe Welsh."

He has been courted by the rich and famous though he refuses to let power turn his head. "That's what neck muscles are for," he tells puzzled undergraduates. Many an aspiring and indeed established politician has felt the venom of his scathing pen if they try to hoodwink him with bluff and bluster. He has sources in every corner of Dublin 15, even the circular bits, and it is well known that he has a pair of eyes and ears in the James Connolly Memorial Hospital, which are often used for medical research.

Throughout these hundred issues, he has consistently championed the cause of the poor, especially those without much money. "The pen is mightier than the sword," he is often heard to say, though friends admit that he is reluctant to put it to the test. "It is easier for a rich camel to enter the kingdom of heaven, than for the eye of a needle to," is another of his cryptic sayings.

The *Community Voice* has become a beacon of hope for many of the oppressed and underprivileged in the world today. As they lie in their beds in Charnwood and Diswellstown, they feel comforted by the fact that there is a newspaper out there that gives them a say, gives them a voice. Let us raise a glass, preferably containing some kind of drinkable liquid, and pray that the *Community Voice* may continue fighting tyranny as well as bringing heartwarming good news stories to Dublin 15 for another hundred issues.

(September 2007)

Giving blood

Probably my biggest regret in life, apart from the incident with the Swedish air-hostess and the apricot jam, is that I never gave blood sooner.

Of course, such was my lifestyle in the early years of my so-called adulthood that anyone benefitting from one of my donations would have felt more than pleasantly merry and might well have been stopped by the Gardaí as they drove home from the hospital. But once the last vestiges of adolescence had fallen off my shoulders and I became boring and flatulatory, there really was no good reason why I shouldn't have started giving blood.

Of course, I told myself I was too busy, though I could always make time to go and see Shelbourne. I had no car and Pelican House was on the south side but so was Harold's Cross, where Shels played at the time. Years of wasted opportunities, I suppose, looking back.

It was only when we moved out to Dublin 15 that I started giving blood. The clinics were local and the venues were many and varied. I have donated blood in Coolmine Community School, St. Peters in Dunboyne, Castleknock Community College, Hartstown Community

School and Blanchardstown IT, a veritable cornucopia of educational establishments and have admired everything from class projects on Peru, (with the emphasis on anchovy fishing,) to Confirmation portraits while waiting for my turn to lie down on the bed.

The thing that depresses me a little bit though are the questions. Have you ever had typhoid fever? Have you ever fondled a monkey from South America? Have you ever snorted cocaine? Have you ever snorted a typhoid monkey or fondled South American cocaine? It really makes me wonder what sort of exotic lifestyles some people have and puts it up to me how dull my life has been.

But that feeling disappears when you get chatting to the nurses. Blood nurses are the only category of people that are never in bad form. Even hospital nurses have their grumpy moments and nuns have been known to give the odd lash of the tongue when riled but the blood nurses are invariably, almost unnaturally, pleasant. I suspect it's because they do a lot of monkey fondling in their spare time and therefore feel their lives are so enriched.

The first time I gave blood, I actually had a little trouble. I lay down on the bed and the blood nurse inserted the needle. No problems. But when she opened the valves, the red liquid – I was quite pleased to see it was indeed red – merely trickled despondently into the waiting container, as though loathe to leave the safe confines of my body. "Go on, get out into the world, meet new people," I urged it but to no avail. Was my blood donating career over as soon as it started?

"We'll try the other arm," said the blood nurse and lo and behold, there gushed forth a veritable waterfall of crimson liquid. After all this time, this is a phenomenon that I have never come to grips with. Surely your blood is coursing through your veins constantly, starting at your heart and performing a complete loop around your body before being reenergised back in your heart? At least, that's what I remember from my biology classes apart from incubating frog spawn and the explicit diagrams on page 73. Your blood doesn't say "No, I don't think I'll bother with the left arm – too much of a detour and the traffic can be dreadful." The blood nurse's explanation of "It happens," doesn't quite satisfy the scientific probing of my mind but there you have it. This is probably what political commentators call 'The Arms Imbalance.'

Apparently, for I have no way of confirming it, I have Blood Type O. At first I was a little disappointed in this, having hoped for an exotic blood group that only a dozen people in the world have, thereby being put on a worldwide data base and called into action to fly to Venezuela at a moment's notice.

However, it was patiently pointed out to me that it was far more useful to society that I had the most common blood group, as there were potentially so many more people that I could help. And also if I urgently required a transfusion myself, they wouldn't need to disturb Jimenez in Caracas on my behalf.

The thing about giving blood though is the tremendous amount of well-being it brings you. I don't know who said that there is no such thing as a truly unselfish act (possibly Lionel Ritchie) but the psychological benefits of giving blood must rank almost as high as the physical effects of receiving it. You've given up an evening of slouching in front of the telly and made a huge difference to someone's life – maybe even saved their life. And all because you've made the huge sacrifice of sitting in a classroom and lying on a bed.

On about my ninth or tenth visit, I was lying on my bed in Blanchardstown IT filling my bottle (intravenously I should add) when I was approached by a blood nurse in the manner of a raincoated man recruiting for the CIA.

"Psst!" she hissed, through gritted teeth. "You ever thought of giving platelets?"

I assured her that, far from the action being at the forefront of my mind, I had no idea of what a platelet was, no idea of what one looked like and no idea that I had any to give, not having progressed much further than page 73 of my biology book.

A quick biology lesson ensued, wherein it was pointed out that platelets are an essential component of blood, along with red blood cells and white blood cells and lord knows what else. They are particularly of benefit for leukaemia patients and premature babies and, as I had a particularly high concentration of them lazily breast-stroking around my veins, I considered it somewhat selfish of me to hang on to them, when it was a matter of life and death to other people.

So now every month, I go to St. James' Hospital and spend a very

comfortable 45 minutes to an hour attached to a centrifuge, while I try and make as many words as I can from the nine letter word square in the Independent. Being strapped to a machine sounds dodgy but in reality it is extremely relaxing. You lie on a bed and can watch telly or a DVD – Quentin Tarantino movies I find are particularly apt – or simply watch the Luas glide past outside the window. Occasionally you might get a bit of tingling on your lips but that is all.
The other big thing – though possibly not such a big thing for people less egocentric than myself! – is that you get two points for every platelet donation and, as you can donate every 28 days as opposed to 90 days for blood, your tally mounts up really quickly. Together with our partners, we were all brought out for a lovely meal and presentation night in the Burlington Hotel, when we reached 50, and I am already licking my lips as my 100th donation approaches.
So perhaps monkey fondling does have a down side.

(October 2007)

The book of loud lamentations

And lo, it came to pass in the fifth month of the third reign of King Bertie that a great darkness fell upon the land of Blan-chards-town. And a plague of crane fly descended upon the people and it got into their houses and it covered their asses and their oxen and their kith and kin and the people were sore afraid.
And they ran out into the street and they rent their teeth and gnashed their garments and they cried out, Lord, why hast Thou set this plague of daddylonglegs upon us?
But the Lord remained behind a cloud giggling and made no answer.
And the spider who lived in the window frame cast out his net upon the left side and he cast out his net upon the right side and soon his net was heaving with the weight of crane fly and the spider gulped.
And the sky drew dark and more and more daddylonglegs descended upon the land. And the children of Blan-chards-town had great fun removing their legs on the one side so they ran around in circles. And

some children removed the legs from one daddylonglegs and stuck them onto another daddylonglegs to make the second daddylonglegs go faster.
And the Lord grew red in the face trying to suppress his laughter.
And the sun went down on the first day.
And then the great prophet Va-rad-kar spoke unto the people.
I am a doctor, he sayeth. Let me through.
This plague is all the fault of King Bertie. In his court is great wickedness and sloth and the Lord is punishing us for following the path King Bertie has shown us. For surely the jackass may lead the hyena into the wilderness and his tongue will cleave to the roof of his mouth and he may lose one tenth of his body fluid but the lamb will not lay down with the lion unless it is a very foolish lamb.
I call on the people now to give thanks and praise to the Lord and to call upon the great prophet Enda to lead you out of the darkness and banish this plague of daddylonglegs for ever. For though I am a great and powerful prophet I am not worthy even to tie the sandal of the great prophet Enda who lives in the land of Ma-yo.
But the people paid no heed to the great prophet Va-rad-kar and passed by on the other side. And the sun went down on the second day.
And the people called instead upon the wise men of the Sanhedrin who lived in a magnificent palace in the centre of Blan-chards-town where people came from all over the county to worship and pay homage. And the wise man in charge of the administration department sayeth that it was not his issue for the daddylonglegs were in the houses of the people and he told the people that it was a housing issue and the wise man in charge of the housing department sayeth that it was a matter for public lighting as the place was dark with the plague of daddylonglegs and the wise man in charge of public lighting sayeth to the people that they must contact the environment department as this kind of problem layeth under their domain and the wise man in charge of the environment department put the people onto environmental health and the wise man in charge of environmental health said he was away from his desk yea verily until the 18th but if you leave a message he would get back unto you. Yea verily.
And the sun went down on the third day and the people went to bed

with daddylonglegs skimming over their faces and they woke on the morning of the fourth day to find their houses crawling with these insects and they had taken over the sitting room and the remote control and the people could not watch Strictly Coming Dancing for the daddylonglegs kept flicking onto David Attenborough.
And then the great prophet Hig-gins who had been banished unto the wilderness rode back into Blan-chards-town upon his ass and the people lined the streets and sang hosannas and laid palm leaves beneath his feet or used dandelion leaves when palm leaves could not be found. And Hig-gins addressed the people thus.
Good citizens of Blan-chards-town. This plague of daddylonglegs is the result of selfish and wicked ways. Thou hast followed the teachings of the property developer who sitteth down at the table of the politician and shares his wine. For as the lion attacks his prey the hyena will follow and the hyena may fill his basket a hundredfold from the table of the lion. Just as the ivy cannot live without the cedar, so the property developer cannot live without the politician.
I am urging you now to cut down this vine and hunt down this lion and rid this land of the scourge of daddylonglegs.
But the people looked mystified and walked over on the other side. And the sun went down on the fourth day.
And on the fifth day the people called upon the great Brian son of Brian to save them from the plague of daddylonglegs which had now taken over the public transport system and were driving the 39 into town during off-peak hours.
And Brian son of Brian told the people that he had made representation to the holy Green Party members within the sacred cabinet upon their behalf and that the holy Green Party members had promised to look into it and report back in due course.
And the people bowed down in thanks and gave praise to Brian son of Brian, saying, He is indeed a wise and holy man.
But still the daddylonglegs kept on appearing. And the sun went down on the evening of the fifth day.
And on the sixth day the daddylonglegs had assumed control of all the light industry and service industry in Blan-chards-town, yea even the shops in the Centre and all the bottles of insect repellent mysteriously

disappeared from the shelves in Atlantic Homecare. And all the plugs were removed from all the hoovers in the land and the sweeping brushes were hidden and the people blamed it on global warming and immigration and the EU and George Bush and the younger generation. And they packed the churches in great lamentation and wailing and called upon the Lord to deliver unto them salvation from the great pestilence that lay upon the land, though some secretly said the public transport sytem was now a big improvement on Dublin Bus. But the Lord was on a pilgrimage to Fatima and had forgotten to turn his out of office on.
And the sun went down on the evening of the sixth day.
And on the morning of the seventh day the people woke from their fitful slumber to find that all the daddylonglegs had disappeared, save for the few still caught in the nets of the spider on the window frame. And they were sore puzzled and scratcheth their heads and furroweth their brows and peepeth nervously behind curtains.
And the great prophet Va-rad-kar addressed the people and claimed the credit.
And the even greater prophet Enda addressed the people and claimed the credit.
And the wise men of the Sanhedrin addressed the people and claimed the credit.
And the banished prophet Hig-gins addressed the people and claimed the credit.
And Brian son of Brian addressed the people and claimed the credit.
And the priests and pharisees addressed the people and claimed the credit.
But the people cared not and there was much drinking and carousing and revelling and barbequeuing, yea, even past the setting of the sun.

(October 2007)

The stop and go man

A few weeks ago, that delightful company Eircom decided to spend a week or so digging a long narrow hole down one of the distributor roads in Littlepace and then filling it in again. Naturally the work entailed one man sitting in a JCB eating sandwiches, while another five sat around reading the Mirror and arguing over Mourinho.

However, sitting morosely at the head of the queue of the cars waiting for our turn to pass, I suddenly realised that it was a long, long time since I had actually seen a Stop and Go man. And, such was the length of the hole that was to be filled in, it doubled my delight when I spotted that there was actually a similarly-engaged youth at the far end and that the two, through a series of knowing looks and gestures, were working as a team to ensure neither queue grew too large.

Of course in days of yore (a large vegetable of the brassica family which has sadly fallen out of favour,) the Stop and Go man was ubiquitous, wielding his mighty sign wherever there was a blockage on the thoroughfare. Young Peter O'Loughlin, who "stopped the whole street with a wave of his hand" according to Percy French's "Mountains of Mourne," was obviously a Stop and Go man who chose to bring his talents across the water.

The profession was an honourable one, ranking just above zoologist and slightly below gigolo in Debrett's annual "List of Notable Professions," and it seemed as though the Irish had a special knack for it. While the English and the Germans frantically experimented with signs that read "Stop" on both sides and took copious notes on the ensuing gridlock, the Irish had long since perfected the system and were leading the way in freeing up the highways. The Japanese too tried to muscle in on the act, flooding the market with cheap signs which, though clearly displaying the words "Stop" and "Go," failed to differentiate between the two in terms of colour, both sides being a hideous shade of orange and today there is a large landfill site near Ibaraki which contains ten million of these returned prototypes. Even Marcel Proust, the notable French pastry chef, found his revolutionary new sign with "Allez" on both sides fraught with difficulties and it was only after several years of pranged Renaults that he discarded it in favour of the Irish version.

It seemed as though every town and village in the land had their own

Stop and Go man, just as they had a policeman, a postman and a florist. It was not an uncommon sight to see students of this great art practising out in the fields in all winds and weathers with bemused cattle, trying to perfect the roll of the hand that signalled, in the great AA quote of our times, that a contra flow was in operation.

Generally the first son inherited the family business, the second became a priest and the third went to the big seminary in Borris-in-Ossary (now the Whining Moon Chinese Restaurant) to study the art of Stop and Going. "My son, the Stop and Go man," was a phrase uttered casually by proud mothers who used to relate to small clusters of other excited women after mass, the latest exploits of their offspring. "Working down on the N7, hundred and fifty cars an hour," they would whisper, nodding sagely, while their audience listened in wonder.

The advent of that most hideous of Man's creations, the Temporary Traffic Light, signalled the end. In Britain, riots ensued at picket lines as the Stop and Go Union Leaders warned that its introduction would spell the end for this honourable profession but the Lady, and it seemed, the road diggers, were not for turning and these automated monstrosities were soon adorning the tarmac wherever a hole needed to be dug. Disillusioned Stop and Go men sat morosely in Job Centres, reminiscing with shepherds and executioners about the good old days, while despairing clerks tried to find modern uses for their skills. Their plight was beautifully summed up by Pete St.John in his sentimental ballad, "Bloody Traffic Lights:"

"And now I lie
Abed and cry
As 'lectric lights now glow
To indicate
If cars should wait
Or if it's safe to go."

Of course, the Temporary Traffic Light was a godsend to the Road Digging Contractor, who did not need to pay it wages nor arrange for it to have toilet breaks but for the harassed motorist, it has merely increased the frustration inherent in modern day driving. Waiting for ages as these yellow machines dictate that it is unsafe to proceed while nothing is coming the other way, does little for the blood pressure of the driver trying to get home in time for "Deal or No Deal" and it is little wonder that contractors have returned to work in the morning to find their little red-eyed gods adorning ditches and hedgerows.

Thus I was delighted to see the renaissance of this noble art in Littlepace and spent several minutes marvelling at the almost telepathic skill of the two operators as they rolled their signs around in harmony after the briefest inclination of their heads. In fact it was with great reluctance that the incessant and frustrated beeping of horns behind me forced me to move, though on leaving the scene of the roadworks, I immediately executed a 180 degree turn to experience this personalised service from the opposite direction.

And then, only last week, I was travelling down the Clonsilla Road to return a Lionel Ritchie album that I felt was not up to his impeccably high standards, when I came across another Stop and Go man. This time, as the roadworks were considerably shorter in length, he was working solo, his head constantly moving from side to side as though watching a tennis match, as he appraised the length of the queues in either direction. A small crowd had gathered on the opposite path and they applauded him every time he swivelled the sign around, though, like a true professional, he simply bowed and continued his watchful post.

One swallow, as they say, does not make a summer, and certainly a veritable flock of swallows didn't make any kind of summer in Ireland this year, but I couldn't help wondering if the sighting of these two separate Stop and Go operations heralds a shift in the tide of progress. Is the seemingly all-conquering reign of the automated machine coming to an end, with a return to manual labour? Will horses be reintroduced into the fields of Ireland while Massey Fergusons lie rusting in barns? Will comely maidens return to dancing at the crossroads? Will this column go back to being written in longhand with the numerous spelling mistakes being laboriously corrected with Tippex?

Er, probably not. But with the reintroduction of the Stop and Go man, there is a chink of light for the future of mankind. The next time you pass one of these artisans of vehicular logistics, I urge you to shout a few words of encouragement to him and maybe slip him a fiver for a pint.

(October 2007)

The curious case of the prison conversation

"You seem agitated, Watson," said Sherlock Holmes, as he battered an old violin into submission with a horse-hair bow. "Come and sit down, old friend, and tell me what is the matter."
I withdrew my head from the gas oven and flopped down heavily into one of the Georgian armchairs that adorned Holmes' Baker Street apartment. "I can hide nothing from you, Holmes," I stated wearily. "My mind has been puzzling over a conversation I heard some evenings ago and I must confess, its meaning has been driving me to distraction."
Holmes flung the wailing fiddle out of the window and began pacing up and down. Then he began pacing from side to side. "Tell me all about it," he exclaimed patiently. "I can't keep this pacing up forever."
"It was the other night," I began. "I happened to be taking my evening constitution by the walls of the prison, when suddenly a young girl started calling."
Holmes' ears pricked up at this. "A young girl?" he repeated. "How old? Seven or eight?"
"More like twenty, old chap," I replied. "She was evidently calling to someone inside the prison as there was nobody else around at the time."
"How very singular," Holmes ejaculated.
"How so, Holmes?"
"Well… in so far as it isn't plural," replied my friend impatiently. "But tell me, do you manage to remember anything of what she said?"
"Why certainly, Holmes," I answered. "I took the trouble of writing it down in my notebook just as you have advised me." Here I withdrew a vellum notebook from my breast pocket and began to read slowly.
"Michael," I read. "They have taken you away."
"Surely this Michael, being in prison, would be aware of this salient fact," snapped Holmes. "Did this girl seem simple?"
"Not at all Holmes."
"Then proceed. Did she say anything else?"

"She called out at the top of her voice that this Michael had stolen Trevellyan's corn so the young might see the Mourne," I answered after consulting my notebook.

"The young? The young what?"

"She didn't say, Holmes."

"Hmm," replied the detective, stroking his angled chin and pacing diagonally across the lightly furnished room. "So, by calling this out at the top of her voice, she was alerting the prison service to the fact that this Michael had indeed carried out this act of larceny?"

"It appears so, Holmes. May I continue?"

"Pray do."

"The next thing was, she bawled out that a prison ship was lying waiting on the kay," I continued doubtfully.

Holmes head snapped up. "On the kay?" he asked. "Are you sure you heard this conversation correctly? It wasn't a quay by any chance, for I happen to know that at this very minute a convict vessel is lying on the quay" – he stressed the word – "waiting to sail to Botany Bee."

"Well, okay, it may have been a quay," I conceded ruefully.

I was about to continue when the sound of feet came scurrying up the stairs and came to a halt outside of Holmes' apartment, to be followed by several sharp raps on the door.

"Who can that be Holmes?" I asked in bewilderment.

"A woman, aged in her mid forties. She has obviously served in India for a considerable time. She has a tattoo of Victor Hugo on her left ankle and has a fondness for Lionel Ritchie, though she prefers to keep this latter fact from the public's gaze."

As I gasped in astonishment, Holmes strode to the door and swung it open.

"Pizza," said a young boy. Holmes grunted and took the two boxes, flinging the Pepperoni at me in disgust.

"Anyway, Holmes," I continued tactfully. "This girl then proceeded to shout out that the fields of Athenry lie very low and that she and the prison inmate had evidently spent some time together watching – how did she put it? – "small free birds" flying there."

Holmes flicked the last of his peppers into the fireplace and ruminated this information. "So, she has an interest in the topographical contours of east Galway, yet her knowledge of ornithology is somewhat vague," he murmured. "Yet why should she be imparting this to the man inside the prison?"

"Maybe it's a code," I offered.

Holmes jumped up and smacked me smartly on the back, causing a bit of crust to go shooting across the room and land on the piano.

"You have it, old friend!" he announced smartly. He strode to the bookcase and pulled out an old volume called "Rugby players of Connaught." This he proceeded to open and flick through at great pace. "Tell me, Watson," he asked. "This young lady didn't happen to mention a sporting personality of yesteryear that she and the young man were intimately acquainted with?"

"Good Lord, Holmes," I gasped in wonderment. "Her very next words were "Our love was on the wing." How could you possibly know?"

Holmes read quickly from the journal. "Lionel Edgar Mentary. Rugby player of some note in the nineties. Played for Galwegians. Went into business with a young couple after they got the franchise for Merry Green Giant sweet corn for the West of Ireland. Currently under investigation by the fraud squad." He closed the book triumphantly. "L. E. Mentary, by dear Watson."

I doffed my cap to the great detective, despite the fact that I wasn't wearing one. "That's amazing, Holmes," I said at last. "But pray, who is Trevellyan?"

"Ah, poor Trevellyan," said my friend wistfully. "He was the loser in all of this. He had been selling tins of sweet corn around the towns and villages west of the Shannon for years, until these three reprobates tried to muscle in on his act. Poor man. When he woke up one morning to find his warehouse broken into and his total supply of sweet corn missing, he was so distraught that he got a blockage in his – what's the name of that canal that runs through your body?"

"Alimentary?" I ventured.

"Alimentary, my dear Watson. Come we have no time to lose. We must alert Inspector Backwall of the Yard that a consignment of sweet corn is currently being stored near the River Mourne ready to be dumped in Strangford Lough."

"But what about the code, old chap?"

"It's only a sniffle," replied my friend impatiently and ran out of the door.
(November 2007)
A Christmas altercation

If Blanchardstown City were the Rolls Royce of European Football, then Roy Neake was the engine. Or maybe the glove compartment. Suffice to say he was a vital cog in the machine that had purred to the European Cup Final the previous year, scoring the goal that had knocked out arch-rivals Sporting Fingal FC in the semi-finals.
They said Roy was the complete footballer, having all the attributes that a top class footballer needs, namely good vision, a full complement of legs and the ability to cram at least four clichés into every interview. However, like every tragic hero of history, he had one fault in his character that was liable to be his undoing. In his case, it was anger. With the other six deadly sins, he held no truck. He wasn't avaricious, although he had no idea what the word meant. Sloth he associated with a tree-hugging mammal from South America. Even lust never crossed his mind, which gave rise to the sarcastic nickname "Stud" amongst his team-mates.
But the red mist had always been his bugbear. He had missed the FAI Cup Final of 2019 when he decapitated an opponent for looking at him sideways. He had been suspended for one match by UEFA for taking a hatchet to a Romanian opponent who had been smirking at him. And even this season, a match against Tralee FC had to be abandoned when Roy kicked down a goalpost when a penalty decision didn't go for him.
It didn't help that the team had not been firing on all cylinders since their European exploits. Their form had slumped and manager Lee Sammy was not a happy bunny.
Not that Lee was the master of jollity at the best of times. He was a big, brooding Sligo man with a face that seemed to have been carved out of Ben Bulben itself and then gone to work on by a drunken builder with a Kango hammer.
They said the only time Lee was happy was at his recently purchased farm in Kildare. Despite his rural upbringing, he knew little about farming but had found a certain happiness whilst shearing his cows and

leaving his fields fallow.

That happiness was little in evidence after Blanchardstown City's home game against Shannonside Invincibles at the end of November. As the team trooped off dejectedly after a 2-0 defeat (Richie L, 47, and Neake, 89 (o.g)), Lee Sammy was already waiting for them in the dressing room.

"Ye bunch of useless pansies!" he yelled furiously, turning the key in the lock as the last mud-bespattered player trooped in. "Ye couldn't get stuck in to a bowl of porridge! I've seen more grit and determination at the local apathetic society!"

After these sympathetic words of welcome, he then went through the team individually, singling out each player for individual censure in a hairdryer of a rant that lasted ninety minutes.

"Safe Hands" Molloy, the keeper, was like Dracula – he was afraid of crosses. Gary Byrne, the right back, had as much timing as a broken Rolex. Gary O'Brien, the left back, should apply for a monthly ticket on the 39 bus, he was that much of a passenger. And so it went on. And on.

Observers said later that Roy was not particularly singled out for special blame, despite his thunderbolt back pass to the keeper from thirty yards in the last minute of the match. However, he did not escape the manager's ire either, with Lee accusing him of both greed and sloth, which left the midfielder scratching his head in puzzlement. His teammates looked on aghast, as they all knew that Roy's only sin was anger. Roy however did not react in his normal Tasmanian-Devil way to the insults. Slowly and calmly and still wearing his football kit, he walked over to the dressing room door, unlocked it and went out. A few people who noticed him climbing into his Porsche in the car park of the Lenihan Stadium (named after Dublin 15's most generous benefactor, Lenihan Stadium) described his face as "steely and determined" and his legs as "muddy."

Roy drove down the back roads to Leixlip and then on to the outskirts of Celbridge. He pulled in to Lee Sammy's farm, waved genially to Lee Sammy's wife who was watering the chickens, and climbed on to a tractor that was conveniently parked next to an outhouse. Slamming the tractor in gear, he performed a 180 degree handbrake turn and roared

forward to the nearest barn.
Lee Sammy's wife looked on in horror as the tractor ploughed through the gable-end wall of the barn, sending newly-sheared and shivering Jersey cows running for cover. The structure came crashing down, a mass of twisted aluminium, but the tractor didn't stop. It continued on its destructive odyssey, gathering hay bales and a rather sleepy-eyed Friesian before exiting the far end of the barn in similar fashion.
Then Roy calmly stepped down from the vehicle, surveyed the carnage with a satisfied grin, stepped back into his Porsche and drove off.
Of course, when the press got a hold of the story, news of Roy's retribution was spread across the world, with many papers making much of Lee Sammy's sarcastic jibe that Roy couldn't hit a barn door with a tractor. It seemed that Roy's days at City were not only numbered but lettered too and many fans were found disconsolately wandering around the Shopping Centre after dark bemoaning the impending transfer of their star player.
Lee Sammy however knew which side his bread was buttered on as he had once worked in O'Brien's sandwich emporium. Though furious about the destruction of his barn, he told the Board that he would not insist on Roy's transfer. If some sort of agreement, some sort of compensation, could be reached, Roy could remain at City.
The solicitors and agents got to work but it was a long, slow job, as they were working on an hourly wage. December came and with it the first cries of a disorientated cuckoo. Santa's elves grumbled constantly about their hours. The gridlock around Blanchardstown Centre grew steadily worse and two emaciated bodies were found in a Corolla on the Snugborough Road junction.
But still no news of a breakthrough in "Roy-gate" as the papers unimaginatively called it. City fans were glued to Blanch TV, hoping for breaking news but none came. They feared the worst and many had already called the Joe Duffy Show to voice their despair at the situation. It was the Saipan of their generation and divided whole communities.
But at last on Christmas morning itself, the news broke. Not, as it happened, through the usual media of television or radio, but by carol singers. A compromise had been reached and the club, in recognisance

of the day that was in it, sent out teams of woolly-scarved carol singers to the furthest reaches of Hansfield, Porterstown and Tyrrelstown to convey the good news to the citizens of Dublin 15.

Thus it was that many people awoke that bright and sunny morning to the sound of angelic voices proclaiming the good news outside their windows:

"One-sin Roy'll stay with City –
Stud'll owe Lee cattle-shed."

(December 2007)

Biscuitgate

A recent, if somewhat unreliable, poll of Dublin 15 residents threw up the rather startling fact that most people were less concerned by transport and education issues than the parlous state of the Rich Tea biscuit. In fact the recent "Prime Time" special on the subject, using actors in graphic reconstructions, only served to underline just how bad the situation has become.

Years ago, the odd one or two biscuits at the end of a packet were occasionally found to be broken. The old joke was that manufacturers should therefore leave the end one out. No, not very funny but neither were a lot of comedians back then.

A much better joke is - who sang lead vocals on "You're once, twice, three times a biscuit?" Lionel Rich Tea.

To get back to the main point of this mini rant, however, for the past year or so, it is quite rare to get even one unbroken biscuit in a packet, as most Rich Tea aficionados will attest. In fact the common practice has become to end up with 600 pieces all the size of an old sixpence – little bigger than crumbs.

There is of course a finger Rich Tea biscuit but these are rarer and don't have quite such a malty taste. For the purposes of this discussion the Rich Tea is circular, designed to fit precisely into the average mug, unlike the much sweeter digestive which you can only dip an end in before turning it round to fit in the mug.

The Rich Tea has always been my favourite biscuit. Of course, there are others like Hobnobs and Jaffa Cakes which are much tastier but they are more expensive and we're only allowed to have them on special occasions like Christmas and St. Swithin's Day. The RT, as it is affectionately known, is only 31c in Dunnes for 300g – by far the best value of all the appetising bickies in that aisle.

Naturally we buy others from time to time. Ginger nuts are great for dunking and you can only eat about two or three at a time. Bourbons and custard creams (the biscuit equivalent of 'ebony and ivory' living in perfect harmony) are also good value. I like Malted Milk too, mainly because of the fine bovine artwork involved, but find the Mariettas a bit bland.

So we always buy RT, though we always have to have a packet of chocolate digestives at the ready in case of visitors. Visitors would evidently be very offended to be offered a Rich Tea and it is not the biscuit of choice in social circles, though it is rumoured that the Duke of Edinburgh keeps a packet or two in the shed at Balmoral. The Rich Tea is rich in name only and should really be called a "Poor Tea," due to its social standing.

The RT is a "base" biscuit, which doesn't mean it has low moral values but, together with Digestives and Nice, are one of the primary colours of the biscuit world. It has guided many a recuperating child back to health and, together with toast, is one of the few foodstuffs recommended by the World Health Organisation to be eaten after a stomach upset.

Peter Kay derides the Rich Tea mercilessly for its lack of dunkability but generations of Irish people have had years of pleasure dipping them in and out a "nice cup of tea." There is an art to this of course. One dip, hold for about a half a second and retrieve. Eat immediately. If you don't leave it in for long enough, the inside is still crunchy. If you leave it in too long it ends up as a soggy mass at the bottom of your cup and is actually quite tasty to scoop out with a teaspoon. If you don't eat immediately, it slowly bends over on itself before dropping with a giggle into your lap.

As I mentioned though about a year ago, something happened in the manufacture of what Terry Wogan calls "The Lord of All Biscuits."

Perhaps they decided to cut down on the glue that holds the mixture together. Perhaps the man who carves the letters "Rich Tea" on each biscuit started going a bit heavy handed on the chisel. Whatever the reason, these biscuits now end up in the biscuit tub in thousands of small pieces and, despite the opinions of a certain person not a million miles away, this is not down to the way that I open the packet.

I am fully aware that there is a blue strip that you're supposed to pull to release the wrapper but everybody knows you use the carving knife and slice through the diameter two biscuits from the top. Even if the first one seems intact, you only have to look at it sideways and it goes to pieces. It would have been no good if it had fallen into the hands of the Gestapo as it would have been broken before they even turned on the spotlight.

Perhaps, my wife goes on to suggest, it is that particular brand. Not so. I tried another brand (who shall be nameless but who bear a Scottish name that rhymes with 'pity') and the very same thing happened. This is not an isolated case – this is a Rich Tea pandemic which is threatening the enjoyment of the tea-dunking public on this island and as far as I can see, the Government are showing little enthusiasm in resolving the situation. Sadly there is no election coming up in the foreseeable future, so we have little leverage with the politicians at this moment in time, but in four years time I expect they'll all be clamouring to condemn Biscuitgate, as I expect it will come to be known.

I knew a man once who used to spread butter on the backs of two Rich Teas and then stick them together like a Custard Cream. In fact it formed part of his thesis at UCD. Obviously he can't do that now unless he has plenty of time to spare trying to reconstruct the biscuits from the myriad of pieces, like archaeologists trying to piece together a Grecian urn. His fun is gone and it is only a small crumb of comfort to him that he has been forced to take up the social art of dunking, though with pieces the size of your fingernail.

(January 2008)

In love with the library

I love the library, particularly on cold winter days when the rain slices down. It is a haven of calm and piece in a maelstrom of whirlwind shopping activity and if I had my way I would cheerfully spend three hours there while my wife tries on every jacket in the centre before deciding that there is nothing that she likes.
The best thing about the library, apart from the calm and relaxed atmosphere, is the books. My Lord, have you ever seen so many books? Hundreds, nay, thousands of them, spines facing out, arranged on shelves as far as the eye can see.
The interesting thing about the books in the library – and I'm going on hearsay here, for I haven't got around to reading them all – is that they all contain more or less the same words. If you open a book on quantum physics (the pop-up version) and compare it to Jordan's autobiography, for example, you will be amazed to find that the same words appear in each. Of course, they are in a completely different order and, as such, totally alter the meaning of the text, which is a good thing, as it helps to maintain interest in literature.
You can find books on any subject under the sun and a few on subjects behind the sun and over its left shoulder too. And they are all arrayed with different covers, which is a great help in differentiating between them. Imagine if every book in the world had a plain brown cover, what confusion there would be!
Be warned though! If you go into the library looking for a book with a red cover, you will have to look long and carefully, for the books are not arranged by colour. There might be a couple in the poetry section, a few more in travel and maybe an oddball on the poets-who-died-of-consumption shelves.
So, millions of books and you can borrow most of them (though not at the one time) and bring them home at no cost. Then when you are finished with them, simply bring them back. This is a concept unique in the retail world and it is surprising that it hasn't caught on more. You

could go into Penney's, pick out a nice swimsuit for the summer holidays and then, when you come back, simply return the item to the store. Seems a good idea to me and would cut down on those endless queues at the tills, wondering why "yer woman" hasn't got her purse ready if she's been standing there for the past ten minutes.

Of course there are other things in the library apart from books. There is a music section too containing what I am told the young people of today call Compact Discs. These are a new-fangled invention, smaller in size than a 45 but capable of holding as many songs as a regular album. Be warned, though, you need a special contraption to play these Compact Discs and many don't come cheap.

Again, the variety is breathtaking, anything from Mozart to 50 Cent (an American gentleman with a whimsical approach to lyric writing). It even contains that magical moment of music history when Lionel Ritchie broke into Bob Dylan's set on Live Aid to announce that "Hey, America, have we got something special for you tonight?!" before launching into "We are the world."

There are also DVDs but don't bother with these unless you are very technically minded. They are so complicated that very few people even know what the initials stand for.

You can also take out paintings, which is another brilliant concept. Remember how that dappled picture of the whitewashed cottage on the Algarve looked so fresh and vibrant when you first hung it on the kitchen wall and now looks completely jaded? Well, the library has the answer. This week, a painting of a lake in Connemara, next week a basket of fruit with a dead pheasant by the side of it, the third week a horrendously ugly naked couple and an apple. Home decoration was never so easy. Forget those swanky and expensive home interior places – Blanchardstown Library has all the answers.

There are also computers in the library, ranged in circles and generally faced by dishevelled young people who know how to use them. Here, if you know what buttons to press, you can search the World Wide Web for any information that you require, though, if you don't know what buttons to press, you get a paperclip man who tells you that it looks as though you are writing a letter.

A sign at the bottom of the stairs reads "Have you ventured upstairs yet?" Pretty spooky, eh? I prepared myself well. I stuffed a packed lunch, my Swiss army knife, several changes of clothing, a hairdryer and some Kendal mint cake into my haversack before slowly beginning the ascent, accompanied only by several Sherpas and a back-up team that waved me off from base camp. Slowly, I climbed, higher and higher, pausing every third step to reacclimatise myself to the more rarefied altitude. Soon my erstwhile companions were lost to view far below me and I pressed on alone. And then, suddenly, I was there, at the summit, with the broad sweeping panorama of Adult Fiction and European History spread out below me to the distant horizon.

I looked around at this brave new world. Here too were books but strangely different books to the ones I had left downstairs. These were "Reference books" and quite frankly, I wouldn't really recommend them to those people who like a good yarn with a clever twist at the end. One book I picked up was a Government report on something, which was written in a language that seemed familiar but I couldn't quite put my finger on it.

There were also magazines, though not many with "Britney reveals all!!!!" splashed over the front and newspapers and periodicals, which I had previously thought was some kind of flying dinosaur. Loads of luvverly things and I feasted my eyes on them like a child in a sweetshop before taking a few photographs for the scrapbook and abseiling back down the stairs.

In fact the only fault I can find with the Library is that it doesn't stay open 24 / 7 like Tesco's in Clearwater. How good would that be, spending an hour or two reading the latest Patricia Cornwell before heading into work or swatting up on the archaeology of the ancient Incas at three o'clock in the morning? Throw in a hammock or two and some futons and coffee and ginger nuts and it would be my idea of heaven.

Yes the library is a wondrous place and if my wife ever throws me out in favour of a toy boy, I think I could cheerfully move in. The chairs are very comfortable and they even provide you with a variety of newspapers to start your day, though the staff looks dimly upon you when you look for more toast to dip into your egg.

(*January 2008*)

A warning to all house buyers

The recent case of the Pigg brothers that made headlines across Ireland recently should serve as a salutary warning to all those first-time buyers who launch themselves into the property market without researching fully the implications of their actions. While putting money into real estate and property is generally regarded as a sound long-term investment, the tale of two of the Pigg brothers shows exactly what can happen if a few simple steps are not followed.

The three brothers grew up in the countryside (a green place the other side of Clonee) and on reaching maturity were promptly handed a puckle of money and kicked out of the family home by their mother, who claimed they kept their rooms like a pigsty. Each of them caught the Expressway into Dublin, alighting in awe as the Q building came into sight on the N3.

On opening their puckles, each brother found they had enough money to invest in the property market and promptly set about securing lodgings in that mythical suburb known as Dublin 15.

The first Pigg brother entered a very dodgy estate agents and decided that a cheap house would be the best bet. That way, he would still have enough money left over to go and have a good time. Accordingly, he purchased an "idyllic rural retreat made from traditional materials – may need some renovating" up near Hollystown. With the money left over, he was able to go to Heaven every night with a Swedish flight attendant on either arm and life was great.

The precise events of the night in question are still sub judice but according to local sources, there was a sudden gust of wind and the whole house simply collapsed. Rumour has it that the traditional material used in the construction was in fact straw and not even good solid Irish straw at that but a substandard variety imported from Taiwan. It is believed that Mr. Pigg then absconded to the Costa del Sol after the house insurance company issued fraudulent proceedings against him, though the presence of a solitary pork chop in amongst the

rubble has fuelled macabre speculation amongst local residents.
The second Pigg brother decided to go down the eco-friendly route. Convinced by another shyster estate-agent that chopping down 145 trees to construct a house was the only way to safeguard the planet, he opted for a wooden chalet built alongside the railway track on the far side of Clonsilla Railway Station. He bought the site and then drove up to Ikea in Belfast where he purchased a flat-pack house and garage. He found that, after all this, he still had time to go to the Vortex in Dunshaughlin every Saturday night and sometimes managed to score with one of the young wans that had travelled up in the minibus from Dunboyne.
However, a similar tragedy befell this brother. One night towards the end of November, locals said they heard a strange huffing and puffing, which might well have been the last train out to Maynooth, but could equally have been something more sinister. When daylight dawned, as it is wont to do in Clonsilla at that time of year, the house lay in ruins and the eager locals took it away for firewood before somebody thought to call the police. With much of the forensic evidence crackling away in neighbouring fireplaces, whispers soon began to circulate about the sturdiness of flat-pack housing until Ikea threatened court action.
Again the second brother appeared to have vanished completely, though sightings of him in a Kibbutz outside Tel Aviv remain unconfirmed.
The third brother bought a lovely two bedroomed semi-detached house in Latchford from a reputable estate agent. Of course, he was fleeced by the bank whose interest rate charges bore no relation to the current economic situation and he was only able to get up to the Hartstown House for a solitary pint every month with his neighbour, Nigel, but he was pleased with his investment and felt very secure in his compact abode.
Latchford of course is built on the site of the Great Scaldwood, a huge forest that once spread from Cabra to the River Tolka and home to hoards of marauding bears, spiders and wolves. Having done his research and not entirely believing the history books that claimed that these wild beasts had all been eliminated, he purchased security chains

and an alarm and a cowl for the top of his chimney.
One night, he wrote, in a letter to the Times, he fancied he heard a strange scraping on his roof and a mysterious panting noise. Having just watched a David Attenborough programme about how wolves had learned to remove cowls from the tops of chimneys, he boiled up a big pot of water in the microwave and placed it in the fireplace.
Sure enough, within a few seconds, a big hairy beast landed in the pot with a yelp and disappeared back up as quickly as he had come down. A photo fit description of the intruder closely resembled a wolf, though police still called at the home of Fingers "The Beard" McGee and questioned him closely about his whereabouts on the night in question. The third Pigg brother naturally wrote a book about his experiences called "Huff and Puff" which topped the bestseller list for non-fiction over Christmas, following his appearance on the Late Late Show. Although the book reads well as an adventure story, Citizen Advice Centres have recommended it as essential reading for all first time house buyers as a guide to the pitfalls inherent in a foray into the property market.

(Property Supplement February 2008)

The drive of death

Occasionally, just occasionally, and a lot more rarely as you get older, you experience something that thrills you and excites you to the very marrow of your being. Something that you know is a whirlwind knuckle-clenching ride to oblivion as you laugh in the face of danger and dribble in the face of certain death. For some people, it is parachute jumping, or white water rafting, or maybe the new series of Desperate Housewives.
I have just had one of those experiences. As I type this, my body is still shaking with the sheer excitement of it all. I am on a high and my body has not yet adjusted to the dull, maudlin reality to which it has returned. I need to tell the world about it.
Yes, I have just come down the New Ongar Road at 60kph.

For those of you who live in the south of Dublin 15 and have never had occasion to venture out into the sticks, the New Ongar Road is a brand spanking super highway that links the Power City Roundabout (not the official name!) on Blanchardstown Road South with, well, New Ongar. It has liberated a whole generation of Littlepacers and Ongarites from the horrors of the N3 and the Blanchardstown Centre slip-road and given them an alternative route to the holy shopping Mecca only two miles away.

In short it is a godsend and I always include the Roads Department of Fingal County Council in my nightly prayers by way of thanks for their divine and munificent intervention.

It is a wonderful road. It consists of a lane for ordinary traffic, a bus lane, a murderous and psychotic looking pink strip (commonly known as a "complete cycle path" – sorry, but the old jokes are always the best) and a pavement for pedestrians. And there's another set of four travelling in the opposite direction too. It is an eight lane, straight as a dye, ultra highway that would have your average American drooling in envy.

There are no houses on the New Ongar Road. The good citizens of Mount Symon, Allendale, Lohunda et al, whose estates border this infrastructural jewel in Dublin 15's crown, may sleep soundly in their beds, protected by a long high wall that runs the length of the road in both directions. Just the kind of wall that the deafened citizens of Pheasant's Run and Swallowbrook on the N3 would give their right ears for. As it is, nobody is inconvenienced by the high pitch scream of traffic tearing up and down the New Ongar Road at 50 kph.

I say 50 kph (that's 31 mph for those of you still operating in pounds, shillings and pence) because up until this year, that was the speed that the Road Traffic Authority had deemed it unwise to surpass. And rightly so. A long, straight stretch of road with a bus lane to separate the cars from pedestrians and cyclists and no houses on it? Sure, you'd want to be as mad as a Lionel Ritchie fan to want to risk exceeding 50 kph.

However, and I know it is hard to believe, some drivers felt that tearing along at 50 kph was too slow. They had this reckless habit of overtaking on the inside – nipping into the bus lane to try and get past the car in front. No matter that a bus is very seldom seen on the New Ongar Road since its official opening – a bus lane is still a bus lane, whether any buses use it or not. Of course such despicable activity soon drew the attention of the local Gardaí whose radar gun soon put a temporary stop to this practice.

But the RTA, or some man in an office somewhere, acceded to the pressure to raise the speed limit and since the beginning of the year, the red bordered circle with the black six-oh in it was planted at either end of this Formula One track. Again for the benefit of English and American readers, I convert this as 37.2 mph, a speed, I'm sure you will agree, that is physically very difficult for the human body to endure.

Purely in the interests of research for this column, I have just driven down the New Ongar Road at a speed that approached this limit. (For the purposes of clarification, I always regard the journey from Ongar to Blanchardstown as 'up' and the reverse as 'down.' I realise it may well be an optical illusion but I fancy the latter run would make a damn fine ski slope, should our oil run out and global freezing make a comeback) The G-forces as you approach 60 kph have to be felt to be believed. The loose skin on your cheeks is pulled back and it feels as though your hair is being pulled out by the roots. It was only with great difficulty that I managed to prevent my head from snapping back, knowing that to take my eyes from the road ahead would mean calamity. Now I know what those brave astronauts go through whenever the Space Shuttle is launched.

Despite this, and I cannot verify this for certain as I was struggling to maintain my grip on the wheel, I have the vague impression that I was still being passed on the inside by cars going even faster. Now, my knowledge of quantum physics is decidedly sketchy but I am sure that Einstein had a theory somewhere about what happens when speeds of 60 kph are exceeded. Time begins to warp and you actually reach the end of your journey ten minutes before you began, I think he said, which is great if you are late for an appointment at the hairdressers, but would have poor Gay Byrne turning over in his grave, if he were dead. In his wisdom, the man in the office somewhere has placed three sets of traffic lights along the New Ongar Road, perfectly synchronised that, although you may get through one and possibly two of them, the third will always pull you up. The worst one is at the junction with Shelerin Road, obviously designed by the same man that designed the infamous Snugborough Road interchange. Each road gets a go in turn – and there's about five of them, then the pedestrians. Just miss a green light and you have time to read another chapter of "PS I Love You" (why this work of art was not even shortlisted for the Booker Prize is one of the great travesties of modern literature) before the lights turn green again

Of course, as the traffic coming up the New Ongar Road builds up, waiting for the green light, some drivers at the back nip into the bus lane at the lights, afraid that they will not make the next green. Or maybe it is important to them to get three cars ahead, I don't know. Whatever reason, not only is this practice extremely dangerous, as it runs a risk of colliding with the bus that has hardly ever been seen on the road, but it also infuriates the drivers in the proper lane.

The Rules of the Road state that the proper course of action in this situation for the law-abiding driver in the correct lane is to make sure the first car in line makes a smart getaway and is followed in close proximity by all the other cars in the line, thus preventing Mr. Impatient from getting back in line and keeping him in the bus-lane where he is summarily nabbed by a waiting traffic policeman thirty yards up the road.

In practice though, the first car normally makes an extremely slow getaway or the car ahead of yours obligingly leaves a large gap to allow him to come back in. And of course the traffic policeman has more important things to do than dealing with traffic.

I am calling on the Minister for Transport to step in here before somebody gets seriously annoyed.

(February 2008)

Alternatives to childminding

(Over the years I have been writing these articles, my wife has censored them stringently, mainly because they reveal too much of the idiosyncrasies of our daily life, which she doesn't want revealed to the world. Sometimes whole paragraphs are erased and once or twice, complete articles.
There has only been one occasion though when Fergus himself has rejected an article, on the grounds that it was "a bit disturbing." This is it)

The cost of childminding these days is fast causing a whole generation to become celibate. Queues form daily at the Rotunda with young mothers claiming that "there's been a dreadful mistake" and can they have a set of rustic placemats and an electric blanket instead? Orphanages are putting up "House Full" signs. Crèches are becoming so successful and enjoy such a high income per capita that many are threatening to secede from the Republic and set up their own thriving autonomous theocracies. Grizzled old prospectors no longer dream of striking oil but now yearn to strike children, to coin a phrase, so to speak, in a metaphorical way.

The whole childminding issue was very much to the fore in the last bye-elections in Kildare and Meath and there is no reason to believe the temper tantrum has abated any in the past two years. Parents in Castleknock are so incandescent with rage about the whole issue that they have been known to tut and shake their heads despairingly whenever the subject is raised.

But what can be done about these toddlers that are breaking their parents' hearts and bank balances?

The more enlightened companies in Ireland today actively encourage their employees to bring their children to work, though it is hard to complete an urgent report on last month's unexpected downturn if your three year old is sitting on the keyboard picking her nose. Of course there are still some professions – mountaineers and astronauts come to mind – where bringing baby along is actively discouraged, for some reason.

A taskforce was recently set up by the Minister to pursue the possibility of finding gainful employment for these two to five year olds. If they could prove useful to the economy rather than being serious non-contributors, if they could somehow pay for themselves, then perhaps the social and financial drain on parents would not be quite so acute. A proposal to send them down t'mine seemed to be on a winner until it was discovered that the last coalmine in Ireland had closed more than a decade previously. Suggestions that "we could send them down anyway" fell on deaf ears, as it was generally seen to be unprofitable to have toddlers wandering around deserted mines eating charcoal.

One of the members of the taskforce, a Mr. O. Schindler, suggested that maybe you could rub them in petroleum jelly and push them up the inside of armament casings to clean them. Again, a quick flip through the Golden Pages revealed a complete absence of munitions factories in Ireland and the plan was reluctantly discarded. A similar suggestion that maybe you could strap them to a pole and use them to clean first floor windows was dismissed when it was pointed out that a simple squeegee incurred far less running costs.

Nappy adverts appear to be almost the sole gainful employment of our country's pre-schoolers and sadly there are far more applicants than jobs on offer. Unsuccessful auditioners, rejected by Pampers' equivalent to Simon Cowell, have been known to hit the bottle in an alarming way, sometimes pouring the entire contents over the floor in a fit of temper. Many simply become demoralised and roam around the back streets disconsolately until Barney comes on.

One solution that the Government is seriously promoting is the notion of child farming. Farmers on the outskirts of the capital are frantically seeking profitable usage from their land after the latest round of subsidy cuts has seen them forced to keep their current BMW for more than six months. Some are opting for eco-tourism – hiring out the leaky barn to couples with zithers – though most have developed a sudden yen for growing apartments. Still, child farming is becoming quite a popular alternative.

Farmers drive down to the local market – normally Tesco or Dunnes – and round up all the stray youngsters sitting on the floor in a strop. These are then herded into a trailer by a sheepdog invariably called "Boy" and then the farmer drives them back and sets them loose on his land.

"You have to round them up in the evenings and bring 'em into the barn," says Vladimir Duffy of Whitechurch Farm, Kilbride, who wishes to remain anonymous. "The noise does get to you at times but once they get a handful of Hunky Doreys they're generally quite docile until morning."

The E.U. subsidy on child farming is still comparatively large compared to turnips or sugar beet and many farmers can have a quota of up to 300 toddlers an acre. On the better run estates, farmers employ local lads to go around pulling faces and blowing raspberry noises on their forearms to amuse the kiddies, thereby significantly increasing the tonnage.

Generally the farmers keep the livestock until they are ready to go to school and then send them back to shell-shocked parents, providing they haven't moved in the meantime. As well as pocketing a sizable amount from Brussels, the farmer also receives the cost of comics and rusks from the parents.

But though the financial rewards are high, anybody venturing into a child farm enterprise should realise that it is not a big bowl of cherries, as Farmer Duffy, his face in silhouette, explains.

"Its hard work rearing childer," he states, spitting on the palms of his hands and rubbing them on his trousers to emphasise the point.

"They're very dirty animals and mucking out is not a pleasant job at all at all, so it isn't. I've heard some people actually let them into their houses but you couldn't keep the house intact if you did that.

"Most of the time they're quite content to wander around foraging for worms and the like, but sometimes you've got to sit down and read 'em Goldilocks and the three bears or some other fanciful nonsense, just to stop 'em hyperventilating. But no pain, no gain – isn't that what they say?"

He is critical of human rights organisations who claim that the children are treated like cattle and forced to exist in barbaric conditions. "My childer are the happiest childer y'ever saw," he claims. "We shear them three times a year and dip 'em every week or so. They have all manner o' biscuit tins and cardboard boxes to play with and sure they're well used to the branding by now."

(February 2008)

A Pancake Tuesday wreath?

On January 6th, which very helpfully fell on a Sunday this year, I was co-opted by a certain party into taking down the Christmas decorations. Apparently this is the day that they have to come down or else you get penalty points on your house insurance or something, so I quickly started untangling wires and unplugging the fibre-optic Santa that my daughter finds so unnerving.

To me of course, it seemed very soon to be taking them down, particularly as we don't normally put ours up until the weekend before Christmas, on the basis that we'd be fed up of them by the time Christmas comes around. Every year somebody bursts into the kitchen at the end of November to announce that they've just seen a house with a Christmas tree in the window and we all tut deprecatingly and say "That's ridiculous" and "It's getting earlier and earlier every year." Although I didn't actually see it myself, I read on the Beechfield Residents' website that somebody on that estate had their tree up and lighting on the 1st November, which has to be some sort of a record. But I duly went about unhooking, untangling and unplugging while my wife wrapped and put them in the boxes that were to go back into the attic until next year, making sure that the unused cards, wrapping paper and crackers were packed in a box to be left next to the attic door, so it should be easy to see if we need to buy any of same next November. (This is supposed to be a foolproof method but we've actually accumulated enough wrapping paper to last us into the next century, so next year I have decided I will set up a stall at the farmer's market in Ongar and sell it off. I've already been practising my "Fifty cent de wrapp'n' paper. Would ya like a roll, luv?" spiel.)

Finally, when the house seemed as bare as a Minister of Finance's bank account back in the eighties, I removed the wreath from the front door and was proceeding through the kitchen to hang it on the apex of the shed roof, as is our tradition, when I was stopped by our interior designing expert.

"Where are you going with that?" she asked.

"To the shed, like always," I answered.

"Oh. I was going to leave it on the front door. There's nothing wrong with it."

Of course I know my wife well enough to know that this was not a wistful remark but rather a direct command to go and put it back where I had found it. And, being the dutiful husband that I am, I did so with alacrity.

The wreath remained there all through January. As the needles did not turn brown, there was no reason to consign it to the back garden and here I must complement Dunnes Stores on the wreath's longevity, which they should use in their advertising next Christmas and if they want to pay me a few shillings for this endorsement, so be it.

If it is still perfectly good, as my wife stated, what is the point of taking it down and leaving it out in the back garden? What was the point, indeed?

Of course, we had to field the occasional puzzled remark from callers. We used up the Russian orthodox Christmas excuse and also the Chinese New Year excuse and I scoured the internet to find other possible feast days that might explain away its presence. A Pancake Tuesday wreath or an Easter wreath, anyone?

It was naturally very handy for giving people directions to our house. "We're the one near the end of the road with a wreath on the door" became a foolproof way of locating our abode.

I spent a large period of what little leisure time my wife allowed me scouring the local estates to try and see if anybody else still had the wreath in situ. By mid-January, I was starting to widen my search and eventually found such a house in Kilcock, which was a great weight off my mind, and I could stop fretting that we were perhaps unique in the western world.

However it became evident that we had to face up to the reality of the situation and admit that we were the only house in Dublin 15 with a Christmas wreath still on the front door by the time February rolled into town. It was a statement, I told myself. We were telling a disposable world that we would not discard an object simply because society

dictated that we should; that we were trying to maintain the natural biodiversity of our house and garden; that we were sending out a signal that a wreath, like a dog, is not just for Christmas.
On my meanderings around the area though, I did notice quite a few icicle lights and one "Merry Christmas" sign still adorning the walls of houses. These unilluminated remnants of the festive season indicated perhaps that they would save the residents time next Christmas. Instead of risking life and limb hanging them up on a freezing cold December afternoon, they need only flick a switch and on they'd come.
However when I suggested to my wife that perhaps we ought to leave the Christmas tree up throughout the year and simply turn it on again in Advent, she gave me one of her famous withering stares that can reduce a man to jelly.
My daughter tried to turn it into a joke. She got a teaspoon from the kitchen drawer (after asking directions from us) and threaded it carefully through the tightly woven foliage.
"Who's that?" she declared.
Seeing our blank faces, she gave the answer immediately.
"Wreath With a Spoon."
I have since written her out of my will.
Of course I suspect that many of the neighbours thought that we were just too lazy and could'nt find the time nor the energy to remove the damned thing. The social embarrassment was acute and I took to leaving the house only under cover of darkness and then with a jacket over my head. Eventually, when my wife was up in HMV one day looking for the new Lionel Ritchie album that was rumoured to be the best thing he had done since "Hello," I decided to take matters into my own hands. Rooting out an old paintbox set, I coloured in a portion of the wreath in a convincing light brown.
"I see the wreath's starting to go," I murmured over dinner, as she failed to spot the offending withered patch such was her disappointment following her fruitless shopping trip.
The hapless object is now adorning the shed in the back garden, at last genuinely brown and a sad reminder of a Christmas passed all too quickly.

(*February 2008*)

Painting the town yellow

It has never happened in the past and it will probably never happen again but I am going to use this column to formally congratulate Dublin Bus. Now, please excuse me while I go and sit in a darkened room with a wet towel pressed against my head.
That's better. You may be wondering which of Dublin Bus's many marvellous attributes has earned this eulogy. Is it the far-sightedness of the route planners giving commuters on the 39 route a complete and inclusive tour of every housing estate in Dublin 15 before arriving at Ongar? Or maybe it is the legendary punctuality of the buses which always come when they say they will and never leave passengers stranded? Or perhaps it is the professionalism of the drivers who take roundabouts and sharp bends at such a gentle speed to avoid discommoding the many standing passengers that delight in using the service?
The answer is – and here I'm paraphrasing the great Lionel Ritchie - none of the above, though all are worthy of mention in helping to keep Dublin Bus at the cutting edge of suburban transportation. No, I have been enraptured by the poles.
Not, I hasten to add, those East European bus drivers whose quick, witty banter help dispel the traveller's winter blues – I mean the poles at the bus stops.
You must be severely snow blind not to have spotted them. Where once they were navy blue, in keeping with the circular DB logo on top, they have now been painted a glorious yellow that brightens up even the dullest thoroughfare. Even Picasso, during his little known and ultimately ill-fated yellow period, never had the temerity to produce a yellow so vivid. Canary yellow is probably the nearest I can come to describing it, though any small songbird coloured so vividly would undoubtedly attract the attentions of every sparrow hawk in a twenty

mile radius. It is like radioactive custard, a bold sweeping corporate statement of intent from one of the biggest movers and shakers in Ireland today.

Frankly, this country is now light years ahead of our European neighbours in terms of bus stop colouring. The Germans are still experimenting with a rather mundane emerald green, while the Belgians are firmly rooted in the past with their robust but sombre black poles. Even the Spanish, normally renowned for their love of all things florid, have not progressed much past the terracotta so favoured by Franco.

Purcan Daul, probably Ireland's most earnest poet of the last thirty years, has been quick to put pen to paper in praise of the new poles. "So come, yellow crane legs / And shine your bounteous gait / 'Pon those who patiently wait," he wrote in his epic poem "Bus," which was premiered at the Coolmine Poetry Slam recently to rapturous applause. The question of course is – what is the reason for this sudden eruption of colour from Dublin Bus?

Busologists are naturally split on this and the forum message boards on the internet have been hopping with theories. "The Travelling Wilbury" from Hartstown maintains that this is Dublin Bus's response to the advent of spring, echoing the annual explosion of daffodils on the centre lane of the N3. "Regina the 39er" suggests that at last the company have got a female marketing manager whose keen eye has insisted that the bus stops blend in with the new buses in an attractive and easygoing way, rather like the way that women seem to think that curtains and cushions should match, (although that is somewhat of a sexist viewpoint not at all shared by this observer.)

A certain cynical section of the bus-hopping public have now been wondering if the luminous bus stops might be an ingenious device to even more fully attract the driver's attention and thus prevent him or her from sailing past crowds of frozen commuters when the bus is only half full. As if that ever happens!

Others have caustically remarked that it is a Government ploy to divert the public's attention from the recent revelations at the tribunals and the parlous state of the health service, though as everybody knows this Government has much to be proud of and does not deserve such scandalous vilification.

Whatever the reason, Dublin 15, like the rest of the city, has now exploded into a riot of colour that makes the Dutch tulip fields look positively drab by comparison. Distributor roads shine when you turn onto them and passengers have taken to wearing dark glasses for fear of too much exposure to the brightness. Approaching pilots have been warned not to confuse the rows of brightly painted bus stops with the landing lights at Dublin airport after a Ryanair flight from Carcassonne recently discharged a plane load of puzzled tourists onto the tarmac at Diswellstown.

Critics have pointed out that the vividness of the new colouring will attract the black marker in much the same way that a Wet Paint sign attracts a curious finger. "Macker loves Natalie" will now stand out much more against a yellow background than it ever did on the navy, when people had to squint fiercely to decipher the enigmatic messages contained thereon.

I'm not sure this is true. In fact, I have every confidence that our much maligned disaffected youth will view the aesthetic values of the new posts with pleasure and reverence and will not seek to adorn or indeed deface them in any way.

Sadly the name of the man or woman who came up with the idea to paint all the bus stops a lurid shade of yellow will probably never be known. It is possible he or she is merely a disgruntled employee who utilised the company's suggestion box in a moment of merriment, little realising that his or her facetious suggestion would be pounced upon by the company's marketing department with such rapturous enthusiasm. Maybe they're sitting in the Clonsilla Inn or the Bell now telling a doubtful audience that it was their idea to paint all the bus stops and how much money they have made out of it. It is a tale they can tell their grandchildren when they grow up happy and content in the wonderfully colourful new neighbourhoods of Dublin 15.

Whoever you are, sir or madam, I salute you.

(*March 2008*)

Of Blogs and Blogging

On a recent radio programme, the very lovely John Waters, of the Irish Times and Eurovision fame, waxed lyrical on the subject of bloggers. "I have never actually met one," he opined, "but they are all stupid. If I meet somebody for the first time, I ask them if they are a blogger and if they reply in the affirmative, I ask them to leave my presence immediately."

For those of you who are not fully computer literate, a blog is simply a "web blog" or an online diary set up generally by individuals. And a blogger is naturally someone who hosts a blog. (Again, "hosts" might imply finger food and cheap chardonnay, but, despite the great advances in technology, scientists have yet to come up with a way to serve food online)

Of course I have never actually met John Waters but he is stupid. If I meet anyone for the first time, I ask them if they are John Waters and if they reply in the affirmative, I ask them to leave my presence immediately.

That statement is not strictly true. I put it in to be facetious, much as I hope Mr. Waters was doing with his original pontification. In fact, I met him briefly last year at the Strokestown Poetry Festival just before he flew out to Finland to represent Ireland and we had a brief, but perfectly polite conversation on Dervish's chances of taking the musical world by storm.

I find I am somewhat perplexed by Mr. Waters' assertion and not merely because he chooses to offend so many people who have discovered a new and harmless pastime. As a columnist in the Irish Times, he writes a log, which over a period, builds up as his own personal record of the times we live in. Which to my admittedly stupid eye, doesn't seem a million miles from what bloggers do, without of course the web connection. But of course, he gets paid for it and bloggers do it for free.

I must confess that I am a recent convert to blogging, thanks to the very worldly Tony Devlin of the Phoenix Writers Group who, á la John the Baptist, showed me the true path to literary fulfilment. Until that seismic day last August, I had always believed that setting up a website was for highly qualified computer geniuses who speak in terms of gigs and megabytes and it would cost an awful lot more money than I was prepared to spend.

Tony – he actually does bear a resemblance to JTB in his pre-decapitation days – pointed out that all you need to do is to set up a free account in Google (not more than two minutes) and then set up your own blog from a series of templates given to you (again, not more than two minutes) I couldn't believe I had my first one up and running for absolutely no cost in less time than it takes to do the Daily Star crossword.

It is possible to blog on any subject that you desire. Some use it simply as an online diary: "Met John Waters today. When I told him I was a blogger, he asked me to leave his presence immediately. God, I feel so stupid." Others use it to lambaste traffic wardens, or raise awareness of shingles or to praise Brian McFadden's musical output.

I have a number of them set up now. I have a blog on Shelbourne 2008, blogs for my light verse, a blog for my "seriouser" verse, a blog on the various Irish lighthouses I have visited (don't ask!) and a blog on the Irish football team. Even this column goes onto my "Musings" blog. On the John Waters scale of intelligence, I must be pretty close to the height of stupidity.

Of course, as you get more and more used to the set-up and play around with it, you can blog more and more things. You can add pictures. You can add links to other sites. You can host cheese and wine parties (only joking) Some people have podcasts, which I am still highly suspicious of as they sound quite contagious.

I have open access to my blogs which means anyone with the internet can come in and have a look. Naturally I don't put in personal details, address or phone numbers but people are welcome to leave comments if they want, provided they are fulsome in their praise of my blogs.

Actually, not many people leave comments, which is probably a good thing, as a host of negative comments might cause me to close the site down.

One little device I have found fascinating is the Stat counter. You may have already seen them on websites – "You are the 24,709th visitor to the site" Again, free and easy to install, you can actually go into the counter and find out where all your "hits" are coming from and how they found your site (in my case, normally by accident!)

Of course, most of my sites don't attract too much interest. Can't think why! Some have barely crawled into double figures since I installed the Stat counter in January. Others are getting up to thirty hits a day from around the world. It fascinates me that I can see that someone in Surinam spent two minutes on my site reading a poem about a frog. More worrying is that a lot of Americans seem to google "Poem about goldfish." Whether this is a commentary on the forthcoming elections, or if there is a lucrative goldfish poetry competition happening over there, I don't know, but I have caught myself more than once darkly brooding over this phenomenon.

If you get a successful blog, with loads of hits, companies will pay you to put ads on your site. I have decided against this route for two reasons. Firstly, I consider myself an artist and I feel that any commercialism of my work would compromise my integrity. Secondly, and far more truthfully, I don't get near enough hits to entice any self-respecting advertising executive to part with even the tiniest portion of his budget.

One suggestion I gleaned in order to increase my Stat count was to simply include the words "Christine Aguilera Naked" on the site. This will ensure a great deal more hits from all around the world. In fact, as this column goes onto a blog, I expect the stat count to soar immediately. Or you could include "Britney Spears Naked" or "Brian Lenihan Naked" or "Joan Burton Naked" or "Lionel Ritchie Naked," whoever you feel is the most popular object of desire.

Apparently, every year at this time, the Irish Blog Awards are held. They have lots of different categories – humorous, political, arts and crafts – and they publish a very long shortlist before whittling it down again. And then they have a ceremony like the Oscars in a city centre hotel and everyone goes along to meet other bloggers and make acceptance speeches, break down and cry and dedicate the trophy to their mum.

In sheer hard neck brazenness, I nominated a few of my blogs for an award and was dumbstruck to find some of them making that long shortlist and was even more amazed to find this Musings blog making

it onto the "Best blog from a journalist" shortlist. However, after a quick phone call to a dress hire shop enquiring about the cost of renting out a tux, I decided that my artistic integrity would again be compromised if I were to go for the populist approach.
So when I read that it didn't win, I concluded that John Waters was nearly right after all.
It's the blog judges who are stupid.

(*March 2008*)

The lamentable letterboxes of Latchford

Up in the further reaches of Dublin 15, between the townlands of Rosedale and Ravenswood and nestling in the foothills of the old and now deserted Hansfield Road, lies the quiet and ancient township of Latchford.
It is said that residents can trace their history back to 2004 when a merchant called EP Lynam first had the vision to turn a barren and featureless field into a strong and vibrant community and embarked on a plan of building that would be undreamt of today. Quite why he decided to name the estate after a bearded Everton centre-forward of the 1970s is unfortunately lost in the mists of time but certainly modern day Latchfordians are proud of their heritage.
Latchford has been called "The Zurich of the North," particularly by those who have visited both places and have commented on the similarity and indeed the resemblance is striking. Both have roads and houses and footpaths and green areas and enjoy an almost winsome mix of apartments and semi-detached and terraced housing, so the moniker is well-founded, though perhaps Zurich's financial district is slightly larger.
Every fortnight I have the pleasure of visiting this delightful estate in order to relay the tidings, glad and otherwise, contained in this very newspaper. In days of yore, naturally, this would be done by a stout man with a very large voice and a bell, shouting out "Hear ye! Hear ye!" in the middle of the village green, but sadly my bell lost its clapper

a while back and I got special dispensation from the editor to simply post a copy of the paper through every letterbox. That's modern technology for you.

As newspaper rounds go, Latchford is pretty okay. The doors are close together and thankfully there are no garden walls to treble the distance around the estate. With a fair breeze and a good head of steam, I can give every resident his or her fix of community news in one hour. However, despite all its fine attributes, its honest, hard-working citizens, its picturesque and homely street layout, its sturdy yet attractive housing and the stunning view towards the hedgerows of Ongar, Latchford appears to be deficient in one specific area – its letterboxes.

Most of us, I am sure, take letterboxes for granted. They are there as a decorative means of blocking the draught that would otherwise surge through the rectangular hole in the front door. A letterbox is a letterbox, as Iago cunningly tells Desdemona in "Othello."

The lamentable letterboxes of Latchford, however, are different.

They are as much use as sunglasses in a coalmine.

Oh sure, they look the same as any other letterbox, rectangular and brassy and possessing that enigmatic glint when caught in the sun's fleeting rays, but the proportion of houses that have defective letterboxes is quite staggering. This of course has gone unreported for many years but the inclusion of the Letterbox section in the next census will doubtless shed light on this whole murky affair.

I must admit I am only viewing these sorry pieces of door furniture from an on-street perspective. I have no idea as to the condition of these letterboxes hall-side as posting newspapers is generally a task performed al fresco.

A lot of houses simply have no letterbox on the outside, merely a rectangular strip of rubber. Whether the letterbox blew away in a storm or was purloined by the hares that bound suspiciously around the field at the rear of the estate or simply melted in heavy rain, I have no idea. In some cases, the delinquent contraption lies forlornly on the window ledge, pleading to be reattached to the front door. (Incidentally, a note to any apprentice newspaper deliverers – do not try to post through these letterboxes, as there is no corresponding hole in the window ledge)

Some letterboxes have been ingeniously reattached with what Buzz Lightyear called "unidirectional bonding strip" (or "sellotape") or masking tape. Others have been carefully balanced back into position so that, though they look perfectly sturdy, glancing sideways at them causes them to fall off. As I was delivering to one house for the last edition, the whole letterbox came away in my hand and I was suddenly affronted by one of those Game of Scruples type moments when the thought flashed through my mind that perhaps I should just place it on the windowsill and walk away quickly. Thankfully the prophet Elijah appeared to me in a dream and I heeded his advice and gingerly replaced the offending article as I had found it.

Strangely, not every house has been affected by this curious phenomenon. There are still many houses that boast sturdy letterboxes, grinning intactly (?) from their proud vantage points, oblivious to the mayhem that surrounds them. However, many of these have a rough edge on their bottom lip, which rubs against your hand when inserting a newspaper.

After the first time I had completed the round, my hand resembled one of those roughly chopped hunks of meat which zookeepers throw to the lions and I have since been obliged to purchase one chain-mail armour-plated glove to complete the round as per current health and safety guidelines.

I have been doing some research into what Doctor Watson would doubtless call "The Curious Case of the Latchford Letterboxes" and have come up with three possible explanations for this sad state of affairs.

Firstly, EP Lynam, hardworking and honest merchant that he was, was sold a dud consignment of letterboxes. Apparently there have been a lot of fraudsters operating in the letterbox trade in recent times and it is possible that several have moved to our shores for tax reasons. It is hard to believe that EP could have been hoodwinked by charlatans but they might have caught him at a weak moment.

Secondly, and equally unlikely, is that the lad who affixed the letter boxes was in a hurry to get home and listen to his new Lionel Ritchie CD and cut a few corners (not literally.) Maybe he used insufficient glue or glue of an inferior quality or glue for indoor use only – a classic case of spoiling the ship for a ha'porth of tar, though a ha'penny doesn't buy you much tar in today's market.

Thirdly and much more likely is the uncorroborated tale I heard fourth hand from a friend of someone who once drove somebody past Latchford. Apparently a fair damsel approached Mr Lynam and asked him if she could purchase one of his houses. After lengthy and protracted negotiations, he refused her on the grounds that she "hadn't any money." Flying into a rage, she turned into an ugly old hag with a hooked nose and a pointed black hat and screeched, "A curse on you, Lynam. From henceforth, all your letterboxes shall in time wither and fall off! Yea, even those of your children and your children's children! And I shall hide all but two of the letters of your first name in a place where nobody shall ever find them, except maybe an amorous prince a hundred years from now!"

Of course, this is only rumour, but it does appear that Latchford's lamentable letterboxes have been bewitched in a way not seen since the great Castleknock garden gnome hex of the late 1700s, when 40 of these six inch figures ran away to Benidorm and set themselves up as property developers.

In the meantime, I will keep you posted.

(March 2008)

Still fighting the bin war

(This is an article I decided not to submit as, on re-reading, it came across as a complete rant!)

A few years ago, at the height of the bin tax controversy, our family was featured in an *Irish Independent* feature called "The families fighting the real bin war." In it, we, or rather my wife, detailed how, through careful household waste management, we had got recycling down to a fine art and only needed to put our black bin out every six weeks or so. My wife was photographed, seductively posing next to a green bin and that was that.

The secret of our bin tag bill reduction is my wife's system of management, in which every item of recyclable material, from plastic bottles to bacon rind, has a home, leaving very little to go to landfill. It is a great system and I am thinking of writing a book on it and talking about in on "Richard and Judy."

Of course it must be stated that recycling takes a little effort, which, in today's disposable, dishwasher, car-wash society is very much out of fashion. Bottles have to be rinsed and dried; plastic bottles squashed, tetra packs cut open, unfolded, rinsed and dried. All the inside bins have to be emptied regularly into the green bin and/or the shed; trips have to be made to Coolmine; the compost needs to be removed from the composter at regular intervals.

So we are doing our bit for the environment. We take a little time, take a little effort and are happy in the knowledge that under the insightful leadership of Fingal County Council, the polluter pays.

This is great for me financially. We recycle so assiduously that we only pay for a black bin tag eight or nine times a year. We could probably go less but it starts to smell. We break down all our cardboard in the green bin and the Oxegen truck comes around every four weeks and our bin is only three quarters full. All our kitchen waste goes in the composter and if, in the summer, we have any pruning to do in the garden, Coolmine accepts up to two bags of garden waste free of charge.

All in all, we're saving money by our recycling efforts and minimising our environmental footprints at the same time. So, I am happy, right? In a word, no.

From this year, Fingal has decided that the waste disposal system is operating at a loss and so every household in the county will have to stump up €110 to pay for this, on top of the normal charge for bin tags. I am unsure where it has been decreed that waste disposal should be self-sufficient. Is the library self-sufficient? Will we have to pay a standing charge to use this facility, on top of a charge per book? How about all the wages of the council officials? Surely, administration costs are 'operating at a loss?' (Actually, I'd better shut up in case some bright spark in the Council reads this and thinks it's a brilliant idea.) However, Fingal tells us, for our €110, every household in the county will get a brown bin collection and they will also double the regularity of the green bin collection.

Yippee. Trouble is, I don't need a brown bin collection as I either compost all my green waste or bring it to Coolmine. And if my green bin is only three-quarters full when it is collected every four weeks, what on earth do I need an extra collection for?

This is similar to the Government turning around and saying "We're going to raise income tax to 25% but in return, we're going to double the amount of street lights in the country. Instead of having them every thirty yards apart, they're now going to be every fifteen yards apart." Unfortunately, there is no opt-out option. I can't say, "No, its okay, leave them at thirty yards, it's perfectly adequate."

As a reader commented in a recent *Community Voice* Letters page, the whole concept of the polluter pays has now been thrown out of the window. Now we all pay, whether we embrace recycling or not. I am now obliged to fork out €110 to subsidise people who don't bother recycling and in return the Council are spending extra money on two services that I neither need nor want.

In fact, the inference is that, reading between the lines, because our family has only been putting out its black bin every six weeks or so, it's somehow our fault that the Council hasn't been able to meet its waste charges! Naturally, if we'd just thrown everything into the black bin and put it out every week, the revenue from the Goulding household, and similar green households, would have been much higher!

My wife points out that the green bin service, the brown bin service and the recycling centre in Coolmine is still free of charge and that a €110 annual charge is a small price to pay for these services, particularly when you hear how much the private contractors are charging in Ballyjamesripoff. And I agree. In fact, up until recently, I have always included Fingal County Council's environment in my bedside prayers for their enlightened polluter pays policy.

But why should we pay for recycling? If anything, the Council should be paying us for saving reusable material from landfill. We are doing them a service and they are charging us for it.

At this point, I must interject that a recent private operator's leaflet came through our door and their standing charge of €280 per year worked out at far more than my estimated Fingal cost of €110 plus 9 x €8 = €182 per year. So the option of changing to private enterprise for the avid recycler is not really there.

But I am annoyed with Fingal, facing a 300% hike in my refuse charges? It is the old Eircom trick of paying for standing charges, whether you use the service or not. I sincerely hope this policy will not lead to illegal dumping or other such dodgy activities as throwing your rubbish in someone else's skip or burning it. Personally, I would not resort to simply using the public waste bins in the street for my one tiny bag of daily rubbish – though it's very tempting – and I will probably end up paying the €110 charge, though with a bad heart.

I feel as though I want to start another bin war.

(*April 2008*)

Just desserts

I have to admit that I have a sweet tooth. To be honest, the rest of them are pretty sweet too and when eating out, I find it hard to resist the dessert menu.

It does not matter if I have wolfed down a huge starters and a massive main course, as well as polishing off the remnants of the plates of the rest of the party. It does not matter if I have already loosened my belt two notches and am starting to doubt whether I shall ever rise from the chair without the aid of a winch. The fact of the matter, as doctors and surgeons around the world will attest, is that desserts go down a different compartment and thus can always be squeezed in.

My grandmother, with whom I lived for a period of my childhood, was a great dessert woman, although she referred to them as 'pudding,' or 'afters.' Dessert, or sweet, was what the nobility had after dinner and implied something light and insubstantial, like a fruit salad. For us, 'afters' were big, thick chunks of jam roly poly pudding or spotted dick, or rhubarb crumble, or treacle sponge, each bowlful probably containing our recommended annual allowance of carbohydrate and starch and drowned in a vat of thick yellowy custard, brimming with sugar.

Seldom do any of the puddings of my childhood appear on the menus of the restaurants I occasionally frequent. When they do, a wave of nostalgia sweeps over me and I am tempted to try and recapture a part of my youth. I am usually disappointed. The bread and butter pudding somehow doesn't taste quite as creamy as I remember it and the bakewell tart is made with thick, comparatively tasteless pastry.

But then of course, I am being unfair. The puddings of my formative years were prepared by an old lady with fifty years experience who had nothing better to do than sift a bowl of flour for twenty minutes and careful grind lemon onto a saucer. Modern restaurant kitchens can hardly be expected to spend three hours nursing a jam roly poly to fruition!

But the dessert menu today (strange how the word 'dessert' now has no class connotations!) very often appears to be an afterthought to the main menu, with very little variation between restaurants. I first came across Sticky Toffee Pudding ten years ago in Windermere and now every restaurant worth its custard seems to contain it (or Sticky Chocolate Pudding or Sticky Toffee and Chocolate Pudding.) Profiteroles, cheesecake and ice cream make up the other staple ingredients with one or two other specialities completing your choice. Whereas I can understand the reluctance of restaurants to tackle spotted dick (recently re-named as Spotted Richard by one large British retail chain, in response to people being "too embarrassed" to ask for it) due to time constraints, I have no idea how some of the tastiest desserts in Christendom, Muslimdom and Jewdom are criminally ignored at the end of a perfect meal.

Semolina. Have you ever seen it on a menu? That luscious and rich creamy texture with just a hint of grit is conspicuous by its absence. Oh what fun we had adding a spoonful of strawberry jam and stirring the whole thing into a pink paste.

Rice pudding, too, and tapioca have never come into the reckoning when proprietors have chewed pencils concocting dessert menus, though zabaglione often rears its foreign-sounding and therefore exotic head. My mother-in-law makes a wicked banana bread, whose like is unequalled in the annals of Irish baking, but you never get the opportunity to complement your carvery lunch with it. When was the last time the waiter suggested evaporated milk to pour over your bowl of Sunny South peaches?

And then there is my own personal favourite, the Emperor amongst Desserts, the King of Cool, the John, Paul, George and Ringo of the sweets world – Butterscotch flavoured Angel Delight.

Just the merest spoon tip of this light and fluffy dessert melts on the tongue before suffusing the taste buds in an ocean of pure delight. Even the act of digging in to that smooth coffee-coloured surface to reveal the deeper texture beneath is pure unadulterated joy, a visual preamble to the taste extravaganza that is to follow.

Not only is it never seen in restaurants but Dunnes have also stopped stocking it, concentrating their merchandising power on strawberry, raspberry and banana, all fine desserts in their own right, but lacking that ultimate frisson of excitement supplied by the butterscotch.

But find it on a dessert menu in the Greater Dublin area? You may as well be looking for a witness with a good memory at the Mahon Tribunal. Okay, I can accept the connotations of adding "Butterscotch Angel Delight" to the menu, when everybody knows how much it costs in the shops, but you could maybe add a slice of kiwi to it and sprinkle the plate with icing sugar and bits of Flake and call it "Butterscotch sensation – a serving of aerated and finely whisked butterscotch mousse topped with fresh fruit and chocolate slivers" which sounds a lot more upmarket.

In defence of Irish dessert menus, as anyone who has travelled at all will vouch, they are a darned sight better than in many countries, which simply serve pre-packaged ice-cream in a plastic Disney figure mould. The Americans, despite their many accomplishments in combatting terrorism and promoting world peace, are blissfully unaware how good desserts can really be. A few European countries treat desserts with the deference they deserve – notably Germany, Switzerland, Austria and Italy – but by and large in many foreign restaurants you are obviously expected to be too stuffed after your main meal to continue eating.

I once ordered the only item on the dessert menu in a restaurant in the Siberian town of Irkutsk. With the menu being in Cyrillic I had no idea what it was until it arrived. To my untrained eye and nose, it looked

and smelled like a bowl of milk that had gone lumpy and sour after being left out in the heat for a week, with streaks of blue and green coursing through it.
It remains to this day the one dessert that has refused to go down the separate compartment.

(*Eating Out Supplement April 2008*)

Solving the schools problem

Last year, I outlined my solutions to this area's chronic traffic congestion problem, though it has to be said the Government has been very slow in investigating my idea of a giant slide with the steps in Blanchardstown and the bottom in the Temple Bar area. Still, I can only offer up my vision for the good of humanity – I have neither the money to see it through nor the desire to get up off my backside and do something about it.
Since then I have been putting my frankly amazing intellect to the problem of the provision of schools for the Dublin 15 area and this time I'm certain that I have come up with a solution that will have winsome little Mary Hanafin rubbing her hands with glee.
The problem, as it stands, appears to be that nobody envisaged that the huge population growth in the area would mean that we would have to provide more schools. Probably they just imagined that all the new residents would arrive fully grown and educated and without any children in tow. You can't blame the Government for that – it was a perfectly reasonable assumption to make and it is certainly not their fault that many of our home buyers started procreating once the keys were handed over.
Anyhow, the schools we do have, are now bursting at the seams with children squashed up against the windows and very often it takes the teacher ten minutes simply to squeeze into the classroom. So the very lovely Mary is under pressure to build more schools and this is where the problem arises.
First of all, she can't mix concrete to save her life. You tell her five

shovels of sand to one of cement and she still manages to get it wrong. Or else she digs down too deep and ends up with half a bucket of soil in the mixer.

Another reason she often cites is a lack of money, and I've definitely noticed that she keeps a firm hold on her handbag whenever the subject comes up. Apparently, and I find this hard to believe, we are being ripped off by those lovely people, the property developers.

The law, which in some people's eyes is some kind of donkey, states that for every x amount of houses, the developer must set aside x amount of land for a school. (I have no idea how much x is and frankly couldn't be bothered to go and find out) However, and this is a big however, and this – HOWEVER – is an even bigger however, the developer then sets the price for the land he has reserved for a school site. And then, if, after x amount of years, the Government fails to take up the option of buying the site for the very reasonable sum of €50 billion, the developer can then go ahead and build apartments on it. Or something like that.

Society's problem is that it has traditionally seen a school as a building with a collection of classrooms, a staff room, toilets with very small facilities and a playground. This seems a very narrow definition of a school. I think it was that great philosopher Peggy Mitchell of Eastenders fame who once said, "Leave it aht, Phil! A school is a state of mind. 'Tis the harbinger of the soul and the exerciser of wit."

That other internationally renowned educationalist Alice Cooper was probably thinking along the same lines back in 1972 when he uttered his famous dictum, "School's out for summer." Out, certainly. Out in the open air. Out of the classroom.

Out in the hedgerows.

Hedgerow schools were once an integral part of the educational life in this country and I think the time is ripe for them to make a comeback. Nobody who attended a hedgerow school ever hotwired a Ford Focus, or bullied people by text message, or indeed failed CSPE and I think society would do well to look to the past as a way forward.

Just think of all the advantages! Low maintenance costs in running the school. All it needs is for the caretaker to give it the once over with a pair of shears in summer and it's as good as new. No water rates, lighting and heating costs, no school photographs in the corridor of the 1984 hockey team that reached the Leinster Final.

Both children and teachers would be liberated from the pressure-cooker, claustrophobic environment of the classroom and out in the healthy fresh air, closer to nature. You need to build an extra classroom? Just move further down the hedge.

The problem of graffiti on school walls would come to an end as it is very difficult to spray paint any meaningful sentence on even the thickest hawthorn. Environmental issues would have more immediate impact on the students and those taking meteorology would have a distinct advantage over their more traditional contemporaries.

Of course there would be still be the usual queue of young miscreants lined up outside the Principal's thicket but the heinous crimes of running in the corridor, impersonating wood pigeons and throwing cubes of jelly up onto the classroom ceiling would all be rendered obsolete. Macker wouldn't be able to fall asleep at the back of the class due to the thorns piercing his backside and footballs would be more likely to break themselves rather than any school windows.

Most importantly, the Government wouldn't be held to ransom by those nice developing people, who refuse to give a site big enough to put up even one pre-fab unless they get planning permission to erect a hundred apartments at the same time. Mary Hanafin would be able to hand three quarters of her capital budget back to the Minister of Finance and we'd all be happy, safe in the knowledge that our money would be well spent.

As with all great plans, (and I believe this great plan deserves to be known as a Great Plan, if not The Great Plan,) there is one tiny flaw which needs to be overcome. With all the developments that have been erupting everywhere, there are in fact very few suitable hedgerows left in the area in which to build a school.

Leave it with me, I'm working on it.

(April 2008)

The Roquefort terrorist

A while ago in this column, I urged the down-trodden citizens of Dublin 15 to take up cudgels and throw off the yoke of 800 years of oppression by seceding from Ireland and declaring an autonomous republic, tentatively titled The Principality of Castlehuddart.

The response was very encouraging with a 100% increase in membership in the past two years, though I suspect my wife is only humouring me. I daresay the take up would have been greater but for the exorbitant price of cudgels in Dunnes, which is yet another example of financial repression.

What we needed, I told my wife, was a coup.

"Cooooo!!!" she said sleepily. And thus I knew I would have to work on this by myself.

After months of feverish planning, the first blow for freedom and liberation was ready to be struck. We would announce the arrival of the Dublin 15 Liberation Army in style, grab world headlines and call on socialists around the world to rally to our cause.

So, armed with only a credit card, I entered the Ryanair website one night and purchased two return tickets to Rodez in France. This is a new addition to the Ryanair schedule and we chose it as we felt that airport security there might not be up to speed yet. It lies in the Aveyron département of southern France and is well known for being quite near other well-known regions of France.

We travelled there in mid-April, posing as tourists, ostensibly on a three day weekend break. Security, we noted on arrival, was perfunctory, with a sleepy-eyed custom official barely glancing at my proffered passport.

We checked in to our hotel in an otherwise deserted village in the Cévennes countryside and, in order to maintain our pretence, we acted like tourists. We visited the spectacular Tarn Gorge and the mediaeval hilltop village of Conques, gasped in awe at the highest viaduct in the world at Millau and then unselfconsciously made our way to the little hillside village of Roquefort sur Soulzon.

Following an EU directive – I am as yet undecided if our autonomous principality will secede from the EU or not. It probably depends on the size of the subsidies – only cheeses matured in the caves of Roquefort sur Soulzon may bear the name Roquefort. Known in France as the

King of Cheeses and in Ireland as That Smelly Mouldy Stuff, Roquefort is produced by injecting penicillin found in a particular species of mushroom into the ewe's milk cheese and allowing it to spread. I am still wondering who first thought that it might be a good idea to try that out.

Whistling with an air of complete unconcern, we made our way to the visitors' entrance of Societé, by far the largest Roquefort producer. We paid our €3 and took the guided tour, which did not particularly add to our knowledge of the cheese making process, as neither of us had got much further than "le chat marche au bibliothéque" in our rudimentary French.

We did discover that there were three main types of Societé produced, depending upon the cellar in which they were stored. There was Original (That Smelly Mouldy Stuff) Templier (That Very Smelly Mouldy Stuff) and Baragnaudes (That Smooth Smelly Mouldy Stuff.) At the end of the tour, still whistling unselfconsciously and thus attracting a lot of curious stares, we purchased a gift box containing a 200g wedge of each of the three Roqueforts.

On the final morning, I stuffed the cheese in amongst my used socks and jocks in my hand baggage, figuring that any nosey customs official would choose discretion over valour. We donned sunglasses to make ourselves look inconspicuous – even though it had rained solidly for the three days – and drove to the airport at Rodez.

We only had cabin luggage so proceeded directly to security. My wife went first and I could see from the beads of sweat on her forehead that she was either very nervous or very warm. She got through okay and then I stepped through the metal detector. It didn't beep and I breathed a sigh of relief which in my experience is the best thing to do with sighs of relief.

"Arriverderci!" I beamed affably at the security girl, who regarded me warily. "Is this your bag, monsieur?" she replied, indicating my holdall.

"Si, si," I answered and felt a lump in my throat, the remains of the croissant I had hurriedly devoured that morning.

"Will you open it, monsieur?" she said. I felt the cold tendrils of fear clawing at my stomach as I slowly unzipped the bag.

"And remove ze contents please."

The game was up. Although I dallied, hoping she might get bored, she watched my every movement and the moment the three pieces of Roquefort came to light, she pounced on them with glee.

"Zees are forbidden," she said and handed them to the guy at the x-ray machine. I couldn't help marvelling at the technology that had allowed a machine to pinpoint cheese through myriad layers of underwear.

To my surprise, she didn't lead me to a little room where I would be confronted by anti-terrorist police, forced to strip naked and then driven in an armoured convey to the offices of the Sûreté in Paris. Instead she just waved me through.

I clenched my right fist and yelled "Freedom for Dublin 15" at the top of my voice. Well, actually, I muttered it under my breath and stretched my arms as though yawning. Not only was my fiendish plot scuppered but I had cunningly been denied access to worldwide publicity by their failure to arrest me.

"Serves you right," my wife said.

The plan had been simple. Under the pretence of going to the toilet, I would burst in through the cockpit doors and put the pilot out of action with the Baragnaudes. I would then hold the Original Roquefort to the co-pilot's throat and demand to be flown to Dublin, even though that what was where the plane was bound anyway. In the meantime, my wife would hold any have-a-go heroes at bay at the cockpit door with the Templier.

We would demand the release of all Dublin 15 Liberation Army prisoners around the world and an Urbus to bring us back into the rebel heartland. The resulting publicity would advance our cause and bring the day of our glorious independence a step closer.

Later that night, at home on the Web, my wife discovered that all liquid-based foodstuffs are prohibited in hand baggage. No wonder my Roquefort had been summarily confiscated.

I am not by nature a bad-minded man but I earnestly hope that the penicillin in the Roquefort was from a faulty batch and that whichever security official got to take it home suffered violent stomach pains as a result.

Vive le fromage!

(May 2008)

Dead tigers

As some of you may be aware, there are not too many tigers rambling around the general Littlepace area and consequently my knowledge of the lifestyle of this great and beautiful animal is somewhat limited. I presume that when he is about to die from natural causes, he slinks off into the undergrowth, watches his life pass before him in a series of mental flashes and then pops his clogs, lying there for a long time until the hyenas figure out that he can't still be asleep and start giving him the odd nervous nudge.

I occasionally wonder – and with increased frequency of late – what will happen when our own special brand of economic tiger crawls away into the Maumturk Mountains for the last time. I suppose we'll all be waiting at Oughterard for a while in case he returns, but eventually we'll have to bite the bullet and accept that Tiddles (well, nobody else has bothered to give him a name) is no more. He is an ex-tiger. He has ceased to be.

Now my tenuous grasp of economics is matched only by my tenuous grasp of reality but I predict that as soon as Tiddles has departed for that great wilderness in the sky, there will be a mass exodus from the country. Already there are rumours of a Polish Tiger – or whatever animal the Poles have chosen to represent their economic upturn – sniffing around the steelyards of Gdansk and doubtless, Lithuanian Panthers and Nigerian Cheetahs will also appear in due course.

Even if Tiddles doesn't actually die but just goes around grabbing people by the sleeve and telling them what a great tiger he used to be in the old days, people will soon realise that a fit and healthy Moldovan Leopard cub is more attractive than a Tiger with a gammy leg and a hearing aid. There will be a mass movement of Jah people and a lot of other people as well.

And it will not only be the new communities who will leave. As happened in the fifties and again in the eighties, our young people will head for the shores of Americay and some might even venture inland,

wondering why the letter "Y" has been mysteriously added to the name of the country. Or they'll go to Brussels or Munich or Melbourne or Abu Dhabi, wherever there are jobs worthy of their qualifications.
And what will that mean for those of us left here at home in Ireland and particularly those of us in Dublin 15? Life will probably carry on as normal for settled communities in Malahide or Dalkey but for areas that have expanded hugely to cope with the massive demand for houses – Lucan, Swords, Blanchardstown, Hansfield, Ongar and so on – the effects will be seismic.
If you live in one of the newer estates – say, one built in the last fifteen years – imagine what your particular stretch of road would look like if all the members of the new communities and say 20% of the indigenous 18-30 year olds moved away. How many empty houses would there be? The actual answer, calculated statistically with all available data, is – a lot.
With all these empty houses all over the place, it is pretty obvious that house prices in the area will, like the walls of Jericho, come tumbling down. This won't affect those of us who live here and have no intention of moving, although those people with mortgages will be paying for a pig in a poke. And they don't even know what a poke is!
But it will affect those who have speculated to accumulate – landlords who could now find themselves with no tenants whose rent pays for the mortgages on their expensive houses. Neither can they sell because there is nobody to buy. House prices will tumble again as they try and cut their losses.
And of course with dole centres full of lines of people pining for Tiddles, there will be no need for people to commute into town because all the jobs will have gone to enlightened countries like Burma and Tibet. The brand new Navan rail line – formally opened by President Ahern – will fall into disrepair and garden centres will buy the sleepers at a knockdown price and sell them to people in Howth for rose garden borders.
With poverty rampant, many household pets – fearful of ending up on the Sunday dinner table – will pack up their belongings and head for the now boarded-up houses in Dublin 15, claiming squatter's rights and playing Kanye West at great volume at all hours of the night. They will

grow their hair long and tie-dye their collars and doubtless engage in depraved acts such as free love and civic studies.

As disaffected animals take over the neighbourhood, humans, powerless to act due to current species-equality legislation in the Constitution, will move out. After all, who wants to live next to a house full of tibetan terriers singing protest songs till four o'clock in the morning?

As whole families wander the highways and byeways of Ireland with their belongings piled high on carts, the BBC will do a major documentary on our plight and food aid will come pouring in, though many children will perish because there will be no tomato sauce to accompany it.

(Actually this is turning into quite a promising synopsis for a science-fiction novel. If anybody wants to finish it for me, I'll only take 50% of the royalties.)

And then, if all this homelessness and eviction and ghetto-creation were not enough, finally the true horror of the situation would kick in as a whole new generation of ballad singers would spring up and drown the country in an ocean of gut-wrenching songs about "strong Irishmen and true" being forced out of their houses by uncaring building society managers and ships bound for the mythical land of Americay. Low lie the fields of the Hansfield SDZ indeed.

Now before you all start to get palpitations and reach for the valium, this is just the product of my rather fertile imagination which, as my wife often tells me, could be put to much better use. I am neither economist nor sociologist. In fact, I am nothing that has an "ist" on the end of it, except perhaps a motorist.

So do not take my idle speculations seriously. I am sure that the good citizens of Dublin 15 can sleep soundly in their beds knowing that our new and astute Minister for Finance will keep Tiddles well and truly pampered for another few years yet.

(May 2008)

Oh what a divine war

Greetings, fellow inhabitants of Planet Bisto!

As you know, I have broadcast reports from the most deprived and depraved regions of the Known Universe but today I bring you a tale that will bring a shiver to both spines of all readers. It is a tale of inbistoriaty from an insignificant planet circling an insignificant sun in an insignificant galaxy in Sector V of the universe.

The unimaginative occupants of this planet call their sun "The Sun" and their planet "The Earth." The part of the island they inhabit is called Littlepace and the island is called "Ireland."

The humans – as they call themselves – that reside in Littlepace are the planet's most intelligent race and follow the same basic life-cycle as most creatures in Sector V – they are born, they grow to maturity, they mate, they moan about their children and then they die. All this happens in but three Bistorian hours, so as you can imagine these humans spend their lives rushing about from place to place in an awful hurry.

However, in addition to their very short lifespan, Littlepacers also live in fear of their great god, Fingal.

Fingal is a massive snarling god that comes down to the Littlepacers once a week. A jealous god, unlike our own beloved Tayto, Fingal is cruel and demands sacrifice from the natives. They are forced to feed a small black plastic pet called "Wheelie Bin" and, at the beginning of the week, they wheel him out to the street and leave him there.

Imagine what this poor Wheelie Bin must go through as he hears the ferocious deity entering the estate! Imagine the dread as the god rounds the corner and his minions – all dressed alike in chilling blue uniforms – grasp the Wheelie Bin firmly by the ears and lead it to the sacrificial site! Nearer, nearer, the growling monster approaches and then suddenly it happens!

The poor Wheelie Bins are chosen in pairs to pay homage to Fingal. They stand side by side trembling and then suddenly they are hoisted into the air and are summarily disembowelled. With a great gulp, Fingal flips off their heads and gorges himself on the intestines. It is almost too horrible for me to describe in words. They are then released, discarded, thrown aside, often many hundreds of yards away from their owners, alone in a strange part of the estate, violated and disorientated. Occasionally the natives are so keen to keep on the good side of the incarnate deity that they stuff the protesting Wheelie Bin with too much food. The bloated bin then stands groaning on the street until some black feathered angels swoop down from the chimney pots and relieve its distress by scattering much of the excess around the neighbouring lawns and pathways. The residents are afraid of the wrath of these angels and the residue sometimes lies in the gardens for weeks afterwards.

Sometimes it happens that the natives forget to leave their sacrifices outside the door on the appointed day. It is not uncommon on these occasions to see scantily clad men come running down their driveways dragging a petrified Wheelie Bin by the ears begging the god's minions for forgiveness and pleading with them to intercede on their behalf. Such is the terror in the natives' eyes that the minions at least show some propensity for mercy and accept the sacrifice.

Like many gods though, Fingal keeps demanding more and more. Once a month, in addition to the offering of the black plastic Wheelie Bin, he sent down his sister-God, Oxygen, demanding that a rarer green Wheelie Bin be sacrificed. He has now stated that two green Wheelie Bins a month must be offered up to placate her. There is even talk that he will soon demand that the incredibly rare brown Wheelie Bin must also soon be filled and left on the street for him to gorge upon.

Naturally the residents are petrified at the thought of such excessive demands and have petitioned the Church to intercede. The archbishop – more commonly known as the Director of the Environment of Fingal County Council – has wrung his hands and reported back that the sacrifices must be made or else a plague of rats, locusts and other creepy-crawly things will be visited upon the heads of the householders. In addition to this, the god Fingal has levied a financial punishment upon the heads of the householders because, he is reported as saying, not enough of the natives have been putting out their black Wheelie Bins in homage.

But of course there are downtrodden races all over the universe. What is so special about these Littlepacers?

The answer, oh Bistorians with but a single loving father figure, is that a new god has arrived in town and is trying to woo the natives away from Fingal with promises of eternal redemption. His name is Panda and already some of the natives have turned their back on Fingal and offered up their sacrifices instead to Panda. If more natives go over to Panda, Fingal will become angrier as his share of the sacrificial market declines and his appetite for Wheelie Bins of all colours will increase. Other gods, like the omnipresent Greenstar, are said to be viewing the situation carefully with an eye to picking up enough disciples to make divine intervention worthwhile.

The archbishop and bishops in the Church of FCC have all denounced the interloper as a false god and are urging the natives to shun the new road, no matter how brightly the sunlight falls on it. "Fingal is the Word, the Truth and the Light" appears to be the Church's watchword. Thou shalt have no other gods except him.

It is all shaping up to be the greatest religious pitched battle since the gods Fluffy and Nigel squared up to each other in Sector III at the end of the last uranium age. And you can be sure there will be casualties with the helpless residents of Littlepace wedged firmly between a rock and a solid mineral-based molecular structure, to use a well-known bistorianism.

The people of Littlepace urgently need your help. Please send money – notes of large denomination only - to my intergalactic / off-planet / non-residential account where the funds will rest prior to their eventual distribution to those most in need.

(May 2008)

A green fingered lament

A very learned man once told me that if you stand on top of the Quinn Direct building in the Blanchardstown Shopping Centre and look out over the sprawling metropolis of Dublin 15, you will be struck by the amount of greenery. Our planners may be accused of a lot of things from traffic gridlock to the spread of fundamentalism in world religions but, if anybody still wore a hat, he or she would have to take it off to them when it comes to environmental awareness and picturesque settings.

Developers, though much criticised for the constant building of new estates, have not skimped on the provision of grass verges, roadside trees and landscaped gardens. Many of us new arrivals are faced with a decent sized lawned garden, and in the same way that an artist squares up to a blank canvas, we have launched ourselves into making the most of our outside spaces. The provision of plants has doubtlessly been a big industry in this area.

Like many others, we were enthused with the gardening bug when we first moved up here eight years ago from Arbour Hill. A huge back garden – at least, compared to the postage stamp we had previously– was a challenge and an opportunity for us to design a piece of heaven that would have Diarmuid Gavin drooling in envy.

We shared the work according to our talents. Basically, my wife chose the plants and I dug. I found out I was pretty good at digging, particularly after I bought a spade. If my wife needed the lawn trimmed back a bit for a hebe? No better man.

Of course, at the start, this gardening lark necessitated a lot of time spent at the Phoenix Park Garden Centre on the Castleknock Road. Not wanting to return home to a bombsite, it was deemed necessary to take the kids along and so the four of us would hop into the car on a Bank Holiday afternoon and head off. The fact that three of us moaned like mad at the prospect of spending hours there when we could be sitting on our backsides watching Indiana Jones did not deter my wife unduly and when we arrived, she would be out of the car like a shot, the three of us trailing dispiritedly in her wake.

The only good thing I could say about the garden centre was that it afforded me the opportunity of smoking in comfort. At the time, I was a smoker and my wife counted exactly how many cigarettes I had gone through in the last hour / four hours / twelve hours. She was also not behind the back door when it came to telling me if I was overstepping the mark with my nicotine allowance. And like most smokers married to non-smokers, I always maintained that I smoked less than I actually did.

So while she was off examining fuchsias, I'd be wandering around the gooseberry bushes having a crafty fag. The problem was that I found the garden centre excruciatingly boring and when bored, I smoked. So I'd smoke a lot more, always keeping a wary eye out for my wife suddenly appearing around a dwarf conifer.

Itchy and Scratchy of course spent their time annoying the goldfish and playing hide and seek in and out of the bedding plants. My wife seemed to think she was obliged to examine every plant in the centre in case it had mildew or liver fluke or whatever plants get. And I'd wander, round and round and round, my eyes glazing over as I passed the alpines for the twenty fourth time.

Whenever I encountered my wife – and I felt obliged to bump into her every so often to show her that I wasn't smoking – she would invariably ask me what I thought of this or that plant. My stock answer would be, "Yes, it's very nice, but where are you thinking of putting it?" I found this worked much better than actually offering an opinion. (The equivalent these days is when she asks me to comment on wine. I always reply that it is "very fruity," though I think she may have cottoned onto that one now.)

I have to say I did admire my wife's attention to detail in the garden centre. Coming, like myself, from a distinctly un-green-fingered background, she was determined to inform herself about the whole subject of horticulture, while I couldn't be bothered. Give me a plant and tell me where you want to put it and I'll dig a hole for it. All the difficult stuff like soil types and aspects and pruning, I left up to her so it was hardly surprising that she took hours making up her mind whether to take the spirea and put it in beside the viburnum or should she take the pyrracantha and move the heathers out from the back wall? Even when she had made a choice, there was still the problem of selecting which of the ten thousand geraniums (gerania?) on offer should have the honour of adorning our garden. This one was too scrawny, that one had already bloomed too fully, that one was the wrong shape or had a hole in the leaf where caterpillar vandals had thrown a brick through it. By the time the choices had been made my throat was raw from nicotine inhalation and the kids were being told off for chasing each other up and down the aisles with a goldfish.

Our garden could now be accurately described in an estate agent's brochure as 'mature.' After a lot of trial and error, we have the climbers along the back wall, roses in the sunny corner, a veritable jungle of shrubs along the sunny wall and a couple of large japonicas along the shady wall. Suffice to say that we haven't bought an outdoor plant in ages, as the lawn has been reduced in size enough.

It is not a route I normally take, so driving down the old Castleknock Road recently, I was surprised to find that the Phoenix Park Garden Centre – oh paradise of my middle-age! – is no more. Further enquiries elucidated the fact that "it's been gone for years, you big eejit."

This kind of makes me wonder where all the newer residents of Dublin 15 are buying their plants. It seems peculiar with such a huge potential consumer base that there is no dedicated indigenous garden centre to cater for the hordes of green-fingered enthusiasts out here. I would have said that the fuchsia looks bleak but my wife says that cheap laughs are something we should be garden against.

The Phoenix Park Garden Centre – RIP.

(June 2008)

Rain magnets

I'm beginning to think that either my wife or I is jinxed. The way that things are going, one or other of us, or maybe both, are going to be physically ejected midflight the next time we take Ryanair in the same way that Jonah was dumped overboard in the Bible as a harbinger of bad weather.

I suppose it started last year with the abysmal summer that we experienced here. Although, to be fair, it had its good points for I had a readymade excuse for not cutting the grass for months on end. But all in all, I'd have preferred to put in the hours for a patch of blue sky. The only two good weeks in the whole year that were any way decent was the first fortnight in April, when two million burnt lobsters turned up for work, rubbing their hands and saying they had a feeling in their water that it was going to be a great summer.

And where were we during that halcyon fortnight? Why, we were on a once-in-a-lifetime trip to Orlando, where we had to make regular mad dashes for cover to escape sudden downpours and where the CNN news was full of "the coldest Easter since records began."

But of course, that was just unfortunate.

In recent times, I have become a Ryanair junkie. Yes, the seats are ridiculously narrow and yes, the airports are sometimes nowhere near the places they purport to serve and yes, the fact that you have to pay a credit card handling charge per person each way is a rip-off, but the fact remains that they can get you to the furthest reaches of Europe for cheaper than the cost of a taxi from Dublin 15 to the airport.

Some people like to spend their money on home improvements. Others choose to buy new cars or eat out in restaurants. We treat ourselves with short trips at home and abroad.

As someone who can't resist a bargain, I have consequently visited a lot of places on the Continent that would have hitherto been beyond my budget and I have dragged my wife around with me. We have enjoyed the delights of -25°C in Vilnius in January, blundered our way through springtime fog in Trieste and negotiated the interminable road works in Wroclaw. As someone who considers himself a good environmentalist, I do worry about this carbon footprint Achilles heel of mine and tell myself that the next trip is the last one but something tells me that cheap airfares won't be around forever and I ought to make hay while the iron is hot.

Last October, to compensate ourselves for missing out on the two weeks of summer in early April, I booked us in for three nights in Pula in Croatia, a town now strangely removed from the airline's list of destinations. The guide book assured me of very pleasant weather in October – not the oppressive heat of summer but like a nice spring day here.

It was a beautiful spot, rich blue waters and green headlands, but, oh my God, it was freezing. And when it was not freezing, the rain came down in bucketfuls. Driving back from a day trip to Slovenia we got caught in a shower that threatened to put dents in the roof of the car. It was reminiscent of another Ryanair trip to Perpignan, via Girona, when we both got soaked to the skin running ten yards to the shelter of

McDonalds.

This rain thing was starting to infiltrate in my consciousness. I booked two nights in December in Frankfurt to see the Christmas market and sure enough it rained on one of the days, though to be fair we weren't expecting hot and sunny in Germany at that time of year.

This year, I was determined to break our string of bad luck. Rodez, a small city near Castres in the midi-Pyrenees promised us April sunshine but yet again failed to deliver. We marvelled at the way the water just kept on coming down hour after hour with no let up in its intensity.

Surely three nights in Biarritz in mid-June would break our duck? Close to the border with Spain and with a reputation for long sandy beaches and sun worshipping, where could we go wrong? Sadly, the duck, far from being broken, positively revelled in the conditions. When the first drops started to fall at 1pm on our first day, I just shrugged helplessly. Subsequent persistent downpours on the second and third days were only exacerbated by the blue cloudless sky on the morning of departure. And, just to rub rainwater into the wounds, the plane home decided to let us off about 400m from the terminal building back at Dublin and we got drenched in the length of time it took us to gain refuge.

The other day I got a call from Met Eireann, wanting to know if we had plans to go away anywhere in the near future. Satellite pictures can only tell so much, he said, and he had heard our ramblings around Europe were a much more accurate barometer of weather trends. The Timbuktu tourist board left a message on the phone wondering if we might consider holidaying in the sub-Sahara this year as the rains there had failed again. The Ombudsman is currently ruling on privacy laws and whether airlines are obliged to disclose to other passengers if the Gouldings (or, more colloqially "that shower from Dublin") have booked themselves on a particular flight.

Sympathy among our kith and kin for our plight is somewhat lacklustre, particularly among the kith, who have always been a bit harsh. If we choose to swan around Europe like the Royal Family, they say, we should accept whatever Fate launches in our direction.

Of course, the other side of the coin is that we are providing a valuable

social service to the weather weary residents of Dublin 15. As our Ryanair plane heads southwards, the sun will peep out nervously from behind a cloud to make certain we are gone before leaping out with a big grin all over his face and spreading warmth and bonhomie all over Blanchardstown. T-shirted neighbours will smile at each other and remark that "the Gouldings must be away again."
I think we should be recompensed for this. At the very least, Fingal County Council should sponsor our trips abroad, seeing as how, just as in a Pink Panther cartoon, we're fated to exist with our own personal black rain cloud above our heads.

(*June 2008*)

The legacy of Scaldwood

I was waiting in the barbers in Ongar recently and among the reading material was an ancient manuscript purporting to document the true history of the establishment of townlands in the Dublin 15 area. Blowing off the dust, I opened it carefully and noted that it was dated MDCLXXVII, which to the uninitiated means it even pre-dated numerals and was thus Very Old.
Long, long ago, it seems, a vast, deep, impenetrable forest covered the land between the River Liffey and the North Pole, or at least as far as the Tolka River. This forest was called Scaldwood and it was marked on maps with terrifying legends such as "Here be beasties and creepy-crawly things." Within the forest lived wolves and bears and hedgehogs and all manner of bloodthirsty creatures, though it is unclear how anybody knew this, seeing as nobody had ventured within its green-leafed canopy.
Scaldwood was a name that struck terror into people's hearts and often other parts of their anatomy as well. An early version of the "Teddy Bear's Picnic" for example – used as a lullaby for young impressionable children on the north side of Dublin - detailed how going down to the woods today would doubtless mean getting your head bitten off by a rabid wolf.

And then in the seventeenth century, there appeared on the scene a band of young men who did not know the meaning of the word 'fear.' Of course there were a lot of other words they didn't know the meaning of, for Samuel Pepys hadn't brought out his famous dictionary at that time.

There was Leopold Blanchard, strong, fair and the bearer of the most magnificent moustache in western Christendom; Randy Luttrell, the movie star; Denis Diswell who, legend had it, could perform cartwheels with both hands tied behind his back; the four amigos, Billy Blake, Hughie Hunt, Harry Hart and Willy White, who had long dreamt of building four towns linked by a semi-circular distributor road; Igor Carpenter, the aptly-named carpenter; Alan Ash, the railway buff; Peter Pellett, Fintan Phibble, Wally Holly, Kieran Kelly, Tony Tyrell and the peculiarly named Warren Warren.

This troupe of gay young blades used to meet in the Undamaged Wall (now the Hole in the Wall) pub on Blackhorse Avenue, where they would drink and carouse and play dominos. Occasionally they would play Spin the Bottle and on one occasion, Alan Ash wagered Leopold Blanchard he "dared not venture a half a league into Scaldwood." Reliable witnesses say that all faces turned from the telly at these words and silence fell. Then all faces fell and silence turned from the telly. After what seemed like a minute but was more likely sixty seconds, Blanchard spoke.

"Ha!" he quoth. "I will venture into Scaldwood my lily-livered dandy. Not only will I venture therein but I will travel to the very middle and there construct a town with a wondrous shopping centre."

"And I shall hack down a portion of forest and construct a whole new estate with management companies!" roared Tony Tyrell.

"And I shall clear a large space and make a fine golf course," said Wally Holly, brandishing his fork magnificently.

"And I shall rezone a large portion of the forest for housing and maybe a secondary school," added Kieran Kelly.

"And we shall build our towns and link them with a semi-circular distributor road!" cried the four amigos, clutching each other awkwardly to their bosoms.

When word got around about this foolhardy venture, the city fathers consulted with the city mothers and declared that "whatsoever portions of Scaldwood were cleared and towns constructed, these could be named after the perpetrators," a handsome declaration made in the expectation that none of the fifteen would ever be seen again.

At 9.17 on a Wednesday morning (the exact date has been lost in the mists of time), after a hearty breakfast of Coco Pops, Leopold Blanchard gave his magnificent moustache a final twirl and led his fourteen companions into the notorious Scaldwood. A large crowd cheered them on, shouting encouraging words about being ripped from head to toe by tigers. Wives and children sobbed bitterly, even those who weren't related to the men.

And that was the last that anyone saw or heard of the gallant band for five years. Lonely light-putter-outers on the fringes of the forest sometimes thought they heard strange sawing noises coming from the interior as they trudged their weary way home at midnight. And Captain Llewellyn in the Ordnance Survey Office in the Phoenix Park repeatedly wrote home to his wife that "I have strange dreams that I hear concrete mixers at work in the forest, even though they will not be invented for another 250 years."

And then one day, a massive spruce fir came crashing down at the perimeter of Scaldwood and fifteen bearded but unbowed men marched out, hatchets on their shoulders and a look of triumph in their eyes. Leopold Blanchard, his moustache more magnificent than ever, unscrolled a sheet of parchment and, in a large, powerful voice, proclaimed to a passing small boy that Scaldwood had been well and truly spanked and that henceforth no-one need ever fear its terrible name.

When word got around about the men's return, there was a clamour to visit the townships that the men had created. Randy Luttrell gleefully showed visitors around his castle and charged them well for dining in his restaurant. Denis Diswell performed handless cartwheels for amazed onlookers around the new estates named after him and Alan Ash proudly showed people around his railway station.

But the most awe and reverence was saved for Leopold Blanchard and the bustling High Street complete with church, pubs and bank that he had constructed. A site had also been reserved for a shopping centre, he told the press conference, with work expected to begin in the next 300 years or so.

And this was how the Greater Blanchardstown area first evolved, hewn from impenetrable forest by fifteen strong men and true who spat in the face of the danger and stuck their tongues out at peril. Today all that remains of Scaldwood is two square yards of woodland in the back garden of 73, Lohunda Avenue. A survey conducted in 2002 reported that "there appears to be no wolves, bears or other wildlife of any significant size currently surviving within."

As I was ushered to the chair and draped in voluminous cloths that failed utterly to keep any stray hairs from getting down the back of my neck, my mind was filled with the great and heroic deeds of those brave men who risked all to give me a safe place to have a haircut.

And I suddenly felt very humble.

(July 2008)

The old school tie

I remember being very concerned about that tie.

I was four years old and it was blue and yellow and grey and I knew that somehow I would have to master the art of putting it on. It had hung on the bedroom door handle for a week, along with the rest of my uniform, and I had eyed it nervously every time I passed in and out.

I made a few half-hearted attempts but the "knot," such as it was, came apart if I looked at it. What on earth was I going to do when the Big Day arrived?

Thankfully Dad came to the rescue and the night before my first day in school, we went through the procedure until I had it perfected. Left hand, little end. Right hand, big end. Big end six inches longer than the little end. Hold out little end in left hand. Pass big end in between tie and arm, let go, catch it and go around again. Second time, come up by neck and down through the gap in the tie just created. Raise knot to neck and adjust to correct size.

Soon I was able to do it subconsciously and without looking in the mirror. If it had been an Olympic event, I'd have qualified easily and would doubtless have been in contention for a medal place.

Like every other schoolboy, I soon learned the trick of pushing the thin end of the tie through the buttons of my shirt, ingeniously overcoming the need to redo the knot if the thin end was too long. I recall excitedly imparting this information to anyone in earshot, with all the eagerness of Sir Isaac Newton explaining the laws of gravity.

Of course, the state of the tie leaving the house was a far cry from the state of it on my return, much to my mother's frustration. Red-faced and sweaty, I would bound in through the door with the tie loose around my neck and tilted over to the side, or else it would be rolled up in a ball in my pocket along with all the fluff, sticky sweets and other treasures I had managed to accumulate during the day.

The school tie was great for tying around your head and pretending to be an injun. In fact, I would say that any passing Cherokees or Mohicans would have to look again to make sure we weren't compatriots, such was the uncanny resemblance of the blue, yellow and grey school tie to traditional Native American headwear.

It was also great for tug o' war, though mums doubtless tended to disagree. You could also tie your mates to their chairs and, in the summer, when jumpers weren't worn, they would also do for goalposts, though disputes often broke out over their exact delineation.

Over the years, the way that the school tie was worn reflected the fashion trends. At the end of the sixties and the beginning of the seventies, it was considered "hip" and "groovy" to make the knot as large as possible, often the size of a small football and obliterating the very wide lapels on the shirt. It was a great source of amusement to us in those days to grab the thin end of someone's tie and yank it very tightly, until it was down to the size of a marble and impossible to undo without the aid of a chisel.

This practice ceased with the advent of punk rock when it became distinctly uncool to wear the knot of your tie large and floppy. It was much more anarchic to yank it down to the size of a cherry stone and the more frayed it looked, the better. These were the days when the honour of the school was repeatedly invoked in order to stop the growing trend of cutting other people's ties with a pair of scissors.

Doubtless the founding fathers would be rotating madly in their respective sarcophagi at the carry-on.

By the end of my secondary school career, I was thoroughly fed up with the old school tie, both in a literal and also a symbolic sense. I found it rather difficult to convey respect to a bit of cloth that you wore around your neck for merely decorative reasons just as I was developing a rather deep antipathy to the notion of a school as a kind of father figure that should be venerated due to having been in existence for many years. I had toyed with the idea of going to the doctor, Alex Higgins style, and claiming that the tie chafed my neck but in the end I spent my money on going to see the Clash instead.

The worm, naturally, turns. As a father myself, I was rather looking forward to helping my son master the intricacies of cravatology (okay, I made it up) on his first day at school but it was not to be. My wife returned home with one of those ties with the elastic around it that you simply slip over your neck. What kind of fun is that? Yet another labour-saving device that means schoolchildren now have an extra ten seconds to play with at the start of every school day. And if you try wearing it on your head, any self-respecting Sioux or Navaho would spit on the ground contemptuously.

I could not however share my wife's righteous indignation when my son returned home with the tie rolled up in a ball or full of mud stains. This was partly due to the fact that it was not me who washed and ironed it but also I was secretly rather pleased at my son's antipathy to the state of his tie.

My secondary school tie went out in a blaze of glory on my final day at school. It was a cheap and unimaginative shot but it felt good, as though the flames were cleansing my soul.

I did however come across my old primary school tie in the attic recently. My mother must have packed it away with my three-legged race second place certificate and my certificate for swimming twenty five yards without drowning. Despite the battering it had suffered, it still seemed in remarkably good shape and I realised that it was probably the article of clothing that I had worn most often in my life. Wow, I thought sentimentally, and threw it in the bin.

(Educational Supplement September 2008)

Sunrise, sunset

So there we were in southern Crete, in an idyllic little town on the coast and somebody suggested we book an evening meal in the village above on the mountain "and watch the sun set."
Okay, a bit yuppie but it seemed like a good idea. We ascended the steep winding path at around 7.30pm and got a steep, winding table for eight on the terrace with fabulous views of the bay below. And it was warm and the food was delicious, even the olives, and the company was great, but the sunset? The sun was like an aspiring actor that has waited all his life for his big part but then proceeds to fluff his lines. It showed no desire to turn luminous red or paint the skies with fantastic oranges and purples but simply sank with a bit of a groan behind the headland to the west. When it had gone, a little strip of cream bordered the headline for a while and then all went black.
I remember sitting on my balcony in Tenerife with a bottle of beer and watching the sun (it was the same one – I recognised it) set over the sea. I was prepared for the spectacular and again was roundly disappointed. Far from crashing into the dancing sparkles of the ocean in a cacophony of colour, the sun never actually made it to the horizon. It became enveloped in a kind of a haze three inches above the sea, shrugged its shoulders dispiritedly and simply petered out.
Now Crete and Tenerife have great advantages over Dublin 15 in many areas, particularly the weather. You may not have noticed but the last couple of summers in this part of the world have been a little on the moist side. However in other parts of the continent, the weather has been veritably Scorchio, to borrow a phrase. One would have thought that entry into the EU would have resulted in some more equal distribution of weather but it appears that this is still a long way off. But where Dublin 15 wins out every time is in the quality of its sunrises and sunsets. For the benefit of any teenagers reading this, sunrise occurs in the early morning when the sun ascends above the horizon. In

our case, the horizon is somewhere over Damastown and some of the most spectacular sunrises I have seen have emanated from behind the large beech tree in Littlepace Woods.

A few weeks ago, the sun was about to burst forth upon a world that, while not unsuspecting, was largely asleep. There was a large grey cloud that looked a bit like the island of Madagascar (without the lemurs) hovering above the Spar and the hidden sun illuminated it in oranges and greys, so that it looked like a stream of molten lava or those hot coals that very silly people run across in the South Seas. This was set off by an absolutely pure pale blue that the whizz kids at Dulux can only dream about, which stretched from the N3 to almost overhead, where it gradually became darker until merging with the night sky above Beechfield. On the far side of the N3, pinks and creams were splashed on this magnificent canvas in what was a veritable riot of colour.

Sunsets can also be quite spectacular, with flamingo pinks and dusky oranges sometimes covering up to a third of the sky. Red clouds, isolated and seemingly on fire, are commonplace and must have terrified prehistoric Dublin 15-ers, before they figured out what they were.

It is very likely that the history of the art world would have been very different if Paul Gauguin had decided against Tahiti and come to live in Blanchardstown instead. What a world of colour he would have tried to recreate, sitting at an easel outside Mace at six o'clock in the morning and gazing in awe at the panorama above Corduff!

In Channel 4's recent programme "The World's 100 Greatest Sunrises," hosted by Brussel Rand, Dublin 15 had seven sunrises all told and three in the final ten. Critics may argue that the eventual winner (the very first sunrise after God created dark and light on the Fourth Day) was somewhat of a bizarre choice as there exists no photographic evidence to back up its claims of brilliance, save for some rather grainy black and white snaps, which prove nothing.

Similarly the morning after the Krakatoa explosion in 1883 may well have produced a fantastic sunrise but solar commentators all agree that this was due to particles of molten ash in the atmosphere and cannot be attributed to a merely naturally produced luminary phenomenon.

For those of you who have difficulty struggling out of bed at such early hours, the Sunrise Channel (number 834 on your digital box) broadcasts repeats of the best ones throughout the day for those of you who missed it first time around. This is normally accompanied by some atmospheric music such as the panpipes or Slade's "My Friend Stan," to further enhance the effect.

Of course, you don't get good sunrises or sunsets every day. Certain criteria have to be met in order to produce a multi-coloured extravaganza such as I have been talking about. The time of day is important. Very few sunsets take place in the middle of the afternoon or at nine o'clock in the morning, so timing is essential.

Also, a good scattering of cumulo-nimbus clouds seems to augment the show, which of course is where the likes of Crete and Tenerife fall down so badly. These sun-kissed islands don't appear to have the ability to produce good, sunlight catching clouds and frankly, they are the poorer for it. Of course, the mere presence of clouds indicates the possibility of rubbish weather but every cloud has a silver lining, so they say.

Just as Hollywood attracted film-makers with its brilliant blue skies at the turn of the last century, so I feel that Dublin 15 could easily become the sci-fi capital of the world. The alien skies above this portion of the capital would save millions on film sets and push back the boundaries of what is possible in the world of cinematography.

I have written to an Bord Fáilte, suggesting to them that they come to Dublin 15 and record some of our sunrises and sunsets. Then they can play them in audiovisual rooms in Blarney Castle or the Burren Interpretative Centre, with a diddley-i-doh soundtrack and encourage rich Americans to come and sample the delights of Carpenterstown and Mulhuddart. We could establish sunset interpretative centres, where we could explain the complicated astronomical dynamics involved in sunrises and sunsets, with little models and an interactive video game and perhaps an adventure playground.

So far, I have not had a reply but I feel it can only be a matter of time.

(September 2008)

Reclaiming the game

This morning I listened to a conversation in work between two very loquacious groups of colleagues. It was in essence the same conversation that has taken place every morning since time began and went something along the lines of "Liverpool are muck, United are great, Liverpool are great, United are muck, hurray, boo, hurray, boo." Among the Wildean repartee, there was, as usual, the tendency to refer to the football club of their choice in the first person plural. "We'll stuff you when we meet you next." "We need to sign a striker." "We are the greatest." Call me a cynic, but I doubted very much whether the persons uttering these claims have obtained the necessary permission from their respective clubs to speak on their behalf. However I decided not to intercede.

Of course, the 'we' is indicative of feeling a part of this entity called a football club. They are the supporters, the faithful, from the day they are born until the day they die. Blue and true, or red and true or pink and true or whatever. True football supporters one and all.

The only problem with this little scenario is that football is a sport played in three dimensions. Nay, I jest not. In the real world, football consists of real people, the smell of deep heat, humorous crowd chants and a need to take evasive action when the left black decides to boot the ball out of play in your direction.

The other sport, about which the workplace arguments revolve, is a sort of virtual football called The Premiership. It is a soap opera for (mainly) men, featuring a cast of thousands from around the globe, all earning the kind of money that Matthew Perry and Courtney Cox could only dream of.

In a sort of "Who's your favourite Desperate Housewife" kind of way, the very young are peer pressured into deciding which Premiership team they will buy into for the rest of their lives. Then they are encouraged to purchase the shirt and buy the Sky package and follow their team in the print media and the two-dimensional screen whenever it might appear.

This is actually not very different from what real football used to be like. There would be peer pressure also from a young age to go and follow the local team and buy the shirt and follow the team in the print media and the three dimensional arena whenever it might appear.

Of course, with the meteoric rise of the Premiership, there has been a corresponding decline in interest in real football. This has happened globally and now kids from Vietnam to Venezuela play in the streets in their Manchester United shirts, while down the road Ho Chi Min City and Caracas Casuals play to half-empty stadia.

Whenever I mention the subject of League of Ireland football, I am informed that it is rubbish, or words to that effect. To back this up, they tell me that they went to a match once and it was dire. When I point out that they have just been lamenting how awful their team was on the box last night, I am regarded with pity. I am often asked which Premiership team I follow, which is akin to asking me for my favourite member of the Royal Family.

By claiming that they don't follow League of Ireland football because its rubbish, Premiership fans – and we are really talking Big Four here – are really admitting that they only follow a team because they win trophies. Why else are Celtic so popular and Hibs, who are much older and just as Irish, ignored? Why don't they follow Middlesborough or Aston Villa in such numbers? Dublin fans will never win anything, yet they don't all go off and support Kerry.

Shels will never win the European Cup and even the League of Ireland looks out of bounds for the foreseeable future. Yet I am convinced that winning our first League title for thirty years in 1993 and beating Hajduk Split at Tolka in 2004 gave me far more pleasure than United fans here had on winning their 800th trophy last year.

It is estimated that by 2012, half the world will be of Chinese extraction and 47% of the global population will claim to support one of the Big Four in the Premiership. In England there is a campaign called Reclaim the Game, which aims to promote real football with mud and crowds but they are small and pitted against Murdoch's billions.

This season Sporting Fingal joined the League of Ireland. They play in

Morton Stadium, Santry and unfortunately are doing rather well in their first season. I say unfortunately as I am a Shelbourne supporter and they stymied our push for promotion recently.

Most Shels fans dismiss the club as a sporting franchise, a Fingal County Council plaything and, based in Morton Stadium in Santry, they are hardly 'local' to Dublin 15, despite Fingal's attempts to make us all feel that we belong to their little empire.

They do however play real football, sometimes badly, sometimes well, but it does actually exist in the real world. You can actually go down to a match, pay your €12 in and actually shout at players and officials in a situation where they can hear you. Sometimes they will even answer you!

Now I am not advocating that everybody climbs down off their barstool and goes and watches Torpedo Fingal. I'd prefer if they came and saw Shels. Or Clonee United or Verona or Castleknock Celtic or some team that is putting a huge amount of time and effort into representing the local community, whether they are good, bad or indifferent. But at least go and watch a real match! You can still follow your soap opera for the rest of the week!

In my confirmation class, I once had the temerity to ask if you could be a good Christian and not go to Church. In reply, I was told the parable of the boy who wanted to be a boy scout (this was back in the mists, when Baden-Powell infamously promoted Scouting for Boys!) He purchased the uniform, practised his reef knot and bowline until they were perfected, lit campfires from two pieces of flint and sang all the campfire songs. Yet he never attended a meeting. Could he claim to be a real Boy Scout?

In the same way, a true United follower can tell you how many goals Giggsy has scored and how many they beat Valencia by the last time they played them and how much shopping Rio Ferdinand bought on the day he was supposed to take a drugs test.

But if he never goes to a match, is he a real football supporter?

Support your local team.

Reclaim the game.

(*September 2008*)

Junk mail

The other morning a slip of paper came through our letter box, not, I hasten to add, of its own accord, but thrust there by person or persons unknown.
I bounded down the stairs three at a time in a state of high excitement only to discover that my wife had leapt up from her armchair and dashed out of the sitting room before me. As she read the contents quickly I hopped about from one foot to the other, as though bursting to go to the toilet.
"It's only a flyer for blinds," she said, handing me the paper and returning to Fair City.
My face fell. I suppose you are either a curtain person or a blinds person and I am the former. My experiences of blinds is limited to holidays in Kerry or Sligo, where I quickly found that I don't have the necessary hand/eye coordination to operate them successfully. When I'm trying to raise them, they lower further and further or else I end up with one side up and one side down in a very art nouveau but impractical way.
Consequently I trooped out to the kitchen and placed the flyer in the empty cornflakes box that stands by the back door. The box saves us having to go out to the green bin every time we have a piece of green recycling. When the box is full, we bring it out and empty it. (This ingenious invention has actually been patented by my wife and is under copyright. Bill Dyson is said to be raging that he didn't think of it first.) Not all junk mail goes straight in the recycling though. If the flyer is of the non-shiny sort and is blank on one side, it is added to the bundle of scrap paper in the drawer held in place by an elastic band. This is handy if I need a piece of paper to work out why the taxman has taken so much money off me or if I need to write a note to my wife to tell her that I've gone out to buy the new Lionel Richie album.
The point that I am making, very long-windedly, is that it doesn't

require a lot of physical effort to transfer one small piece of paper from the front door to the green bin. There is no need to hire a hand trolley or a fork lift, unless you are very feeble, although admittedly there is a need to walk six yards from front door to back. However, this unnecessary trip can be obviated by leaving the flyer at the foot of the stairs until such time as someone is going into the kitchen.

I have no problems with junk mail. The green bin truck comes around every second week now and we never find that our green bin is overflowing. I am sure that the nice men in the recycling centre get quite a buzz out of reading all the leaflets they receive every day.

We do not often eat out but if a new establishment opens in the neighbourhood, a flyer would remind us to "give it a bash." I do not need any handy jobs done around the house, as I simply close my eyes and work around the problem. I am not thinking of buying or selling a house in the area, nor am I thinking of buying a new Peugeot, though I am sure they are very nice cars.

I do not need my shirts ironed and, as my youngest is twenty, I do not need a childminder, though at times I'm not so sure. I will glance through Lidl's catalogue to see if they have anything "on special," and do the same for Aldi, even though I can't be bothered to travel to Maynooth to pick up a pair of retractable garden shears. Nor am I likely to join Leo Varadkar's blue-shirted army in the near future. Sorry Leo. Probably the only piece of junk mail I object to is the one that asks me if I want my lawn cutting. Without knocking on my neighbours' doors, I am unsure if I have been specifically targetted for this leaflet because of the length of my grass out front or if everybody on the street has received it. I suspect the former, as I never receive this type of flyer when my grass has been freshly cut.

But although 99% of junk mail holds little or no interest to me, I will defend to the death the right to deliver it to my door. (Well, not quite "to the death" – more "till I get bored" really. I have no deep desire to be martyred for this cause and become the patron saint of junk mail.) Junk mail is produced, in the main, by local businesses trying to promote a service to the local community. They have used a bit of initiative and gone to the trouble of producing a flyer that, they hope, will attract more customers and I applaud them for that. I am sure there are less stony ears than mine out there in the community and I hope their efforts are successful. More customers equals more jobs, as I've been trying to explain to Brian Lenihan.

It saddens me therefore that a few people are feeling the urge to put little "No junk mail" signs on their letter boxes. Despite what people maintain, we are hardly burdened down by the weight of junk mail pouring through our letter boxes. We don't need to call out the fire brigade when we return from holidays to help us force open the front door. At most, what do we receive – three, four pieces of junk mail per day? It is hardly back-breaking work to cope with all of it.

It also raises the question as to what constitutes junk mail. Does notification of evening classes fall under this heading? Public information leaflets? The Community Voice? Census information forms? Warnings of an imminent nuclear attack? Does junk mail have to be trying to sell you something?

One letter box in the vicinity is adorned with an essay threatening prosecution under the Litter Act to anybody who dares to drop a leaflet, a menu or a newspaper through it. This person seems very angry. The only explanation I can come up with for this litigious fury is that perhaps there is a baby in the house who is constantly being wakened by the sound of the letter box clattering.

Of course, I feel he is missing out because of this. I have often had the urge to rifle through my green bin and post out all the previous fortnight's flyers to him in one large A4 envelope. This way he can show support to his local community without the baby being constantly woken.

But I jest. I accept that some people might find the task of transferring junk mail from front door to green bin onerous in the extreme. I am consequently considering offering my services in this regard, calling out to people's homes to perform this task for them for a nominal sum. In order to promote this piece of entrepreneurship, I will be sending out a flyer to all houses in the near future.

(September 2008)

The joys of strimming

One of the unforeseen consequences of global warming that doesn't seem to appear anywhere in the Kyoto agreement is the fact that people's lawns now grow in the winter. Whereas before, you could safely pack the lawnmower away at the end of September and know that you wouldn't have to clap eyes on the damned thing again before April, these days the sprouting jungle both back and front is a constant nagging reminder during the winter months that you really should get the finger out.

Being a traditionalist when it suits me, I put even the vaguest thoughts of lawn cutting out of my head and make up spurious excuses why a trip to the shed to retrieve the lawn mower should be shunned. The ground will be too wet, I maintain. The grass needs to grow and breathe for a while without being ruthlessly scythed down every couple of weeks. I feel a twinge in my back.

It was therefore with great satisfaction last week that I cut the grass for the final time in 2008. Due to the inclement weather and a bout of sheer laziness, it had not been done for a month previously and, despite the fact that it hadn't rained for five days – surely some sort of national record – the ground still resembled Strangford Lough at high tide.

But I persevered, squelching through the mashed grass and finally finding a use for the brown bin which had been put out empty for the recycling people the last few times.

Finally I took the strimmer – which had come free when we purchased the lawnmower eight years ago – and proceeded to laboriously unravel the flex which had somehow become tightly woven around the body of the strimmer like a thin python asphyxiating a sausage dog.

The strimmer.

Surely this model of modern technology has to be the most useless invention ever devised by man? Is there anybody in history who has managed to cut five yards of edging without the bit of cord snapping off?

Sure enough, as I began, I knew that a particularly sturdy looking dandelion three yards away was going to cause problems. There was no escape. We had to go into battle. I whispered a few words of encouragement into where I imagined the strimmer's ear should be, shouted "Death or glory!" at the top of my voice, startling a jackdaw on my cotonaster, and ploughed into the fray.

It was all over before it began. The green cord was no match for the soft juicy flesh of dandelion stalk and, after the all too familiar "zip" and the change in tone of the strimmer, the two inch green strip went sailing into the hebe further down the herbaceous border, as we fancifully call the few miserable plants straddling the lawn. (My garden is littered with two inch green strips of strimmer cord. One day, I am going to go around collecting them all and construct an astro turf football pitch out back)

I uttered the word that is worse than "feck" and turned the strimmer upside down, tutting impatiently while the rotating bit of plastic slowed to such an extent that it wouldn't take the skin off my fingers. As I removed the cap, the tightly wound coil of cord sprung out at me like a joke toy and I sighed and commenced re-winding.

It was then that I glanced up. Declan, my neighbour from two doors down, was similarly engaged. As was the man with the white van further up the street. And the man with the dog further down. It seemed that a good fifty per cent of the street was at that moment engaged in trying to thread the required two inches of green strimmer thread through the tiny hole in the base and a blue haze hung malcontentedly over the estate as expletives punctuated the afternoon balm.

Suddenly I realised what a brilliant marketing ploy it had been to hand out a free strimmer with every lawnmower. Yes, it would have cost the company millions but they would have made a tidy profit in the intervening period with all the spools of strimming thread sold to disgruntled lawn cutters who saw the cost as a necessary extra.

Now we like to think of ourselves as a modern society at the cutting edge of the technological revolution sweeping the globe. I work for Intel and their level of expertise is so great that I have no idea what they produce. We can split atoms, whether for profit or simply for amusement, and we have devised machines that can actually tell you that you have just taken a wrong turning and I told you to turn left at that petrol station, you dumbkopf.

Would it be possible, I meekly enquire of our budding inventors and teams of research scientists nervously wondering if they are the next for the dole queue – would it be possible for someone to come up with a strimmer cord that didn't actually break in hand to hand combat with a thistle or a daisy or a dock leaf? One that flashed brightly like a scimitar in the hands of a crowing Mongol, scything down all that stood up to it?

Maybe – and I am no scientist, so I am open to correction – the material used in the strimmer cord is not up to the job? Perhaps if tungsten steel were used instead, or at least something that didn't give up the ghost when confronted by something thin and botanical?

Naturally there would need to be limits. We wouldn't want one that knocked down your garden fence when you tried to decimate the sprouting grass springing joyously up against it or sliced through the breeze block that your shed is standing on but surely there must be some happy medium?

Personally, and I realise that I am abandoning all my principles of snapping up free gifts, I would be happy to pay a modest amount of my hard earned cash for a strimmer if I didn't have to perform a cycle of running repairs on every circuit of the lawn.

Anyway, all you budding inventors out there, you have until next April.

(October 2008)

A leafy suburb

Nature, they say, abhors a vacuum, which to me seems a strange thing to get het up about. Labels that stick into the back of your neck, umbrellas that turn inside out when you look at them sideways, the hit record "Dancing on the ceiling" – these are all subjects that I could wax vehement on for hours. Vacuums, I have no particularly strong feelings about either way, which shows that, in this regard at least, I am not really "at one" with nature.

Where my thinking does coincide with that of nature is in our joint abhorrence of waste. At least I assume that nature abhors waste, though

I've never actually heard her mentioning this fact personally. Bushes grow berries, bird eat berries and spit out the seeds in disgust, young birds grow, new berry bushes grow – it is all what Elton John was talking about in "The Circle of Life." Nothing in nature, it seems, should be wasted.

I got to considering this fact the other week whilst striding down to Dunnes in Ongar to see if they had any Werther's Originals, for which I have developed a sudden and unaccounted craving. I found myself pondering the now nearly-naked young trees that lined the Littlepace Distributor Road and the vast array of brown and yellow leaves that adorned the pathway.

Leaves. Millions of them. If I were Dustin Hoffman in "Rain Man" I would have counted them but I'm not, so I didn't. Just lying there on the road, the path and the black strip that we assume is the cycle path. Never mind what becomes of the broken-hearted – what becomes of all the leaves that nature annually discards at this time of year? Where do they all go to? They don't gradually decompose and enrich the tarmac, that's for sure.

I assume of course that in the great circle of life in years gone by, this latter scenario would indeed be the case, when the leaves would rot into the soil, forming compost and so on. But nowadays, it just seems such a waste for these leaves to fall on stony ground, like in the parable. Nature doesn't seem to be adapting very quickly to the new blanket of tarmac that has smothered our landscape.

When you come to think of it, though, discarded leaves have very few uses apart from the aforementioned composting, which is disappointing, because a leaf is a thing of beauty in itself. When you hold it up to the light and view the veins and the colours and the shapes, it is a work of art that cannot be reproduced by the hand of man – it is natural art, like the Giants Causeway or sheep's droppings in Connemara.

The only good thing you can do with leaves is to shuffle through them, when they have drifted up against a wall, or maybe kick them in great quantities around the street. The only problem with this is that there is not much money in it. My Uncle Balthazar did this for a living for five years before his wife complained.

As a young man in a bedsit in Ranelagh, I gave 99% of my wages to my landlord and Arthur Guinness and had very little left for luxuries like food. One day I did indeed try to make a homemade soup out of leaves that I picked up in the street. Let us say it was not a complete success and I was obliged to stay within sprinting distance of the toilet for a week afterwards.

Similarly, though striking examples of natural beauty, the leaves do not make good wallpaper. I tried it once on the wall of the kitchen when my wife was away at her sister's and though it initially looked very striking, as the leaves dried and became wrinkled, the effect deteriorated somewhat over time till it just looked like a load of leaves stuck on a wall. And be warned, its murder trying to match up the pattern.

I have tried to think up a way of gainfully using all these leaves but the only thing that I can think of is that we should abandon the Euro and adopt the Leaf as our unit of currency. I realise that my grasp of how world currencies work rivals that of Idi Amin ("The country's broke? Then we'll print more money") but there would be enormous benefits if we were to follow the Green Pound through to its natural conclusion.

Firstly, it would encourage people to plant more trees, which would help to counterbalance the effect of all those greenhouses that are heating up the sun. If you are literally being paid to go green, then that can only be beneficial to the health of the world. More trees equals more carbon dioxide equals more ozone layer or something like that, so we could save the world and get rich doing it. Of course, we would need to enlighten the populace on the difference between deciduous and evergreen and which of them would provide a regular source of income.

Secondly it would get rid of banks and their constant ripping us off. There would be no need to keep our leaves in financial institutions as there would be more than enough to go around for everyone. Just go out into the street if you're getting a bit short. It would also be a fallacy for parents to admonish their profligate offspring with the words, "Money doesn't grow on trees, you know."

Of course, we would have to tighten up our customs and excise operation to stop people smuggling large quantities of leaves into the country and devaluing our currency. We could employ sniffer giraffes at docks and airports, though naturally you'd have to slip them the occasional five leaf note to keep them happy.

Back gardens in our leafy suburbs would become veritable jungles of shrubs and small trees as we all wait for the autumnal windfall. Farmers would employ Securicor to collect their harvest, though doubtless they would still demand subsidies from the government for doing so.

Medical costs would plummet as whole families would get fit by going on long forest walks with big sacks.

But of course, all this will only happen in a post-apocalyptic society when the few survivors emerge from our bomb shelters and gaze around at the devastation outside. It will be like the dove returning to the ark with a leaf in its mouth or maybe the coast of Greenland being discovered by Leaf Eriksson.

(October 2008)

Printed in the United Kingdom by
Lightning Source UK Ltd., Milton Keynes
138063UK00002B/16/P